EMPIRE
OF THE
SAVIOURS

A J DALTON

First published in Great Britain in 2012
by Gollancz
An imprint of the Orion Publishing Group
Orion House, 5 Upper St Martin's Lane,
London WC2H 9EA
An Hachette UK Company

This edition published in Great Britain in 2013
by Gollancz

1 3 5 7 9 10 8 6 4 2

A CIP catalogue record for this book
is available from the British Library

ISBN 978 0 575 12314 4

Typeset at The Spartan Press Ltd,
Lymington, Hants

Printed in Great Britain by Clays Ltd,
St Ives plc

www.ajdalton.eu
www.orionbooks.co.uk

To Siouxsie, Mum, Dad, Chris, David, Galen, Caspar, Lachlan and Katarina with love.

Beware those who speak of faith and the betterment of the people yet say magic is the work of the devil.

With a salute to my vigilant reading group:
Paul Leeming (stalwart), eagle-eyed Mike Ranson, the as-yet-unmet Sandi Wakefield, the commentating Becky Unicorn, the effusive Phil Sharrock, the ever-busy Maggie Milne and the energetic Kevin Burge.

With thanks to Matt White, Nick White, Tom Martin and Kasia Martin, for their unstinting support.

CHAPTER 1:

Magic is the first evil

In the beginning, the blessed Saviours had rescued the People from the pagans and barbarians, and then built fortified towns within which to keep their new followers safe.

Each town had a standing force of Heroes along its walls to guard against any sudden attacks by marauders from without, and to keep any of the People who became distracted or disorientated within. For it was not unknown for a pagan magic-user hiding somewhere in the deep woods to attempt to cast a dark influence over the minds of the People. There was a story whispered among Jillan's classmates that one such spell-caster had caused the People of New Sanctuary to rise up against their own Heroes, and that it was only a sudden and unexpected visit by one of the Empire's Saints that had saved the town from being entirely lost – praise be to the Saviours for their foresight in commanding the Saints to travel between communities in order to administer ongoing care to the People!

It was said that the pagans and barbarians were brutal savages – many of them shape-changers – who were elements of the Chaos. In the olden days, it was from the Chaos that the Saviours had created lives of order and safety for the People. That had been so long ago, of course, that everybody now knew about it even if they hadn't been alive when it had happened. The Empire of the Saviours was ancient and had always been – older than old Samuel even, and he was the oldest person in Godsend – older than Jillan's grandfather, great-grandfather, great-great-grandfather, whoever he had been, and even the one before that.

Minister Praxis said that just as the Empire of the Saviours had always been, so it would always be; that the Empire was *eternal.* The only ordered life that existed in the world was the Empire and everything else was the Chaos. At the beginning of time, the Minister told his young students, the forces of good and order had come together as the Empire in order to prevent the Chaos and its dark pagan gods from ruling absolutely and from ultimately destroying the world. The Chaos constantly railed against the Empire and tried to tear it down, jealous that the People had been wrested from its clutches. Thus, every community needed its walls and Heroes, and all of the People needed to remain vigilant and guard their thoughts and minds against any unholy instinct or temptation.

Jillan had lived all his thirteen years within the walls of Godsend. Each morning, he would be sent off to the school at the centre of town, just off the wide and open Gathering Place. His mother and father – along with most of the other adults – would spend the day beyond the walls, his mother working in the fields and his father hunting with a skilled few in the woods. The adults were always escorted and protected by a squad of Heroes, although the pagans would rarely attack while the sun was in the sky. In fact, there'd never been an attack while Jillan had been alive. Minister Praxis said that the pagans had learned to fear the Heroes and preferred to use dark, sneaking ways rather than risk any sort of direct confrontation. Minister Praxis always looked at Jillan when he used the words *dark* or *sneaking*, but Jillan was never sure why. It made him uncomfortable and his face would flush. He'd feel guilty and afraid and Minister Praxis would smile and nod knowingly, reminding all the students how important it was to guard their thoughts against any secret and selfish desires sent to them by the pagans and the Chaos.

Jillan was afraid of Minister Praxis and didn't like going to school to sit beneath the tall man's glare every day. The boy knew he should be grateful to hear about the Saviours, because of what they had sacrificed and done to free the People from the corrupting grip of the Chaos, but Jillan's mother would have to shout at him several times each morning before she could get him out of his bed. Sometimes he found himself wishing that the night and his sleep would last forever, and that the sun would never rise again. Then he'd realise such a desire was sinful – that it was *dark* and *sneaking* – for the night belonged to the pagans, and in wishing for a night that lasted forever, he was actually dreaming of the final triumph of the Chaos. Of course he wanted the sun to rise again! How could he not? If it didn't, he'd never awake to see his school friends and parents, and he loved his parents dearly, more than anything else, even though he knew he should love the Saviours more.

Jillan was scared of his own thoughts and feelings sometimes. They could be sinful and threatened to get him into trouble, threatened to let the Chaos claim him completely one day. And the way Minister Praxis looked at him in class meant that the Minister *knew*. He had to know that Jillan had such thoughts. He saw it every time Jillan's face flushed, and perhaps even sensed some of his thoughts, for those who were strong in their faith were gifted with an ability from the Saviours to see where and when the Chaos was at work. It was why all the other town elders listened respectfully to the Minister whenever an important decision needed to be made or whenever one of the People brought some grievance to the council.

'Do I *have* to go? I feel a bit sick,' Jillan complained as he sat eating breakfast with his parents. Then he brightened: 'Maybe I can stay home today, and you could stay with me, Mother!' Jillan used his most pleading eyes, the sort that usually persuaded his mother to give him his birthday present early or give him an extra helping of one of her wonderful puddings.

But his father was too quick for him today. 'I'm not surprised you're sick, spending all night cooped up in here. Fresh air is what you need, lad. You can get plenty on the way to school. You'll feel right as rain by the time you meet your friends.'

Jillan refused to adjust his expression and kept his eyes on his mother. Her face became worried.

'Perhaps he really is sick, Jed.'

Jed snorted and set down his mug of light beer on the table with a bang. 'My sweet and trusting Maria, didn't you see how he polished off that bread and honey? A boy with that sort of appetite can't be so sick, now can he? It can't be contagious whatever it is, since you and I are fine, so whether he spends the day sick at home or at school makes little difference. Better he spends the day in school then, learning his numbers and letters so that he doesn't have to end up in the fields or woods like us when he comes of age.'

Jillan silently cursed – he should have thought to resist the bread and honey, but honey was his favourite. He knew he would have to change tack. 'But I don't want to work with numbers and letters, Father. I want to be a hunter like you! I've been practising with my bow and can hit a tree from forty paces!'

Jed, who was a bear of a man, nodded his head in approval and clapped Jillan heavily on the shoulder, all but flattening him. 'Yes, son, you have the eye, but you do not yet have the strength to draw the sort of bow that can stop a wild boar in its tracks . . .'

Jillan eyed his father's bow leaning in the corner by the door. It was as long as he was tall, and when he'd secretly tested himself against it just the week before, he'd been unable to bend it more than half an inch.

'. . . and you cannot yet read the spoor of an animal, or navigate the trails of the forest. Look, it's only another six months until the Saint is sent to Draw all those coming of age. Then you will be a man. I will begin to teach you to hunt, but it will be several years before you are ready to have a full longbow. During those years you will have to work at something to contribute your share to the community . . . and to support any wife you might choose to take.'

Jillan flushed and suddenly found the pattern of the table's wood fascinating.

'So learn your numbers and letters well and you might yet be offered work with Jacob the trader. He has no son and his back is too bent to load that cart on his own. You've always said you wanted to see other places, rather than being stuck out here in the far and wild reaches of the Empire. Well, the trader can offer you chances to travel, for you know well that he visits Saviours' Paradise every month and sets up a stall there on market day on behalf of Godsend.'

'And Jacob's daughter, Hella, is a sensible girl.' Maria smiled. 'I hear she has the sort of eye for you that could hit a heart at forty paces.'

Jillan flushed even more furiously than before. 'I'm going to school!' he announced hotly and stood.

Jed took pity on him. 'Maria, don't tease him so. It's all right, Jillan, all in good time. And the choice will be yours – we will not arrange and insist on such things as some other parents would. All right?'

Jillan nodded. 'I have to go or I'll be late. I need to get my slate and chalk for school. Can I be excused?'

Jed hesitated, debating with himself for a moment. 'If you tell me why you were trying to avoid going to school.'

Jillan's eyes widened in panic.

'Jed, he's distressed enough as it is,' Maria warned. 'This can wait.'

Jed kept his eyes on his son and lowered his voice to a growl. 'Is Elder Corin's son giving you trouble again?'

'No, no!' Jillan protested. 'He's just an idiot. I'm not scared of him.'

'Then what is it? You know you can tell us anything. We're your parents, and we love you no matter what.'

Jillan shifted his weight uncomfortably from one foot to another, and then back again. He glanced at his mother for help, but she only watched him with a mix of concern and curiosity. Finally, he couldn't help blurting, 'The Minister hates me! He always picks on me. And I haven't done anything wrong, not really. But don't say anything, pleeease, because that'll only make things worse! It's only six more months. It'll be fine!'

A terrible anger came into his father's eyes, an anger Jillan had never seen before and one that scared him more than Minister Praxis did. Jed seethed, 'I knew that snake couldn't be trusted to leave well enough alone!'

'Jillan!' Maria snapped, demanding his attention. 'Get your things and be off to school. Now! I need to talk to your father. Don't worry, all will be well.' Her eyes blazed as she turned on his father.

Heart pounding and blood roaring in his ears, Jillan fled to his room. He grabbed slate board and chalk and then took up one of his special rocks from its niche in the stone wall of his bedchamber. His collection of strangely coloured and oddly shaped rocks had started when he was young enough to believe they had special meaning and magical properties. He now understood that his father only brought him such rocks when the hunters had failed to catch enough rabbits for everyone's dinner pots. Nonetheless, today, he put the smooth red pebble that he associated with feeling brave in his pocket.

Jillan ran back through the small kitchen and eating area of their small house, hardly daring to glance at his parents, and out into the daylight. His mother's voice filled his ears.

'. . . if you really do love us, then you will leave it be. When we came here, you promised me you'd cause no more trouble, so that we could raise our son in some sort of peace and safety. You promised me, Jedadiah, and I mean to hold you to that promise!'

His father rumbled something in reply, but Jillan couldn't catch it.

'No!' his mother rejoined in her high pitch. 'That died in New Sanctuary, along with many good people. If you're going to start on that again then – as the Saviours are my witness – you can do it without Jillan and me. I will not stand idly by while you put this family in danger.'

Jillan blinked as he tried to make sense of what he'd just overheard. What did his mother mean by *when we came here*? Had his parents lived in a different part of Godsend at some point before he was born? And how had they known of people in New Sanctuary, a place of such shame and blasphemy that its name was only ever whispered in conversation?

As far as Jillan knew, the only home he'd ever had was their small cottage squashed up against the wall of Godsend. The families who had first settled the town naturally occupied the large homes – complete with front and back yards – near the Gathering Place, and usually had a seat on the council. As the town had become more established and the population had grown, however, there had only been hurriedly built crowded homes available for the newer families. Jillan and his parents lived right up against the south wall, behind which were the midden ditches and cemetery, and just beyond which the wilds truly began.

People tended to avoid the south wall. Even the south gate was only guarded by a single Hero, since it was used solely for infrequent burials. It was usually only the very newest families who lived in the higgledy-piggledy warren of the southern part of town, yet while most families moved out as soon as they could, he and his parents had remained in their home even when the houses around them had become deserted and fallen into disrepair. Consequently, rather than thinking of his family as newcomers, he'd always assumed they lived where they lived because his parents liked their privacy. After all, people just brought interference and trouble, with their rules and disapproval. And he really didn't mind the smell from the middens, at which so many people turned their noses up – he'd grown up with it and somehow found its damp earthiness reassuring.

Blinking, he realised he was almost out of the maze in which he lived and close to the busier parts of town. He slowed his pace, wanting to delay the moment when he would reach the school as long as possible. He watched a bird winging high across the sky and found his steps drifting after it. It led him back to the wall and he climbed the long stairs up and round to the Hero keeping a solitary lookout over the south gate.

Old Samnir the Hero nodded to Jillan in welcome and then turned his grey eyes back towards the wilds.

'Anything moving?' Jillan asked as he always did, taking his customary seat between two crenellations.

Samnir continued to scan the landscape. After a second or two, he replied gruffly, 'Thought I saw one of the mountains move to the left earlier.'

Jillan smiled. 'It did not!'

The Hero scowled at Jillan. 'Know much about mountains, do you? Ever even set foot on one? Didn't think so. And who are you to challenge a mighty Hero of the Empire? I should have you flogged, dragged through the streets and then hung on high for all to see, so that you might serve as warning to all those who allow the pagans to corrupt their thinking.'

Jillan's smile broadened. 'The creases in the corners of your eyes always deepen when you're not being serious.'

'Damn this traitorous face of mine!' Samnir sighed. 'It knows me too well. It means I can never play cards with any of the other Heroes.'

'Is that why you're always out here on your own?' Jillan asked without much thought.

The Hero tightened his grip on the haft of his spear until a few of his knuckles cracked. He quickly turned his face back towards the cemetery and the forest. His voice became cold. 'You are presumptuous, boy! I don't owe you any answers. You should get along to school. I don't want the Minister saying I've been keeping you from your studies.'

Jillan was crestfallen. Samnir had always seemed different to everyone else, less judgemental, less disapproving. The Hero had seen the world and wasn't scared of anything, even keeping guard alone in a lightning storm. For a few years Jillan had dreamed of becoming a Hero just like Samnir – with a face as weathered and muscles as hard as rock – until he'd learned Heroes were never allowed families of their own, lest their willingness to do their duty be compromised by sentiment. Even so, they'd spent many hours in each other's company over the years, whether in companionable silence or talking about other communities, trees, animals and all manner of things Samnir had seen – although, Jillan now realised, they had never spoken about exactly why Samnir chose to stay out here on his own. Until now Jillan had always felt safe in Samnir's company, and the world had seemed to make a bit more sense each time he spoke to him.

Yet today something was different. Something had gone wrong. He'd managed to make his parents argue, and now he'd made Samnir angry. Perhaps he'd been fooling himself in thinking he and Samnir were friends. After all, what could a grizzled warrior and a thirteen-year-old boy have in common? Clearly, Samnir had merely been indulging him up till now, or being kind because he felt sorry for the boy from the southern part of town. Angry at himself, and resolving never to bother the Hero again, Jillan shifted in his seat and prepared to jump down and make for the stairs. The sooner he got to school, completed six more months of study and was Drawn to the Saviours by the Saint, the better.

To Jillan's surprise, however, Samnir said quietly, his back still to him. 'Wait.' A sigh. 'Why am I out here commanding nothing but the wind, when I was once a leader of men in the Empire's army? Why am I in the remotest backwater of the Empire, when I once marched side by side with Saints in the campaign against the barbarians in the eastern desert? Why do I now oversee nothing but a graveyard of dusty bones, when I once guarded the temple of the Great Saviour himself?' He paused. 'Because I am like all other men, Jillan. Once, I thought I was better than every other mortal, that my proximity to the sacred heart of the Empire made me special, made me something more. I refused to see otherwise, even when my joints began to pain me as I rose from my pallet each morning and as the weight of my armour began to make my shoulders droop. I began to see younger and more capable men as a threat and began to say and do things to undermine them, even when it was not in the best interests of the Empire. I put my hubris and self-interest before the will of the Saviours, despite everything they'd given me. But the Saviours are all-knowing and saw the blasphemy in my heart.

'I was asked to step aside, and when I refused I was exiled from the holy temple complex. I was denied all sight and sound of the holy ones. I was not worthy to be in their presence, you see. Even then, I was allowed a chance to redeem myself, for the Saviours are merciful even when punishing transgressors. I was put in charge of the Heroes on the walls of Hyvan's Cross, a large community no more than a week's march from the Empire's sacred heart. Yet still I was ungrateful and in my anger sought to blame all those around me. The Saviours forgive me, but I took their name in vain on many occasions.

'Saint Azual was forced to banish me from Hyvan's Cross and after several other unhappy postings I ended up here, on the edge of the wilds. My fall from grace was caused by my thoughts, words and deeds, and they have taken me as far from the sacred heart as it is possible to get. I am all but become pagan, so far have I strayed and so corrupted am I.

'Why am I out here?' he asked, turning back to Jillan with wide staring eyes. 'I have condemned myself to this place! Everyone finds their right and proper place in the scheme of things, Jillan, and this is mine. Ultimately, mortals are only ever victims of their own selves. I am the lowest of the low and must now spend my remaining days doing this lowly duty to the best of my ability, else I may as well leave the Empire altogether, join the pagans in the mountains and embrace the empty Chaos entirely.'

Jillan could not move, pinned where he was between the crenellations by the looming Hero. He'd leaned back as far as he dared, clinging desperately to the stonework with his fingers to prevent himself from falling fully thirty feet to the midden ditch and cemetery below. He dared not breathe lest Samnir's wild and tortured gaze suddenly focus on him, rather than looking through him.

'Do not become like me,' the Hero whispered. 'A ghost wailing in the wind. A being of so little substance and worth that even the spirits of the dead below shun his company and search elsewhere for the warmth of life. Promise me!'

Jillan nodded and swallowed fearfully. His assent seemed to appease the soldier, who blinked several times and then apparently came back to himself. 'I'm sorry, boy. I didn't mean to scare you.'

Jillan dragged himself up and planted his feet safely back on the walkway. 'I-I still like you, Samnir. I don't think you're the lowest of the low,' he mumbled, but then betrayed his words by running for the stairs.

'I'll see you tomorrow?' Samnir called after him. 'I'll tell you more about the mountains if you like! They're a stronghold for the pagans and the Chaos. They are a place so cold and inhospitable that not even the Saints will venture there alone. Boy! If you ever need my help . . .'

The Hero watched the boy go. He turned his bleak gaze towards the forest of nodding fir trees which stretched all the way to the distant mountains. A chill wind rattled his teeth and he hunkered down into his armour. If he was any judge, there would be snow early in the mountains, and that meant a long hard winter that not everyone would survive. The harvest had barely finished. What had happened to the autumn? So short, and gone like his youth. 'Damn that boy! He makes me forget myself,' he murmured.

Shaken, Jillan ran all the way to school. Everything had been turned upside down so far today, so he was eager to see the familiar faces of his few friends and have some sort of comforting routine restored by the school day.

The other children of Godsend stood waiting outside the large oak door to the school. They mainly kept together for shelter from the wind that whistled across the expanse of the Gathering Place at the centre of town.

'I was worried you'd be late!' Hella said with a dimpling smile.

Breathing hard, Jillan only nodded by way of reply.

'What's that smell? Middens are strong today!' Haal, Elder Corin's son, said loudly. His friends Karl and Silus snickered.

Haal was heavily built like his father, but where Elder Corin was something of a gentle giant, Haal used his size to get the other students to do whatever he told them. Jed had told Jillan that nature sometimes gave those who were slow of wit extra strength, as otherwise they would not be able to survive in the world. Jillan didn't know if that was true or not, and it really didn't matter either way, since Minister Praxis knew better than to be hard on the elder's son for being dull and lazy. As far as Jillan could tell, Haal could be the stupidest and weakest person in the world but he would still survive more easily than others, and stupidly think to mock them while doing so.

Normally Jillan would have ignored Haal's comment, for he'd been saying such things for years, but Jillan wasn't feeling normal today. Today was not a normal day. Today was a day when parents argued, Heroes faltered and friends became angry. Today was a day when Jillan had confessed his fear of the Minister, told his dream of becoming a hunter, looked forward to being Drawn and worried about finding a wife one day. Today was a day when Jillan could no longer pretend to be a child. Today began the fight that would last the rest of his life.

He squared his shoulders, faced Haal and glared at him. Jillan was gratified to see uncertainty creep into the other's eyes.

'Jillan, don't do this!' Hella breathed, sensing Jillan's mood and becoming nervous.

'What you are no doubt smelling, Haal, is your own breath, for the rubbish that comes from your mouth is as foul as any midden. One wonders what you eat to be so malodorous and bloated. What festering garbage do you gorge on and where do you get it all from? You haven't been sneaking out to the ditches in the dark of the night, have you? With such a creature abroad, no wonder the pagans fear to come near Godsend. The Chaos itself fears the enormity of your appetite, and that you will pig it down whole!'

There was silence. Even the wind stilled as if in shock.

'What, Haal?' Jillan sneered. 'So stupid that you don't even know when you've been insulted?'

Karl and Silus stood with their mouths hanging open. Their eyes flicked from Haal to Jillan and back again. All the other students instinctively drew away.

Haal's face began to redden and swell, rage sparking in his small black eyes. Speechless with anger, he choked and spluttered. Then he lowered his heavy brows like a wild boar preparing to charge.

'No! Don't!' Hella squeaked.

Jillan was strangely calm. Let the Chaos come then. It would either destroy him totally or he would put down his enemies. It was simple. It was clear. There was no doubt in him to confuse things or cloud his judgement. There was only focus, purpose and poise. He would not fail. The storm raged around him, but he stood in the still centre of its eye. He watched with a strange detachment as the eddies of power swirling around him began to buffet Haal . . .

The school's large door suddenly swung open, showing only darkness beyond. It was a cavernous mouth yawning wide to consume its prey whole. A cold breath issued out of the portal.

'Come in, children!' creaked the voice of Minister Praxis. 'Quickly now, for we should spend whatever time we may learning of the blessed Saviours for our own improvement.'

For once most of the students wasted no time hurrying into the darkness. Jillan suddenly came back to himself and staggered as dizziness overtook him. Hella reached out to steady him, her blue eyes fearful.

'What happened?' she whispered. 'It was so strange.'

Haal still stood glaring at Jillan. He silently promised that things would be settled between them after school and then turned on his heel, followed by the pale Karl and Silus.

'I-I don't know,' Jillan wheezed. 'Maybe I'm coming down with something.' Yet he forced himself to straighten and seem bright, so as not to upset her any further. 'Come on then, let's get inside. Otherwise, the Minister will decide we need punishing for being lazy.'

But Jillan's thoughts were not so easily straightened. They swirled as if the storm was in his head and desperate for release. A pain started at his temples and it was a struggle not to wince. He concentrated hard on placing one foot after another evenly on the stony ground, and managed to force everything else into the background, reducing his headache to a dull throb. It itched and nagged at him, making his shoulders twitch every now and then, but he was satisfied that he had it largely under control. He managed a smile for his friend and pulled her inside the school.

Minister Praxis stood looking down at each of them. He was so tall and thin that he seemed unnaturally upright. His eyes were like water, sometimes colourless, sometimes taking on the hue of everything around them. Jillan felt as if he were drowning whenever the Minister looked at him. Everything else about the Minister was hard lines – an unbreakable brow, ruler-straight cheekbones and a spiked nose. He was the rod of discipline every community needed if it was to remain close to the will of the blessed Saviours.

'Good morning, children!' the Minister creaked.

'Good morning, Minister Praxis!' they chanted back, having to brave his gaze. Jillan could not help shivering, the back of his neck feeling wet and cold. He swayed slightly and his chair scraped.

'Jillan Hunterson, do you know no manners?' the Minister asked. 'You others may sit.'

Haal made no effort to hide a smile. There was the shunting and scraping of chairs as the class settled behind their desks. Jillan looked down at his feet.

'Well, Jillan Hunterson? We're waiting. Or do you seek to keep us from our study of the blessed Saviours?'

'Sorry, sir, it won't happen again.'

'Stop mumbling, boy! Are you trying to swallow your apology before it can be heard? Are you not genuine? Are you not honest? Lift your head up and apologise clearly to us all.'

His head and eyes never having felt so heavy, Jillan slowly raised his head and said, 'I'm sorry.' He hunched his shoulders slightly to hide the twitch that stabbed him in the middle of his back.

'You know, I'm curious, boy. Is it a poor upbringing or dark and sneaking thoughts that are to blame for your ill behaviour? Well? Which is it?'

His mind a muddle, Jillan could think of no easy answer. The Minister's question had him trapped. Either he had to blame his parents, giving Haal and his cronies the chance to smirk, or he had to confess to succumbing to the temptations of the Chaos.

'I . . .'

'He's coming down with a cold or something! That's why he's shaking,' Hella blurted.

Minister Praxis turned an ire-filled gaze on the bright-haired daughter of the town's trader. He said nothing for a few moments as the class held its breath . . .

'The Saviours gave him a tongue, Hella Jacobsdotter! If he cannot speak for himself in front of the Saviours' own Minister, then what use is that tongue? And we must wonder what secret it is that prevents him from speaking. Beware, Hella, that you be not unwise in your selection of friends and choosing for whom you speak up. Do you understand me, or should I perhaps ask your father and the town elders to explain it to you?'

Her bottom lip trembling, Hella managed a nod and a stuttering, 'Y-Yes, Minister. I understand. I-I'm sorry too.'

The Minister nodded and snorted at Jillan. 'Sit down! You have already wasted enough of our time. You are not worthy of our attention a moment longer when we should be contemplating our blessed Saviours. Now, attend me, children, for some of you will soon be of an age when you will be Drawn to the Saviours by the divine Saint Azual. You will then be ready to take your place as full members of this community, when you can begin to repay us for the years of food, shelter and betterment with which you have been indulged . . . and with which some have likely been spoiled.'

Jillan resisted the urge to shift uncomfortably under the Minister's glare.

'The visit of the holy Saint to this humble community and the Drawing are to be much celebrated. There will be dancing in the Gathering Place on the night of the Drawing, but those who attend should be careful not to overindulge in the revelry, lest their judgement become impaired and the Chaos find entry to their thoughts. Those who are to be Drawn will see the holy Saint alone during the day. Whatever goes on between yourself and the holy Saint must remain a sacred secret of which you never speak, else the pagans learn too much and plot ways to intrude upon the sacrament. You will need to confess your darkest thoughts and then be tested to see if you are worthy of being Drawn. Some will inevitably be found to carry the taint . . .'

Jillan's scalp itched and he dropped his eyes to the plain surface of the wooden desk.

'The tainted will be cleansed by the Saint. It is not a pleasant process, but you must obey the Saint's instructions without hesitation, lest the taint martial its strength and resist its removal. I will say nothing more of the testing and cleansing, for it is part of the sacred secret. Fear not, for the Saint will do much to remove the sacred knowledge from your mind in any event. Only allow yourself to be guided by the Saint, no matter what is asked of you, and all will be well. Do you all understand?'

'Yes, Minister Praxis!'

The Minister nodded, for once pleased. 'Nonetheless, we would do well to remind ourselves of the terrible sacrifices Saint Azual made in the name of the Saviours, so that we are sure to understand the great honour he does us with his visit. As the Book of Saviours tells us, he was once a child like yourselves, in a community like this one. But his community had become proud and wilful, seeking to decide its own future rather than be guided by the will of the Saviours. The Chaos had corrupted the minds of his parents, causing them to subject him to awful temptations in the dark of the night. His soul was in constant peril and there seemed none to hear him when he cried out for help or cried himself to sleep.'

There was the knowing look. There was the hot flush rising in Jillan's cheeks.

'One of you will now read to us from the Pages of Azual. Listen closely, children – without fidgeting – for I will test your understanding immediately afterwards. Hella, you seem eager to exercise your voice today so please approach the Book and find the proper page.'

Minister Praxis often asked Hella to give the reading, for he knew she helped her father with his record-keeping and therefore had a good grasp of numbers and letters. Many of the other students struggled with their reading, and the Minister could little bear to hear the sacred words of the Book of Saviours mangled in the mouths of the illiterate.

Hella went up to the simple lectern next to the Minister's desk and lifted back the heavy cover with her two small hands. The pages were illuminated with gold and lit up her face. She looks like an angel, Jillan thought. He stared, entranced, as she found the marked page and began to read in a slow, deliberate voice.

'And, in their wisdom, the blessed Saviours gifted a boy-child to the People of Downy Gorge. He was raised with the name Damon, as it was also his father's name. The boy-child was a joy to his parents and all who saw him, for in his innocence he was beloved of the Saviours and therefore drew all hearts towards him as the sun draws a plant from the earth, and as a flame draws and consumes the fluttering Chaos creatures of the night. Yet the sun will oft cast a shadow through no fault of its own when any seek to block it. And even a newly grown plant will attract a blight, and that is no fault of the sun. In the same way, the corruption of the Chaos sought out the young Damon in Downy Gorge.

'His father became envious of his wife's love for their son. He was further envious of those who spent time with his son when he could not. Therefore, he turned on Damon, his beloved child, and kept him locked away in a small room in their home. Further, he forbade his wife from ever seeing their son, for he was intent on owning and loving his son completely. In the darkest hours of the night, when the influence of the Chaos was at its strongest, he then visited Damon and sinned against him.

'Yet although the sun will set for a while, it cannot be held back. And so Damon was freed by his mother, who could not deny her proper motherly love any longer.

'Terrified that his father would be lost to the Chaos completely, Damon went to the town council to denounce his father and any who would not bow to the will of the Saviours. Even then, in his heart, Damon forgave his father for his sins, for Damon's was a selfless act, born of a care for the People.

'Yet the town council had long allowed pagan magicks and blandishments to work upon them. They saw the world not as it was, but as they wanted to see it, for then they could be happy no matter what went on in the world and what happened to the People. They mocked Damon and criticised him for resisting the discipline required by his father. They called his claims spurious and spiteful. And then they demanded he recant. When Damon would not, for he only understood the ways of truth, the council passed judgement that he should be exiled and never be permitted to return to Downy Gorge; and this was despite the pleas of his penitent mother and father.

'And so Damon was cast out into the wilderness, with nothing but the shirt on his back. Long did he wander, living off berries, mushrooms and plants, until he came to the sacred heart of the Empire. The Saviours were greatly dismayed to hear what had been done to the young and innocent Damon. Further, they were aggrieved to hear what had become of Downy Gorge and swore revenge, to push back the Chaos for the good of the People and the Empire.

'The Heroes of the Empire were sent forth to protect the People, Damon at their head, for he knew the land well, but also because he wanted to do all he could to save as many inhabitants of Downy Gorge as he could. Despite the trials and tortures to which he had been subjected, Damon still wanted to offer the inhabitants forgiveness and every chance to repent. As an honest and faithful member of the People, he was intent upon following the example of the blessed Saviours, intent upon saving the People and Drawing as many as possible to the Saviours.

'And so it was that Downy Gorge was overthrown, once honest Damon had shown the Heroes the secret ways through the walls of the community. Many were killed, for they were beyond saving; many were saved, and some few escaped under cover of darkness. Damon led the army of Heroes in pursuit and found out many pagan enclaves in the deepest parts of the forest. The fighting was terrible. The ground and rivers ran red with blood, and the fields were buried under the bodies of the fallen piled several deep. Yet, with the will of the Saviours to protect him, brave Damon prevailed. He cleared all the land to the south of the sacred heart, pushing the unrepentant pagans into the teeth of the mountains.

'The People and land were thus saved and allowed to flourish anew. New settlements were established, called New Sanctuary, Saviours' Paradise, Heroes' Brook and Godsend, in thanks for the wisdom and actions of the blessed Saviours. In recognition of his honesty and faith in the face of extreme temptation and hardship, Damon was beatified by the Saviours and reborn as an eternal Saint, he who is called Saint Azual. He was further charged by the Saviours to keep the lands to the south of the sacred heart always under his protection, so that never again would the Chaos be allowed sway over the People of that region.

'And so it was that the temple of Saint Azual was established at Hyvan's Cross, so that the blessed Saint would have a fitting place to receive pilgrims from the region, and a place of succour to which he might return every few months once he had administered the holy sacrament of the Drawing to those coming of age in the communities of the south.

'Here endeth the lesson,' Hella finally pronounced and looked to Minister Praxis.

The Minister nodded slowly and gestured for her to return to her seat. His eyes swept the class, looking for any who might not be paying their fullest attention, and finally settled on Jillan.

'Jillan Hunterson, what were the three miracles performed by Saint Azual when still known as Damon?'

Jillan only heard a rushing noise in his ears. He saw the Minister's lips move but could not decipher them properly. He felt a pressure behind his eyes and before he knew it he was asking, 'Sir, it is my duty to understand the reading better. Could you tell me if some of the pagans escaped into the mountains? And does Downy Gorge still exist?'

There was a quiet gasp from the class. Instinctively, they knew Jillan had crossed some line, had dared to go somewhere that was forbidden. They didn't understand why it was wrong, they only knew it *was* wrong, and that that was all they needed to know.

The Minister's face became as severe as they'd ever seen it. His cheeks were hollowed with shadow, his nostrils pinched and his lips bloodless. 'You dare?' he whispered. 'You presume to question *me*, a Minister of the Empire? What corruption is in you, boy, that you are so fascinated by the pagans?'

The noise roared in Jillan's ears now, but he was not going to let himself be trapped this time. 'They are our terrible enemies, sir. We must know enough of them to know how best to guard ourselves against them. Do they survive still in the mountains?'

Menace in his voice, his eyes narrowed, the Minister said very quietly, 'Our best defence against the dark and sneaking ways of the Chaos is a proper understanding of the Saviours' will, and that is all we need to protect us, as you should already know, boy. A close study of the holy book and the guidance provided by the Saviours' own Minister in Godsend is defence enough!' Now his voice became louder and his words came faster: 'Is that holy teaching not enough for you, boy, in your pride and arrogance? You are too inquisitive to keep your thoughts controlled and safe! Beware, Jillan Hunterson, for the Chaos lurks to either side of the righteous path of the Saviours' will, and should you start to wonder whether the lights and glints to either side are a better welcome of a lost treasure, then you will all too easily step from the path and become lost forever!' Spittle sprayed from the preacher's mouth and caught the thin light that made it through the shutters. 'If you were a better or more faithful student, Jillan Hunterson, then you would not so quickly forget the salutary lesson of Kaspar the Curious from the holy book! What is it that clouds your mind with forgetting? Well? You know yourself, do you not? It is a taint of corruption, is it not!'

The other students stared at Jillan in horror. Even Hella's face showed doubt and fear.

The Minister was shouting and wild-eyed now. 'You are too wilful for your own good, boy! Wayward like your parents, I say! It is that which makes you dangerously inquisitive. Until you learn the error of your ways, you are a danger to all your fellow students. They should shun you lest the taint spread to them also! Shun you, yes! Out, children, out! Go to your homes and pray for the Saviours' guidance. Hella and Jillan, you will stay here with me and study the holy book and seek salvation. I will then talk to the council to see what we can do about having you isolated from the others until the blessed Saint comes to Draw the taint from you. Out!' he shrieked.

The children scrambled to their feet in panic, a few crying out in fear as they were pushed and shoved by the others. Jillan blinked in shock, struggling to understand what was happening. Was he tainted after all? Was that the explanation for the trouble today and why everyone seemed so angry? And what did it mean that his parents were *wayward*? He looked at Hella, but she'd begun to cry and wouldn't meet his gaze. Her shoulders shook, but he dared not go to her.

The Minister shooed the last of the children out and proceeded to pace back and forth in animated fashion. He stared at them every so often and mumbled to himself. He clasped his hands together and shook them in fervent prayer. Jillan's shoulders twitched violently, but fortunately the distracted Minister failed to notice. Finally, the Minister stopped, some decision apparently made.

'See what your corruption has done, boy! See how it has disrupted our proper study of the Saviours' will. Do you see what a danger you have become?'

Caught between shame and denial, apology and refusal, Jillan found it impossible to speak. He managed to nod miserably, however, as his twitching became all but continuous.

'Let us pray we are not too late! Confessing your own corruption is the first step towards salvation, boy. If you repent and then show yourself genuinely penitent, there is still some hope for you. The Chaos may yet be defeated, and the taint exorcised by the blessed Saint! All will then celebrate your return to us! So you must not despair, Hella Jacobsdotter, for to give up hope is to lack faith in the eternal Saviours. We must instead become stronger and more determined in our faith, for we need the Saviours now more than ever before! Show me that you understand this: repent of your despair, Hella Jacobsdotter!'

Hiccuping through her tears, and wiping snot from her nose, the young girl answered, 'I repent, sir, truly I do. I try to be a good girl and learn the lessons as well as I can.'

'That is good, Hella, that is good. Now, approach the holy book and read to us from the Pages of Damnation, so that we may better understand the horrors that the taint of corruption stores up for us. Let us hear of the pagan hell towards which the Chaos tries to lead us, a place that is buried deep, just as Saint Azual piled the bodies of the pagans several deep. It is a place of decay and corruption, where the Chaos feeds on the unwary and those who have strayed from the safety of the Empire; and it is a place of dark concealment where the Chaos secretly schemes and burrows in an attempt to topple the Empire, while all the while cringing away from the exposing light and shining glory of the blessed Saviours and their Saints. Come, Hella, and read for us, while Jillan sits racked and shaking with remorse! See how the corruption within him twists in pain now that it has been found out and must hear the purging words and truth of the Saviours' will!'

Minister Praxis did not release them until the sun had begun to set on the world. He ordered them straight home, telling them to talk to no one – especially each other – and to let their parents know to expect a visit from himself and several elders later that same evening.

Tormented by guilt and visions of horror, Jillan stumbled sightlessly towards his house. He was exhausted, but there was something in him that wouldn't rest. It was the taint, he was now sure. It was never satisfied and it burrowed in him like a worm. If he'd had a knife, he would have cut himself open to try and get it out. 'After all, *Sacrifice and duty safeguard the People against the Chaos*, don't they?' he repeated to himself. He should be prepared to cut himself open to save all those he loved. It was the only way; otherwise, he would be a danger to others and allow the taint to spread.

They were waiting for him around the second corner. Something hit him across the back of the neck and then he was pushed forward.

'Pagan!' spat a voice behind him. It sounded like Karl.

Jillan staggered, having to run to stay upright and avoid pitching straight into the ground. He saw Silus ahead of him, the boy's fists clenched and ready. Knowing he wouldn't be able to stop in time, Jillan increased his speed and tackled Silus at waist height. The boy went over, banging his fists ineffectually against Jillan's back. Silus landed with a *whoof* as the air was forced out of him. Jillan lifted his head up sharply and caught the other under the chin, snapping his head back. Then Jillan punched Silus hard in the face.

A large shadow loomed out of the darkness. It was Haal. With a grunt, he swung a heavy stick in a flat arc. In the dim light Jillan didn't see it coming until it was too late. It caught him just above the right eye and knocked him back into the dirt. Blood filled his eyes and he groaned. He was kicked savagely in the side, but as he curled up in pain he managed to grab the leg of his attacker and topple him.

'Saviours curse him! Karl, get him! Beat the taint out of him!' Haal shouted.

And then the corruption finally broke free. The storm that had been trapped in Jillan's mind blew up around them and began to tear at their clothes. Jillan saw only red as bloodied lightning arced and crackled out from where he stood. Deliberately, he directed the raw energy at Karl, and the boy screamed in terror as it struck him. There was a deafening detonation and then a concussion wave flattening them all, Jillan included.

In the aftershock the only noises to be heard were whimpers from Haal and Silus. Karl lay prone and unmoving. The smell of smelted metal and cooked pork hung over them.

Jillan struggled to rise and then sagged back to the ground, no strength left in him.

Quavering voices began to shout out in the night.

'Here!' Silus sobbed.

'Magic!' wailed Haal. 'Murder!'

Jillan growled and the boys yelped and rolled away. His voice slurring with tiredness, he said, 'Keep quiet or I'll kill you too!'

They obeyed him and watched with animal-scared eyes. Jillan slowly got up, fighting against a wave of nausea and trying not to swoon. He only just kept a grip on consciousness as he took a lurching step into the dark. His eyes wouldn't focus and his limbs were reluctant to obey him. It was like that night when he'd decided to try some of his father's beer. His stomach turned over and he threw up against the stone wall of the nearest house.

'Who's there?' challenged a man's voice.

Jillan pushed himself away and tottered towards the next house, and the next. Suddenly, strong arms were sweeping him up off his feet and the forest smells of his father filled his nostrils.

'It's all right. I've got you. You're safe now,' Jed rumbled.

Gratefully, Jillan rested his head on his father's shoulder. He wanted to cry, he was so tired. His eyes began to close.

'No, no,' Jed whispered as he strode quickly towards their home. 'Stay awake!' He shook his son gently. 'Come on, tell me what happened, quickly, before we get home.'

He didn't want to think about it, but there was no hiding. They would be coming for him. Tears began to run down his cheeks and he began to shiver. What had he done? 'I am t-tainted, Father!' he moaned. 'They attacked me. I-I killed Karl.'

In a tight voice Jed asked, 'Are you *sure* he's dead?'

Jillan shook his head. 'He wasn't moving. Father, I am tainted!'

'No!' his father insisted with unexpected force. 'There is nothing wrong with you. Karl was probably just unconscious is all. There's no such thing as any taint. It's the Minister filling your head with nonsense. You were simply defending yourself.'

'B-but there were lights and a loud noise. I was rude at school. The M-Minister and some elders are c-coming to see you.'

His father held him tightly and began to move more quickly. 'Listen to me!' he whispered fiercely. 'Whatever happened was completely normal, and never let anyone tell you otherwise, you hear me! They made it happen. There's nothing wrong with you.'

Jed was running by the time their small house came into view. There were already welcoming candles in the window, and there would be a cosy fire inside.

'Maria!' his father shouted between heavy breaths. 'Maria! I've got him.'

The door flew open and his mother came out, took one look at them and then hurried back inside.

'Some warm tea or broth, Maria, quickly! Or even water if there's nothing else ready.'

Everything began to blur to Jillan. There were shouts. Shadows. Images faded in and out. He was in the big chair by the fire. Lifted again. A blanket. His mother's drawn face. His head resting against something hard. 'Drink this!' A spoon. 'Jillan! That's it.' Light hurting his eyes.

'. . . pack our things. We have to run!' his father was saying.

Another spoonful, half the contents dribbling down his chin.

'What are you talking about? There's nowhere to go,' his mother said with forced calmness.

'There was some accident with a boy. Maria, you know the sort of accident I'm talking about. And you know what they'll do to him. I won't allow it.'

Another spoonful, the contents slightly too hot, but he was unable to do anything but swallow.

'Jedadiah, do not panic! We must think. Listen, we will say things got confused. It happened on the way home, yes? Then who can be sure what happened in the dark? The children were tired and overwrought after a long day at school, and got overtaken by a night-terror. Many of the elders are sensible, despite what you might think of them. They will not want any sort of trouble here, not after what happened in New Sanctuary.'

'No! You know what that Minister is like. And the Saint will know what happened. They *always* know! They will take Jillan away and he will be lost to us. We'll probably never see him again.'

Another mouthful and he could taste again. His mother's flavoursome vegetable soup filled his senses.

His mother was silent for a few moments. He could sense her anguish. 'But we have nowhere to go, Jedadiah,' she said with a tremor in her voice. 'They will send Heroes after us. We have no horse. We will not even be able to get out of the gate unchallenged.'

'Samnir will help!' Jillan coughed, the room beginning to right itself.

His parents exchanged a glance. Suddenly, Jed was in the bedchambers and pulling blankets from the pallets. He grabbed sacks from the kitchen and began to fill them.

'Jedadiah, no! Hear me! Stop this!'

Jed did not stop.

'I outrank you in these matters; you will stop at once!' Maria commanded in iron tones.

Jed slowed and then stilled. He gazed at his spouse, his face tortured even in the firelight.

'You will listen to me, old bear. Listen and think! If we all leave together, they will start to search for us beyond the walls almost immediately. Yes, you know the forest paths better than most, but the other hunters will be set to track us. Jillan and I will not be able to keep up with you. They will ride us down within hours.'

'So what do we do?' the large man pleaded.

'It pains me beyond words, beloved, but you and I must remain.'

'What? How? He cannot go into the woods alone! He is just a boy!'

'When they come to our home searching for Jillan,' Maria insisted, 'we will be here waiting anxiously for him to come home. They will then search the town for him all night, giving Jillan time to get away. It would be inconceivable to them that any Hero would let him out of the town and not report it.'

'The Saint will know!'

'But will not be able to get here in time to stop him getting away. As parents, what would we not be prepared to suffer by way of reprimand from the Saint? Nothing, beloved! And Samnir will have his own reasons for helping us, reasons I doubt we could not even begin to guess at. Always was a strange fish, that one.'

'I should be there to protect my boy!' Jed said helplessly, his shoulders bowing and his voice breaking.

'You can protect him best by letting him go. He is almost of age, husband, no longer a boy. These events must show you that clearly, no? Do not seek to keep him a boy, therefore, else it prove his undoing,'

Jillan's mother replied firmly, apparently becoming stronger as she saw Jed weaken. As fragile and small as his mother had sometimes seemed next to his hulking father, it was now she who stood over Jed and filled the room with her presence. Then, more gently, she said, 'Now is the time for speed, beloved. Pack Jillan's things into a leather bag while I get some provisions together. Quickly! Jillan, are you strong enough to finish the soup yourself?'

'Yes, Mother.' Jillan nodded, fresh tears in his eyes, knowing it might be the last time he ever tasted his mother's wonderful soup. 'Father, remember my rocks, please?'

Jed's face became pained and he self-consciously turned away. 'Of course, son.'

Maria began a constant chatter as she set about gathering dried meat, hard cheese and small apples into a cloth. 'Jillan, make for Saviour's Paradise, where there is a man who once knew your father and me. He goes by the name of Thomas Ironshoe, if he hasn't changed it. Repeat his name so I can hear it.'

'Thomas Ironshoe.'

'Good. When he asks you what you want, tell him you seek Haven. Say it!'

'I seek Haven. But what is Haven?'

Maria glanced at him. 'I don't know, and it is not important. Thomas Ironshoe will either take you in as his own, until your father and I can come and join you, or he will send you to other good people. No, don't interrupt! Every second is vital. You will leave by the south gate and circle around to the north. Follow the road, but stay off it during daylight. Travel through the woods to the side of the road and always keep the road in sight. If anyone should meet you by chance, you are on a pilgrimage to Hyvan's Cross, to worship at the Saint's temple. Do you understand?'

'Yes, Mother,' Jillan replied, although she was talking so quickly that he found it hard to follow.

'Ready!' Jed declared, thumping the bag down on the table and placing Jillan's bow and quiver next to it.

Maria bundled the food inside the leather. 'The bag is heavy, and when you tire you may be tempted to throw something away, but resist. The things in here will keep you alive on a cold night. Never lie on the bare ground, as it will leach the heat from you and you might never awa— ' Her voice caught at the last and she shut her lips tightly, not trusting herself to continue.

'Enough, Maria,' Jed said softly. 'I will tell him the rest as we go.'

Maria nodded and finally managed a shuddering breath. She threw her arms wide and bent down. 'Then come kiss your mother goodbye, my baby boy and young man grown! Look upon my face and remember its lines. Feel no guilt as it fades with time; just know that I will always love you and will always be thinking of you, no matter what happens or where you are.'

She hugged and kissed him till he couldn't breathe, and even then he thought she would not let him go. Finally, she pulled away to wipe her cheeks and straighten up. 'If they come while you are gone,' she said to Jed, 'I will tell them that he never came home from school and that you have gone into town to look for him, imagining that he is dallying somewhere with Jacob the trader's daughter. Go now, for I need to replace blankets and food so it does not look like anything is missing. Go!'

Jillan stared back at his mother, not wanting the last look to come. No one was more beautiful than his mother, not even Hella. There were care lines at the corners of her mouth and hazel eyes, but they only helped to make her look loving and kind. She complained of white hairs among her long fair tresses, but to Jillan's mind they caught the light like gold and silver. And then there was the look she had just for Jillan, a look she never bestowed on anyone else, not even his father, although there was a different, special look for him too.

But then the door to the house was closed and his mother was lost to him. He turned round and saw nothing but darkness. He waited for his vision to adjust and then trailed after his father, who shouldered the bulging bag and Jillan's weapon.

'You can walk on your own, yes?' Jed suddenly thought to ask.

'Yes, Father, if we can go slowly at first.'

They reached the stairs up to the south rampart and began to climb.

'Who goes there?' Samnir called from above.

'It's me,' Jillan replied as loudly as he dared.

A pause. 'Jillan? What are you doing out at this time?'

Jed and Jillan climbed in silence until they reached the walkway. The two adults nodded a wary greeting to each other and then Samnir looked to Jillan.

'I need to leave, Samnir. I'm in trouble,' the boy explained without preamble.

Samnir sighed. 'Aye, I heard some sort of ruckus earlier and there are a lot of folk running back and forth all in a tizz. I don't miss much from up here, you know.'

Jillan wondered if Samnir had actually seen and heard everything. 'I need your help,' he said simply.

'Aye, and I promised it to you, lad, I promised it to you. My help you shall have, and I've already had your generous company and friendship in return. By my reckoning, a bit of excitement's good for the town anyway. Shakes them up a bit and reminds them they're still alive, if you know what I mean. You'll be leaving through this gate with no one else the wiser, though I hate to see you go, lad, really I do. Still, leave you must, so follow me.'

'Thank you,' Jed offered. 'You don't know what this means.'

Samnir stopped and looked back at him with an unreadable expression. 'Ah, I know all too well what it means, Jedadiah the hunter. But let us not think of such things, lest we tarry too long.'

A minute later Samnir and Jed were levering the heavy bar off the south gate. They swung one of the heavy doors inwards until there was a gap big enough for Jillan to squeeze through.

Jed rested a hand on one of Jillan's shoulders and turned him back towards him. 'Be brave, Jillan, for you are a man, as your mother says. Know that I am always proud of you, no matter what happens, or what you say or do. Always remember that there is nothing wrong with you, and that there are things far beyond the ken and experience of the simple people of Godsend or the simple words of the Book. Perhaps you will discover some of them and have an adventure of sorts. There is little advice I can give you about the Empire, my son, for to my great shame I have seen little of it. But I will tell you this: there are many bad and dangerous things that are not even deserving of a quick death. Even so, if you are ever to be a hunter, you must not hesitate to kill, else you be undone in that moment of hesitation.'

Jillan nodded silently, not really wanting to think of the death he was sure he had already caused. Karl's collapse had been so quick, he could only wish he had hesitated longer.

'Jillan, I would take it as a personal favour if you would take this blade with you,' Samnir interposed. 'It is from the Great Temple itself and will always find you should you call. It is freely given and therefore yours to command.'

'Thank you, Samnir,' Jillan said softly, the short ceremonial sword cumbersome in his hands.

An owl screeched in the woods and the night stilled as the predator's shadow swept over the trees.

'Goodbye, Jillan!' Jed choked. 'Your mother and I will see you soon. We will follow on as soon as we may.'

'Goodbye, Father! Tell Hella . . . tell Hella that I . . . liked her a lot.'

'I will, son, and I'm sure she already knows,' Jed whispered and gave his son a fierce bearhug and an awkward kiss on the forehead.

Jillan looked at the dim faces one last time and then stepped out into the darkness. Long seconds later the gate closed behind him with a soft *boom* of finality.

Jillan followed the path past the noisome midden ditches and weaved his way across the uneven ground of the cemetery. He looked back once to scan the ramparts. There was no sign of his father, who had no doubt hurried home to play his part in the deception of the Minister and elders. Yet there was the silhouette of Samnir, a lone sentinel against the corruption of the pagans, the pagans among whom Jillan was now numbered.

Jillan wanted to run and scream to be let back in. He wanted to deny he had done anything wrong. He wanted to be forgiven for having asked Minister Praxis questions and for what had happened to Karl. Yet such things were far beyond forgiveness, he knew.

Instead, he peered tiredly at the higgledy-piggledy graves and wondered where they would put Karl's body. If he'd had a flower, he'd have placed it in some open area. He half wanted to lie down with the dead himself, but this was not a cemetery for pagan bodies, so he dragged himself into the woods. After all, the bad things in this world were not deserving of a quick death, he'd been told.

*

Samnir watched the small figure disappear among the deep shadows beneath the trees.

He sighed and shook his head. 'Damn that boy!'

CHAPTER 2:

And character is the second

She had been born in darkness and had grown in darkness. Her earliest memory was a scream. Whether her own or her dying mother's, she had no way of knowing. Cries, a wet slap, sticky warmth and bad smells. The instinctive need for milk, minerals, sustenance – anything! Lying on her side there in the dark, she'd sucked in whatever she could, swallowing water, grit and something that was half-congealed and had a metallic tang.

The dark was timeless. There she remained in the womb of the earth until she found the ability to move and grasp at different places and textures. She gorged on new thicknesses and slurries, physical need forcing her to eat even the ones that smelt bad. Afterwards, she would sometimes feel bad, and her body would spasm and physically reject what she had just eaten; but she would take the stuff down again, and again, until her body became used to it and she could start to grow more.

She began to hear . . . well, not herself . . . the darkness rather. Whenever she moved, sound came from the womb around her. The sound repeated and shifted, allowing her to get a sense of where substance was thick, thin or absent. Movement and sound, limit and space. She began to perceive differences in the darkness without having to move. What lay beyond the gaps? she wondered.

She moved freely through the darkness to the largest gap. Suddenly, there was a terrible rumbling and the womb shook. She moved back quickly and crouched down in fear. The rumbling continued, finally became quieter and then stilled. She decided she would not go near the gap again, but then she heard cries from the other side, cries like her earliest memory. Perhaps there was another one of her through the gap.

She waited. The cries became quieter and more infrequent. Worried that they would disappear and leave her alone again, she ventured closer to the gap once more. There was no rumbling this time. She went through and then moved into the absence beyond, following the cries, chasing them before they could escape.

'Who's there?' wheezed a voice.

Sounds she didn't understand. Not a movement and not cries exactly. Something different. She turned this way and that, trying to make it out.

'Is someone there? Help me, please! The cave-in has me pinned. I can hardly move. For the love of the Overlords, help me!'

The other her seemed stuck in the thickness. It couldn't move freely in the way she could. The sounds it made were unpleasant to listen to, as if it were . . . scared. It smelt odd, but not scary. Her mouth watered hungrily, but she was not used to eating something that moved. And if she ate it, she'd be alone again. So she pulled the other her out of the thickness instead.

'Aieee! Careful! Thank you, thank you! Who are you? How are you so strong? Do you have any light?'

Unintelligible sounds. The other lay hardly moving. She remembered back to her earliest time. She had been like this once, lying in the dark. She'd needed darkness she could eat, the runny kind. She scooped it out of a nearby hollow and poured it into the other's mouth.

A gasp. 'Thank you, that's better. I was so thirsty!'

Physical contact. She grunted and shuffled back, uncertain.

'Oh! I'm sorry. You have the blight, you poor soul. I didn't know. May the Overlords bless you. And I don't mind, truly.' A pause. 'My name's Norfred. I thought I was a goner that time. Probably would have been if you hadn't happened along. They don't make much effort to find the old ones like me, you know.'

The other was not as thick or hard as she was. It was not the same as her. And it still didn't move much. She nudged it.

'Here! What are you about? Man who's just been through a cave-in needs a moment to recover, you know. Who do you think you are, one of the Overseers?'

The other had flailed out and slapped her. Startled, she hunkered back. She wasn't used to feeling something that wasn't hunger. She wanted more. She came back and nudged him again and waited for the slap.

'All right, all right! No rest for the wicked, eh? Help me up then.'

The other made contact in different places at the same time. She froze, utterly overwhelmed by the sensation. Here! This was otherness! An infinite wonder beyond the womb! She wanted to consume it entirely, wanted to be consumed by it entirely. It was everything she wanted and could ever want.

'Okay, okay. I'm fine. Let go now! Overlords, but you're heavier than the cave-in. Easy, easy! Oww!'

The other was making the unpleasant scared noises again, so she eased her hold on it, but did not let go completely.

'We need to go this way, but there'll be tons to be moved. Don't know another way to the home chamber, do you? Didn't think so. Then we'd better get started while our strength lasts, eh? If we're lucky, they'll hear us working and start digging from their side.'

The other scrabbled feebly at the thickness where it was mixed with areas of absence. She sensed that the other would get stuck in the thickness again! The thickness was not as hard in places as it needed to be. Couldn't the other tell?'

With a grunt, she pulled the other back and started to shift the thickness herself, but only where the thickness was hard enough and would not make them stuck.

'Oh! Thank you. By the Overlords, that's amazing!'

She pushed through and past the thickness with ease, more familiar with its nature than anything else in her life. It was the substance of the womb that had fed and nurtured her from the beginning. She'd eaten it, slept on it and clung to it in the dark since she could remember. And she'd become as hard as the thickness itself, becoming just an extension of its substance, albeit a moving one. When she passed through it like this, she almost felt at one with it and fancied she could understand its vastness, could feel its infinitely slow movements, and could glimpse its strange thoughts, although none made sense to her.

The other stayed crouched directly behind her as she went.

'You move through the rock as if it were water, or the air itself. Truly, you have an amazing skill. You must be the greatest miner in the world!'

Sounds from the other that were not unpleasant to listen to. In fact, they were nice and created a feeling in her she could not remember experiencing before. It was like wanting to be consumed by the otherness. It made her want to do things for the other, do everything for the other.

She moved all the thickness aside until she broke into the great absence beyond. And then the darkness disappeared and she became blind! She cried and made unpleasant noises to tell the other that she was scared. And then the other was there helping her.

'It's just the light from the miners and the home chamber up ahead! Here, cover your eyes until they get used to it. Give me your hand! Here, over your eyes. That's it.'

Gone was the texture, depth and differentiation of the darkness, all washed away by something that was . . . not darkness, was the opposite of darkness.

The other guided her forward through the blindness, just as she had guided him through the dark and thickness a moment before. Was the blindness then the substance and nature with which the other was most familiar? Had this substance fed and nurtured the other during its beginning? Had the other eaten of it, this thin substance that was not darkness, slept on it and clung to it? Was that why the other was soft and thin where she was hard and thick? Was otherness then precisely what she was not? Was that why she felt completed by it? Was that why she wanted nothing but the other?

Sounds came towards them, sounds that were more others. So many! The sound swamped her and she tried to block it out with her hands, but then the blindness flooded in. Trembling, she turned away.

'Back, back!' the other cried. 'Don't crowd it! It saved me! Yes, I'm fine. It brought me through the cave-in. Quietly, quietly! It seems scared.'

'Is it the rock blight? I've never seen it so bad.'

'But it moves freely. It hasn't petrified or turned to stone like so many do. How can that be?'

'Its skin seems hard enough though.'

'How is it not a statue, fixed?'

'It's a female,' the other sounded. 'But mute, I think.'

'Poor thing. Let us women take her with us.'

'No, she has the taint. She'll infect us all!'

Contact all over her. She lashed out.

Unpleasant sounds. Cries.

'Aieee! My arm! It's broken! Bitch!'

'Leave her!' Sounds from her other. 'Back! All of you! Don't touch her. You're scaring her.'

'My arm! My arm!'

'Someone help Gang-leader Darus. I'll calm her and take her to my tunnel,' the other said.

'She's a danger. Ah! Careful, you dolts!'

'We shall deal with her in good time, Gang-leader. It's more immediately important that we see to your own immediately. We are nothing without you. Quickly, take the Gang-leader to the healer.'

Contact again, but this time she knew it was her other, for she could sense its particular texture. She clung tightly to it, knowing she must be hurting it, but there were no unpleasant sounds. The other was helping her. The other completed her. All would be well while the other was with her.

The other led her through the absence. She sensed them both entering a vast area of absence and then a smaller place.

'Here we are. This is my burrow. It's small but cosy. Sit here. That's it. Now, let's see what we can do about your eyes. I'll wrap some cloth around your head and you can get used to the small light that gets through that for a while. Everything will be fine, you'll see.'

And so she entered the world of the Overlords. Every morning Norfred would speak to her and teach her words. He gave her the name Freda, and she was pleased because it was a gift from him, although she wasn't sure why she needed it or what it was for exactly. And the others referred to her via other names and words anyway, although she wasn't sure what any of them meant. Then he would test her eyes without the cloth, and she would suffer the blindness for a while to humour him, although she could sense far more when her eyes were closed and she moved through a world of darkness.

After their morning lesson, they would go with the others to work at the thickness, or *rock* as they called it. The others were soft and not very good at moving through the thickness despite the things they had called *tools*. She, however, had no trouble pushing though it. The others were amazed at how she worked, and made excited noises. Norfred was happy too, and that pleased her, especially because he seemed to need more help than a lot of the others to move the thickness.

'It's because I am old, Freda,' he said when she asked him about it one day.

'Old?' she gurgled.

'Yes. After a certain amount of time, people start to get weaker, Freda, until they are so weak that they simply stop altogether.'

Freda scratched at her head and flicked away bits of skin that had crumbled where she had caught her head against a low-hanging piece of rock. 'If they stop completely, they become like the rock . . . or slurry, yes?'

Norfred tilted his head as he thought about it and then nodded. 'Yes,' he smiled, 'just like the rock and slurry, waiting for miners to find valuable bits left in among them.'

'Once they have stopped, how do they start again, Norfred?'

'They don't, Freda, I'm afraid. It's called being dead.'

Freda was quiet for a long while. Then she gurgled unhappily, 'I don't want you to stop, Norfred!'

He patted her on the arm. 'Don't worry, Freda, it won't be for a long time, especially if you're around to save me from any cave-ins. It's a blessing for us that you always know where the rock is too weak to venture. There hasn't been a single accident since you joined us, you know. Even Darus has to listen when you say where we should and shouldn't work, although I don't think he likes having to do so, eh?'

'Darus doesn't like me, Norfred!'

'Ah, don't worry, Freda – he doesn't like anyone. That's just his way. It's his job as Gang-leader not to like anyone or have any favourites, as that way he makes sure we all work as hard as possible. Our Overseer made Darus the Gang-leader precisely because Darus was the meanest of everyone here, you see. But Darus is in a far better mood these days now that you help us find so much sun-metal. The Overseer is very pleased, I hear, and there's talk that Darus might soon ascend as reward. He would be the youngest of us ever to do so. It is the just reward for hard work to which we all aspire, Freda.'

Freda's nose cracked as she wrinkled it. 'I don't like the sun-metal, Norfred. It frightens and blinds me. And it hurts to touch.'

'It's just the way it glows, Freda, that's all. Your eyes aren't used to it. But many think it is as beautiful as it is rare, and the Overlords need it to make their weapons for the war they fight on our behalf. There is nothing stronger than sun-metal, you see, and it burns our dark foes terribly. We supply the sun-metal to the Overlords, and in return they make great sacrifices above to ensure that we remain safe down here. And they will often go without food to ensure we eat properly.'

Freda nodded, although she didn't understand much of what Norfred said. He'd talked of such things many times before and it seemed important to him that she understood and agreed. But she didn't eat the food of the others because it made her feel weak – she was far happier with the slurry that came from the thickness. It meant her bones were never soft or breaking, unlike the bones of the others.

'So, you see, the sun-metal is important, and you are a blessing to all of us. And you are a blessing to me in my old age, Freda, for I'd never thought to have anything like a wife or child again. But the Overlords have been kind, for I have lived long enough to see the day.'

Freda was very familiar with the idea of children, for there were always some of them running and playing about the main home chamber, and the larger ones tended to work side by side with the adults. And there seemed to be two types of adults: husbands and wives. They tended to stay in pairs, for companionship and to look after a child or two. Freda was not sure she would know how to look after a child, though.

'What happened to your wife and child from before?' she asked curiously.

Through the gauze over her eyes, she saw Norfred scrunch up his face in a way she associated with him being unhappy.

'The rock blight took my dear Tasha, but our son Jan was done the great honour of being chosen for the army of the Overlords. He's a handsome and strapping lad, you see, and those like him are often selected by the Overseers. There was a great celebration in the home chamber, for a whole level of the mine takes pride when one of its own is taken like that.'

But Norfred's voice sounded sad rather than proud. 'Are you sorry you do not see and touch him any more?'

Norfred smiled. 'Of course, Freda. I miss him dreadfully, even though he was taken so many years ago. I fear that the fighting is bad, I wonder where he is and I imagine he has a wife and a child of his own now. A grandchild, you see. And maybe that grandchild looks like my dear Tasha. Ah, but listen to me going on. It's nothing but fanciful talk, best not dwelt upon.'

'Maybe we can go and look for him if that will make you happy, Norfred.'

'What are you saying, Freda? There is a terrible war up there. It would be far too dangerous. And every miner must work as long and as hard as they can to find sun-metal. If they were all to go off looking for their children, there would be no sun-metal, no weapons and no army. All would be lost, Freda! The Overlords depend on us. If I were to go off, all the other miners would have to work harder, but they already work as hard as they can, so it would break some of them, and I cannot have that on my conscience, truly I can't. Besides, the Overseers and the miners of the levels above guard the way and wouldn't let us up.'

Freda puzzled and then said tentatively, 'We can go our own way up. I can take us through the rock like I did with the cave-in. We can go now.'

Norfred became tense now, as if upset. In a low voice, he said, 'I . . . This is my home, Freda. I was born here, like my father before me.'

'Are you scared, Norfred?' she asked in confusion. She'd thought he wanted to see his son more than anything else. And she only wanted to make him happy.

'Freda, I . . .' He paused for a long moment. 'I have never been above this level, let alone all the way up. What you're suggesting is . . .' He gave up again. 'I am at this lowest of levels because it is my place. When I have worked long and hard, then I will ascend. Even that is not certain, because I am weak. But we don't know what's up there.'

'You're weak because of the poor food you eat, and your son is up there.'

'Wait, wait. Freda, we're happy here. You're happy here, aren't you?'

'Yes, Norfred. I am happy when with you. You will be happier with your son, though, will you not?'

'Enough, Freda! I don't want to talk about it any more. I'll think about it later, but I don't have time right now. You heard the bell – we have to go and start work with the gang. We don't want to be late.'

'Yes, Norfred,' she said miserably. 'Don't be angry with Freda, please.'

He sighed and patted her arm again. 'I'm sorry, Freda. I'll think about it, I promise I will. Come on, let's see if we can find enough sun-metal to make even Darus smile. Now that would be a thing to see, eh?'

'Yes, Norfred,' she said more happily.

'It's not enough!' Darus spat at Norfred.

Norfred frowned. 'But it's more sun-metal than we've ever collected. In just one shift we've found more than we did all of last year!'

'Just because we've finally found a rich vein doesn't mean we can slacken off and waste our time with celebration! Quite the opposite! We should be inspired to work even harder now that our efforts are finally beginning to bear fruit. We have kept the Overlords desperately short for far too long. We need to get the sun-metal to them as quickly as possible, so it can save us all, and perhaps even tip the balance of the war in favour of the Overlords. So stop your selfish and shameful whining, Norfred, and get that brute back to the workface.'

Norfred placed himself between Freda and the Gang-leader. 'She's exhausted! You've had her working two shifts straight. Push her any further and she'll become ill. Then where will we be? Don't risk all we've achieved for the short-term!'

'Are you forgetting who is Gang-leader here, old man?' Darus sneered. 'Are you becoming addled in your dotage? Do you forget who instructs who?'

'It's a-al-all right, I can work for a little more,' Freda groaned.

Norfred ignored her and drew himself up to his full height. Freda knew his back would suffer for it later. 'Darus,' Norfred rasped, 'I am not so addled as to forget when I dandled you as a babe on my knee. I am not so addled as to forget having to tan your hide for stealing apples from the stores when you were a mere boy. I am not so addled as to forget you asking my advice when you were made a Gang-leader not so long ago. And I am not so addled that I cannot see when a man's better judgement has been undone by his selfish ambition to ascend!'

'How dare you!' Darus blazed, his voice so loud it echoed throughout the level. Eyes wild with fury, he stepped forward and violently back-handed the old man.

Norfred crumpled to the ground, Darus shrieking as he discovered he'd again fractured his arm that had only recently mended.

With a roar louder than any rockfall, Freda surged towards the hated Gang-leader. Darus had brought two of his biggest men with him, and they came forward now to meet her. One slammed a giant fist into her chin, but she barely felt it, while the bruiser cried out as several of his knuckles broke. She smashed her forehead into his nose, instantly turning his face into a bloody mess. Then she swung her right arm and hit the other miner across the chest with it. He flew backwards into the cave wall, his head cracking sickeningly against the rock. He slid to the floor and blood began to pool around him.

She advanced on Darus now, intent on pounding him to dust. The Gang-leader whimpered in fear and she smelt urine.

There was a weak cough and Norfred called to her. 'Freda, don't! I need your help. Leave him! Freda, come lift me up and take me somewhere safe. Freda, I need you.'

She hesitated with her two boulder-like fists raised above Darus's head. Then she lowered them slowly and turned back towards the other, he who made her complete, he whom she only wanted to make happy and protect. But she had not done enough to protect the other, and now he was hurt. She was suddenly terrified that he would stop completely. She stumbled to him in haste and lifted him as gently as her clumsy hands would allow. He was so light and fragile. She could tell he was weakening. She sensed something like a small cave-in in his head, but this time she didn't know how to save him.

'Freda is sorry, Norfred!' she moaned.

He ran trembling fingers across her cheek and whispered, 'Do not be sad, Freda. I have had a long life, longer than most. And I am happier than any that ever lived that I got to know you.' He coughed weakly and his rheumy eyes clouded with pain. 'Promise me?'

She lowered her head closer to his lips. 'Anything, Norfred!'

'Promise me that you'll go to the top of the mine and beyond. You deserve to be free of Darus and his cruelty. I wish I had listened to you before, and now it is too late, my dearest Freda. If you see . . . if you see Jan, tell him I . . . I miss him and love him.'

'Don't stop, Norfred, pleeease!'

The life in him guttered like a miner's candle. 'There's no pain now, Freda. Take me to the women. They will know how to tend to my body. Be free and happy, my dearest Freda.'

And then all was darkness. Where once she had found comfort, nurture and texture in that darkness, now it was empty. It was a void where the silence was eternal and deafening.

'You'll pay for this, you freak,' Darus promised quietly as he watched the monster retreating down the tunnel, cradling the old bag of bones.

The women had always been kind to Freda, although she didn't understand the look of sympathy that was always in their eyes when she spoke to them. She was grateful for it now though.

'Place him here, you poor thing,' Mistress Widders said gently. 'That's it. We'll look after him and see to it that he's prepared in the proper way. He'll join the spirits of those who went before him, dear. He'll be cast into the bottomless pit, which is one of the eternal places.'

Freda's sharp ears picked up shouts in the distance, but no one else seemed to have heard them yet.

'It goes on forever, you see. There is no death or unhappiness there. He'll be welcomed by the Overlords who have gone before him, and he will be treated as if he were their equal. They will celebrate his life and name him an Underlord of this world. And he will wait for you, Freda, and you will see him again one day.'

'I will?' she asked in wonder, suddenly filled with hope and smiling so widely that flakes of skin rattled off her cheeks. 'If I cast myself into the bottomless pit, maybe I can see him straight away!'

Mistress Widders's face fell. 'No, Freda, that would be wrong. The Overlords will not receive us in the eternal world until we have first finished all our work for them in this world. Do your duty by them here, and then you will be welcomed by them. They will call you to them when the time is right. It was Norfred's time, but it is not yet yours. Norfred will wait for you and watch over you. Do you understand?'

She nodded heavily. The shouts were closer now. The anger in them was plain to hear.

'What's that commotion now?' Mistress Widders asked in exasperation. 'Will these men never abide? There is grieving to be done, respects to be paid and prayers to be said. Is it beyond them to keep the peace?' The head woman sighed, touched Freda on the arm and asked, 'Freda, be brave now and tell me how Norfred passed.'

Freda shifted her weight from foot to foot and shook her head. She didn't want to think about the terrible moment again. She would see her kind Norfred again one day and that was enough for her. They should just leave her alone now. Why couldn't they leave her alone now?

'Come on, dear. Save for the bottomless pit, there is nowhere that is deep or dark enough to hide from the Overlords. I need to know, Freda, if you have done anything wrong. Tell me, quickly now.'

'It was my fault!' she choked. 'I didn't want to work any more, and that made Norfred and Darus argue. I know I am meant to do what the Gang-leader says. But he hurt my Norfred so I hurt him back. I'm sorry! I didn't mean to.'

'Shh!' the head woman said, patting Freda. Her face became stern. 'Darus hurt Norfred, yes?'

Freda nodded miserably.

Voices erupted around them as a large group of miners carrying flaming torches charged around the bend in the tunnel that led to the women's chamber. The light dazzled Freda's eyes and she was forced to turn away.

'The freak murdered the old man! And killed good Sol too! She must pay!'

'The rock blight has made her a mad beast. She must be thrown down before she can turn on the rest of us!'

'Or before she can infect us!' Mistress Widders squared her shoulders, lifted her chin and deliberately stepped into the mob's path. She stared them down and they quailed before her.

'How dare you!' she shouted at them. Then she pointed an accusing finger at Darus. 'You! Why didn't you bring Norfred's body here for care? You were too busy stirring up your gang, is that it?'

'There is justice to be done,' the Gang-leader replied smugly. 'And we should see to that justice quickly, else we do Norfred's memory a disservice. Isn't that right, men?'

'Ayeee!' the mob chorused angrily behind him.

'It is just one man's word against another's,' Mistress Widders said with a shake of her head. 'Gang-leader or not, man or woman, when there's a trial one miner's word has as much weight as any other's.'

But Darus had gained his position by dint of his shrewdness and was not about to let this woman take the momentum out of his mob. 'One *man's* word, she says. One *woman's* word, she says! But I ask you this, men: is that freak born of any man or woman? You've seen how the monster walks through walls! It isn't natural! Is it natural? Answer me! Is it natural?'

'Nooo!'

'Now stand aside, woman, or be put aside!' Darus said through the din and stepped forward with intent.

Freda panicked as she saw him take that step. He'd moved forward in exactly the same way when he'd struck down Norfred. She could not let him do the same to Mistress Widders, *would not* let him do it!

Releasing a roar of rage, Freda rushed at the mob. How she hated the others now.

'Freda, no!' Mistress Widders cried, but she had already been pushed to the side by miners eager to reach the creature they believed to be a killer.

Freda smashed into them, immediately knocking two burly men to the floor. She hammered her fists into chins and torsos, snapping necks and shattering ribs. The point of a pickaxe came down on the back of her head and she staggered, slowing for a moment. A flaming brand was thrust into her face and she was blinded. Blows rained down on her from all sides and she was kept off balance. She was forced onto one knee and had to use her arms to cover her head so she could find a moment's respite.

It was tempting to give up, to admit that it was her laziness that had killed Norfred. Perhaps she did deserve to be punished. Maybe then it would all stop, all the fear, sadness, pain and ugly words. Maybe then she would stop and become stone and slurry. Maybe she would be thrown into the bottomless pit and she would finally see her beloved Norfred again.

'Stop it! Shame on you! You're nothing more than murderers yourselves! Look at yourselves. The Overseer will be told of this!' someone was shouting. Was it Mistress Widders?

But she had promised Norfred she would go to the top of the mine and find his son. And Mistress Widders had said Norfred was watching over her. She could not bear the thought of letting him down again.

Gritting her teeth so hard that she chipped them, she surged back to her feet and bludgeoned the miners nearest to her to the ground. She clapped her hands on either side of another's head and crushed his skull. Spraying blood filled the air and covered her face, until the red liquid was running down her facial channels and into her mouth. It tasted good and only increased her hunger.

'Use your torches!' Darus cried. 'Go for her all at once! Now!'

She swept them aside and trod heavily on those unfortunate enough to lose their footing.

Yells and screams echoed and boomed through the mine as if some gigantic beast had been uncovered and the entire place was collapsing. People began to run, and Freda went after them.

She lumbered down tunnels, through the home chamber and then made for the steep incline up which only the sun-metal and Darus were ever allowed. Her lungs were burning painfully now but she did not slow. She hurled herself forward, not caring that chunks of thick skin were torn away on outcroppings or where the walls of the passage narrowed.

'What in the name of the Overlords is amiss down there?' called a deep voice from up ahead. 'Answer me.'

Freda growled and burst up through the opening. A large bearded ogre of a man reared back from her and raised his spear shod with glowing sun-metal to the ready position.

'What, have the Underlords driven this horror out from among them? What have you done with Gang-leader Darus, fiend?'

Then he lunged forward powerfully with his weapon and impaled her through the shoulder. Her skin was no defence against the terrible burning metal and she bellowed in agony and fear. The passage of the sun-metal blade left energy trails in the air that scored across her vision. Thick black blood bubbled out of her wound and sizzled as it met the spear. Acrid smoke billowed around her and she found it hard to breathe.

The Overseer yanked his weapon free and prepared to plunge it back into her, but she cringed away and fell back into the rock for refuge. She moved through the thickness as quickly as she could and pushed upwards.

She soon began to slow, as exhaustion, blood loss and shock overtook her, but she did not stop climbing. Ever higher. Her head swam, but she dared not stop for fear she would lose her sense of up and down. She had visions of becoming disorientated and ending up back at the lowest levels of the mine, perhaps even plummeting into the bottomless pit and a hell of eternal punishment.

The rock began to change, to become softer, and she realised she must be coming close to the top of the mine and whatever lay beyond. There were strange wriggling things in the soft mulch that replaced the rock, but they seemed harmless. Surely these small things were not the Overlords, were they? What were they then? They burrowed, tunnelled and scurried, but largely ignored her and refused to answer any of the questions she asked.

There was more water here, and the mulch clogged her ears, nose and eyes. She didn't like it, and it took everything she had not to start thrashing around in panic. She kicked violently and propelled herself further upwards, where it was drier again. At least the wet mulch had soothed her troublesome wound somewhat. Now, there was almost as much air as mulch making up the thickness.

And then she broke through into the largest and brightest cavern she'd ever seen. She glimpsed a large shining disc of sun-metal somewhere far away and high up but was otherwise blinded, even when her eyes were shut as tightly as possible. She felt like she was falling upwards as she left the thickness. She did not understand anything she heard or smelt and her skin felt like it was constantly shifting around independently of the rest of her because it was never the same temperature all over.

She had entered the most terrible place of the Overlords, a place that was a hell of constant warring. So there was hell below and a hell above.

She was tempted to return to the limbo of the rock between the two hells, but Mistress Widders had said the tireless miners of the Overlords would eventually find her there. She had promised Norfred she would suffer this upper hell to find his son, so suffer it she would. She now knew that the fear, sadness, pain and ugly words never stopped and were the nature of existence for creatures such as she. Why else would she be allowed such strength and such a thick skin?

Panting hard, Jillan hauled his heavy pack through the dark woods around Godsend. While at the beginning his breath had billowed in the cold air, he could now hardly see it – he realised he was already losing body heat. *Don't panic*, he told himself. But he pushed on urgently nonetheless.

Keeping the walls of the town always in sight, he circled around to the north and found the road. Staying in the trees, he paralleled the way to Saviours' Paradise until Godsend was well out of sight, and then moved to walk on the wide flagstones.

Don't think. Ignore the strange sounds in the woods. Don't imagine horrors for yourself. Keep going. Don't worry that this is the furthest you've ever been from home. But with that last thought, others came creeping and stealing into his head. Of course, it's not your home any more, is it? You can never return there again, unless you want to put your parents at even greater risk. They'll be better off without you in all likelihood . . . unless they were already being carted off to the town's punishment chamber by the Heroes, because they had been accused of hiding him somewhere by the Minister and the elders. Should he turn back and throw himself on the town's mercy in order to save his parents any further pain?

His steps slowed. *Don't think! Keep going!* He swung his head up and round to look back down the road. He experienced a moment's giddiness and realised he was light-headed with cold, tiredness and maybe shock. *You're not thinking clearly. Find somewhere to rest for the night and you'll be better for it.*

But he needed to put some sort of safe distance between himself and the town before he could allow himself any respite. He increased his pace in the direction of Saviours' Paradise once more. How far did he need to go until it was safe? As far as possible to be as safe as possible.

Yet there was no such thing as safety for him any more, was there? The further he got from the town, the wilder the woods would become and the greater the threat would be from the pagans and the other Chaos creatures, especially on a moonless night like this. The dark and sneaking enemy had probably already found his trail and begun to hunt him.

He broke into a jog, which was as fast as his cumbersome pack would allow. The trees began to give way on either side to a stretch of open fields. Here was where his mother and many of the other adults worked during the day. There were long furrows of cabbages in the field to the right, while the field to the left was empty. He didn't like cabbages too much, so left them – besides, people might notice the next day if there were some missing and might put two and two together.

He imagined his mother toiling in the fields and was tempted to camp in the trees just further on so that he might catch a glimpse of her the next morning. But the logical part of his mind shook his head for him and told him he was becoming crazy again. There would be Heroes patrolling the perimeters of the field all day. He would be at risk of being caught if he came too close, and he certainly wouldn't get a chance to talk to his mother.

Keep going. The road passed beyond the fields, and the trees began to crowd in on either side. There was moss growing between the flagstones now too. Clearly, the road was less used from here onwards. And he couldn't see a thing. His skin prickled as the woods around him began to moan in the gusting wind. He was definitely moving beyond the ordered environs of Godsend and into the wilds where the Chaos lurked. It was as if he was entering an entirely different realm; passing out of the light and civilisation of the Empire and into a dark and untamed world of haunting ghosts and ancient pagan magic. He fancied there was a cold malevolence in the air and that he was being watched. It was all he could do not to break into a flat-out run – but he knew he wouldn't get more than fifty metres or so before collapsing in exhaustion and making himself entirely vulnerable to whatever horrors were inclined to prey on him.

He jogged deeper into the darkness, his labouring breath filling his ears. He wouldn't hear it if something was creeping up on him. *Keep going!* He needed to keep going till morning, and then he could rest during the day. If he only travelled at night, the road would be fairly safe for him and he should be able to make it all the way to Saviours' Paradise . . . as long as the Chaos didn't find him before then.

Yet he was struggling to stay on his feet – he was still drained from the confrontation with Haal. His pack pulled down on his shoulders more and more, like the burden of his guilt. His steps wandered and he constantly had to squint with his tired eyes to make out the way forward.

Suddenly, the horror came for him. There was a shriek off in the woods to his left that definitely wasn't human. There would be no time to string his bow and ready an arrow, he knew. He immediately swerved off the road to the right and went towards the only opening between the trees ahead that was wide enough for him to get through . . . only to slam into a stone wall of a broken-down old tower. He was thrown back and unceremoniously dumped, what with the added weight of his pack, on his behind and back.

Winded, he lay blinking up at the structure. *Who put that there?* he thought stupidly. Then he gasped as he realised his pursuers would be gaining on him every second he continued to play the town idiot. *Up!* Yet he didn't hear anything off in the woods. No growling and snuffling of a predator following his spoor. Not even the sound of dry leaves shifting in the breeze as something stalked him. All was still.

He released the breath he'd been unconsciously holding and clambered to his feet. *You are an idiot, Jillan, panicking every time you hear some forest creature.* He leaned for a moment against the wall and then made his way round to the entrance. Ivy and other plants had long since pulled any door away and had even begun to wrest stones from the forlorn structure. The walls sagged badly in places, but Jillan was too weary to worry about the danger. He put his head through the doorway and smelt damp, decay and something worse. Some animal must have died in there, he decided. And he could see the sky up through the tower, so it didn't offer that much shelter.

He stepped back out of the small building and tiredly considered it. What was it here for? It seemed older than Godsend, so who had built it and why? Did it guard something? With a shrug, he turned away and saw a lighter area of the forest past the line of trees ahead. Curious, he moved towards the greyness and emerged into a wide field with what looked like ruined hovels and cottages on the far side.

He still couldn't see well, but the field seemed to be entirely covered with dead branches and twigs. Had someone felled the trees hereabouts, hauled the trunks away and left all the smaller branches here? It didn't make sense. What was this place, and how had he not heard of it when it was closer to Godsend than even Saviours' Paradise?

He peered more closely at the ground, looking for secure footing, but the murk was too thick to make much out. He shuffled forward, the wood crunching and crumbling strangely under his weight. He detected the same sort of unpleasant odour as he'd experienced in the tower, albeit not quite as strong.

As he edged further out into the field, the ground around him began to tremble and . . . creak? Then it gave way beneath him and he crashed down through the branches for six or so feet before he hit the ground.

Jillan coughed and groaned before weakly trying to move. Nothing seemed injured, so he took a moment to catch his breath. He looked up at the small patch of grey sky above him where he had fallen through the treacherous surface. He sighed. It looked a long way off from where he lay, and he wasn't sure if the branches would take his weight if he did try to climb out. If he started flailing about in this midnight hollow then there was a good chance he could bring everything down and bury himself forever. It was probably best to wait until daylight, he persuaded himself.

At least it was dry where he was, and he was sheltered from the wind above. He even had the advantage of large predators not being able to get to him across the branches, unless they wanted to end up trapped as well. Fate had apparently decided he would sleep somewhere safe that night after all. *Praise be to the Saviours,* he thought as his eyes closed, and then realised that was probably not the most appropriate thing to be thinking any more. He resolved to worry about it the next day, and was asleep in seconds.

Jillan dreamed dreams of blood and misery. He was standing shoulder to shoulder with what looked to be field workers and shouting abuse at a group of soldiers some distance away. He realised the soldiers were Heroes, and they looked grim-faced and determined indeed. Their brown leather armour was scarred from recent fighting and there were notches in their swords and spearheads. By contrast, those standing with Jillan shook pitchforks and mattocks, and wore only heavy homespun clothing.

'Don't worry, boy,' the spotty young man next to Jillan said in a strange thick accent and gave him a wink. 'We outnumber them a good bit, so they'll not be forcing us off our land.'

The man's breath smelt strongly of ale, and Jillan couldn't help wrinkling his nose and turning his face away.

'Aye,' said a tall man with an unkempt black beard on his other side. 'And with our shaman back from the mountains now, the oncomers will soon find their bowels turned to water and themselves impotent, you'll see. Shush, here's the headman now, looking to talk to them. 'Swaste of time, I reckon. The oncomers don't know any reason 'cept for taking what they're wanting, and killing any as tries to tell them nay. There's no bargaining with them so as all can live through winter.' He spat. 'Hard bargain, hard winter, all know that.' He gripped his staff more tightly.

'I heard they let the people of Malmsby live, but set them to work building up the place as some sort of fort,' the pimpled youth said.

Blackbeard snorted contemptuously. 'Aye, they'll keep you alive while they need a job doing. But they'll take a man's freedom to roam the land, which is as bad as taking a man's life by my reckoning.'

The youth didn't look inclined to agree, but thought better of saying anything to that effect. Instead, he asked, 'Can you hear what they're saying?'

'I could if you impatient youngsters would keep quiet for more than a moment!'

A large white-haired elder in gold-inscribed leather armour, whom Jillan took to be the headman, had gone striding out from the ranks of the villagers towards the line of Heroes. He was broad-shouldered and had a pronounced jaw. Despite his advancing years, his body had not yet turned to fat, nor had it wasted – he was clearly still a powerful man. At his side a small man in animal furs stepped nimbly across the ground, waving his hands in the air and speaking as if to himself. The hairs rising on the back of Jillan's neck told him there was magic in the air and this was the village shaman.

From among the Heroes, an abnormally large individual came forward. Jillan could see the man's eyes even from this distance, for they were a mix of red and purple and seemed to shine as if with an inner light. Jillan gasped. Was this a blessed Saint of the Empire – or a Saviour even? The man's high cheekbones, aquiline features and gentle brow certainly seemed noble enough and matched some of the descriptions he'd read in the holy Book of Saviours.

Jillan's legs became weak and he was about to fall to his knees in awe when the young man caught him under the armpit. ''Sall right, boy,' he whispered. 'Ain't no shame in turning pale and shaking with fear when facing the enemy. 'Tis a natural reaction that is but the beginning of rage and indignation. Your brothers are with you and will hold you up.'

Jillan nodded and gulped. 'Th-thank you.'

'Nothing for you here 'cept mud and a mean living,' the headman's voice rumbled to the emissary of the Empire.

The emissary's voice thrummed with fervour and the power of righteousness in response, easily carrying to everyone on the field. 'Come now, villein, this is but the building material for greatness. Would you hold the People back with your selfish desire to own the land, when the land is no one's to own?'

The shaman chuckled and bobbed his head up and down like a bird. 'Pretty words, pretty lord. We are made of mud too, for do we not all return to the mud when the land is ready to receive us once more? So why then, pretty lord, do you seek to command and own us, while yet accusing us of the same? Just as the land cannot bend its knee to you, neither can we.'

A reddish mist began to drift across the field from where the Heroes were standing. They seemed unaffected by it, however, so there was no alarm raised. The emissary, meanwhile, affected a bored yawn. 'Always the same confused, circular riddles with you pagans.' Then he sneered and spat: 'Always the same self-justifying and selfish trickery as well! You purport to speak for the land, and bind the People by it. They are enslaved by it, imprisoned! None should be so imprisoned. None!'

The mist reached the emissary, headman and shaman. Their hands and faces became speckled with it, but they were otherwise unharmed.

'I will free these People,' the emissary continued, his voice dripping with malice and his eyes flaring brightly, 'whether you like it or not and no matter who seeks to prevent me! I will *save* them in the name of the Saviours, raise them up out of the mud and protect them from the base nature and Chaos of their current existence! Will you yield?'

The mist drifted towards the villagers. It would soon envelop them.

The headman sighed and shook his head. 'We will never yield to your cult. It would be the annihilation of all we hold dear, of all that makes us what we are. I beg you—'

'Then see how you cause your People's suffering!' the emissary screamed. 'See!'

The shaman hissed as he suddenly realised the threat. He spun and shouted words of power, but the mist had already reached the villagers. They began to cough and choke, unable to clear their lungs. Jillan found that he couldn't breathe and clawed at his throat. Then he put his sleeve over his nose and mouth to try and filter the mist, and that helped a bit, but it was too late for it was already inside him and had begun to burn. His stomach cramped and he fell to his knees. The youth next to him was writhing on the ground, his eyes bulging from his head and an engorged tongue hanging from his mouth. He gave a final kick and didn't move again. Blackbeard cried piteously, blood running from his mouth and nose, as well as from his ears and even the corners of his eyes. As Jillan watched, the man's extremities took on a bluish hue and then blackened. The villager made a croaking noise and then died.

In desperation, Jillan looked to the shaman, only to see the emissary slash him across the throat with a long glowing knife he'd had concealed somewhere about him. The emissary laughed gleefully and then plunged his knife into the headman's stomach. But the man's armour deflected the shining weapon, giving him a chance to grab the emissary on each side of the head and squeeze. The white-haired chieftain thumbed the emissary's eyes and the representative of the Empire screamed hideously.

Then the Heroes shouted their eternal battle cry – *For the Saviours!* – and charged. There could be no hope for the villagers now. Jillan cried blood as he watched the emissary blindly stabbing down at the headman. Twice the blade's point skidded off the top of the headman's armoured shoulders, but on the third strike the tip found its way down between the headman's neck and the edge of his armour. The emissary howled in triumph as he pushed down hard.

The headman flinched and twisted in pain, but he did not release his grip. He grinned fiercely and bellowed, 'The Geas receive me!'

Now the emissary abandoned the knife and forced his hands up through the headman's guard. Rather than trying to break the elder's death grip, however, he got his hands around the other's neck and crushed his windpipe with an inhuman and surely Saviour-blessed strength.

The two struggling giants were lost to Jillan's view as the Heroes swept past them, weapons raised and intent on slaughtering the few villagers still on their feet or twitching in the mud. Jillan did not even have the strength to beg for his life.

He woke up gasping, a coldness like death in his lungs. His chest heaved painfully as, close to panic, he gulped air. *It's just a dream, just a dream! You're alive, you're alive!* The dawn sky spun up above him and he kept his eyes fixed on it until he'd got his breathing under control.

Jillan blinked and felt a rime of ice on his eyelashes come away. His whole body was numb and he realised he'd been lucky to wake up at all. It had been stupid to fall asleep without even getting the blanket out of his pack. He needed to get moving and warm again as soon as possible.

As his eyes became accustomed to the weak light down in his hollow of sticks and branches, his breath suddenly caught in his lungs again. Even before his eyes fully confirmed it, instinct and the haunting vestiges of his dream were telling him that he was not lying within rotting piles of wood. The smooth curves of those evenly spaced sticks, all coming off a main column . . . they could only be ribs. And that was a shank bone.

He lay among the dead, and they were piled six deep! In horror, he backed away from the side of the hollow closest to him, only to bump into a teetering pile behind. Thinking something had reached out to touch his shoulder, he spun his head round quickly and pulled it away. Jillan let out a yelp of fear as he came face to face with the vacant eye sockets of a skull. A pronounced jaw detached itself and clattered down the wall of bones to land between his splayed legs. The headman!

He threw himself away, but his stiff limbs were uncoordinated and he sprawled on his face, splashing mud up from the ground. He uncovered the face of a smaller skull and its top ribs and shoulders. There were signs the skeleton had once been wrapped in animal furs. The shaman!

Jillan clambered to his feet, desperate to be free of this place. Something glinted at him near the headman's skull, although how one of the rays of the rising sun had managed to find its way down into this Saviours-forsaken grave he had no idea. It glinted again and he stilled. Curious despite himself, he crept forward as if approaching some altar of bones, and spied the headman's gold-emblazoned armour in the wall.

He tugged on it carefully, ready to jump back in case he was about to be buried by the dead. To his wonder, the armour came free without stirring anything around it. It looked as if it were newly fashioned, and its strange designs dazzled and bewitched his eyes.

He couldn't resist trying it on, so raised it over his head and lowered it over his shoulders. There was no way the armour of the towering chieftain in his dreams should fit his boyish frame, but fit it did. It was not too heavy either, not even when he hung his pack off the back. If anything, the armour spread the load and gave him more freedom of movement than he'd enjoyed previously.

Pleased at his luck and strangely energised, Jillan scrabbled out of the dark pit and into the warm light of the new sun. Light-footed, he ran for the road, eager to leave the field of the pagan dead far behind him. They'd come close to draining all the life from him, to keeping him down in the wormy mud and decay forever, and to making him one of them; but he'd managed to escape their cold clutches and would be more wary the next time the Chaos came to try and steal his soul.

The only slight worry he had was just how angry the pagan spirits would be that he'd taken the armour.

CHAPTER 3:

For we are permitted life

Saint Azual shook off the warm muzzy feeling that came with drinking down the magic of one of those coming of age and waited with ill-contained excitement for the moment of ecstasy that always followed. It never disappointed, even though it would inevitably seem too brief. He spasmed as the charge radiated out through his body and sharpened his senses and mind. His one good eye blazed and understood the nature of every stone that comprised the mean temple of Saviours' Paradise. He saw the fleeting lives of whole worlds as they were born and then consumed in the smoking flames of the torches on the wall. He saw the collapse already beginning in the body of the young girl whom he'd just drained, saw decay beginning to nibble at her extremities.

He yawned and stretched, revelling in the temporary increase in his power – it was the one thing that made life worth living, the one thing that never paled or managed to bore him. It was always new, always different, as if he were reborn to see the world through inexperienced eyes once more. It made the repetition of his long existence bearable, the tedious round of visiting the communities in the south every six months, the endless days of listening to the same empty praise and prayers for aid, the interminable centuries of seeing to it that every generation feared and revered the Saviours.

The death of the young girl was a shame, but only because he'd now have to listen to the high-pitched exclamations of grief from her kith and kin, and that would grate on his nerves. He'd have to trot through some facile explanation of how the girl had been tainted but not been strong enough to endure the purge. Her kith and kin should celebrate, he'd declare, for the girl's death had been overseen and blessed by the Saint himself, so there was no doubt her spirit would be welcomed by the eternal Saviours.

The truth, of course, was that he'd become distracted while he'd been tapping her of her burgeoning energies, and had only realised when it was already too late to save her. It had happened to him several times over the years, as the tedium of inserting a channelling tube into one child after another, after another, had caused him to lose concentration. The first time it had happened, he'd almost been intrigued to see what would happen as a result, for it was a change from the norm. But nothing much had happened, in truth. There'd been a bit of wailing, tears and a few speeches, and that had been that. Everything had carried on just as before.

Such was the value of the life of one of the People. Nothing but wind and noise marked their passing. They left no other meaningful mark on the world or eternity. They were a type of cattle, really, penned into their compounds and bred in the numbers required by the Saviours. And the People were worthy of nothing more, for left to their own devices they would fight among themselves and scratch around in the mud their whole lives. They would seek to find happiness by making others more miserable than themselves.

It was the Saviours who gave the People the potential to be something more, gave them a vision of the glorious civilisation that could be built, a sense of order within which they could start to better themselves, instilled them with ideas about themselves in a larger scheme of things, a sense of meaning beyond a primitive hand-to-mouth existence. With the coming of the Empire, this mean world had discovered wonder, magnitude and awe for the first time. It was still largely a place of mud and filth, to be sure, but every now and then the search for betterment uncovered the odd glint of something more valuable. And then there was the eternal presence of the Saviours themselves, and their temples, to inspire and reassure generations of the People from cradle to grave.

Naturally, the People knew they were unworthy ever to see a Saviour, and could not be properly protected if they were free to move through the Empire. For such reasons, the People were rarely permitted to travel beyond the environs of the town in which they were born, unless they had a trading licence, undertook a pilgrimage or were chosen to become retainers in the Great Temple. And so it fell to the Saints to visit the towns of the regions and see to it that the People's ignorance was constantly corrected, their base behaviours were punished and their sullied blood was cleansed. For, not surprisingly, the lesser nature of the People exhibited itself not just in their behaviour, but also in their blood. As they became older, a corruption of sorts manifested itself in them, a type of chaotic energy that was rarely controlled and would seek to spill out to cause untold damage. Azual tended to think of it as a virulent infection or a dangerous illness. Sometimes, with particularly bad cases, he would have no choice but to put down the individual for the good of the rest.

And the corruption appeared in all of them because it was essential to the nature of this festering world and all life born to it. All was mud and decay. A child might seem pure, innocent and full of life, but it was conceived by those already corrupt so, as soon it began to grow, the corruption would begin to work, ageing it and breaking it down until it died and returned to mud.

The only ones to remain uncorrupted were the Saviours, and as a result they were eternal. It had never been recorded how it was they came to be uncorrupted, but Azual had overheard Saint Dionan from the east speculate that they may originally have been from a place beyond this world and therefore did not share its essential nature and corruption. Azual had his own belief, though, that the Saviours had once been like him, and had, through strength of will, come to control the chaotic energy within: as a consequence, the corruption had no longer been able to age them, and they had become eternal. Was that not indeed how it had happened for Azual himself? Was that not how he had come to live for centuries? Despite the suffering inflicted upon him by his own corrupt community when he was a child, he had remained true to the teachings and discipline of the Saviours and refused to submit to the Chaos. Both the Saviours' and his own righteousness had been shown when he'd ultimately *saved* his community; and in recognition of his true faith, Azual had been named Saint and set to purging the People of their corruption.

Azual knew he must be close to becoming a Saviour himself, for he had been becoming stronger with each passing generation of the People that he drained of their chaotic energy. In contrast to his early days as a Saint, he no longer had any difficulty hearing the thoughts of the People in the communities of the south beyond Hyvan's Cross. He even perceived a shape and pattern to all the different thoughts to which he was connected, and could sometimes anticipate large events before they happened. Imagine what it must be like to understand the thoughts of all living things in this world, to be able to predict the destiny of all things! Surely that was the power of the Saviours that would one day be his. He would be a living, omniscient and eternal god!

Were it not for the wretched pagans. They refused to join the Empire and, even more wilfully, refused to die out completely. They lingered like one of the elderly on their deathbed: no longer any use to their community, a constant burden to their family, infirm of bowel and a hygiene hazard; yet selfishly clinging to life in a final vainglorious bid for the sort of attention of which they were fully unworthy in life. The vision of an eternal future for the world would not come to pass while the pagans survived. They resisted the Saviours' desire to bring all living things together; they held the People back; they constantly sought to undermine the civilisation the Saviours had built; and they prevented this world realising true godhead.

How he despised the mud-worshippers! True, they'd given him some of his greatest moments of joy when he'd slaughtered them in such large numbers coming south for the first time, he reflected while knuckling his empty, itching eye socket through his patch. But then they'd scurried away in all directions and hidden in the darkest or most remote parts of this world, just as insects will burrow and race when the rock under which they have been scheming is lifted and they are exposed to the light.

So now he must abide and wait for the last of them to emerge from their lairs or to gather together under some new rock where they might be caught all at once. And so he would wait, patiently tending to generations of the People and seeing to the growth of the Empire, all the while keeping a constant and careful watch with his one all-seeing eye for the mud-worshippers to betray themselves.

And there could be no doubt that they *would* betray themselves. Just as he inevitably became stronger, and the Empire inevitably grew, so it was inevitable the desperate pagans would be forced out into the open. He could all but read it in the shape and pattern of things. The pagans had been in continuous decline since the beginning of the Empire. More than that, though – and this was the delicious irony of it all – corruption, death and decay were essential to the nature of the pagans. The mud-worshippers could never hope to outlast the eternal and patient Saviours. The pagans could only fail – only find defeat for themselves – in themselves. If they could but see it as he did, they would probably surrender and save a lot of grief, bother and wasted energy.

Still, if they surrendered too simply, there'd be no fun to be had through the hunting and harrying of them when they did break cover. In many ways, the waiting only increased the anticipation and hunger, meaning the kill – when it finally came – would be all the sweeter.

And so he would abide, patiently tending to the tedious People, just as a cowherd will sometimes sleep in the same shed as his cattle or a shepherd will sleep beneath a tree to be near his flock. He would abide in this manner for centuries more if necessary, although he felt the change in all things would come far sooner than that. He would continue to purge the People of their dangerous and chaotic energies, and what did it matter if he killed a few – or more than a few – along the way? It mattered not one jot. It might actually be kinder in the long run, not that the simple People often understood that.

He looked at the twisted agony of the dead girl again and sighed in irritation. He should probably pull her limbs straight and close her eyelids – it would make for less fuss from the People waiting outside, meaning that he'd have to put up with less of a headache in turn. The People of Saviours' Paradise were feistier than those of Hyvan's Cross, because they did not live day to day in the shadow of his home temple or under the watchful gaze of his elite and personal squad of Heroes. As a result, they had developed an inflated sense of their own worth and the worth of their lives. Perhaps a few more deaths like the girl's would disabuse them of such preposterous notions. Perhaps he should ban the town from holding a monthly market, to prevent them from seeing themselves as more important than the other communities.

He checked himself as he realised he was experiencing the characteristic bad mood that followed the high of drinking down the magic of one coming of age. Some decades previously, he'd all but wiped out one of his communities when in a fit of dudgeon like this. What had been the name of the place? Yes, New Sanctuary. To be sure, the People were his to do with as he saw fit, but he'd spited himself by giving in to such pique because he'd slaughtered a lot of his own prime breeding stock, which had taken him generations to replace; meaning that he'd therefore missed out on generations from which he could drink magic. He'd made himself weaker in the long run. Even worse, it had caused the blessed Saviour to whom he was devoted to contact him, something that had not happened in a long, long time.

Are you well, Damon? the serene, sexless voice had suddenly asked in his mind.

Azual had fallen to his knees where he was – amid hundreds of dripping carcasses in the town square, with his legion of Heroes looking on – and begun to tremble violently. The holy one had addressed him by his old name, not his Saint name! The full horror and consequence of what he had done hit harder and far more painfully than any pagan chieftain ever had. Bile rose in his throat and it felt as if he could barely keep from vomiting his stomach, heart and lungs onto the red-stained grass. His own body was in revolt, so disgusted was it with the being of which it was a part.

H-h-holy one! he mentally cried in torment. *What have I done? I did not mean it.*

Why do you say so? Nothing is hidden from us, Damon, you know that. We always know. Know thyself, Damon, know thyself. I will not tell you again.

H-holy one, instruct me! Do not leave me. How might I best know myself?

But there'd been no reply, as much as he'd pleaded. It was a punishment to him, but it also required him to become a solution in and of himself, in the same way that he'd become the problem. He sighed as he remembered the difficult years of self-doubt and self-recrimination that had followed. It was then that he'd truly understood that there was always a terrible price to pay when drinking of the beguiling, chaotic energies of this besmirched world: just as there was the moment of ecstasy and transcendence, so the moment of loss and pain would follow; just as his personal power would increase, so he would lose something of himself and his self-possession. He must never forget that this magic was corrupt and corrupting in its essential nature. He must seek to control it at all times, therefore. Lapses like the young girl might happen from time to time, but they should not become a habit.

Azual frowned. Just what had gone wrong today? There was something nagging him. He threw his mind out across the thoughts of all the People to whom he was connected. There was a disruption somewhere; something wasn't right. Where there were usually smooth and regular shapes and patterns in the web of the People's thoughts, today there was a particular area of randomness. He looked closer and pursued the fragments of thought there. What a mess! He ended up following a number of loose strands and coming up against a few dead ends before he had it.

His one good eye flared in surprise. Godsend? Just what sort of trouble could have occurred in that miserable backwater? There'd been a death. That wasn't out of the ordinary by any means . . . but as a result of magic! He sat bolt upright. Not since the days of conquest and settlement had there been any display of magic from the People. What could have triggered it now? What did it mean? Were there pagans involved? It wasn't clear.

Wasting no time, he arranged the dead girl so she looked more at peace, sealed the final flask so that it was ready for transport to the Great Temple complex and ducked to exit the damp and draughty stone temple. How he was glad to be free of the rotting mausoleum of a building. Like most temples, it had been designed to make a statement to the People more than for the comfort of the Saint who resided there whenever he visited. Thus it had been built of giant stone blocks which spoke of the permanence of eternity; it had low entrances and a low roof so that worshippers would always keep their heads bowed; and it had large, unshuttered apertures so that it was open to the light and elements of the world. It was a home for higher beings who thought nothing of the cold, wind, and rain, for such elements were theirs to command. It was a place for those who had no need of rest or sleep, for they were so close to eternity.

He would have stayed elsewhere, anywhere, but that would have been to erode the community's focus on the temple. In turn, that would have threatened the community's devotion to the will of the Saviours, and thus the community's very cohesion. Chaos would have ensued and then the Heroes would have been forced to put the People down. So staying in the temple was just one more sacrifice Azual had to make for the care of these troublesome cattle. Once they had fully served their purpose and he'd attained almost godlike power, he'd exterminate them to pay them back for all that he'd had to endure, every humiliation, every indignity, every injury.

But now there was some sort of trouble that demanded his attention. A young boy, was it? Hmm. Surely the magic he could drink from this one would be beyond anything he'd tasted before? Could it be that, at last, the power he needed to complete his transformation was within his grasp? The boy must be his at all costs! Drooling with anticipation and truly excited for the first time in who knew how long, Azual strode across from the temple to the Captain of his personal guard of fifty Heroes and hurriedly issued his orders: 'Have several men collect the flasks and ride with them to Hyvan's Cross. You and the others will mount up and ride hard for Godsend. I will go ahead of you.'

'Yes, holy one!' the Captain replied with a respectful bow of the head and set about repeating the orders to his underlings.

The Minister of Saviours' Paradise dared to place himself in the Saint's path with a low bow. 'Holy one, the girl . . .'

Of course, the girl. 'Is dead!'

The Minister's eyes widened in distress. 'I understand, holy one. I shall inform the parents. I will ensure that their grief does not overshadow tonight's celebration of your visit to our community. Shall I tell the other children that they will be Drawn to the Saviours tomorrow?'

What was this fool's name? In his distraction, he couldn't remember and couldn't be bothered with extracting it from the shapes of the thoughts around him. Minister Baxal, wasn't it, or was that the one who'd died some years before? He resolved to pass an edict whereby all Ministers would bear the same name from now on. 'I am leaving now. The others will wait. Out of my way.'

'But—'

Saint Azual turned the full fury of his burning eye upon the simpering priest and, using his connection, the Saint squeezed the other's mind. With a shriek, the retreating Minister tripped over his own heels and landed heavily.

Azual ignored him and moved with purpose in the direction of the gates. People threw themselves out of his path or fell on their faces in front of him. He trod on them as necessary and without a care. His destiny awaited him, and he moved towards it as a wolf would come for a deer.

His blood churned and his muscles twitched as the magic he'd recently drunk demanded release. He loosened his long limbs and began to flow across the ground at an ever-increasing speed. He was soon flying along the road to Godsend. Now let the hunt begin!

Looking back on it now, it was almost as if the gods had conspired against him, to see him exiled from his own people. What sort of life or meaning could there be when both gods and mortals turned their faces away? He did not know and was not sure he wanted to find out either. Maybe he'd be better off not moving from this exposed spot on the mountain – he could instead become a part of the stone itself, unmoving and unmoved. It endured, separated gods from mortals, and eternity from fragility, and yet was unanswerable to either. He would sit and slow his thoughts and breath to almost nothing, where there was no difference between one moment and the next, whether alive or dead. Except then his stomach would growl peevishly and ruin everything . . .

And it had been his damned stomach that had got him into trouble in the first place. He'd been about to head for home with the young mountain hare he'd managed to snag after a long day of otherwise fruitless hunting, when he'd suddenly spotted a deer straying above the snowline where he currently lay. As it had drifted back again for the better foraging, he'd begun to stalk it.

The deer had led him a merry chase for hours. Several times he thought he'd had it cornered in a ravine, only to find that it had scaled an impossible, sheer rock face. He'd then had to spend an age finding a way around and back up to it. It was only when he'd sensed the weather beginning to close in and had admitted defeat that he'd turned round to find it waiting docilely for him. It was almost as if it now wanted to be caught.

Carrying the carcass back up the mountain was far harder work than he'd anticipated, and far slower too. He glanced anxiously up at the sky: it was a flat white without any depth and the wind was high. He could feel the temperature falling by the second. He'd spent his sixteen years of life here in the high mountains, and everything he knew told him that there was a cruel and terrible storm coming, the sort that reminded all men, women and children that they were not the most powerful things in this world, that they lived only so long as it pleased the gods, and that any right-minded person would be wise to pray to and bend to the will of those gods.

He prayed fervently under his breath as he deliberately planted one foot ahead of the other, and as the snow began to fall thick and fast. If he didn't reach the high pass soon, he would probably be cut off from his tribe's villages for weeks. Worse, if he found it impassable, he would be surrounded by snow as well as exhausted, so his chances of survival would be virtually nil.

You're a fool, Aspin, he remonstrated with himself and dumped the deer on the ground. *It's not worth dying for. Now get moving!* He leapt into the face of the storm, his short powerful legs propelling him upwards and his muscled arms pulling when his footing chanced to slip. Even among the mountain people, he was considered small for his age, but that meant he had good strength for his size and was one of the fastest when it came to scaling a rock field.

He rose quickly, fighting against himself as much as everything around him. The snow forced itself into his eyes and made him miss his steps and holds. It was only a matter of time before he broke an ankle or wrist, and then it would all be over. His lungs burned and he gasped for a clear breath, but fists of snow forced their way down his throat. He realised he was in the jaws of what some of the elders called a Wolf Winter, a sudden snap that arose with so little warning that none could outrun it. The best that could be done was to hide yourself well and pray that it couldn't find you.

Aspin now knew he would never reach the pass. He had to find shelter instead. Perhaps a cave . . . but there were none in this part of the range. Could he descend back beneath the snowline? The firs there might offer him some sort of cover, but never enough to protect him from the cold or exposure. There would certainly be no chance of a fire either.

With a sinking heart, he realised there was only one hope, although that word was the last he would have normally used about the crazy old man called Torpeth. Only the truly desperate, those harbouring evil desires or those who were similarly crazed, sought out that lunatic. Some of the elder tribe members referred to him as *the holy man*, saying he was touched by the gods, but the way the man harangued the tribe's youth on festival days – about some payment or other being due, always some payment – Aspin thought of him as a demon more than anything else.

Torpeth had always lived well away from the rest of the tribe – some might consider him holy, but they didn't need him worrying their goats, urinating on the main fire of the large tribal home or leaping out at them on a dark night. He was the only one on these particular mountain slopes – who else would be crazy enough to live in such close proximity to the territories of the blood-soaked lowlanders? But now he was the only one who might offer Aspin shelter and any hope of survival.

The wind howled around him, all but knocking him from his feet, tearing at him like a frenzied pack of wolves. He knew he wouldn't last much longer in this storm and that he couldn't afford to hesitate for even a moment. Life or death. Choose now, warrior. He ploughed forward and then broke left onto a rapidly disappearing goat-track along a ridge. The footing was treacherous and the wind was intent on hurling him from the top of the mountain, to be smashed on the rocks below, but he had the balance and sure-footedness of one of the mountain people and was not about to give up his life easily.

Head down and teeth gritted, he reached the end of the ridge and plunged down into a more sheltered gully, where he could at least draw an unencumbered breath or two. The wind above shrieked and snarled in frustration, hurling down snow at him and reducing visibility to little more than a few arm lengths. He made his way carefully along the gully, worried that at any moment he would stumble into a hidden chasm, and finally emerged onto the top of a large slope. He glimpsed the dark shape of a long, low turf-walled construction below and threw himself down the incline towards it.

As he slid, he was helpless to slow his momentum and smacked into the back wall of the house with bone-jarring force. Dizzily, he made his way round to the other side of the dwelling and pounded on the door.

The door creaked open several inches and a beady eye peered out at him from the darkness. 'Took your time!' whispered a voice with unidentifiable emotions running through it. 'Left it any longer and you wouldn't have survived at all. Then how would you have made me and the gods look, huh? Embarrassing it would have been. Last thing we need is the next chieftain doubting our holy and wise words just because you can't be bothered to pick your feet up. Bit full of yourself, are you, huh? Wouldn't be surprised. Often the way with warriors, particularly young ones. And now you're letting the cold in! You must be crazy.'

With that, the door slammed shut in Aspin's face. He rocked back on his heels, confused and at a loss for words. Crazy man! Aspin pounded on the wood again. Nothing. And again.

The beady eye ogled at him. 'Go away!'

'Let me in, Torpeth!'

'Why should I?'

'I'll die otherwise. I'll give you payment!'

'Not so crazy after all then. In, quickly!'

Aspin squeezed through the small gap he was permitted and entered near darkness. A small fire crackled in a hearth at the other end of the room and he wasted no time heading for it. His teeth chattered and his hands were shaking as if he had the palsy. Shadows near the fire shifted and he suddenly realised there was someone ahead of him.

'So, come to challenge me, have you?' growled Braggar, the chief's brawny and cruel-eyed son. 'Torpeth said a challenger would come, although I found it hard to believe any would dare stand against me.'

Aspin was already shaking his head in denial. 'Nay, chief's son, I bring no challenge. All agree you will be the next leader of our tribe.'

Torpeth was suddenly at Aspin's shoulder. 'Ah, but you promised the gods payment, son of the snow! You bring a challenge in with you whether you know it or not. During the weeks of snow ahead, Braggar will abide here and learn the tribe's secrets so that he may one day rule. Son of the snow, you have insisted on abiding here, so you will also learn these secrets. You will be a challenge to Braggar's rule whether you will it or not. You have made your choice, warrior.'

'B-but I didn't know! I had no choice.'

Torpeth tutted. 'There is always a choice. You may leave if you wish. That will mean your death, of course, but the choice is yours.'

Aspin frowned at both of them and then shrugged. 'Then it appears I must be a challenger.'

'You will regret that!' Braggar promised darkly.

Torpeth giggled and pushed Aspin closer to the fire.

The days that followed blurred one into the other, for there was little to distinguish them. There was little light in the place, whether it was night or day; they ate from the same giant pile of pine nuts for every meal, and they did and said very little of significance.

Aspin would always awake to find himself lying closer to Braggar and Torpeth than was comfortable, but there was as little heat as light in the place, so it was not surprising their bodies would look to share warmth. Unfortunately, Torpeth snored loudly and smelt so bad that he would often keep Aspin awake. On one occasion Aspin had been determined to shake the holy man and push him away, but the lunatic's wide and rolling eyes had scared him off.

Once Torpeth was up, he would insist the other two keep perfectly silent – he called it making observances to the gods. If either Braggar or Aspin moved too noisily or even breathed too heavily, he would scream in outrage. He would froth at the mouth and pull handfuls of matted hair from his head or beard. Then he would invariably start to cry, snot running freely from his nose, begging for forgiveness from the roof, the chimney and the cellar. He'd attacked Braggar once, his movements so fast that they'd blurred and Braggar had been unable to defend himself. Just as it had looked like the chief's son would collapse, Torpeth had become distracted, stopped and started talking nonsense to the air. Another time the holy man had thrown himself into the fire on his back and begun to writhe around like a dog scratching its back: they'd had to drag him free by the heels and then pull him out the door into the snow.

After they'd made their observances to the gods, Torpeth would stare at each of them as if for the first time and mutter to himself. He'd absently scratch at his armpits or crotch, and then pick his nose. Aspin was sure the holy man had fleas. Then Torpeth would ask them the same inane questions as he did every day – what were their names, who were their parents, what was their favourite colour and so forth.

In the afternoon Torpeth would wonder out loud if they needed more firewood, and Braggar and Aspin would argue for the privilege of going to collect it from the covered store at the side of the house. They were both eager to leave the claustrophobic and smoky home of the unpredictable holy man whenever they could. They weren't just revolted by him, they were also scared of his violent passions. Whichever of them it was who was left alone with Torpeth while the other got firewood, they would try to stay at the other end of the room and avoid eye contact.

In the evening Torpeth would gather them round the small fire and tell them some crazed tale or other. He would add a strange evil-smelling fuel to the flames – Aspin suspected it was dung or something like that – the smoke from which made them choke but also experience the occasional hallucination. Braggar's eyes would become overly dilated; he'd sweat profusely, and his face would take on a haunted look. He would request the tale of the naked warrior again and again.

'There was a man,' Torpeth whispered and whistled through his brown teeth, 'who was faithful to the old gods of our people. He spent his days watching the sky to read the whim of Wayfar of the Warring Winds, bathing to know the course of Akwar of the Wandering Waters and working the earth to understand the ways of Gar of the Still Stone. Where the sun bespoke the earth, the warrior saw himself directed by Sinisar of the Shining Path, saw himself instructed to bring those lit by the sun to the worship of the old gods. And so he waged war across the world wherever the sun touched.

'Much was the suffering, but finally all people bowed down as the warrior demanded and commanded. The people were united but they did not prosper as the warrior had hoped, for Wayfar remained warlike, Akwar still wandered, and Gar was unmoved.

'The warrior realised the people simply bent the knee rather than embracing the old gods with their hearts and minds. Therefore, the warrior continued his war on all people touched by the sun, punishing them for their lack of faith.

'So great was the suffering, and so little did the people have left to lose, they decided to throw off the warrior's rule and put aside the old gods, even though it cost them many a life. The gods became angrier than ever before and sent storms, droughts, plague and famine against the people.

'When the others came, they found a broken land. There was dissent among the people, disarray among the gods and terrible division between the two. There were none who could stand against the others and all was theirs for the taking.

'Most of the people had no choice but to bow to the rule of the others. The old gods were overthrown and their few remaining followers were forced into the mountains, a place of merciless winds, frozen waters and cruel, stony ground. Even when Sinisar dared show something of himself, he no longer illuminated anything with sufficient power to transform it into anything god-touched.

'As for the warrior, he was left with nothing and he realised that it had been his desire to understand and have everything that had been his very undoing. He had sought to encompass the people and the gods themselves, when he was still one of them, and this had been the undoing of the people, the gods and himself. He had nothing, he understood nothing and he was made nothing.

'No weapon or armour was left to him. His mind was undone. Truly, he was a naked warrior, fit to fight none but himself.'

In the dim and crackling light Aspin and Braggar watched Torpeth in owlish silence. Surely this holy man, who wore nothing but his own dirt and hair, couldn't be the naked warrior, could he? The coming of the others must have happened many ages past.

'Did the naked warrior die?' Braggar asked thickly, making Aspin start. Neither of them had ever asked a question before.

Torpeth giggled and farted. 'Where would the lesson be in that, silly ox? The naked warrior exists still, fighting himself forever and ever. It was his punishment to witness the undoing of the people and the old gods forever more. Where once he had been god-touched and lived in a god-touched world of life and death, now he is but a shadowy memory or cry on the restless wind.'

And the night would always end with Torpeth jumping and scampering around the house, apparently becoming angry and then demanding to know if they'd learned anything that day. The young warriors would invariably nod, as that was all that ever seemed to mollify the holy man.

Whispering brought Aspin out of his dreams of complaining, shouting and rowing gods. Torpeth was crouched near the sleeping Braggar and murmuring in the ear of the chief's son. The holy man yelped and leapt back when he saw Aspin watching him. Then the filthy creature hissed, 'Braggar, awake! There is your enemy.'

With a roar, the chief's son threw back the goatskin under which he'd been sleeping and rolled to his feet. Aspin got unsteadily to his own feet, trying to shake the remnants of sleep from his head. He moved to put the small fire between the two of them.

'Braggar, I'm not your enemy! I've only just woken up.'

Torpeth clapped his hands and capered in the corner of the room. 'You are the challenger, son of the snow! You are Braggar's enemy. Unless he can defeat you, his rule is forfeit.'

Braggar pulled a bright branch from the fire and hurled it at Aspin. Then he leapt over the fire pit and sought to lay hands on his adversary. Yet Aspin was not so simply caught, despite his disorientation. He easily ducked the branch, rolled forward beside the fire and away from Braggar's grasping hands. As he rolled, he dashed embers back over his head in a cloud.

There was a shout of anger as Braggar was stung by the glowing motes of wood. Aspin hoped the chief's son had been blinded in both eyes and had inhaled a deadly amount as well, but he felt the other's breath on the back of his neck and knew he'd not been so lucky. Instead of coming fully to his feet, he kept low and swept one leg back round. He took his opponent at the ankles and knocked him flat on his side. He considered following in with fists and elbows, but the savage grin on Braggar's face made it clear that coming too close would be a grave mistake.

Aspin skipped forward and then ran flat out for the far end of the house, where he knew Torpeth kept a small pile of stones, although what purpose the holy man had for them Aspin had no idea. He took one up and turned to face the enraged warrior bearing down on him.

Braggar was only six long strides away. Aspin raised the stone. He envisioned it striking Braggar in the middle of the forehead and imagined he heard cracks in the bone radiating out from the point of impact. He felt the soft part of Braggar's brainpan compressing and beginning to bleed. Pain, darkness and then death. The tribe would be grief-stricken and all would gather round to watch the old chief struggle to break the cold stony ground so that his only son could be buried. Then the families with sons would begin to argue as to who should be the next to lead the tribe. Factions would emerge and the tribe would be slowly torn apart. There would be foul murder and feuds to last generations.

All because of this small stone in Aspin's hand. Why didn't Braggar stop? Surely he knew he was all but forcing Aspin to kill him. But Braggar was not himself. He was not behaving with any care for himself; it was as if he'd taken complete leave of his senses.

Aspin hurled the stone at Braggar's leg. It had the desired effect – staggering the chief's son and knocking him off balance – but Braggar's forward momentum was such that there could be no escape for Aspin. Braggar slammed into his small challenger and pinned him against the back wall of the holy man's house. The large hands of the chief's son found Aspin's neck and began to squeeze.

Aspin thrashed wildly, but Braggar used his weight to bear him to the ground. Aspin tried to claw at Braggar's eyes, but the chief's son had the greater reach so managed to hold his head up and out of the way. The pressure around Aspin's neck increased and he heard his spine creaking where it joined his skull.

Maybe he should have hurled the stone at Braggar's forehead after all. If he'd pulled the throw slightly, maybe it wouldn't have been fatal and would have just knocked Braggar out instead. Now he would never know. Stupid to die like this in a filthy turf-walled building that was hardly fit for goats. Stupid to die like this because of the whispered ramblings of a mad man. Stupid to die so young. Stupid to die because of a deer. Stupid to have lived at all. It had been no life of which to speak. Stupid.

His vision darkened at the edges and narrowed to a small point as if he were lying at the bottom of a deep well and looking up. Then Torpeth was at Braggar's ear and whispering again. Braggar's grip slackened, his eyes closed and he slumped down on top of his victim.

'Heavy ox!' Torpeth panted as he hauled Braggar off Aspin. 'He will be a good chief though, and breed strong sons and shrewd daughters.'

Aspin didn't give a flea for Braggar's future husbanding skills right at that moment. He was too busy trying to get his throat to open so that he could breathe. He coughed hard and then gulped in half a breath. How sweet, if uncomfortable, it tasted.

'Wh-why?' he asked hoarsely.

'Well, no need to thank me!' Torpeth harrumphed, acting as if he were the injured party.

Feeling far from solicitous, Aspin struggled up so that he was sitting with his back to the wall. He glared at the holy man crouched before him. 'He could have snapped my neck!'

Torpeth snorted. 'Might have saved me having to listen to your childish wheedling.' He looked at one of his long cracked fingernails as if seeing it for the first time and chewed on it hungrily.

'Why? It's not a lot to ask.'

Torpeth sighed and shook his head, glancing at Aspin sideways. 'Not a lot, he says. It's everything. Maybe he hasn't learned anything after all. Too young perhaps, but he wouldn't have come here if he were too young. Perhaps he's right though. Perhaps it is all nothing.' Then he shrugged.

'Damn it, Torpeth!' Aspin tried to shout in exasperation. 'Make sense for once, would you!'

The holy man blew a raspberry at the young warrior and then shuffled round so that he had his back to him. Aspin wouldn't have been surprised if the wretch had chosen to defecate at him, but Torpeth muttered loudly instead. 'Sense, he says, as if he knew anything. He's ignorant, so how's he to know what sense is? He can't even see that Braggar needed to think he'd completed some sort of trial so that he'd be confident in himself as a leader for the rest of his days. Ignorant, ignorant! He can't even see that I deliberately put those stones there for him. Can't see that he too was being tested in a way that would help him learn something. Torpeth wasting his time with this slow ox. Worse, Torpeth wasted all his pine nuts on the greedy ox! Took ages to gather those nuts. Will probably starve now.'

Aspin couldn't help feeling slightly guilty. 'Well, why didn't you say so before?' He paused to massage his sore throat and thought through the implications of what he'd just heard. 'So you put those stones there on purpose? But they were there even before I arrived. How . . .'

Torpeth didn't move or reply.

'So you knew I would throw the stone then. But you knew I wouldn't kill Braggar, is that it? You must have because you've wanted him to become chieftain all along, a strong chieftain, right? But how could you know that? Why put me in such a position? What were you testing and showing me? That I would be able to predict the consequences of killing Braggar? That I would see he wasn't himself? What's the point of that? Far too risky and dangerous if you ask me.'

Torpeth rummaged in his armpit, caught something between thumb and forefinger and then crunched down on it with his teeth. 'Hmm. Not as nice as pine nuts.' He shuffled back round and fixed Aspin with one eye while the other continued to roll around in his head. In a low flat voice, he said, 'Risky? The life of a scrawny child like you is as nothing. The alternative is a chieftain with no confidence who will see to the demise of the entire tribe, ensuring that the triumph of the others is complete. Once the others take this world, do you think they will be satisfied? Or once they have raped and pillaged the power of this world's Geas, will their force and appetite become even greater? Will they move onto and consume yet another world? And then another? Where does it end, little warrior and son of the snow? Does it end when all worlds are become nothing and the others are everything? Risky? You are a scrawny ox, nothing!'

Aspin was shaken. He didn't understand everything Torpeth had said, but he understood enough to be scared. He wanted to remain ignorant, wanted nothing more to do with this place and its insanity. 'Very well, you are right. It was worth it to give Braggar the self-belief he needs. And now there's a slight thaw, we'll be returning to the village.'

Torpeth tutted and shook his head. 'Braggar can go, but you can never return.'

Aspin went cold. 'What?' he asked quietly.

The holy man yawned and his eyes drooped.

'Hey! Wake up! What do you mean I can never return? Answer me!'

Torpeth looked at him blearily, suddenly seeming old beyond counting. 'Come, come, son of the snow, the thing you are good for is soul-reading. I showed you that, did I not? You needed to see it if you were truly to believe it. You are many types of ox, but not a simple ox. You know what will happen if you try to return.'

Trembling, the young warrior nodded. He could see it in his mind's eye. 'Braggar will attack me and kill me on the way back to the village. He will ambush me. I know too much of his time here. Every time he would speak as chief, I would be able to second-guess him or undo his words, since I would know from where they came. I would undermine his confidence and leadership because I know his secrets. Even if I never spoke out, he would always fear I would; he would always have misgivings and doubts about himself. As a strong chieftain, he cannot afford to let me live.'

'Quite right. So, as I said, you can never return, soul-reader.' Torpeth nodded drowsily.

'But my parents!'

'I will explain it all to them, tell them you love them and so on.'

'Where will I go, Torpeth?'

The holy man shrugged with a sleepy smile. 'Who knows? Follow your nose. The lowlands, perhaps, which were once ours but where the others now dwell. To our ancestral lands, son of the snow, where the gods once dwelt and perhaps hide there still.'

Anger. 'It's not fair!'

'As you will. Make your own way then, but I would have thought you'd learned by now there will always be a deer to lead you or a stone waiting for you to throw.'

'No! I decide my own actions. I decide my future. My will is my own.'

'Have it your own way, but do not forget payment is due. You were allowed to live, to survive the storm, and now payment must be made. The naked warrior once sounded like you, you know. Maybe things will turn out better for you than they did for him. Let's hope so, else it'll be the end for good this time, the end for all of us. The others will finally search out and seize the Geas and this world will be no more. Now begone, soul-reader, little warrior and son of the snow, for I am tired beyond imagining and Braggar will wake all too soon. Begone!' Torpeth waved vaguely.

Bemused and confused, Aspin got to his feet. Both Braggar and

Torpeth were snoring now. He turned his back on them, collected his hunting bow and quiver and went to the door. He could not believe he was now exiled from his tribe through no fault of his own. He would have to leave behind everyone and everything he'd ever known. He had nothing and would be less than nothing in the lowlands. What life could there be without a tribe?

He stepped out into the snow and shielded his eyes from the sun glaring off it. It warmed him a little and he wondered if Sinisar of the Shining Path was trying to reach out to him. Could he search him out? The search would give him some sort of aim for a while, even though the old gods were meant to be fallen and broken like the land and the people.

At least he now had clean air in his lungs, rather than the fetid smells of Torpeth's house. And if he never saw another pine nut again, that would still be too soon. Even so, he'd been stripped of everything he'd ever known, as if he were the naked warrior and the one at fault. Could it be that he had made some mistake after all? Chasing that damned deer had done it. And then electing to come to Torpeth's house. Letting Braggar live for the good of the tribe. Yes, the flaw was in him just as much as it was in everything else. There was no escaping it . . . but he would try nonetheless, even if it cost him his life. It wasn't so much to lose, after all, as he was naught but a scrawny child according to Torpeth. And if he failed, well at least he wouldn't then be around to worry about it.

Aspin turned his back on the mountains and bent his steps towards the lowlands and the avaricious others. He dreaded to think what welcome they would offer him when even his own people turned him away.

Jillan trudged through the trees at the side of the road. He walked on a thick carpet of pine needles and dried leaves that had stopped the undergrowth from growing in most places, so the going wasn't too difficult. Even so, whenever he came to a long straight section of road, on which he would be able to see traffic long before it got near him, he would take to the flagstones to make better time.

As it was, he didn't see anybody travelling all that day. He marched from early morning until it was close to dusk. His feet were more than a little sore by then and he looked forward to some sort of rest. It would also be a relief to get out of the cold wind, which had chilled his face and thoroughly numbed his ears, nose and lips. Whether it was wise or not, he intended to make himself a fire tonight. Otherwise, he thought with a smile, whenever he tried to drink anything, he'd end up dribbling half of it down his front.

The pagan armour he wore had been a real blessing, for not only had it spread the load of his pack, but it had also kept his body warm throughout the day. He wondered just how he would have fared without it. Perhaps he would have had to spend the day sheltering in a cave or ditch somewhere, getting no closer to Saviours' Paradise. In fact, he could have found himself having to shelter day after day, running down his food supplies and becoming weaker and weaker, until . . . No, it didn't bear thinking about. It was just the taint in him trying to make him dispirited and desperate, so that when the Chaos did come for him he'd have little left with which to resist it and would be all the more tempted to embrace it.

It's just the taint; ignore it. It was so difficult though. Did the pagan armour actually make the taint in him stronger? Was it cursed armour? The thought horrified him. He should pull it off before it was too late, before it had a chance to mould itself to him fully. Once the parasite had a proper grip on him, there'd be no getting rid of it. It would bond completely with him and replace his skin. It would sink roots and tendrils into his heart and mind and draw his life blood and thoughts through its own organism, filling them with black contaminants and poisons. The two of them would merge until they were of one flesh. He would become a living corruption, a creature of the Chaos. He would shun the light of the day and Empire and instead lurk among the shadows, waiting for a chance to leap out on the unsuspecting or unwary traveller.

The image terrified him as he fumbled with the buckles securing the armour, but it would not clear from his eyes. He blinked furiously and realised that the grey sky had drifted down to obscure the road in a mist. It had caught him unawares. What else did the mist conceal? Was there something stalking him or rushing towards him even now? Something glowed an angry red ahead of him. It was still some distance away but coming towards him at speed.

Giving up on his attempts to remove the armour, Jillan threw himself into the trees at the side of the road and buried himself beneath a layer of dry leaves. He stilled and hardly dared breathe lest he make the leaves rustle, as the panting creature came rushing out of the mist. It was enormous and strings of drool flew from its snarling mouth as it ran. Its feet hit the ground with such force that it cracked the road's flagstones. But worst of all was the blood-red eye that glared from one side of its face: it roved back and forth and burned away the mist wherever it looked. There was a power in its gaze that promised to unmake all it beheld.

Jillan stifled a gasp as he recognised the saintly emissary from his dream. The Saint of Jillan's region was Saint Azual, and was he not said to have but one eye? Jillan knew he should throw himself on his ruler's mercy, but he was too frightened to reveal himself. Instead, he closed his eyes and turned his face away, praying he would not be seen. Then, as quickly as he had come, the Saint was gone.

Jillan got to his feet as thunder sounded in the distance, echoing off the horizon. The storm was coming closer. He dropped back onto his stomach and covered his ears. The ground shook. It was on top of him now. Dark horsemen galloped down the road in the wake of the Saint. A large number of Heroes, pushing their beasts to the limit to keep their master in sight.

His ears ringing, Jillan got up unsteadily. *Keep going!* Saint Azual and the Heroes had been heading to Godsend. Word about him must have spread already. And they'd sent for the holy Saint himself! The holy representative of the blessed Saviours! Jillan shuddered in terror. He was in so much trouble. He would be damned and punished for all eternity.

He took to the road and began to run, his feet slapping tiredly. He had to leave Godsend as far behind as he could. Slipping on the mist-slick flagstones, he put his hands out in front of him to try and break his fall, but jarred his wrists painfully, and then his face and knees were scraping across the stones.

The pain was excruciating and he lay with his head ringing. He sobbed a few times, fighting off tears. *You're not going to get far if you run yourself into the ground, you idiot! Better to get some proper rest and set out early in the morning. If you go breaking your leg or neck in this gloom, you won't be getting to Saviours' Paradise anytime soon, now will you?*

Wincing, Jillan eased himself up and checked everything still moved properly. He started to limp down the road, looking for some track leading off through the trees towards what was likely to be higher ground rather than a bog.

The mist ahead of him thinned as he went, so he decided to go a little further. He was rewarded as a warm glow was revealed around a slight bend in the road. A building, out here? He couldn't be near Saviours' Paradise already, could he? There was no way he could have come far enough. He limped closer and realised he was approaching a fork of sorts in the road.

He made out a white signpost and hobbled over to it. The arrow pointing down the road he'd just come along read GODSEND, the arrow pointing to the left read SAVIOURS' PARADISE and that to the right HEROES' BROOK.

He looked at the building across the road. It was a solid two-storey construction of large blocks of a grey stone like granite, with thick wooden pilings and cross-beams. There appeared to be some sort of wooden side building, which was presumably a barn or stable, although there were no animals in evidence. The main building's door was large and sheathed in some dark metal, no doubt for defensive purposes, but the door was not currently tightly closed – rather, light shone around it as if it were only on a latch. Jillan then saw the large side-on sign swinging above the door and bearing the name MEETING O'WAYS INN and a picture of a knife and fork. At that moment, the aroma of cooked meat assailed him and his mouth instantly watered. He had not realised just how hungry he was, and he was prepared to risk entering an inn that must mostly be used by Heroes.

Jillan wasted no time crossing to the door, rapping on it and then turning the heavy ring handle. He entered an open wood-beamed room with plenty of tables and chairs clustered around the wide fireplace against the back wall. Flames danced merrily beneath a cooking pot suspended from two hooks, and the smells of a stew coming from it were now all but enough to make him faint.

'Ah, so we are to have guests tonight after all!' boomed a voice from a room to the right, and a fat, balding man came out to greet him. He had a moustache that was an alarming shade of orange and his small black eyes were lost in the folds of his face, but he had a broad and welcoming grin. 'I was worried we'd fallen out of favour when so many horsemen passed without so much as stopping to wet their lips.' He extended a meaty hand towards Jillan. 'I am Valor, the owner of this fine inn. Come over to the fire, to warm yourself. What name might you go by? And do you have a mount that needs stabling?'

Jillan shook the innkeeper's hand, which was surprisingly clammy, and found himself dragged over to a table across the room. 'I am . . . er . . . Irkarl. I'm on foot.'

'Irkarl, eh? You passed the horsemen, yes?'

'Yes. That is, I mean, no. I heard them on the Godsend road, but I've come from Heroes' Brook.'

'Heroes' Brook, eh? Last I heard, the road was flooded and wagons couldn't get through. That still the case? You must be hungry, young Irkarl, yes?'

Jillan nodded. 'Of course.' He hesitated. 'I'm on pilgrimage to Hyvan's Cross.' And immediately realised his mistake.

Valor frowned. 'A strange route to come, young Irkarl from Heroes' Brook. Why did you not take the north road from your village?'

'I . . . er . . . am deliberately taking the more roundabout route so that it is a more difficult pilgrimage,' he extemporised.

Valor nodded slowly, watching Jillan carefully. 'A fine sentiment indeed.' Then his toothy grin returned. 'But listen to me wittering on when you must be in want of sustenance. Where are my manners? Ingrid, you lazy girl, where are you? Come serve our guest at once. Ah, there you are. Irkarl will be wanting some of our famous mutton stew, I'll be bound, so step to it, girl!'

Ingrid, who was around Jillan's age and whose orange hair declared her Valor's daughter or close relative, nodded with her eyes kept down and mumbled that she would get a bowl from the other room.

'And you'll be staying the night, Irkarl,' Valor ventured. 'Our rooms are clean, vermin-free and aired every day. Indeed, they are so comfortable that I shall have to come wake you up in the morning lest you sleep the whole next day through, if not the whole week!' With a laugh, the innkeeper went to the cooking pot and stirred it with a ladle so that generous amounts were lifted out and shown before they were allowed to fall back into the pot.

Jillan found himself staring and nodded.

Valor was suddenly standing over him and smiling. 'And how will you be paying, good Irkarl of Heroes' Brook?'

Jillan's face fell. 'I-I don't have any coin with me.' He felt like weeping.

Valor dropped a reassuring hand on his shoulder and squeezed gently. 'Fear not. We will discover some other means by which you can settle your account. At worst, you will tell me the names of your people in Heroes' Brook and I will write to them so that they can send money with the next wagon to venture this way. Now, just you wait there and I will fetch bread and ale to accompany your meal. A man who travels often works up a greater thirst than hunger, eh?'

Ingrid entered with a bowl just as Valor moved over to the bar where he could tap a barrel. She ladled stew from the cooking pot and placed the bowl and a spoon before Jillan.

'Do not drink the ale,' she whispered and was gone.

It had been so quick and quiet that Jillan wondered if he'd imagined it. He stared after the girl and started as he realised Valor was already returning. Jillan snatched up his spoon and shovelled hot stew into his mouth. It burned as it went down, but he didn't care. He did not need to fake his appreciation.

'Mmm, it's wonderful!' he said, looking up as Valor's shadow fell across him.

Valor returned the smile and thumped two foaming tankards down on the table. He took one for himself and sat across from Jillan. 'Well, there's plenty more, young Irkarl, enough to satisfy any appetite.'

Valor drank as he watched Jillan eat. When Jillan finally put his spoon down, Valor pointed encouragingly to the tankard of ale, which Jillan had thus far not touched.

'Might I have some more bread to mop the bowl?' Jillan asked hopefully.

Valor nodded indulgently and moved away. Behind his back, Jillan poured some of the ale out of his own tankard into the cooking pot and then swapped his tankard with Valor's. By the time Valor returned, Jillan was sat composed in his seat apparently having drunk a good draught of the ale.

The innkeeper licked his lips and wiped beads of sweat from his brow as he placed the bread near Jillan. Valor took up his ale and downed it in one, all the while watching the boy. 'Come, young Irkarl, I am sure you must be ready to see your sleeping quarters.'

Jillan nodded and located his pack. 'Yes, I'm suddenly very tired.'

Valor chuckled in understanding and fumbled for a set of iron keys he wore on his belt. 'Thish way then,' he slurred and led Jillan to a narrow set of stairs. 'Up, young Irkarl!'

Jillan was forced to go ahead of the large man and soon found himself trapped with him in a small corridor on the floor above. The sound of the man's laboured breathing filled the place.

Valor was swaying slightly and his head was nodding as he unlocked one of the rooms. 'In!' he said belligerently.

'I don't think—' Jillan began.

'In!' the innkeeper roared, clumsily grabbed Jillan by the scruff of the neck and threw him into the small bedchamber. 'Go to shleep and I w-will be a-along to collect my payment later, you'll shee!'

Valor banged the door closed, trapping Jillan on the inside, and after several stuttering attempts got the door locked again. Then there was the sound of the big man slumping against the outside of the door and sliding to the floor of the corridor. He began to snore loudly.

Jillan ran to the door and thumped and yelled, but the snoring continued uninterrupted. He shouted and cried for help but no one came. He tried to call the storm down to free him, but there was no answer. He tried the thick shutters on the windows, but they too were locked. Finally, he gave in to exhaustion and tears and fell to the hard wooden floor. Surely the Saint would have him now.

CHAPTER 4:

Only as it pleases others

Saint Azual reached Godsend with the first rays of the morning sun. He'd run through the night, leaving his personal guard far behind. He was hardly winded but the magic he'd acquired the day before had been entirely exhausted. He would need to replenish himself here before he could move on again, hopefully with the magic of this rogue boy. What was his name? It was in the minds of so many people in Godsend, even at that time of day, it was easy to pick out: Jillan.

'Open the gates!' he shouted angrily, projecting his command into the mind of every Hero in the town, and shocking a good number of them awake. He would need to have serious and lasting words with the Captain here, make such an example that none of the Heroes would ever sleep again.

The Saint tried to discover the boy's location but couldn't pick out anything clearly. Azual was not yet connected directly to Jillan's thoughts because of the boy's youth and the fact that he had not yet been Drawn to the Saviours. Also, Azual had drained himself by running through the night at such speed, so his senses were no doubt slightly dulled. Curse them, but what was taking so long with the gates! To think that one such as he should have to wait on such lowly creatures! If he'd been replete with energy, he'd have leapt over the gates or simply torn them off their hinges to have done with it. As it was, he had to stand long moments grinding his teeth and knuckling the burning itch in his eye socket through the patch.

At last the great wooden doors across the northern entrance to the town swung inwards. At the same time a bell started ringing somewhere to alert the People to the arrival of their Saint. Azual cursed again. No doubt large numbers would now be turning out, bowing and scraping, begging that he touch and bless them, generally getting in the way and being an annoyance. They'd be stretching, touching and pawing at him. By the Saviours, how he loathed them, with their trivial concerns, their tawdry gifts and their wretched, shrieking children.

A number of Heroes emerged through the gates to honour and salute the Saint's arrival. 'You!' Azual sneered down at the Captain of Godsend, who was by no means a small man himself. 'Have your men form a guard to keep the People back. I want the Minister and the town elders to meet me in the Gathering Place immediately. Tell them to waste no time getting there, as if their very lives depended on it. Do you understand me? And as we go, you can tell me everything that has gone on here under your watch, and why your men are in such a sorry and sluggish state.'

The Captain swallowed and saluted again. 'Of course, holy one. Please, this way. A boy was killed. We have been scouring the town and the surrounding woods day and night but have not found the murderer as yet, one Jillan Hunterson. I've been pushing my men and many have been without sleep for prolonged periods.'

'How has the boy managed to evade you for so long then? Perhaps your men are not that difficult to evade, eh, Captain? Is someone helping him, do you think?'

The Captain half-jogged to keep up with Azual's long strides. 'As the son of a hunter, we suspect the boy has some knowledge of the woods hereabouts, holy one. We have discovered very little from the parents, who say the boy never came home from school. Beyond that, we have questioned his best friend, Hella Jacobsdotter, daughter to the town's trader. She swears by the blessed Saviours that she has no knowledge of the events that occurred, even though she left the school with Jillan. Apparently, the lessons that day were somewhat disrupted and Jillan and the girl were kept back late.'

'Really?' Azual murmured. Credit to the man, the Captain had discovered a useful amount of information in a relatively short period of time, given that he would have no doubt also had to calm the People before getting a search under way. He'd given Azual enough to be able to start trawling the minds of the People for answers as to what had happened. *Ah, yes, that firebrand Praxis had stirred things up in the lessons all right. Jillan and Hella had indeed left school late. Jacob and most of the elders believed Hella free from blame.* Yet Azual could not read the truth in the girl's mind because she had not yet been Drawn. 'Have the girl sent to the temple. I will deal with her later.' He frowned. They'd left the school, but then what? He couldn't read it clearly. Just speculation and hysteria. 'The killing itself, Captain . . . What's your name? What do you think went on there, hmm?'

'Captain Hamir, holy one.' The Hero half-bowed, no mean feat given that he was now all but running to keep up with the seven-foot Saint. He hesitated, clearly trying to choose his words carefully. 'I suspect, holy one, that some of Jillan's classmates had been waiting to catch him before he got home. Three of them.'

Ah, yes, Elder Corin's son, Haal – a bit of a bully. 'They jumped him.'

'I suspect as much, holy one.' Captain Hamir nodded. 'Three against one. The boy will have been forced to use whatever means were at his disposal. As it turned out, he was in league with pagan spell-casters from beyond the walls.'

Azual dismissed the man's ignorant comments with a wave of the hand. 'Surely you've questioned this Haal and . . .' *Who was the other?* '. . . Silus? What did they say? I need to know about the nature of the magicks involved if we are to be properly prepared against them.'

Each of Azual's questions guided the Captain's thoughts towards the bit of information Azual wanted, making that information quicker to extract. The Saint could have found the information in the man's mind anyway, but it was always easier with someone who was cooperating and could be directed. The Saint could also have searched all the minds in the town for what he needed, but using that approach often invited a flood of contradictory thoughts and ideas that then had to be sifted before he could distinguish fact from fiction. Therefore, unless he wanted to learn something that was common knowledge among the People, it was far less exhausting and laborious simply to ask questions of some individual, so that the information he was interested in came straight to the top of their minds. 'Ah, but I see you have *not* questioned them, Captain Hamir. Why is that?'

The Captain rubbed his unshaven chin and grimaced. 'The physick advised against anyone seeing them, holy one.'

What was this? 'Surely the boys were not in a state so fragile they could not be questioned?' Then Azual stopped as he gleaned the answer from the Captain. He dragged the soldier back by the elbow and glared into his face. 'Some sort of illness that can be caught? Plague!' he hissed. 'How is that possible?'

The Captain visibly paled as his face was brought close to the Saint's own, with its terrible eye. 'H-holy one, I do not know, truly! I swear it by the blessed Saviours! The two boys began to lose their hair. Then their teeth loosened. The physick whispered to me that their fingernails and toenails had also blackened and fallen away.'

'You are sure it's contagious? Answer me, man!'

Captain Hamir nodded. 'The physick thinks so. One of my men who took the dead boy and the two others back to their parents fell ill with something similar. H-he is close to death, holy one.' He paused. 'M-might there be anything you can do for him?'

Azual pushed the man away. 'It is not for you to ask me questions. I need to think. I see now why you treated it as so urgent to find the boy – you are looking to contain the plague. Who else knows of the contagion?'

'All the elders, the Minister, the parents of the boy Silus, the physick and myself. That is all, holy one.'

'Good. Make sure it stays that way. The last thing we need is panic. The numbers of people travelling from Godsend is to be reduced to a minimum. The trader is to be examined by the physick discreetly before he is allowed to leave, as are the Heroes who accompany the tithe wagons to Hyvan's Cross. The Heroes are not to recruit any of the youth from Godsend for training at the Great Temple until you hear otherwise from me. Is that clear?'

The Captain saluted smartly. 'Yes, holy one!'

'And those with the contagion are kept away from everyone except the physick, yes? Their bodies will be burned. Yes, good.' As he began to march towards the Gathering Place once more, he found the physick's thoughts and briefly explored them. An illness with similar symptoms occurred every now and then among the very elderly in the poorer parts of Godsend, but there'd never been any sign that it could be contagious.

Plague was the last thing he needed. Every couple of generations there'd be a plague in one of the regions, and whole communities would have to be sacrificed to contain it. He'd even heard a rumour that one of the Saints in the north had caught a plague and died a few centuries back. Well, that was what came of allowing the People too close to one's holy person. Frustratingly, there was now no question of Drawing Haal and Silus to the Saviours in order to read their thoughts about what manner of magic had been manifested by Jillan. Damn the boy! How was it that he could be so elusive?

Azual was too distracted to notice the neat houses and the bowing People lining the wide road that led straight from the north gate to the central Gathering Place. He was deaf and blind to their waves, prayers and supplications. The boy had left school and been attacked. There'd been some magic and a murder, but there were none who could tell him about it . . . unless he got the physick to play go-between with Haal and Silus for him. He might do that later. But where had the boy disappeared to after the murder? Surely it could only be to his parents' place. And they were Maria and Jedadiah from New Sanctuary! He felt sick to his stomach. It could not be a coincidence.

Some decades before, Azual had discovered signs that the People of New Sanctuary had been experimenting with pagan magicks. They'd kept much of what they'd been doing a secret from him because they'd discovered some way to cloud their thoughts. When Azual had visited the town to Draw the next generation of children to the Saviours, one of them had let slip certain thoughts about his parents performing rituals to increase the presence of the Geas in New Sanctuary. Azual had burned with righteous rage that this blasphemy against the blessed Saviours should be committed by some of the People from his region, and in the town square had tortured those who were implicated. When they would not give up the names of others, their defiance provoked a mindless fury in him. He put them to the sword and began to slaughter the People of New Sanctuary indiscriminately. It had only been when the Saviour to whom he was devoted had spoken to him that he'd returned to himself. The few town members who'd survived, or had been captured after fleeing the massacre, had been distributed among the other towns of the south, and New Sanctuary had been razed completely to the ground, as if it had never existed. Since then, he'd not really wanted to dwell on thoughts of the place, although it haunted his memory.

No, it could not be coincidence. Indeed, thus far, it was the only thing that he'd come across that offered some sort of explanation for what had gone on in Godsend. Instinct told him that this Maria and Jedadiah held secrets that would finally see the pagans flushed out of their last remaining hiding places. Along with their son, they held secrets that would see Azual finally gain the power he needed to become as godlike as a Saviour. At last! And it was so close now.

He quickly scanned the pattern of thoughts in Godsend and found the two in a small dwelling at the other end of the town. As he'd expected, there was little to be had from their thoughts at this distance about the night of the murder or Jillan's whereabouts. They had to be hiding something.

'Holy one, the elders and the Minister are at the Meeting House this way.'

'They can wait, Captain, and will do so if they know what's good for them. You and your men are to accompany me to the southern end of the town.'

Godsend was far less presentable in this quarter. Most of the houses, although hovels might have been a more accurate term, were built of a mixture of materials, much of which had no doubt been begged, borrowed or stolen. There was hardly a truly vertical wall in sight and no two buildings seemed to be of a similar shape or size. As a result, the neighbourhood was a maze to any save those who had grown up there.

Azual had always taken a dim view of the place. When a town allowed such poverty-stricken areas to develop, it increased the chances of crime becoming a general problem, as those who were the most desperate stole from those who were conspicuously richer than themselves, formed gangs to run protection rackets or developed black markets that would ultimately affect everybody. Such areas destroyed the cohesion of a community, and that made it harder for the People to act as one in their obedience to the will of the Saviours. And as far as Azual was concerned, the only point to keeping the People alive was to serve the needs of the Saviours and be absolutely obedient to their will.

At the same time, such areas often had poor sanitation and were breeding grounds for all manner of sickness, plague included. Was it any surprise that Jillan had been bred by such a filthy and corrupted place?

Had he been replete with energy, Azual would have simply smashed through every wall in a straight line between himself and the home of Jillan's parents. As it was, he was forced to employ a far more mundane means of navigating the maze, given that he was disinclined to tax himself reading hundreds of random thoughts in order to plot a course. 'Captain Hamir, lead us to the home of Jedadiah the hunter, if you please.'

They reached a small cottage-like building near the south wall. Captain Hamir was about to knock on the door, when the Saint pushed him aside and forced it open. The towering representative of the Saviours ducked and moved inside.

'What's the meaning of—' Jed shouted and rose from where he'd been having his breakfast.

'Where's Jillan?' the Saint demanded without hesitation.

An image flashed of the boy shouldering a leather pack, hurrying out of the small home towards the southern gate. Then the image was smothered and clouded over. But Azual had seen enough.

Jedadiah went for the knife with which he'd been cutting a block of cheese, but Azual had sensed the move coming and backhanded the large bearded man, throwing him back against the wall. Maria ran from the small kitchen to her husband.

'Take these two and hold them in the punishment chamber,' the Saint said over his shoulder to Captain Hamir and moved back outside.

The Saint ran along the southern wall, not caring whether any of the Heroes followed, and sprang up the stairs three at a time until he reached the ramparts. Samnir was there waiting for him.

'You! I should have known you'd be involved,' Azual spat. 'Yours is the worst crime of all, for you have betrayed your oath and the sacred trust of the Saviours again. Your blasphemy is deserving of the most terrible punishment! How could you do this? How dare you do this!'

Unbelievably, the Hero had lowered his spear so that it was levelled at the Saint's chest. Even more unbelievably, it was clear the Hero fully intended to use the weapon. The temerity of this creature!

'You defy me?' Azual hissed. 'I could smite you in the blink of an eye.'

Samnir feigned a yawn. 'Then why don't you? Or are you trying to bore me to death, you meaningless windbag?' Then the Hero's grey eyes narrowed and he sneered, 'Face me like a man or not at all!'

For several seconds Azual was speechless with outrage. In his entire time as a Saint he'd never been sneered at by anyone. Was this the ghost of his father, mocking and belittling him? Would he always be haunted by his disapproving spirit? His eye bulging, Azual choked in a high-pitched voice, 'I could destroy your mind with a mere thought!'

Samnir returned a humourless smile. 'Actually, you couldn't. You were not the one to Draw me, you see. I thought your conniving masters explained such things to their fawning lackeys. Of course, it would be beneath them to explain themselves to such lowly beings as the likes of you and me, eh? They would far rather keep us ignorant, as then it's much easier to take our crops, children, blood, thoughts and very lives.'

Suddenly wary, Azual took a step back. The creature was right that their thoughts were not connected. Depleted as he was, Azual suddenly wondered if this trained soldier could actually be a danger to him – his words were certainly dangerous and intended to keep the Saint off balance. How curious that he was experiencing a certain excitement and thrill at facing this man. It had been a long, long time since he'd met anyone who could stand up to him. He felt a grin spread across his face. 'I shall enjoy this, blasphemer. I shall Draw you to the Saviours for the second time in your life, leaving you a mindless, dribbling idiot incapable of feeding yourself or even changing your soiled linens,' he whispered as he drew his short sword of blinding sun-metal.

'Come then, Saintling, and let us see how quickly I can have that other eye of yours out.'

The ball of sun-metal high above the world of the Overlords burned her sight, causing fluids to run from her eyes, and made her skin itch so badly that she wanted to pull it off in chunks. Freda sank back into the ground, where she could see again and where the dampness soothed her skin.

Although she could not sense much of what went on above her, she could tell from the vibrations in the ground that small wagons were being pushed back and forth to fill a larger one, presumably with sun-metal. A line of people was being escorted by heavier ones to another wagon. Did the Overlords mine people too then, people like Norfred's son, Jan?

She waited, patient as a rock. At one point heavy men carrying sun-metal – weapons? – poured out of the mine entrance and began shouting angrily. The men ran in all directions, just like the crawling creatures in the ground did whenever she moved suddenly. She assumed the men were Overseers looking for her, looking to drag her back down into the mine so that Darus could hurt her. She had no intention of letting people hurt her again if she could help it. Norfred had said she didn't deserve to be treated so, and the things Norfred had said to her would always be more important than anything anyone else said, even if they were an Overseer or Overlord.

She wouldn't let them hurt her. Yet there were so many of them, so many. When they attacked her in large numbers, she struggled to stop them. And there was always the threat of a sun-metal weapon like the one the Overseer had used against her. Why were there so few people like Norfred and Mistress Widders? Why were most people like Darus? Was it because everyone wanted to be an Overseer and couldn't afford to have favourites?

She sighed and waited, content to be safe where she was. After a while, the heavy men with sun-metal weapons stopped running around and returned to the mine, except for one who went to a set of . . . chambers above the ground. The chambers were made of regular blocks of stone and the same soft material that was used for the handles of the miners' tools – *wood*, Norfred had called it. Then, several heavy men came out of the chambers and went to sit in the wagon containing the sun-metal.

She waited and then realised with wonder that the ground was becoming cooler, and that the ball of sun-metal no longer burned so brightly. The world of the Overlords was becoming darker! Maybe the ball of sun-metal was being hauled away in a large wagon, but she didn't hear the vibration of any wheels. Then the wagon of people and the wagon of sun-metal began to trundle away from her. There was a strange four-beat rhythm accompanying the passage of the wheels, and she realised that several big creatures walking on their hands and feet were pulling the wagons behind them. The creatures were strong and uncomplaining, and she wondered what they were.

She decided to follow the wagons through the ground, hoping they would lead her to where Jan had been taken. Then, once the ball of sun-metal had completely disappeared, she travelled half in the ground and half out. It was dark like under the ground now, except for small, silver lights that allowed her to see all the space. One of the lights was much larger than the others, but it did not hurt her eyes. And there were clouds up near the lights. She wondered if they were dangerous gases like those that sometimes built up in the mines. If so, she wouldn't want to be around if the ball of sun-metal came back, because it would probably ignite the gas and cause a terrible explosion and cave-in. She'd need to watch carefully for the ball of sun-metal, that was for sure.

She had little trouble keeping up with the wagons, for they moved slowly, but then she came up against webs of wood in the ground. She could not pass through them as she did the rock. Each web was connected to a tall pillar of wood above the ground, a pillar that had large clouds of a type of moss high above. The moss moved in the breeze and made a sort of rushing noise. She had absolutely no idea what the woody webs and pillars were, but they fascinated her.

Freda went close to one and heard the sound and felt the faint vibration of water moving in the wood. And the wood moved ever so slowly – although far quicker than rock – as if it were alive! Was it growing? She tried asking it some simple questions and listened for a response. There were shifting rhythms and patterns in the sound the wood made, which might have been a language of sorts, but she didn't understand it. Then, when she tore through a fragile area of web by accident, there were high-pitched sounds, as if the wood were in distress or screaming. There was now no doubt in her mind that the wood was alive and capable of some sort of communication, even though it was unintelligible to her.

Unable to proceed any further through the ground without hurting the wood, she went completely above the ground. She felt slightly sickened now to think that the miners used tools made from these dead creatures, and that the Overseers built chambers above the ground using dead wood. More cruelty. Freda wondered whether the Overlords would want to use her dead body to make tools and chambers if they caught her. Imagine if they used her to build a chamber while she was still alive! It was a terrible thought.

She shuddered and realised that the continuous breeze was making her cold. She should find herself some sort of clothing, although it would always get ruined whenever she travelled through the ground. Clothing might also help to protect her skin should the ball of sun-metal ever return.

After an hour or so, the wagons pulled off the track they were following and moved into an open area among some of the wood pillars. The heavy men with weapons got down and began to issue orders to the dozen or so people they'd been escorting, most of whom seemed young, little more than children really. There were both boys and girls among the youngsters, and several of them sobbed quietly. Freda felt sorry for them, knowing that they must have been taken from their parents and would probably never see them again – it was like when Norfred had been taken from her.

Two of the youngsters were set to gathering dead wood from beneath the pillars, and Freda realised that the pillars naturally shed parts of themselves, so perhaps the miners weren't so bad after all with their tool handles. The dead wood was then piled atop a small flame that had been created by one of the heavy men. A number of the youngsters immediately clustered around the fire, and Freda could see them shivering with the cold even from this distance.

Two other youngsters were told to bring food from the wagon, as well as sacking for beds. Then the dozen youngsters were left to settle down as a group while the heavy men moved some distance away to start their own fire. Once one of the heavy men had tethered the strong and uncomplaining creatures to a wooden pillar and fed them with grain poured from a bag, he joined the other five men and entered the murmured conversation.

Moving as stealthily as she could, hunkering down like a boulder whenever anyone looked her way, Freda came in among the wagons and took some of the sacking to serve as clothing for herself. Then she moved back among the wooden pillars and around the clearing until she was close enough to the heavy men to hear what they said.

One of them with a pipe clenched between his teeth was saying, 'Big as Saint Goza hisself, I heard it were.'

'And with skin as hard as rock too, so hard it turned back Altor's sun-metal spear,' said a thin-faced man with a large hairy mole on one cheek.

Were they talking about her? Freda wondered.

'Ain't heard of nothing that can stop sun-metal,' said the eldest of the men, who was cutting himself pieces of something to chew on every now and then.

The youngest, whose face was free of stubble, nodded. 'Apparently, it was sun-metal that did for the old pagan gods.'

There was a moment's awkward silence, and Freda feared they had sensed her presence.

'You ought to know better than to talk of the pagans, boy,' the pipe said by way of reprimand. 'It only attracts their attention, you know. You may not have seen any in your time round here, but they used to be thicker on the ground than the trees. I dare say there's more than a few of them still lurking in the caves and other dark places of the north.'

'Aye,' agreed the one who'd fed the strong and uncomplaining creatures. 'And don't forget this region was sacred to them pagans 'cause of their rock god. They say you could go walking and just pick up sun-metal, diamonds, any type of precious rock you wanted straight from the ground. Where there were lots of 'em, the stupid savages would set up a shrine to the rock god instead of mining anything of value. No wonder the pagans were no match for the Empire, eh?'

The youngest's jaw dropped. 'Serious?'

'The point being, boy,' the pipe sighed, 'that this place was always important to the pagans and one of their gods, so the less said about them the better, see? We don't want to attract any unnecessary attention while we're out here with just ourselves and some green kids.'

'Truth be told, mind, a bit of action wouldn't go amiss,' the eldest observed. 'I may have a sword, but I haven't had to use it in years. See, a lot of the shine has gone from it, even though it is sun-metal. Needs coating in pagan blood to bring it alive again. All we are, lads, is a bunch of nursemaids for wagonloads of kids who can't even make toilet on their own.'

'Big Harold can't make toilet on his own either.' The mole-faced man sniggered, making most of them smile.

Big Harold, who up until now had been too busy drinking something foul and reeking to say anything, lowered his bottle and burped fragrantly. ''Strue! Sometimes this awesome body of mine gets the better of even me. Still, at least no one would say I was too ugly to be a nursemaid, eh, warty?'

Mole-face's smile dropped. 'It is *not* a wart!'

'Catch it from kissing a frog, did you?' Big Harold asked blithely. 'Couldn't find a woman or boy to oblige you, eh?'

'Easy!' the pipe warned.

'Enough, Slim!' the eldest barked as mole-face's hand twitched towards his weapon. 'Draw that and you will have *me* to answer to. I won't just have you up on a charge of insubordination either; I'll rearrange your face so that not even a frog would take pity on you. Honestly, I feel like I spend more of my time nursemaiding you five than I do the kids! Enough, I say. I half wish the pagans would descend on us so you could get this out of your systems. You'd also learn a thing or two about the world and life at last.'

There were a few long moments of tense silence and then Slim overtly moved his hand away from the hilt of his sword. Shoulders dropped around the fire as the soldiers relaxed once more.

'Tell us more about these precious rocks you could just pick up off the ground, Horse,' the eldest ordered to re-establish normal conversation.

The heavy man who'd fed the strong and uncomplaining creatures nodded. 'Everywhere it was, they say. Couldn't walk but for tripping over it. Saviours and Saint Goza took most of it, of course, as spoils of war, which is only right and proper. But I did hear one thing', his voice dropped so that they all leaned in, 'about some temple to the rock god being lost and buried somewhere round here. It is guarded by great and monstrous statues, each made of a different fabulous stone. When the rock god was angered, his magic would bring these statues to life and they'd go out to wreak vengeance and destruction across the land.'

This time the silence was absolute, with only the occasional pop and crackle of wood from the fire.

'And do you think this monster from the mine is one of these statues?' Big Harold whispered.

The youngest gasped in fear.

'Who knows?' Horse nodded significantly. 'But perhaps the monster's listening even now as we speak.'

The youngest yelped and looked wildly around the clearing, his eyes sweeping over Freda but not seeing her.

The pipe chuckled. 'Come now, don't frighten the boy. Easy, lad. It's just a bedtime story told by mothers to their children.'

'Still, it'll keep him awake tonight, which might not be a bad thing,' the eldest observed. 'With this thing on the loose, it's best that we set a guard tonight. You're up first, lad.'

The youngest nodded, licking his lips nervously as the men rose and began to make beds for themselves.

'Don't worry.' Slim grinned. 'As a mine guard, you're lucky enough to have a weapon of sun-metal, lad. With that you can take on the rock god himself, eh? Otherwise, just scream, although you'd better make it loud if you want us to hear you over Big Harold's snoring.'

'I do not snore,' Big Harold said evenly. 'I sometimes breathe heavily though, because I'm having nightmares about you trying to kiss me, Slim. I have this terrible fear I'll wake up covered in warts.'

'Enough!' the eldest said sternly. 'Slim, you sleep over there, and Big Harold, you sleep way over there. Move! I won't tell the two of you again.' The eldest then approached the youngest and put a reassuring hand on his shoulder. 'As Slim says, don't hesitate to wake us at the first real sign of anything untoward. Do not go starting at every shadow or night owl though, for some of these will not thank you for waking them unnecessarily, and they'll tease you about it for years to come. Remember, the rock god is long since gone, broken by the Saviours. Remember that they watch over us, lad. The holy Saint Goza knows all that goes on and will send help long before trouble can ever find us. Remain strong in your faith, lad, and all will be well. The worst that will happen is one of the kids will wet their sacking during the night. Be kind and find them fresh sacking, for it has happened to all of us in our time, eh?'

The youngest nodded and smiled, and then turned his back to the fire so that it would not ruin his night vision.

Freda moved deeper among the wooden pillars and settled down with her sacking. She thought she would stay awake for a long time, but all too soon she was asleep and dreaming: of being cast into a bottomless pit, of a rock god pinned deep beneath the earth by a long shaft of sun-metal and of a giant ball of sun-metal burning her until her skin had turned to powder and there was nothing left of her but dust.

The sound of groaning and weight shifting against the door brought Jillan wide awake. For a second, he didn't know where he was and he frowned as he made out a ceiling and walls in the thin light that crept in around a pair of heavy shutters. Then he knew and he was up on his feet, scrambling for his pack as he heard the sound of an iron key scraping in the lock. There was no time to string his bow, so he pulled two metal-tipped arrows from his quiver and held one in each fist. He stood braced and ready.

'I'm coming for you, boy!' grunted the fat innkeeper from behind the door. 'You've had a meal and a room for the night, and now payment is due. You have no coin so I will have my payment in flesh. As long as you don't resist, there'll be no real discomfort. Are you ready for me, boy?'

Jillan tightened his grip on his arrows and anger began to stir within him. How dare this man imprison him and then try to extort favours from him! Jillan was no innocent or fool; he knew what the man wanted.

'I will work in the stables to settle the bill, or cut wood for you, but I will be no bed-slave,' he said in a voice as deep as he could with warning. 'Try and force anything more from me and you will regret it, I promise you that!'

As the door swung open, the rage in Jillan rose and looked for release. The innkeeper entered the room, his trousers bulging conspicuously. He eyed Jillan lasciviously and fingered his palms. There was a flush of excitement and anticipation in his cheeks, and his moustache fluttered as his hot breath rose through it.

'Well now, Irkarl, if that's your name,' Valor said slyly. 'You're a long way from home, eh? Run away, haven't you? There are people looking for you, aren't there, like those horsemen perhaps? Come over here now, and no one need ever know you were here, eh?'

He knows, whispered the taint inside Jillan. *You will have to silence him. Use the magic. It's the only way. You can feel it like a pressure in your hands. Just let it go!*

'Put down those arrows and take off that silly armour, boy. With its patterns, you look quite girlish.' The innkeeper tittered and took a small step towards him, his meaty hands rising and beginning to reach out.

'Don't!' Jillan growled, no longer recognising his own voice. *No, come closer*, the taint laughed.

Jillan saw red and power danced and crackled between his fingers. He could see the life energy moving sluggishly through Valor with each beat of the innkeeper's overburdened heart. He drew that energy away from the man and Valor suddenly staggered and clutched at his chest.

'No!' the innkeeper wheezed, his small eyes closing in pain.

Then Jillan channelled all the power back at Valor and burst the man's heart. The innkeeper's mouth opened but no sound came out. He fell, smacked his head on the floor and stopped moving. The smell of his releasing bowels left no doubt that he was dead.

The taint laughed and cried in merriment. 'Stop it!' Jillan pleaded, feeling both nauseous and faint. The room felt and looked like it was on a slant. He bent to lift his pack and collapsed on the floor next to the innkeeper's stinking body. The stench was all that kept him conscious as, with a shaking hand, Jillan grabbed his water bottle and managed to slosh some into his mouth and across his face. Gasping, he swallowed and then took another mouthful. After some minutes his vision began to clear, but he was still weak. From one of the pack's outside pockets, he fumbled a piece of hard cheese out of the waxed paper in which it was wrapped and began to chew methodically.

Aren't you forgetting something? the taint whispered.

'What?'

The girl.

'She hasn't done anything wrong. Leave her alone!'

Don't be foolish. She probably knows as well. Either way, she'll raise the alarm.

'You will not hurt her!'

The taint harrumphed and said sulkily, *I suppose if she were dead, the inn would be empty and the next people passing through would know something had happened anyway. It wouldn't take much to put two and two together about this and Karl, would it? Besides, don't they say the Saint always knows?*

Jillan drew a sharp breath. The Saint! He would be coming. Jillan knew he had to get moving, for there was no knowing what the Saint had learned in Godsend. The region's ruler could already be racing back this way.

He chewed more assiduously, until all the cheese was gone. Without looking at the dead innkeeper, he then got his feet under him and dragged his pack out of the room and down the corridor to the stairs. He peered down the stairs at the common room below: all seemed empty and quiet.

He tested the weight of the pack on his shoulders and found he could manage it. He tiptoed down and was just short of the door when he spied Ingrid in the side room. She sat in her nightgown hugging herself and rocking slightly. Her eyes were unseeing and she gave no sign that she was aware of his presence.

'I-I'm sorry!' Jillan mumbled, hurriedly drew back the bolt on the front door and moved to head out into the dawn.

'Don't be,' Ingrid said absently. 'Everything's fine.'

Saint Azual wiped the blood from his face with his hands, not knowing if the blood was his or Samnir's. He licked his fingers. A mixture. The Hero had put up a hell of a fight, even without a weapon made of sun-metal, and Azual's confidence had been shaken. Surprisingly, some of the Heroes of Godsend had tried to intercede on the Saint's behalf – clearly there was no love lost between Samnir and the others – but Azual had roared at them to get back.

Quick as thought, Samnir had lanced his spear forward at the Saint's eye, but Azual had seen it coming and cloven through the spear's haft. It may have reduced the Hero's reach, but the soldier had managed to flip the loose end up off the floor with his foot and then had two shorter poles to use as weapons, which he did with terrible effect, twirling and slashing without let-up. Samnir had battered Azual back to the edge of the rampart, and the Saint had looked to be in real jeopardy. Then Azual had deliberately stepped forward and taken the spearhead deep in the arm just so that he could wrest the weapon from Samnir. Although the wound was deep and the blade had notched the bone, it would not be fatal to one who healed as quickly as the Saint.

Samnir had then been left with a single length of wood, which he used as a short staff to fend off Azual's attacks almost casually. Every time the Saint swiped with his blazing sword, one end of the staff would deflect it at a shallow angle, and the other end of the staff would deliver a debilitating blow to Azual's arms, legs or torso. The Saint had already been thwacked in the same place on the arm where the spear had struck, all but incapacitating it; in the ribs, making it hard to breathe; and on one of his thighs, slowing him down considerably. Now the staff came down on the top of the forearm of Azual's hand which held his precious sword. The Saint only just managed to hang onto his weapon.

Azual retreated, knowing that if Samnir was forced to go on the offensive, the Saint would have a far better chance of meeting the staff head on – rather than obliquely – with the edge of his sun-metal blade. The staff wouldn't last more than a few seconds. But the Hero refused to be drawn and instead rolled his shoulders and his head on his neck as if warming up for a sparring match. The man was mocking him again!

Azual realised that, unlike Samnir, he really hadn't been putting enough time into his martial training in the last few years. He'd come to rely far too much on the fickle and corrupting magic he drew periodically from the People – see how it had betrayed and deserted him just when he most needed it. He should have known better than to trust too much in such tainted power. There was always a price to be paid. He just hoped he would not be paying the ultimate price in the next few moments.

Azual studied Samnir more closely. Weight balanced on feet spaced not too far apart, relaxed shoulders for fluidity and speed of movement, a vague and confident half-smile and a steely, unblinking, unforgiving gaze. Azual had to concede that, incredibly, he appeared to be outmatched by this man because the initial injuries the Saint had received had all but rendered his superior strength and height impotent. And Samnir was a veteran of campaigns against the behemoth barbarians in the east, and hadn't he served as one of the elite guards of the Great Saviour himself? Yes. The man was more than familiar with the fighting styles and limitations of the Saints, not to mention the blessed Saviours themselves! Ageing he might be, but the Hero's experience easily compensated for that.

Azual lowered his sword slightly. 'It appears I underestimated you, Hero. You have taught me a valuable lesson.' The Saint dared take his eyes off Samnir, although he watched him out of the corner of his eye. He moved his sword into the hand of his wounded arm so that he could close his free hand over the bleeding wound.

Samnir watched with shrewd eyes. 'Why do you pause, Saint? Surely you are not going to tell me you have seen the error of your ways.'

'Indeed, I am not.' Azual smiled, letting blood gather in the now cupped hand over his wound. He summoned energy from his core and it slowly rose within him. It was reluctant to answer the call, for his core would be dangerously lessened by its use. If he drew too much, it would likely kill him. Even drawing a lesser amount, he risked losing himself, becoming insane with a need for life energy using any means necessary. He would then be a monster and a threat to all those around him. But the sacrifice had to be made, for he knew he could not afford to look weak in front of the men. The story would spread all too quickly; some of the things Samnir had said would get repeated, and then all the People would begin to see the Saints and perhaps even the Saviours themselves differently. The defiance would grow and grow. It had to be ended here and now, before it began to spread like a plague. Yes, the defiance and the plague in Godsend were the same thing. Perhaps he should raze the place to the ground before it was too late. No, Jillan had already escaped Godsend, and he was the source and focus of both problems. Azual could not afford to destroy the communities in his region too freely, as they were ultimately the source of his own strength. 'No, but I am intrigued as to why you would help the boy. Why put aside your oaths and faith and throw away your life for a young murderer?'

Samnir hesitated, as Azual knew he would, for he had asked the question at the heart of things: he had found Samnir's sacred heart and spoken directly to it. No individual could deny their sacred heart. 'I-I . . .' the Hero stammered, wrong-footed. 'The boy was innocent.'

'He murdered . . . Karl. Did you not know?'

'It was an accident. Jillan was bullied by Praxis. The other students turned on Jillan, no doubt, because of it.'

'Such mitigating circumstances would have been taken into account when I came to hear the trial, if you'd but done your duty and held the boy in lieu of my authority. But no, you blasphemously took it upon yourself to usurp me as the Saviours-appointed judge of this region. In so doing, you have both condemned yourself and put the boy at greater risk. Yes, Samnir, do you really think that a boy so young will survive the wilds alone? Or is it more likely that he will be taken by the pagans or some other Chaos creature? Even if he survives, you have made him a fugitive guilty of refusing to submit to the law of the Saviours. Do you not see what you have done, and how the all-knowing and all-powerful Saviours find a way to punish the likes of you and the boy regardless? The Empire of the Saviours is all-encompassing and eternal, such that those who are tainted and guilty inevitably condemn and punish themselves by their very own actions. People are victims of themselves, Hero.' Azual trickled power from his core into the handful of blood that he held. The blood began to quicken and move, alive to his will.

A few of the nearby Heroes were nodding as they listened. One fell to his knees and began to pray. Samnir's eyes flicked towards them but hardened as they returned to the Saint. 'Fine rhetoric, holy one, and always persuasive to fanatics, the weak of mind and those who have never known any different, but you forget I have seen—'

Yet Azual was not about to let Samnir infect those present with any more of this plague of defiance. He threw his blood into the air in one swift motion and blew the mist towards Samnir. Realising what was happening, the Hero roared and lunged forward, blinking against the blood entering his eyes and expelling breath through mouth and nose so that it could not immediately enter his airways.

Azual staggered back, teetering on the edge of the rampart. One of his knees buckled – the life energy lost from his core already taking its toll – but that chanced to save him from a vicious swipe from the Hero's staff. He only had to survive the assault for a few moments more. His thoughts began to muddle and it took the last of his wherewithal to command the blood landing on Samnir's skin and getting inside his body to intermingle with the Hero's own blood and disrupt his life energy.

Samnir smashed his staff down on the Saint's shoulder and prepared to heave the other's huge frame off the rampart and down to the cobbles far below. But here the Hero lost control of his body and mind. He fell on top of the Saint, losing his grip on the world around him.

The watching Heroes bounded up the stairs and dragged Samnir off their beloved Saint. Azual was too groggy and delirious to refuse their help. 'The sun-metal tube in my tunic!' he croaked. 'Quickly!'

They obeyed him without hesitation.

'Roll his sleeve up!'

Azual plunged the thin hollow tube of sun-metal into one of Samnir's veins and moaned with relief and desire as blood arced through the air. The sun-metal would keep the puncture open and the blood running as long as he needed. He let it rain into his mouth, as if he were drinking one of the fine wines of the east, and swallowed so desperately that any would have thought he'd been wandering the parched eastern deserts for weeks. The magic in Azual's blood latched onto the taint and life energy in Samnir and began to drain it from him. Within seconds, Azual was feeling stronger and more like his old self, yet he continued the purge, drinking more and more, until an ecstasy of power washed through him and there was only just enough left in Samnir to keep him alive. For the Hero must live: to suffer the waking nightmare and punishment of being trapped and helpless in a body no longer under his control and to provide the Saint with whatever information he possessed.

The Heroes of Godsend had backed away from Azual, a look of horror on many of their faces. Of course, they had never witnessed the Saint bestowing the sacred communion on one of the People before, so could not understand its mysteries and wonder. They had experienced it themselves when coming of age, but the memory of it had been largely erased from their simple minds by the Saint.

Azual debated with himself as to whether he should remove all memory of the encounter with Samnir from the minds of the men – but there were a dozen of them, so it would be quite some undertaking, and Azual had decided to be far more cautious from now on about how he expended his power. The boy and his magicks were still at large and there was also the matter of the plague – he might need all the power he could muster far sooner than he liked. Instead, he called Captain Hamir to him and spoke in a voice loud enough for all to hear.

'Do not fear, for the traitor among you has now been purged from your number. The good name and honour of the Heroes of Godsend is restored by my word and gift. I do not blame you for the escape of the boy and your failure to find him subsequently.'

The Captain covered his uncertainty with a low bow. 'Holy one, our oaths and thanks are ever yours.'

Azual nodded magnanimously. 'That is well, Captain. Some of the things that you have seen and heard here today are beyond the ken of you and your men. You will banish these things from your minds and lips, lest your simple understanding were to misconstrue what occurred and serve to unnerve the People. There were magicks in play that could not be seen with the normal eye and which you cannot even begin to imagine. Samnir's soul was tightly bound by dark and cruel pagan magicks. I had to risk myself in order to *save* him, for that is my holy duty and the will of the Saviours. We do this to safeguard the good People of the Empire for all eternity. Do you understand, Captain?'

Azual's eye shone down on the Captain's face, and forced him to kneel. The Hero's own eyes became vacant as he chanted, 'Sacrifice and duty safeguard the People against the Chaos!' All of his men followed his lead, ignoring the discomfort of the stone against their knees and repeating the line from the Book of Saviours that had been ingrained in them all their lives.

'Very well. I am satisfied,' Saint Azual said gently. 'I will take that as a vow from all of you never to speak of these events. Of course, should you utter a word of it, I *will* know and I will be greatly saddened, do you all understand?'

'Yes, holy one!' they chanted, a mixture of passion, fervour and fear across all their faces.

'You may rise now. Captain, have this blasphemer chained in the Gathering Place as a warning to the inhabitants of Godsend to be more vigilant when it comes to the pernicious influence of the Chaos. Let the People pity him or throw food as they wish, for that may suffice to feed him, if his body still knows the instinct for survival. And have a bucket of clean water thrown over him once a week so that all waste is washed away. Show him some mercy, Captain, in the name of the Saviours, for we must punish to teach, but we do not wish to be cruel lest we create martyrs of the corrupt and ill-deserving. Now, take me to my temple, for I must pray and replenish myself.'

*

Azual strode through Godsend, Heroes trotting to either side of him to keep the ardent congregation of People back. Minister Praxis jumped and waved for the Saint's attention, but Azual had no time for the pompous prig. In fact the man was a liability – and if there had been any remoter town than Godsend, he'd have sent him there. *Maybe I should establish a temple at the foot of the mountains for people such as this*, Azual mused, *or better yet* . . . He waved the Minister through the cordon of Heroes.

'Holy one, you have come to us in our hour of need! We are beset—'

'Be silent!' the Saint said out loud and in the Minister's mind simultaneously.

The Minister flinched but did as he was commanded. *Shame. I would have enjoyed seeing his tongue removed.*

'Minister,' Azual continued, not breaking step and no longer deigning to look upon the man, 'you are to be rewarded. Now you may speak.'

The Minister smiled modestly. 'Holy one, I am but your humble servant, vigilant at all times and—'

'And zealous when it comes to instilling a devotion to the Saviours in the People, yes?'

'Of course, it is important to—'

'To instil a fear of the pagans in them? To have them see monsters lurking in every shadow? To wonder always if their neighbours have succumbed to some corrupting temptation or magic? To interpret everyday greetings and actions in such terms just to be on the safe side?'

The Minister's face became guarded. 'Well, I . . .'

'Tell me, Minister, is it not blasphemous to suggest that the Saviours cannot completely safeguard the People from the pagans? Surely if the People fear the pagans too much, then they cannot have true faith in the eternal Saviours. Surely, their faith is nothing more than empty desperation and lip-service. You agree, of course, with the holy representative of the Saviours, do you not?'

The Minister hesitated and then bowed his head in shame. 'Of course, holy one.'

'Come, do not be downhearted.' Azual smiled. 'You have a rare gift, Minister. You have the vision, passion and eloquence of a missionary.'

'I do?'

'Of course you do, and it is for that very reason that I have decided to give you a sacred mission, a mission that I could not give to just anyone.'

'Holy one, you do me a great honour.'

'Indeed I do, but one of which you are most deserving. You will enter the mountains as a missionary of the Saviours, Minister. You will go fearlessly among the pagans to show them you have absolute faith in the power of the Saviours to protect you. You will read to them the holy word from the Book of Saviours, and help them to understand the will of the Saviours. You will show them how they may enter into the Empire of the Saviours and gain eternal life. This is your sacred mission, Minister. You will be an inspiration to all the People. Your name will be known throughout the Empire. Last of all, remember that my thoughts will be with you at all times and that I will be able to see through your eyes how the pagans are disposed. You are doing me an invaluable service and for that you have my thanks and blessing.'

Minister Praxis failed to keep expressions of horror then nausea from his face. 'H-holy one, what of my ministry here? Without me, the good People of Godsend—'

Azual waved away the objection. 'I will have someone sent from Hyvan's Cross. There are many who can offer ministry to the People, but you are the only one I have met with the faith, courage and determination required to embrace this holy mission. Minister, should you survive, then I will see to it that you are considered for beatification. Saint Praxis of the Mountains, you will be known as.'

The Minister's expression now became neutral, but there were tones of wonder and ambition in his voice as he murmured, 'Saint Praxis of the Mountains!'

'Captain Hamir, see to it that the good Minister is furnished with some mule or ass suited to travel in the mountains and properly provisioned this very day. See to it that he has left Godsend before sundown.'

'As you will it, holy one.' The Captain nodded. 'Here is your personal guard arriving.'

Azual looked up ahead to see Captain Skathis, splattered with the mud of the road, marching his men in formation towards them. As he neared, he saluted his master and nodded to Captain Hamir. Azual motioned the two men closer to him so that none could overhear them. 'Captain Skathis, you and your men should immediately get what rest and refreshment you can, for we will have to leave Godsend within a handful of hours. The boy has escaped Godsend. I will Draw the girl Hella and seek to discover where Jillan has gone. Then I will question his parents, but anticipate some resistance from them. They bear some guilt in all this. Then we will take to the road again.'

Captain Skathis cleared his throat. 'Yes, holy one. We will need to change our horses, with Captain Hamir's permission.'

'Of course. It is an honour to assist the guard of the holy one. It is for the Empire.'

He entered the cramped cold temple to find the girl sat shivering and waiting for him. His core stirred hungrily and he had to make an effort to suppress it.

'Be calm, child. You are safe.'

'Yes, holy one,' she replied in a dutiful manner.

'Your name is Hella, yes? And you were Jillan's friend?' Azual seated himself near her, but not so close that he would intimidate or scare her.

She blinked slowly. She would be a beauty when older, if she lived long enough. 'Yes, Jillan and I were *best* friends,' she said in a small voice. 'What will you do to him, holy one?'

The Saint sighed. 'He murdered one of your classmates, Hella. Come, drink this.' He uncorked a glass phial of his imbued blood and gave it to her.

'But he's good, holy one, honestly he is!' she implored. 'They were always picking on him, that's all.'

For once, Azual wasn't really sure what to say. He frowned. Did the girl have some ability to confuse or influence him? 'Well, drink it down so that you may be Drawn to the Saviours. Then they will understand about Jillan better.'

Hella looked down at the blood dubiously. She wrinkled her nose prettily. 'What is it? It smells bad.'

'It's a sort of wine. It will clear your mind and help to Draw you to the Saviours, Hella. Come along now.'

She looked up into his eyes in appeal. 'What will you do to Jillan?'

'I . . .' *Get a grip on yourself. She's just a child.* 'That remains to be seen. Where did he go, Hella? It would help me find him before anything else bad can happen, and that would help Jillan. You trust and have faith in the Saviours and their Saints, do you not? You pray to them, yes?'

'Oh yes, every night, holy one. I don't know where he is. I would tell you if I did.'

'Drink the wine.'

'I don't like wine really. I tried some once and it made me sick. The thing is, Haal didn't like it that Jillan and I were friends. And Jillan was always a bit different to the others, which, I don't know, made them a bit jealous or frightened of him, I suppose.'

Intrigued despite himself, the Saint couldn't help but ask, 'Different how, Hella?'

'Oh, I don't know. He'd say odd things, funny things. He saw things strangely. And they say his parents . . .' she tailed off.

'I know about his parents. Did he ever show signs of using . . . well, pagan magicks before?'

'No, holy one! Well, that is, except for . . . But it was strange.'

She knows something. 'Except for what?'

'Haal and Jillan argued before class. They were going to fight, and I got the strangest feeling Haal was in danger. But it was just a feeling.' She shrugged. 'Then Minister Praxis opened the door and we all went into class.'

'Drink the wine,' Azual said more sternly. He needed to connect with her thoughts if he was to understand things better than her childish ability to describe them. 'It is a blasphemy not to obey your holy Saint's commands.'

She looked at the blood again. 'What if I'm sick? Can't you Draw me to the Saviours without me drinking it? After all, the blessed Saviours can do anything, can't they? And I am faithful.'

Is she stalling? What can she hope to achieve? Never had he had to tolerate a child so full of questions and challenge. Most would not hesitate to follow his instruction, eager to have the taint out of them as soon as they could, so that they would be accepted as an adult by their community and enjoy new rights and freedoms. Where did her defiance come from? The plague, the Hero Samnir, the girl, the parents, and there were bound to be others, all affected and corrupted by this boy. His influence continued even when he was no longer in Godsend. Was he out there spreading his defiance to other communities even now? The boy was clearly some sort of focus for the Chaos, the power that the pagans referred to as the Geas. It was becoming imperative that Azual get answers out of the girl and Jillan's parents so that he could be out hunting the boy before any further time was lost. 'Do you defy me, girl?' he whispered dangerously.

Hella's hands began to shake and she cringed back from the Saint. The glass phial dropped and smashed on the stone floor.

Azual roared in anger. He would have to force her now. His core demanded he take what was rightfully his. How dare she deny him! He snatched her by the wrist and dragged her towards him.

'Nooo! Please, you're hurting me!'

'You bring this on yourself. Your blasphemy and defiance deserve nothing less.'

'Someone help me!'

'There's no one to help you, you wilful child. Are you so corrupted that you would resist being Drawn to the Saviours? Even your own father would want to see you purged.'

The girl's strength was as nothing compared to his. He shook her casually and she was capable of little more fight. Recalcitrant child! No doubt spoiled by her father as well as influenced by the boy. Her eyes glared at him. Was that hatred there? Astonishing. Minister Praxis had taught his students to fear and resent far too much. It was strange that the effects should be so marked, though. Was it another aspect of the plague and defiance, of the wrongness the Geas created?

There seemed to be far too much wrongness in this place whenever he examined the pattern of thoughts. The pattern! There was more wrongness, this time outside Godsend! The boy was at an inn at the fork to Saviours' Paradise and Heroes' Brook. He'd killed again! Cursing, Azual realised he must have passed him just the night before.

He threw the girl aside, not caring how she landed. He no longer had time for her, not when Jillan's parents were bound to know far more. Ducking out of the temple, he called, 'Captain Hamir, gather my guard. I must leave at once. Have the parents chained. We will take them with us so that they can be tested as necessary later. And the largest horse is to be saddled for myself!'

CHAPTER 5:

Or those that came before

Halls of dust stretching to the end of time. They cleaned, of course, constantly cleaned, but the corridors were so infinite that the retainers only succeeded in moving dust from one place to another. Despite the retainers, there was a stillness about these halls that spoke of eternity. It wasn't a feeling of peace as such, more the sense of an implacable and unending patience. All would finally come to pass as intended once sufficient time had been allowed. In this way, their will was inevitable.

The living statues that were the Saviours watched the world through a waking dream. They would only become animated when events in the waking dream were momentous enough to require them to communicate with each other directly or when their gaunt bodies demanded they feed on magically imbued blood to sustain them for another year or so. This physical requirement for nourishment, this *weakness*, displayed itself only in the younger Saviours, those who had been born to this world some millennia before. The elders had no such need when in the waking dream, for they were so ancient that their flesh had long since petrified and become harder than any stone. It was only when they wished to become animated once more that they would demand blood of their retainers.

Something changed. Along one of the infinite corridors, there was a silent whisper. *One of the Saviours stirs!* the retainers suddenly knew as one. *Hide and do not move! See and hear nothing!* The retainers were mute, having had their tongues ripped out so that they could not speak of anything they saw or heard in the labyrinth of the Great Temple, but all were acutely attuned to the vibrations of the place and the will of the Empire's rulers.

It is D'Selle. Clear out of the Saviour's path so that his eyes will not have to suffer our imperfection and will not have to burn us. Move quickly and then become still!

D'Selle drifted through the Great Temple, knowing from the primitive thoughts of the retainers where he would find D'Shaa, a far younger and lesser Saviour. He had been surprised and slightly offended centuries before when the elders had allowed one so inexperienced as D'Shaa to become the organising intelligence for the southern region, but now D'Selle was glad of it because it had ultimately provided him with easy prey. Once he had undone the lesser Saviour and added her power to his own, the elders would surely have no choice but to elevate him to their rank and to share some of the old secrets with him.

He arrived in the vast gallery where D'Shaa stood immobile, and stopped to wait. It was unacceptably aggressive, not to mention dangerous, to wake any Saviour from the waking dream, so D'Selle had to content himself with the hope D'Shaa would soon become aware of his proximity through the dream. She might choose to ignore his presence even then, but he relied on her having little real reason to do so.

To his relief, her eyes opened within the next hour and turned towards him. 'D'Selle.' She nodded stiffly. 'What is it you want from me?'

D'Selle bowed slightly. 'I merely come to enquire whether all is well in your region.'

D'Shaa watched through the waking dream. Like her, her Saint was young but capable. Azual made mistakes, of course, but never repeated them. His power had grown quickly and the southern region had become both stable and prosperous, even trading with the more lawless eastern region with some success. Yet, as she'd feared would happen, Azual had begun to see himself as having outgrown his Sainthood. In that respect, the recent challenges in Godsend were a useful wake-up for him. She was quite happy to sacrifice stability in the southern region in the short-term if it gained her a more humble and cautious Saint in the long-term. It did not do well for Azual to have everything his own way.

The consideration of her Saint aside, however, the challenges in Godsend caused her some disquiet. Instinct told her that these were not isolated events; rather, they were part of a subtle pattern and set of influences. To her frustration, she could not yet see that pattern properly, but she suspected the Geas had finally begun to manifest itself after countless ages in hiding. At least that was what she had suspected until D'Selle had presumed to seek her out.

It was with consternation that she had become aware of his presence in the gallery. Why had he come here? What scheme motivated him? Any why would he so overtly identify himself to her as a potential enemy? Surely he was robbing himself of his advantage, or was he looking to provoke a particular reaction that would then work against her? Of course, given the predatory nature of her kind, every Saviour was a potential enemy to her, but it was worrying that one would choose to signal so obviously that she had his attention. Maybe his intention was to demonstrate that he was fearless of her, so that her confidence would be undermined and her behaviour would change. Maybe he wanted her on the defensive rather than the offensive. Whatever the explanation, she could not help being a bit frightened – so perhaps he was already winning! Her equilibrium threatened, she decided to open her eyes and engage him so that she might glean some information she could use in turn against him.

'D'Selle,' she croaked drily. 'What is it you want from me?'

The older Saviour seemed smug as he bowed and said smoothly, 'I merely come to enquire whether all is well in your region.'

The insult was so great that the elders would not have hesitated to sanction him, but she would be considered weak for taking something like this to them. As an organising intelligence, she should be able to anticipate and pre-empt such an outrageous insult before it was even spoken. So D'Selle was cunning as well as fearless then. Her own fear only increased, although she kept her expression schooled so that she would not betray her weakness.

'How dare you ask such a thing!' she replied severely. 'Again, D'Selle, what is it you want of me?'

He shrugged slightly. 'I merely wish to offer my help should there be anything amiss in your region. The western region is ever ready to serve the wider Empire.'

Unbelievably, he'd followed up the first insult with an even greater one. His boldness and aggression were truly shocking. 'How could there be anything amiss when I always anticipate and pre-empt any problems? If there were anything genuinely amiss and beyond my ability to correct it, for the good of the Empire would I not have brought it to the elders long before it had occurred to anyone to enquire as to the state of my region? How dare you! Again, what is it you want of me?'

'I thought you should know that information can spread more quickly than might be useful when one region seeks to trade too much with others. Traders from the eastern region have come into my western region talking of a plague in the south. I only mention it out of concern for the wider Empire.'

He has spies in the southern region is probably more like it, D'Shaa thought to herself, *and he wishes to discourage the successful trade between south and east too.* Yet nothing so simple could be D'Selle's reason for initiating this confrontation between them. 'You think I would not know this?' she asked incredulously. 'How dare you!'

'If I have caused offence then I apologise.' Her enemy smiled at her. 'I will leave you now.'

She watched him drift out of the gallery and closed her eyes to think. What did he seek to initiate? D'Shaa knew that, usually, the safest course of action in such a situation was for her to do nothing for a long while, so that she could plan for different contingencies and then intervene when circumstances became more apparent. Yet would this approach work when there was a plague spreading? If she left things too late, the results could be disastrous and she would be held to account by the elders. All it needed was for the plague to spread to one other region and the affected Saviour could rightfully make a request that she be undone. She wouldn't have put it past D'Selle to encourage the plague to spread himself, were it not for the fact that the ever-watchful Elder Thraal would know of his thoughts and actions, and if such thoughts and actions were not deemed to be in the best interests of the Empire, then D'Selle's existence would be forfeit.

She considered taking immediate steps to halt the plague, but D'Selle's visit to her had seemed designed to provoke precisely this, and thus she resisted. If he had not visited her at all, then she would have been inclined to wait to see if the plague was indeed the Geas trying to exert some influence in a last desperate attempt to save itself and its world. She would have let it expose itself even further so that it would have no escape when the Empire moved to capture it once and for all. The glory that would come to her if she played a significant part in the capture of the Geas would see her elevated to the rank of elder at least.

And so she understood the dangerous dilemma D'Selle had created for her: she could move quickly to halt the plague but lose the rare chance of capturing the Geas, for which she would be rightly condemned; or she could wait, seek to lure the Geas out and capture it, all the while running the risk that if the plague were something else it might spread and cause her existence to become forfeit. Whether the plague fully represented the Geas or not, D'Selle had built it into his own subtle scheme of causes and events, a scheme that he must have started a good while before, for it had now progressed so far that it could not be undone simply. With horror, she realised he already had her trapped. This gamble was definitely not one she wanted to take, for she was an inexperienced player and the stakes were far too rich for her blood, but there was no escaping it now. The plague was in her region whether she liked it or not. The unleashing of pagan magicks had already occurred, not once but twice.

How had she not seen any of this coming? The elders would have no sympathy for one who could not anticipate and pre-empt such significant events. D'Selle might even be congratulated for his orchestration of the situation, for there was no doubt that he had forced the Geas to become involved in at least some part. Was it D'Selle then who had helped create the conditions in Godsend to focus the influence of the Geas? Was it he who had made sure particular malcontents had all ended up in the same community? Now that she looked more closely at the minds of the Minister called Praxis and the stubborn Hero called Samnir, she saw that they had both lived in the western region in their earlier days! It could be no coincidence. And the forebears of the boy's parents had originally come from the western region to help settle the south. They must have brought specific lore and rituals with them all that time ago and passed them down through the generations, causing disasters like New Sanctuary along the way.

D'Shaa trembled, knowing she was existing on borrowed time, and that it might already be too late to save herself.

Jillan plodded towards Saviours' Paradise, in the woods more often than not in an attempt to avoid the squalls of rain that would batter the road every now and then. There was no real protection to be had, however, because he'd left the evergreens of Godsend far behind: the trees here were iron grey and largely stripped bare. Blades of wind cut and thrust at him constantly. This was an unforgiving place of cold metallic hues.

The sky was heavy and low. It pressed on Jillan's brow just as his pack bowed his tired shoulders. It drove him into the ground and he had to stop, even though there was no decent shelter to be had. He had no appetite to speak of but decided to force himself to eat something in the hope that it would provide some energy. He chewed on a tough heel of bread, but it was tasteless and left him feeling more exhausted than when he had started. *You'd have had more joy eating the soles of your boots.* He found a few old beech nuts on the ground and chewed them for a bit, but they tasted of mouldy wood and mud, so he spat them out.

He dragged himself further away from the road, pulled his blanket out of his pack and curled up under it on a fairly dry area of ground litter. He didn't care what time of day it was. He was desperate for sleep.

'You are a murderer and a thief then, boy,' the corpse of the chieftain accused him, exhaling mulch and decay to fill Jillan's mouth and nose.

Jillan spluttered and looked up at the desiccated body standing over him. The remains of a shock of white hair and the warrior's protruding jaw were still evident. 'Y-you're dead!'

The chieftain chuckled. 'Pretty much. Yet you're still a murderer and a thief. Comfortable in that armour, is it? I suffered much for it.'

'I . . . will return it!'

The chieftain snorted, detritus spilling from his nasal cavity. 'It's of little use to me now. Perhaps you'll have more luck of it than I did.'

'I-I saw what the Saint did to the village. Did they all die?'

The pagan's head lolled as he nodded, and Jillan feared it would become detached entirely and end up in his lap. 'Of course, boy! What did you think? That my people would run like cowards? You insult us!'

'No!' Jillan protested as he retreated from the apparition. 'I just wondered if some had escaped to the mountains and if there was some hope for them.'

The chieftain spat beetles from his mouth and Jillan noticed that things crawled throughout the undead remains, although he tried not to look too closely. 'Hope? Ha! While there's life there's hope perhaps, but I doubt it when that life is an ignorant child who likes to murder and steal. What can you do to help the people of the mountains, boy? You do not even have the good sense to find somewhere properly warm before lying down to dream.'

Jillan's mouth hung open for a moment. What could he do on his own? 'I-I do not know.'

'Precisely. You are ignorant. Worse, you either wilfully ignore or are deaf and blind to the world around you. You grub around and cram your mouth with anything and as much as you can find, not caring if something else has to die so that you can live. Truly, you are a child of the others, looking to consume this world for your own continued existence! You bully others without hesitation, and when they resist do not hesitate to commit murder or steal from them.'

'No!' Jillan cried. He wasn't a bully like Haal. He didn't try and take things by force like Valor. He'd only killed in order to defend himself . . . hadn't he? 'I'm not like them! Don't say that! It's all been a mistake!'

'Was drawing on the Geas for power a mistake, boy? You took that power without any understanding and without any right to it, but that didn't stop you. And you killed with it! You have perverted it, and in so doing have upset the order of life and death that it maintained to keep this world whole. Look at me! I should not be here like this!'

'I-I did not know!' Jillan pleaded.

'The end will come now. You have undone us all, wretched child!' the chieftain moaned.

'No, there must be something that can be done.'

'The Saint is coming for you, boy. He has your scent now. You do not have the strength to resist him, especially now that your parents are his to do with as he wishes. You can only flee now, just as others once fled to the mountains, for you are not one who can stand against this Empire.'

The chieftain's body gave up its last breath and began to break apart. Black ichor ran from its empty eye sockets, the chest cavity collapsed, and its tendons and sinews separated. Bones clattered to the ground and then crumbled. Soon it was indistinguishable from the other rotting matter on the ground.

Jillan started awake, tore the suffocating blanket off his face and scrambled to his feet. Despite the cold, he was soaked in sweat and feeling feverish. Maybe the beech nuts had been mildly poisonous. He pulled a flask of water from his pack and all but drained it in one long drink. His head felt clearer and he threw off the last of the nightmare. He'd had dreams like this before when overly tired.

Stop pretending. You're worried it could have been real. The Chaos has found you, hasn't it? Or is the taint within you taking over your unconscious mind?

'Shut up!' Jillan growled.

You're talking to yourself like the town idiot now.

There was no refuge to be found in sleep. There was only this harsh waking world in which he was constantly hunted. The Saint had his scent and was coming for him. Jillan heaved his pack back onto his shoulders and slogged back towards the road.

The clouds were so dark that Jillan had no idea what time of the day it was, or whether night had actually begun to fall. At least the rain had stopped for a bit, although the sky promised it wouldn't be long before it started again.

As tired as he was, he wasn't sure he wanted to stop. If he did he might fall asleep again, and then the pagans and Chaos would come to tempt and threaten him in his dreams. *If you don't stop soon, you'll probably collapse and never move again.*

He rubbed at his eyes, which felt gritty and sore, and when he looked up glimpsed something glowing deep in the woods. What was it? Some new ghost or enemy to terrorise him? He knew there would be no avoiding it but was not about to be caught unprepared as he had been by Valor. He retrieved his bowstring and then hid his pack in the hollow of a tree. He slipped the loop at one end of the string around one end of the bow. Then he braced that against the foot of a tree and slowly brought his weight to bear until the bow had flexed enough to allow him to secure the string to the other end. He nocked an arrow to the taut string and then began to move as quietly as he could through the woods.

He went slowly, periodically stopping to listen and check all around him. The glowing light did not seem to be moving, which relieved and reassured him that he was not being led astray by some will-o'-the-wisp seeking to trap him in a bog and steal his soul. The oldest man in Godsend, Samuel, used to sit on his porch with a pipe of an evening and tell all the children scary stories about the dangerous cunning of such Chaos creatures. What Jillan wouldn't have given to be back sitting with the other children listening to the old man now.

The trees looked to be thinning ahead. He smelt woodsmoke. He moved behind a bush and peeped out. A straggle-haired man was busy hammering wedges into a felled tree trunk so that the wood would split lengthways and posts and planks could be separated off. A brazier burned nearby, giving the man a certain amount of light by which to work. Extra light also came from the windows and doorway of a small but solidly built cabin set towards the rear of the clearing.

His back to Jillan, the man paused for a breath and wiped his brow. *Jillan, you're either going to wait until you have a chance to slip away and carry on some good distance down the road or you're going to raise your weapon before this woodsman senses your presence.* Jillan stepped out from his hiding place and drew back his bow. The man immediately spun to face him, raising his hammer as he did so, but there were at least thirty paces between them.

The man, who was slightly breathless from his exertions, hawked and spat. 'If you're going to draw a bow on someone, then you'd best be prepared to use it. If you know what's good for you, you'll put it down. I won't give you another chance.'

Jillan did not let his aim waver. 'I am simply travelling through, on my way to Saviours' Paradise. Who are you?'

'And who are you to enter my woods and threaten me?' the man shouted and broke into a run straight for Jillan. He hurled his hammer.

Jillan did not blink as the hammer fell short. He stilled his breath. His father had told him never to hesitate. He released his arrow and it flew straight for the oncoming man's heart. *Murderer*, whispered the voice within him.

Yet, with perfect timing, the man twisted just as the arrow was about to hit him and was again running at Jillan, only now he was much closer. As the woodsman sprinted across the clearing, he stooped, freed a longaxe from a log with a powerful flick of his wrist and screamed as he prepared to cleave the intruder in two.

Even as Jillan had released the first arrow, he'd begun to reach for another. He saw his first arrow miss and wondered how that was possible, but he did not let it distract him. As the man rushed towards him, Jillan calmly nocked the second arrow to his bowstring and reached within himself to limn the arrow with power. This one would not miss; it would fly unerringly, no matter what tricks the man attempted.

The woodsman had the axe raised above his head and was seconds away from bringing it down on its target. He saw the youth ready a second arrow. It shone with red warning as it reflected the light from the brazier. Like the arrow, the youth's eyes were red and unflinching. *Damn! I am too slow. How can that be?* His senses screaming at him, the woodsman suddenly stopped, his breath caught in his chest.

At the moment Jillan was about to release, the man came to a precise halt. Perfect timing again. They watched each other in unmoving silence. The spell was finally broken by the golden patterns of Jillan's armour writhing at the periphery of his vision. Jillan blinked.

'You'll be expecting me to make you tea or some such now, I suppose,' the woodsman grouched.

From where he sat on a low stool, Jillan watched the rangy woodsman as he set water over the fire in his one-room cabin. The man had a dark stubbled chin and an ugly scar on one cheek. His age was indeterminate, anywhere between thirty and fifty, but he moved with an easy strength. He had a heavy brow that often cast shadows across his face, but his eyes glittered fiercely no matter how much light there was.

He caught Jillan watching him and smiled crookedly at him. 'No one's ever managed to sneak up on me before, especially not one so young.'

'My father's a hunter,' Jillan said proudly, only then remembering he shouldn't be giving away such information about himself.

'That so?' the woodsman answered with a raise of his eyebrows, encouraging Jillan to say more.

Jillan became more guarded. 'I am Irkarl from Heroes' Brook, travelling to Saviours' Paradise. Thank you for inviting me to share your fire. Sorry about the manner of my arrival, but I am wary of pagans and so on.'

The woodsman frowned as he took dried leaves from a shelf and added them to the water. 'You may call me Ash. What news from Heroes' Brook, Irkarl?'

Jillan hesitated. 'Ah . . . er . . . the road leading out of town is still flooded, so wagons are not coming to Saviours' Paradise at the moment.'

'I see. Travelling alone is a tad dangerous, though, isn't it, despite how handy you are with a bow?'

Jillan nodded. 'I am on pilgrimage. We must be prepared to suffer danger for our faith. I have chosen to take the long route round for the same reason. Ash, is it not dangerous living out here on your own?'

Ash stared at Jillan for a moment, clearly debating with himself how to answer. With a sigh, he finally said, 'There are no pagans to be afeared of hereabouts, Irkarl, or at least I've never met any. As I said before, there are few that are able to stalk me without my being aware of it. And then . . . Well, bring your beaker of tea with you and we will sit outside for a while.'

Curious, Jillan did as the man bade, and they moved over to the brazier. Ash sat on the ground with his back against a comfortable-looking rock, while Jillan sat on an upturned log.

'We need to wait for a bit,' Ash said simply.

Jillan cupped his hands around the steaming beaker against the cold, and sipped at it. It was slightly astringent – his mother would have added a spoonful of honey to it – but it served well enough to spread some warmth through him.

'How did you end up here in the first place, Ash?' Jillan asked in the dim fitful light coming from the brazier.

There was no response for a long while, and Jillan wondered if the woodsman would bother to answer at all. Then, in a surly voice: 'You are inquisitive, Irkarl. It's not really your business, but I am one of the Unclean. Does that frighten you?'

'Er . . . I don't know what the Unclean are. It's got nothing to do with washing, has it?'

'No!' Ash spluttered. A pause. 'It's far worse than that, certainly not something with which someone on pilgrimage would want to become involved.'

'Really?' Jillan asked in as light a tone as possible.

'Really. I am outcast. The Saint wanted nothing to do with me. He forbade me ever to take a wife or to sire any children. When my parents died, the elders of Saviours' Paradise decided that the house I grew up in should go to a family, so I had nowhere to live. I was effectively banished. They tolerate me visiting the community and trading on market days – the skins I take always go quickly and my carvings seem to be popular – but otherwise they don't tend to like seeing me around. I imagine you'll want to be leaving now.'

'No, no,' Jillan assured him. 'I'll stay a while if you'll let me. But why would the Saint take against you? Did you do something bad?'

'Ha! You really don't know what it is to be Unclean then. You're not Unclean because of something you've *done*, but because of something you *are*! I was born this way. Have you been Drawn yet, Irkarl? You're of an age.'

Jillan was glad that the man wouldn't be able to see his expression in the near darkness, because he would surely have discerned something was amiss. 'Er, no. I will be Drawn when I reach the end of the pilgrimage.'

'Of course. Well, let me tell you something of what happens when a person is Drawn.'

'No, don't! I mean . . . it's a holy sacrament that's meant to remain secret, isn't it?' Jillan tailed off. 'Sorry, forget I said that. I would be happy to hear whatever you can tell me, Ash.'

'Well, make up your mind. So, the Saint asks you to drink a small amount of some thick wine and then sticks a tube in your arm.'

'A tube?'

'Yes, a thin tube. It's made of sun-metal.'

'Really? I've never seen sun-metal. Does it really shine like they say?'

'Anyway, the Saint sticks the tube in your arm so that blood comes out. The taint's meant to come out with the blood, you see. But when the Saint tasted my blood—'

'He tasted your blood? Yuck!'

'When he tasted my blood, he said the taint wasn't coming out and that I was Unclean. I couldn't be Drawn. Then I became outcast, and that was that. But I prefer it this way. Here I can do whatever I want. I don't have to work in the fields or with herds of animals. I don't have Heroes watching me all day. I'm free to come and go as I want. Free.'

'That's . . . that's . . .' Jillan began, but he didn't know what it was really and became quiet as he pondered all that he'd heard. They remained in a companionable silence for a good long while.

Ash brought them out of their reverie when he said, 'Ah, here he is.'

'Here who is?' Jillan asked, looking round. He gasped as he saw a large black wolf lying no more than six feet from them. Its orange eyes burned like coals in the darkness and Jillan's entire head would have fitted between its mighty jaws. Its tongue suddenly lolled out of its mouth and licked its long teeth as if it had heard that last thought.

'Aaash!' Jillan whined.

'Do not fear, Irkarl. The wolf still eats well at this time of year. A month from now, however, with snow on the ground and most prey gone into their winter sleep, you might have left this place with fewer fingers than when you arrived.'

'Ahh!'

'I'm joking, Irkarl! Don't take on!'

The wolf's tongue lolled again and it panted a few times as if sharing the joke.

'Is it friendly?'

'Is not the fact it hasn't eaten you yet friendly enough, Irkarl? But yes, he is the reason I do not fear to live out here alone. None can get close without the wolf knowing about it and warning me. For all that, though, you managed to come here and draw a bow on me. It shows I mustn't become complacent. Maybe the wolf let you through to teach me a lesson. Who knows?'

'What is its name?'

'I don't know. He hasn't told me.'

'How could he tell you? Wolves can't talk!'

'Just because you haven't heard it talk doesn't mean that it cannot. It may simply choose not to.'

'Well, why don't you give it a name?'

Ash shook his head. 'It's not my place to give him a name, Irkarl. Besides, he'll already have one. He just hasn't decided to tell it to me. And why should he? There's no real need to, and names have power, you know. Who am I to have power over this wolf, eh?'

'Hello, wolf!' Jillan said politely. 'My name's Irkarl. Pleased to meet you.'

The wolf growled and bared its teeth at him.

It can't know that I'm lying about my name, can it?

'Easy, wolf! Irkarl is our guest. What sort of hosts would we be if we scared him to death, eh?'

The wolf subsided, but it did not take its menacing gaze off Jillan.

'Well,' Ash said with a smile, 'time to cook something, I reckon. The wolf may feed himself well, but it's never averse to a bit of extra squirrel. Do you like squirrel, Irkarl?'

'I'm not sure – I've never tasted it,' Jillan admitted. 'But I'll come with you,' he added, not wanting to be left alone with the wolf.

Jillan sat back feeling comfortable for the first time in days. They'd enjoyed a roasted squirrel each, Jillan sharing half of his with the wolf to buy forgiveness for his earlier lie, and now they sat out by the brazier drinking some cloudy fermented concoction with which Ash was proudly generous and jealously mean by turns. Jillan had not cared for the muddy drink at first, but after half a beaker or so his judgement shifted and he accepted more whenever it was proffered. With the wolf breathing deeply by his side, food in his stomach and a friend to share his thoughts with, all seemed right with the world. He felt relaxed and safe.

'You know, Asssh, these woodsh aren't sho bad!'

'Of coursh they're not. How could they be, with me living here?'

The wolf groaned and stretched out longer on the ground.

'True, true. But I was . . . thinking.'

'Go on.'

'Well, you know you shaid you were free here? Well, you aren't really, are you?'

'What do you mean?' Ash protested.

'You're not allowed a wife or children, are you? And you're forbidden a larger community. Yesh, you've got the wolf, I know, but you pretty much live in a punishment chamber without wallsh, don't you?'

'Well, you live in a punishment chamber *with* walls, don't you!' Ash shot back. 'Tell me, which one's better, Irkarl?'

'Huh. They're probably as bad as each other. You're right. Can I have shome more?'

'Of course I'm right! Careful, though, that sounds a bit like blasphemy, and you're a good little pilgrim, aren't you, Irkarl? You're trotting along to the Saint like a good little boy to have yourself Drawn, just like your Minister, mummy and daddy told you to.'

'I am not!' Jillan shouted belligerently. 'My parents didn't tell me anything like that! They . . .'

'Oh, he changes his story now! Now he's *not* on pilgrimage! Can never make up his mind, this one.'

'I'm not on pilgrimage! I'm . . . I'm . . .'

'You're what?' Ash asked intently. 'Don't you think it's time you told me the truth, Irkarl, if that's your name? The wolf doesn't seem to think it is. I would think the truth is the least you owe me after I've shared my fire and stores with you, wouldn't you, especially when you pretty much forced your way in here?'

'I . . .' Could he trust this strange man and his even stranger companion?

Ash dropped his voice and made it gentler. 'Look, who am I going to tell? The trees? The sky? You're clearly in some sort of trouble. The way I see it, we're stuck in the same punishment chamber, you and me, and only have each other to help us escape. Here, let me fill that beaker of yours – it must have a leak in it 'cause it always seems more empty than full.'

Jillan sighed and held out his beaker with a nod. 'My name's Jillan.'

'Well, that's a start. And what misfortune has the world forced upon you that sees you end up with a patched-up old man of the woods and a flea-ridden wolf?'

The wolf made a rumbling noise but did not move from where it lay by the brazier.

'Overweight too.'

A louder rumble and then a show of teeth.

Jillan smiled weakly and took a swallow of Ash's forest brew. 'Someone died,' he said quietly.

'Ahh,' Ash breathed.

The brazier fizzed and sighed.

'It was my fault. I ran away instead of letting them put me in a punishment chamber.'

Ash nodded. 'How did they die, Jillan?'

'There was a fight. Three of them. I . . . Well, there was something like lightning and it killed Karl. Then there was the inn. The innkeeper had me trapped in a room, and when he came for me, a similar thing happened.'

'That whoremonger Valor, yes? It's no loss, Jillan, believe me. There's a reason why he had to leave Saviours' Paradise and set himself up in the middle of nowhere. All knew what went on and what that poor girl had to suffer. Her mother took her own life when she found out, they say, although others say Valor did for her when she tried to protect the girl.'

'The Saint is after me, Ash! He always knows everything. And I think he's now taken my parents prisoner. What am I to do? There's no escape.'

'Come now, that's not the warrior who caught me unawares speaking. That's not the man who has come all the way from Heroes' Brook on his own speaking. That's not—'

'Godsend, not Heroes' Brook.'

'All the way from Godsend then. That's not the fellow who finally gave Valor the comeuppance he deserved, now is it?'

'I suppose not,' Jillan conceded morosely. 'But what does it matter? The Saint will find me, and then I'll suffer the worst punishment possible for all the things I've done. I deserve it too.'

'Poppycock and midden water! Like me, you've been born a bit different, that's all. How is it your fault how you were born, eh? No, don't contradict me! I won't hear otherwise, Jillan. You're just going to repeat all the bigotry and irrational fear people have spouted at you over the years. Look, worst comes to the worst, you can stay here with me. The most you'll have to contend with is the wolf's farts when he's had too much hedgehog.'

Jillan shook his head. 'I'm sorry, I can't. My parents told me to go to Saviours' Paradise. There's someone I need to find. If my parents are freed at all, they will also meet me there.'

Ash rubbed his chin in thought. 'There's a good chance the Heroes of Saviours' Paradise have already been told to be on the lookout for you. It's dangerous.'

Jillan shrugged. 'I have to try.'

'Well, there's a market in Saviours' Paradise two days hence. There will be quite a few people from other communities coming into town, and if I go with you you won't stand out as much as someone trying to enter on their own. We can go, ask around for this person for a day or so and then be out of there before you attract too much attention. We can also leave word with someone to watch for your folks in the weeks ahead. That person can pass on the message that you're at my cabin in the woods.'

Jillan thought it through and nodded.

'You'll need to cover up that armour of yours, though. It's quite distinctive. What *are* all those symbols anyway? I don't recognise them.'

Jillan shifted uncomfortably. 'Me neither. I found it in an old barn. I don't think it belongs to anybody, and I don't think anyone has really seen me wearing it, but I can wear a cloak over it.'

'And who is this person you need to meet? I might know him and be able to save us some time.'

'Thomas Ironshoe.'

'Thomas? Nope, I don't know anyone by that name. Still, Saviours' Paradise is a big place and a lot of people come and go. Anyway, that's settled, eh, Jillan, m'lad! We are co-conspirators and adventurers! Let's drink to that! Co-conspirators!'

'Co-conspirators!'

The wolf began to snore.

As night was falling, Saint Azual and his men reached the inn. He was in a foul mood – not used to being in the saddle for prolonged periods and therefore really not enjoying the day's ride through the bad weather. But it had been necessary to conserve energy. *I will make sure the boy suffers for every moment of this blasphemous humiliation!*

He climbed stiffly out of his saddle and threw his reins to one of his guards. He strode up to the door of the inn and pounded on it. Metal-clad though it was, his fists left visible depressions in the surface.

'Open this door in the name of the Saviours!' he boomed, using his power to amplify his voice. 'Open it, or, so help me, I will turn it to tinder.'

Within a few heartbeats there was the sound of bolts being drawn and a pale young face looked out.

'Open the door for your holy Saint, girl! Ingrid, isn't it?'

The girl gulped, pulled back the door with some effort and stood aside so that the glowering Saint could enter. She curtsied as he passed and said tremulously, 'Welcome, holy one.'

'Prepare food and drink for my men, Ingrid, while they stable their horses. Captain Skathis, have the man and woman confined to separate rooms upstairs. You'll find the rooms quite secure, and the girl has keys. I sense no plague here.'

'As you will it, holy one.'

'On second thoughts, girl, leave the victuals for now. You and I need to exchange words in private first.'

'In private, holy one?' she asked faintly.

'Yes, girl, unless you want an audience to your crimes and shame?'

Tears pricked the corners of her eyes. 'Th-this way, holy one.' She led the giant representative of the Saviours into the side room and sat in one of the chairs. Her hands shook as she held onto the front of her dress. Her knees knocked together and then urine began to trickle onto the wooden floor beneath her feet.

Azual wrinkled his nose in distaste – it was at times like this that he wished his senses weren't quite so sharp – but his voice was not unkind as he said, 'You need not fear me, child. My duty is the good care of the People. Come, collect yourself.'

Ingrid nodded and pulled a small handkerchief from her sleeve with which to wipe her nose. 'Yes, holy one.'

'Now, tell me, Ingrid. Where is your father?'

Her eyes showed naked fear. 'My father, h-holy one? Why, he went to town for provisions.'

Azual sighed patiently. 'Did not your father explain to you that the blessed Saviours and their holy Saints know all things?'

She shook her head, tears beginning to run freely down her drawn cheeks.

'I know that he is dead, child. I know that you have disposed of the body. Do you understand it is a sin and blasphemy to lie to a Saint?'

Ingrid began choking and sobbing. Her voice was a wail as she begged, 'Forgive me! I did not know what else to do. He smelt bad, and it's my job to keep the rooms clean. I'm sorry if I did wrong.'

'I am not without compassion and mercy, child. I know how your father mistreated you. Do you really want my forgiveness?'

'Yes, more than anything, holy one!'

Azual smiled. 'Good. Then you will tell me everything you know of the boy.'

'Of course, holy one,' she said without hesitation. 'Yes. It was him who killed my father. He did it! Only . . .'

'I know what Valor tried to do, Ingrid, but tell me anyway.'

'My father tried to lie with him, holy one, and then Irkarl killed him. He left without paying his bill either.'

'Irkarl, you say?'

'Yes, the boy. He said that was his name. Irkarl from Heroes' Brook.'

'I see. Go on. Which way did the boy go? Towards Saviours' Paradise or back towards Heroes' Brook?'

'I-I don't know, holy one. I'm sorry,' she said in earnest distress.

'No matter. Tell me, Ingrid, was there anything else you noticed about Irkarl?'

She bit her lip. 'Erm . . . he was wearing some funny leather, like armour, with gold patterns all over it, but that's all really.'

Armour with gold patterns. Why did that seem familiar? 'What sort of patterns? Could you draw them if you had to?'

'I'm sorry, but I don't really remember them. They were . . . confusing, holy one. Please don't be angry!'

Azual gave her a perfunctory smile. 'But what of you, Ingrid? Running this inn alone is a lot to ask of a child. You don't have anyone to protect you. Perhaps you would prefer to return to Saviours' Paradise.'

Ingrid set her jaw. 'There's never been anyone to protect me from my father anyway, holy one. I all but ran the place even when he was alive. The inn is my home and all I have. Please let me stay!'

'Now you ask a favour of me, after your sin and blasphemy?' Azual sighed. 'Well, I suppose I could Draw you to the Saviours, and then it might be more appropriate. You could become an adult of means and could go into one of the towns on a market day to pick yourself a husband. Should I bestow such a blessing on you, Ingrid?'

'Oh yes, please, holy one! I will try to be better, honestly I will. I will pray both morning and night from now on, and make sure I always thank the Saviours before eating or drinking.'

'Very well. Then do as I tell you, Ingrid. First drink this phial of wine. Hold your nose if it helps with the taste. And roll up your sleeve. This won't hurt.'

Jed hated small spaces, and his bear-like size made most rooms seem small. That was why he was a hunter – so he could be out in the open most of the time. Small spaces made him feel confined and trapped, as if he were in a cage or snare. He'd become panicky and angry if Maria wasn't there to calm him with her soothing words. When he'd been a younger man, friends had got him drunk and locked him in a wood store on his wedding night. When he'd come to and realised he was shut in, he'd felt like he was suffocating and had become wild to be free. He'd slammed his fists into the walls, not caring that his hands bled and his knuckles broke. He'd charged at them with shoulder and head, putting great gashes in his forehead and making everything reel. Just as an animal caught in a trap will chew a limb off to be free before the hunter can come to break its neck, Jed wrecked every part of his body to destroy the wood store around him. The People of New Sanctuary had laughed and shouted to Maria, 'Your man is so hot and strong for you that there'll be no building left standing after tonight!' 'He's so insane with passion that he'll break the marriage bed!' 'Do you want the physick to come call on you in the morning, Maria?' 'Maybe you should have that gold ring put through his nose so that bull of yours can be more easily led.' He remembered little else of the night except the cool hands and whispering voice as she braced and bandaged his injuries.

Now he was not just in a small room, he was also chained. There were locked, heavy shutters on the windows. His chest felt tight and he struggled to breathe. The only thing that kept him in his chair was

Maria's original instruction to remain calm and to wait for her signal before trying to escape. Of course, she'd been right – if he'd tried to fight so many Heroes when they were first taken, he'd be dead by now, albeit with a good number of their corpses lying beside his own. And if he were dead, he'd never see his beloved Maria or dear Jillan again, and never be able to help or protect them as he should.

Maria had always been the smarter one in their marriage, had always known when to fight and when not to, had always known when his temper was about to get them all in a lot of trouble, and had always known just what to say to draw him back from the precipice. She understood the Empire far better than he did: why there were Saints, Heroes and Ministers, why there were silly rules and why people were always trying to confine and trap them. And she knew how to make sure Jed and Jillan got just enough space to save them from self-harm.

It was so hard for Jed to remain calm – especially when there was so little air in the room – but he had to do what Maria told him. Without her, he was nothing. She was a special woman, he knew, one whom most of the men in New Sanctuary had coveted, but she had chosen him. This woman, who had such perception and insight that she seemed almost magical, had chosen him. This woman, who read people and the seasons so well that she seemed to know the future, had chosen to share her life with him. He was the luckiest man who ever lived, or rather, as he sometimes thought, he'd only really begun to live the day Maria had informed him that the two of them would be stepping out together from thereon. He sometimes wondered why she had chosen him, but whenever he asked her she would simply ask him some confusing question like why the sun rose every morning or why leaves fell from the trees in autumn. Then she'd shake her head, smooth his furrowed brow with her palm, kiss his cheek (on tiptoe) and tell him to go chop some wood and think about something more useful.

Their lives in New Sanctuary had been wonderful . . . until that terrible visit by the Saint, which Jed didn't like to think about. They'd had several years in which they'd prospered: every arrow Jed loosed while out hunting had seemed to hit a deer or some other prize, and Maria's leather work, with its unusual designs, became much sought after, even beyond New Sanctuary. Women came to learn her patterns and craft, and everyone in New Sanctuary had treated her with respect.

It was then that Maria had become pregnant and Jillan had been born. Jed's life was complete – he'd never been happier. Yet, by contrast, Maria had become more and more distracted. Others had reassured him that it was nothing unusual in a new mother, but when he'd come home and discovered tear tracks on her face, he'd demanded to know what was wrong. He'd refused to let her put him off.

'Something terrible is going to happen.'

Jed felt the hairs on the back of his neck prickle. He was not so foolish as to dismiss his wife's fears out of hand. 'What will happen, beloved?' he'd whispered.

'I-I'm not sure. But I think it will happen if we don't leave New Sanctuary.'

Jed had baulked at that. They had everything they'd ever wanted in New Sanctuary: friends, trade and good standing in the community, not to mention their beautiful baby son to think of. If they were to leave suddenly, there would be a lot of difficult questions to answer, and the elders and the Heroes might even forbid it. He'd begged her to let them stay a little while longer – half hoping her forebodings of doom would pass – and she'd reluctantly agreed, although she began to store more of their things in easily transportable bags.

Then the Saint had come.

Now the door opened and allowed Jed a few moments in which he could breathe more easily, but then it closed and the face of death was looking down at him. Its malevolent bloody eye saw into him. There was a shining halo of power around the Saint that burned Jed's skin whenever it came close.

'Did Jillan go to Saviours' Paradise or Heroes' Brook, Jedadiah?' Saint Azual asked. 'Answer your holy Saint or be found guilty of sin.'

Jed had clouded his mind so that the monster before him would not simply be able to pluck the knowledge from his head. Maria had taught him the trick back in New Sanctuary, although at the time she'd said it was just to help him control his temper, anger and fear of small spaces. 'Learning not to think of bad things often prevents them happening,' she'd explained. Then, when they'd left New Sanctuary, she'd told him to cloud his thoughts as she'd taught him so that they would not attract the attention of the bad things. 'It's similar to people making a warding sign against evil, Jedadiah. Trust me.' It had seemed to work at the time, but now he had the full and undivided attention of that same evil and he was terrified the trick would not work.

The Saint frowned and tutted. 'I can force it from you if necessary, Jedadiah. Yours is neither a strong nor a trained mind. You are a simple and honest man, though, yes? I am loath to treat such a man so severely. Surely you understand that I only do this out of duty to the Saviours and the People, no? Jillan is a danger to all those around him. I do not seek to harm him, however; I simply need to Draw the taint from him so that he will no longer be a danger to others. He will have to answer for the killings of course – he's killed again, by the way – but I know he was not entirely to blame. I promise you, Jedadiah, that after a few years he will be able to return to a normal life. He can marry Hella, as you'd always hoped, and have children and happiness. Surely you want that for him, yes? You will have grandchildren. You just need to tell me where he has gone.'

'You do not wish to treat me severely, holy one? Just as you did not wish to treat the People of New Sanctuary severely, holy one? You promise me a normal life, holy one? Yet what was your promise worth to the innocent dead of New Sanctuary? You have forfeited your right to anything from me! Why should I trust you will treat my son well when your own Minister in Godsend sought to persecute him? Why should I trust you when you leave a good man like Samnir a dribbling idiot?'

The Saint sighed. His voice was full of contrition as he said, 'Only the blessed Saviours are perfect, Jedadiah. I have had to endure my own struggles and hardship. I regret what happened in New Sanctuary, but there was no doubt that the Chaos had been allowed to influence the People there. You know there was unholy magic at work there, do you not? Yes, I can see you do. I regret the behaviour of my Minister, and he has already been censured accordingly. And I regret what I had to do to Samnir, but he had to be punished for his defiance and an example had to be made of him to the other Heroes. Surely you understand that none may be permitted to defy the holy representative of the blessed Saviours. Otherwise such anarchy would see the Empire undone and the People ruled by the Chaos.'

Jed was not sure what to say. He had never really understood big ideas like the Empire and the Chaos. If Maria had been here, she'd have known what to say.

The Saint immediately took the last thought from his head. 'Ah yes, your dear wife Maria. She is well, Jedadiah. She is in the next room, and I have made sure none of the men have touched her. See, I am not the monster you think I am. She was about to tell me where Jillan was herself, but worry overcame her and she fainted. I know she wants you to tell me what I need to know. We don't have time to wait for her to come round, though, for the sooner we find Jillan the sooner he will no longer be a danger to the People. He's killed two of the People now, Jedadiah. How many more?'

Jed hesitated. Could Maria really want him to tell the Saint where Jillan was? 'You are lying,' he sneered. 'Let me see her and then I'll know the truth of your words.'

The Saint casually squeezed Jed's mind and smiled as the big man winced. 'You see, I could render Maria unconscious quite easily and appear to be telling the truth. But I am not someone who indulges in such deception, not someone who shrouds their thoughts like you, Jedadiah. Shame on you!'

Jed's face flushed.

'I know all of this is confusing for a simple and honest man like you, Jedadiah. Yet I understand your concern is that of a loving husband, as is right and proper. If I do not get the answers I require from either of you soon, then I cannot promise what will or will not happen.'

'If you touch a hair on her head—'

'You threaten me?' the Saint asked dangerously. 'You are simple, Jedadiah, but that cannot excuse such a blasphemy. You are forcing me to deal with you more severely. If I have to force the answers from your head, your mind will probably be so damaged that you will be little better off than Samnir. That will upset Maria terribly. I doubt I would find Maria's mind as easy to break down, but her body is far weaker than yours, is it not? Where a brute like you could endure physical torture all day, perhaps perversely enjoying the scars it won you, how would you feel about Maria going through the same and losing her pretty looks? It would be a shame to have to remove that button nose of hers.'

Jed roared in anger and surged to his feet despite his chains. He barrelled into the Saint and knocked him backwards. Jed pursued and brought his head up sharply under the Saint's chin, snapping the holy representative's head back. The Saint's eye lost its focus and his arms flailed as he tried to keep his balance, but his feet caught on each other and he slammed into the wall of the room, suffering another blow to the head.

Jed hopped and jumped closer but in his haste pitched forward. He fell into the Saint and bit at the holy one's cheek, just short of his good eye.

'No!' the Saint screamed in a high girlish voice. 'Not my eye!'

The panic brought the Saint back to himself. As quick as thought, he seized Jed's mind and squeezed it hard. The hunter's back arched and his mouth stretched wide in silent agony. The Saint threw the big man off him as if he were naught but a rag doll. Jed hit the floor heavily, shaking the floorboards and raising a cloud of dust around him. Blood trickled from the hunter's ears and nose.

'How dare you!' the Saint raged, already on his feet. 'You would attack my holy person? It is inconceivable! Truly you are in the thrall of the Chaos. And all of this had only been a test of you and Maria, Jedadiah, for I have known where Jillan is all along. You have condemned yourself. See!'

The Saint implanted a false image of Jillan entering the gates of a town in Jed's mind. Jed, dazed as he was, held onto the image as a suffocating man will hold onto his last breath. *He has reached Saviours' Paradise safely*. Jed grinned as darkness crept up around his conscious mind.

The Saint gave an ugly laugh. 'Has he indeed? Then you have at last told me what I needed to know, Jedadiah. I will soon find him and he will willingly give himself to me, if he ever wants to see his parents breathe again.'

Aspin fought his way down the mountain through the snow into the ridges of foothills where there was some tree cover from bone-white birch and grey-stone oaks. The snow wasn't as thick here and the air was warmer. There was even the odd bird around, singing a questioning note or two to ask where everyone had gone.

He followed the line of foothills, as they gave him a fairly dry route across the land. When they began to peter out, however, he entered an upside-down place of yew trees. Here there were branches wider than the feasting hall in his village. They grew down to the ground from their trunks, went flat for some distance and then wound up into the sky to make cages for the air. A good number of the trunks had been torn in two by heavy branches growing out of each side of them, and their grey skeletons lay everywhere. It was a graveyard of giants. Yet it was an eternal graveyard, for from the centres of the broken trees came new ones, many crying blood-red berries even at this time of year.

Such trees were hallowed to his people, for the berries were so potent that the merest touch of them on the skin would send an individual to sleep for days or longer and visit tortured hallucinations of possible futures on them. Any sort of ingestion of the berry, even a weak distillation, was almost always fatal. Such an ancient grove of trees, were it to exist in the mountains, would have been a sacred and eternal temple of the Geas for his people.

He stood now in awe, listening to the voice of the wind moaning from the huge hollow bodies of the yews. Were he worthy, he would have been able to understand the voices and will of Wayfar of the Warring Winds and Gar of the Still Stone. Would the voices be telling him to go forward or back? Was he being warned or mocked? Or were the voices lamenting the fall of the gods before the others and their Empire came? This was an in-between place: between eternity and an end, the Geas and the Empire, his people and the others, and god-given life and oblivion. Yet Aspin himself was neither on one side nor the other, for he was exiled, in limbo, suspended between realms.

There was a feel of quiet waiting here, which was closer to peace than anything he'd known in his life. He was tempted to lie on the ground with these giants and their petrified blood-red tears so that he could sleep and dream of possible futures forever more. It was so tempting . . . but he knew his cursed stomach would all too soon rumble in discontent and keep him from his rest. Ah, but this stomach of his was to blame for all his woes. He was tempted to tear it out and have done with it, perhaps devour it to teach it an ironic lesson, but he knew the rest of his body would then all too soon start to protest. Damn this body of his – it was a constant trial to him. Were it not for his body, existence would be far easier, but even the gods had to manifest themselves physically to exist at all in this world. Damn it, the essential nature of this world was of course physical. That was the deal and something he'd agreed to even when in the womb, so what was he complaining about?

What was his cause for complaint? What was his cause? He had no idea. Damn Torpeth for exiling him and forcing him to find a bigger cause. Why couldn't the flatulent old hermit just have left him alone to live out his days as the smartest and quickest of the warriors in the village? Why couldn't he have let him pair with Leesha and have several young ones – the gods permitting – to keep him in his old age while he contented himself with foaming flagons of winter brew by a well-made fire?

Aspin sighed. He knew that he could not spend his life hiding from the others, and his people could not stay safe forever. The others would come eventually, and then it would all be over. Perhaps Torpeth had foreseen that the others would come in Aspin's own lifetime, and had therefore sent Aspin out to learn what he could, so that his people would be better prepared. But what could really be learned that would save them from the might of an entire empire? The only hope was if Aspin could find the fallen gods and somehow raise them back up so that they could fight for the Geas once more.

The idea seemed to have come from nowhere, but it felt right to him. Yet where were the gods to be found? The others must know, since they had toppled them in the first place. So it came back to finding out about the others once more.

Restful as the grove was, therefore, he could not linger here too long. If he lingered, he might never leave, he knew. Besides, there soon wouldn't be much shelter between the realms because there was no longer any balance between them: one realm grew stronger while the other became weaker. It looked like the two realms would soon collapse together, the rule and realm of the others finally prevailing, as the realms and power of the Geas were finally undone.

His people had run out of time then. Maybe Torpeth's hand had been forced. Aspin nodded. Feeling a new weight of responsibility on his shoulders, Aspin passed through the grove before it could begin to visit further revelations on him, revelations concerning the likely future that were no doubt so terrible he would be unmanned completely.

Suddenly scared, he quickened his pace until the grove of yews was lost behind him. Perhaps he would never be able to find the place again.

Leaving the foothills, he found the going easier than expected. No snow had fallen in the lower lands thus far, and he even found he was too warm in his layers of goatskin. There were also plentiful amounts of food to be had: from mushrooms to nuts, to birds, to fish in streams and even a rabbit or two.

Then he came across a wide, wide path made of flat stones. It disappeared beyond sight ahead and behind him. Who had created this path and how long must it have taken? These others must be far more powerful than he'd ever imagined. Guessing that the path led somewhere important – perhaps to the home of the others even? – he began to follow it. He travelled quickly on the wide and level path, and he found there was suddenly hope in his heart.

Aspin whistled as he went and therefore didn't hear the wagon coming up behind him until a distant voice hollered at him.

'Hey there! Jillan, is that you?'

Aspin almost jumped out of his goatskins, so startled was he. He spun and took in the wagon, pulled by two chestnut mares, coming towards him. A lone tubby man with greying hair held the reins of the horses loosely in his hands. Aspin knew he had time to run into the trees if he wanted to, but he'd been seen now, and besides the man had an open face and no weapons in evidence.

'Oh, I'm sorry,' said the wagon-driver. 'You looked like someone I know is all. You've both got fair hair and are of a similar height, but I can see that you're older. Forgive me. My name's Jacob. I'm a trader from Godsend. I take it you're travelling from Heroes' Brook. Road still flooded, eh? Long walk to Saviours' Paradise.'

'I . . . Yes. My name is Aspin, good man Jacob.'

'Tell you what, why don't you take a seat up here beside me and I can take you on to Saviours' Paradise. You'll be going for the market, yes? Looking to trade skins are you, or to find some work?' Jacob winked. 'Or looking to find yourself a maiden.'

Aspin nodded cautiously and then attempted a smile. 'Yes.'

'Come along then, up you come. I'll be glad of the company in truth, for this is a long and quiet road, and Tilly and Floss aren't the most talkative, eh, girls?' One of the horses snorted in answer as Jacob flicked her rein.

Aspin found himself laughing with this jolly man, and settled back to hear his wild, wonderful and sometimes worrying tales of life in Godsend. He was just relieved that the first person he'd met upon entering the Empire hadn't tried to kill him. Perhaps the old gods still had enough power to provide him with some limited fortune.

One of the Saviours stirs! Hide and do not move! See and hear nothing! It is D'Shaa. The Saviour ascends from the level of the sacred to the enlightened! Clear out of the Saviour's path so they may rise with all speed!

D'Shaa drifted up the eternal staircase, each step six foot deep and high. They were no obstacle for one such as her, of course, who could move like the wind or support herself on the air. But the steps were a definite challenge for the paltry beings who were the retainers. She casually crushed them as she would flick dust off her statuesque shoulders. Their lives were so transient and meaningless that they were little more than dust anyway. Indeed, most of the filth that settled out of the air in the Great Labyrinth was comprised of the dead cells that constantly sloughed off their skin. The retainers started dying as soon as they were born. They were a sort of living death that appalled all of her kind and left none in any doubt that this world should be undone before its sickness found a way to spread through the cosmos. To think that their dead cells floated in the air and that she effectively breathed and ate them! It revolted her and made her sickened by her own body, the physical form her kind had to assume in this world. Once the Geas was consumed, she would be free of this miserable muddy world, free to spread her wings and sail through the cosmos wherever her whim took her. Ah, the wonders and power that would be hers once she was free of this tawdry yet binding place. Soon, soon. And as long as she could survive dangerous and conniving competitors like D'Selle.

She drifted upwards more quickly, entering a higher area of the Great Labyrinth usually forbidden to one of her rank. The ever-watchful Elder Thraal would have no doubt foreseen her visit – perhaps even before she had decided upon it herself – and it did not do well to keep him waiting, lest she provoke his ire. Just daring to venture to a higher area was risky enough, but initiating an audience with an elder before being summoned was unprecedented, unheard of in all the time her kind had been on this world. It was all but unthinkable: if the elder disapproved then he would likely not hesitate to destroy her so that the transgression would become indeed unthinkable once more.

Yet she had no choice. She came to the thick stone seal behind which Elder Thraal was entombed. Retainers were not permitted to enter the presence of an elder, of course, since any retainer could only sully such a presence, but also because the power of the elders was such that any life energy in their presence would naturally be Drawn straight towards them, just as air or matter was drawn towards a vacuum. Simply, retainers died when coming near an elder. Even lesser Saviours, those of the rank of blessed and below, avoided contact with the elders whenever they could, since they would be severely reduced by the experience. D'Shaa, however, as one of the sacred rank, would suffer little as long as the audience did not go on for too long.

Finding the crack between seal and rock face, she slid through into the large chamber beyond. The room was lit by orbs of sun-metal in each corner. A cowled figure sat unmoving on a crystal throne, light shifting slowly through the ornate chair. She dared not breathe.

'You dare disturb the Watcher of the Elders?' thrummed the figure.

'I risk my existence, enlightened one.'

'Indeed you do, and you do so when you have not existed that long. The folly of youth, D'Shaa? One of your rank cannot be forgiven for such an act.'

'Yes, enlightened one.'

Silence fell. She waited, for hours, then days. She would for years or decades as necessary, although the plague would not wait that long.

'No, it will not,' Elder Thraal's voice vibrated in her mind. 'D'Selle has you caught on the horns of a pretty dilemma, does he not? You would do well to study and learn from such a one. Your lack of foresight and your carelessness in this matter does you no credit, D'Shaa. Worse, the stability of your region suffers, which in turn damages the stability of the entire Empire. How dare you be so negligent! You are a disgrace to our kind!'

She teetered on the brink of oblivion. 'Yes, enlightened one. I understand the horror of my error and flaw. I have come to you.'

'Speak then, D'Shaa, for they are likely to be the last words of your shameful existence. There are vague echoes in your mind of something you would attempt, but its implications for the future are so unclear that it cannot easily be apprehended. For what is it you seek permission?'

Her tongue was like stone in her mouth. 'Enlightened one, I would ask that the Peculiar be released into the south!'

If she hadn't known better, she would have thought the elder had been rendered speechless, something that was surely impossible with one who was connected to nearly every living thing in this miserable world.

'You do not know what you ask!' the elder thundered, nearly killing her. 'You cannot know!'

'No, enlightened one,' she whimpered, preparing herself for her end.

The elder stilled again. Days passed.

'Child, the Peculiar was here long before us. He is ancient even by our measure of things, as old as the Chi'a perhaps. Pray he never turns his attention towards you, for he is a living armageddon. If we were to unleash him on the Empire, we would risk destroying both it and the Geas, leaving this world nothing but a barren rock. All of our wandering, watching and waiting would have been for naught. Not even the Great Saviour would be able to prevent the destruction. And none of us here would be permitted to exist a second longer than the destruction took, unless the Great Saviour were looking to punish us with an eternal hell. Yet you, D'Shaa, wish to unleash the Peculiar into the south because of a mere plague among the pathetic beings known as the People?'

She couldn't answer him.

'And yet the Great Saviour has spoken to my mind for the first time since the early days of our arrival, D'Shaa.'

She gasped. 'The eternal one has spoken?' What could it mean?'

'Indeed, D'Shaa. There is significance in your making such a request. That is all.'

Significance? She did not understand such things, for the Great Saviour was as far beyond her as she was beyond a retainer. The Great Saviour had travelled through vast and unimaginable expanses of the cosmos. He had crushed entire worlds in his hands. He said there was significance in the request.

'D'Shaa, I do not pretend to interpret the Great Saviour's meaning, but know this: I believe the Geas is finally moving. What you will not know is that in addition to the events in your region, there have been strange stirrings in a mine in the northern region. The mad one we keep deep beneath the labyrinth has also begun to rant and scream without surcease, just as he did in the early days of his capture. None of this is coincidence. We must determine a decisive response. And now you come asking for the release of the Peculiar. By the proclamation of all the elders, therefore, your request is hereby granted, D'Shaa.'

CHAPTER 6:

There being no escape from what we are

The ground rumbled and Freda slowly came awake. She'd sunk into the ground as she'd slept and now she struggled to orient herself. Which way was up? She headed for the sandier earth and her head broke through into the world of the Overlords once more. The whole world was as bright as sun-metal again and she groped around blindly until she found some of her sacking to put over her eyes.

She felt the vibrations of the six heavy men as they moved around rousing the children. A few moved towards the wooden pillars where she was hidden and made water. Curious creatures to expel a substance that seemed such a large part of their bodies – did they do it to stop themselves becoming too big before they were the right age? Then she held her nose as one of the heavy men made water – his smelt bad and of the liquid he'd been drinking before going to sleep. No wonder his body wanted to be rid of that! It smelt like he was ill or dying. The heavy man who had smoked a pipe before began coughing, and he sounded like he was ill or dying. *Very* curious creatures. And the heavy man was already starting to fill another pipe. Norfred had smoked a pipe occasionally, and he'd always seemed happy and relaxed when he did, so perhaps the smoke had a similar effect on these curious creatures as diamond deposits did on her skin – they scratched and damaged her, but oh how good they felt!

The children and the heavy men ate and drank wet, runny stuff and gave some drier stuff to the strong and uncomplaining creatures who pulled the wagons. Then the two wagons were readied and they trundled away once more. She followed along with as much of herself in the ground as the webs of living wood would allow, so as not to expose too much of herself to the painful light of the sun-metal orb suspended up high in the blue wall of the vast chamber that contained the world of the Overlords. She shrouded the portion of herself above the ground in sacking as best she could, but in places the light still found a way in.

Travelling like this for a few hours, her skin became painfully dry and cracked. As long as the cracks didn't spread over her whole skin or go too deep into her, she would be all right. After a few hours more, however, she was beginning to suffer and found she could not move as freely as before. Weren't they ever going to stop? The children certainly seemed to be in need of some respite, judging from the high-pitched noises they made. The light of the sun-metal orb beat down on them mercilessly, and she could sense it burning their skins also.

Just as she was beginning to wonder whether she should stop the wagons herself, in order to help the children, the sun-metal orb began to recede and the temperature fell. The wagons pulled up in a similar fashion to the last time the orb had retreated. The children were ordered around like last time and fires were made in exactly the same way. Leaving her sacking in a safe place, she lay just below the ground where the heavy men sat, and listened to their conversation.

'. . . get to Old Fort early tomorrow, I reckon,' the pipe-smoker was saying, 'since we've not encountered any difficulties on this journey.'

The eldest harrumphed. 'When are there ever any difficulties, eh? Still, it'll be good to be back quickly so that there's time for a bath and a woman in the town before having to get the kids to the fort's Selecting Officers. We'll escort the sun-metal onto Saviours' Smithy the day after, so you lot can have a few hours' free time in the town when it's not your shift guarding the wagon. Stay out of trouble, though, hear me? I do not want to have to come looking for you the next morning in some flophouse, backstreet inn, gambling den, punishment chamber or wherever else your vices take you. In fact, if you're not all present and correct when I'm ready to leave, I'll report you as deserters, get me?'

The men cheerfully agreed.

'You'll find Horse in the stables the next morning, I'll be bound!'

Slim said quietly, eliciting chortles from the others, although what he was implying was beyond Freda.

'At least a horse keeps a civil tongue in its head,' the man who tended the strong and uncomplaining beasts replied carefully.

'Isn't able to complain, you mean,' Slim came back quickly.

There was a loud smack and crack, and Slim was yelling in pain.

'Think yourself lucky I didn't do more than break your nose,' the eldest said with some satisfaction. 'That was your final warning, Slim. If you've got any friends left here, they might see to that for you. Otherwise, if you can't keep a respectful tongue in your head, then I suggest you have it cut out before someone decides to cut your throat instead. Stop your crying as well – what sort of soldier cries about something as minor as a broken nose?'

'Look on the bright side,' Big Harold advised as he lowered the evil-smelling bottle from which he'd been drinking. 'I think the Captain actually helped make you better-looking. You should thank him, you know.'

There were laughs all round. The pipe finally seemed to take pity on the caterwauling Slim. 'Come here! Don't worry. I've done this before.'

There was a loud creak and crunch and Slim was suddenly screaming even more loudly.

'Dying men make less noise,' Horse observed.

'Seems to be getting plenty of air to his lungs. Good sign,' the Captain decided.

'Good vocal range too. Could play a female on the stage,' the youngest attempted, and was delighted when most of his elders laughed or nodded.

'I had to straighten it, Slim,' the pipe explained. 'Trust me – I did you a favour. Crooked, you would have had trouble breathing the rest of your days.'

'Or he would have been able to smell round corners?' Big Harold speculated. 'Useful, that would be, 'cause you'd know who was coming before you met 'em. Maybe we should make Slim's nose crooked again.'

''Strue,' Horse agreed. 'If you were stepping out with a lady friend, like, and then you smelt another of your lady friends coming round the corner, well, then you'd have time to make yourself scarce maybe, or to get yourself posted to the other end of the Empire in a hurry.'

'Den dor lady fren mud mell a lod, eh, Orse?' Slim yelled as best he could.

'What did he say?'

'Say that again, Slim? I didn't quite catch it. It might be my ears.'

'I think he said Horse's lady friends must smell a lot,' the pipe supplied helpfully.

'Really? Wow. You have done this before. I didn't catch a single word of it.'

Horse swung his head towards the eldest and asked mildly, 'Can I hit him this time, Captain?'

The eldest considered for a moment and then shook his head. 'You've all had enough fun for one evening. Much more and you'll become overexcited and won't be able to get to sleep properly. Then you'll be tired and irritable the next day. You know how you get.'

''Strue,' Horse conceded.

'Slim, first watch is yours,' the eldest informed the distressed mole-faced man. 'Try and keep the noise down, could you? The more beauty sleep this ugly lot can get, the better.'

She dreamed of the rock god again. Why she thought it was the rock god, she didn't know, and whether it really was the rock god, she had no idea. After all, it was a dream, and dreams rarely made sense to Freda.

'Why don't you help me?' the vast being groaned as it wrestled in vain with the shaft of sun-metal through its gut.

'I don't know how,' Freda confessed. 'The sun-metal pains me too. Tell me what to do.'

'I do not have long. Find Haven,' the rock god said weakly, his voice dying away.

'I must find Jan first. I promised Norfred. What is Haven?'

There was no reply and she somehow lost sight of the rock god.

'If you will not find Haven, then you defy Gar and are his enemy,' hissed a voice behind her.

She turned and a twisting creature of green stone was weaving through the earth towards her. She quickly backed away. 'I am no one's enemy . . . except maybe Darus, because he hurt Norfred. I am not *your* enemy. I do not even know you.'

'I am the jade dragon of Gar's fabulous will. You *will* find Haven or you will need to beware my wrath. Awake and beware!'

Beware!

Freda started awake. All was dark. One of the heavy men was moving across the camp . . . was it stealthily or in a considerate attempt not to wake the others? Disguised as the footsteps were, she was not sure who it was. She raised her head above the ground and made out Slim in the firelight. A knife glinted in his hand and he was approaching the slumbering Captain!

She dived back into the earth, under the campfire and then back up to clamp her stone hands around Slim's ankles. He yelped and dug down with the point of his knife, blunting it.

Freda continued to rise until she had Slim dangling upside down a foot or so above the ground. He bent and twisted while slashing with his knife. Fortunately for Freda, he'd left his sun-metal sword with his bedroll, since its bright blade would have risked giving him away. Slim realised that he would not be able to win free of her and so began yelling for help.

The other heavy men rolled from their beds and to their feet. The Captain brandished his sun-metal at her. 'Who goes there?'

Freda dropped Slim and lowered her hands to her sides so that she would not appear too threatening.

'Id crept up on me and addacked me!' Slim shouted. 'I was drying to defend myself! Get the freak away from me!'

The Captain's eyes went to Freda.

'I had to stop him,' she said, straining her voice so that it wouldn't be too gravelly and frightening. 'He had his knife and was going to do something bad to you.'

The Captain's face became grim as he turned on Slim.

'No, it's not true, Captain. You can't believe a monster like this over one of your own men. It must be the thing that broke out of the mine, the monster that's killed who knows how many. It'll say whatever is needed to save its own neck.'

'Or it did whatever was needed to save my neck from the likes of you, Slim.'

'But Captain, you can't believe that!' mole-face whined. 'I'd be crazy to try anything like that.'

'What I believe, Slim, is that you're capable of talking your way out of almost anything. Is it so crazy to think someone could slit my throat during the night? Is it so crazy to think that when I was found cold in the morning there would be speculation that some thief in the night had crept into the camp? Is it crazy to think the children would be searched and one of them would be found with a bloody knife nearby, a knife the child disavowed any knowledge of? Is it crazy to think you'd be the loudest when it came to calling for my memory to be avenged, Slim? No, it is not crazy. Be quiet, Slim! Is there any here who would speak in his defence?'

None of the men spoke up, although the youngest looked from face to face before deciding to keep his peace.

'Now just hang on there, Captain. This is no jury or military tribunal,' Slim protested. 'You can't do this! It's murder!'

'It's a hanging now or a court martial at Old Fort. I won't waste a tribunal's time with you, Slim, and I wouldn't put it past you to get through without punishment, so I am exercising my discretion as an officer of the blessed Saviours to see you hanged here and now. Big Harold, Horse, hold him. You,' the Captain directed the youngest, 'get a rope.'

Slim struggled wildly, but Big Harold had him in a vice.

'I demand my right to be heard by holy Saint Goza! The holy one will want to know why you have sided with this pagan monster against one of the People under his protection. There isn't even any proof against me. He'll see all of you executed and damned for all eternity! You dare not deny me my sacred right!'

'I will take full responsibility for the hanging,' the Captain informed his men. 'Horse, gag him and then take him away among the trees. The children do not need to see or hear this.'

'Captain, he has a right to his final words. What if he wishes to repent before he is hanged? Or he wishes to pray to those who have gone before him?'

The Captain was silent for a second. 'So be it then. Let all hear his lies and screams.'

Freda shifted unhappily, her size drawing everyone's attention. 'Y-you are going to kill him? I don't like it when there's killing. I stopped S-Slim just so there wouldn't be any killing. What if Slim says he's sorry and promises not to do it again? Or you could punish him without killing him.'

Big Harold looked at her blankly, the youngest like she was insane.

'See! It's retarded. You can't take the word of a creature of the Chaos over my own. That's it! It's part of the Chaos and a living corruption. It lies by its very nature!' Slim yelled.

'If I were you, Slim,' the pipe suggested, 'I'd keep quiet for a moment. Might be the monster's doing a better job of saving your skin than you are.'

The Captain shook his head. 'I thank you for stepping in to pre-empt Slim's evil intent, but this is now army business. If a man seeks to take my blood, then I may take his in return. If Slim's was a crime just against me, I might be moved to accept some alternative reparation. Yet his was also a crime against a superior officer, the army, the Empire, the blessed Saviours and the Saints themselves. Death is the least that he deserves. An army is only as strong and swift as its discipline and punishment. For me not to enforce suitable punishment now would only conspire with and encourage the crime. Slim can never be trusted again now that he has betrayed the trust and fellowship of his comrades.'

All the men, save Slim, nodded at the Captain's words.

'Take him away.'

'Noo!' Slim cried piteously. 'Have mercy! I haven't done anything. The Saint and the Saviours are watching you!'

Big Harold and Horse half dragged and half carried Slim off into the darkness among the trees. The others trailed after them. The Captain looked back over his shoulder at Freda, who stood rooted where she was.

'Please, make yourself comfortable by the fire. I'll want to talk to you after we've attended to Slim. We won't be long.'

But Freda wanted to get away from this place so she would not have to hear the screams of the man she'd condemned to death. She covered her ears and ran. She dived into the ground, but no matter how deep she went, she could still hear him. *I am a monster*, she moaned.

Minister Praxis tried not to think badly of the holy Saint as he winced in discomfort for the umpteenth time that day as he rode the hard-backed and malodorous mule towards the foothills of the southern mountains. He'd been tempted to name the animal Azual, but had managed to resist such an outright blasphemy. After all, the holy Saint would know everything he said and did . . . perhaps even what he thought.

Yes, he must find a way to banish such blasphemous thoughts from his head. Otherwise, they would distract him from his holy mission to become Saint Praxis of the Mountains. Nothing must be allowed to jeopardise his mission, not even the thoughts in his head. Besides, the thoughts were probably not even his own; they were more likely the whispering voice of the Chaos, which would be a more constant threat now he was moving beyond the edge of the Empire and civilisation.

I bet Azual's mother would have preferred this mule for a son anyway. See, there was another of those thoughts! Yet how to banish them? Pain would distract his mind from the whispering, he knew, so he wasted no time removing his long black coat and rolling up the white sleeve of his shirt, to reveal his milky flesh below. Then he raised his riding crop – which the mule had blithely ignored thus far anyway – and slashed down with it across his forearm. He whimpered in pain and a red weal appeared on his skin. Clearly, his body was too weak to suffer its divinely inspired and correct punishment without complaint. It would require further punishment until it had learned not to be so self-pitying and therefore vulnerable to the indulgent temptations of the Chaos.

How he would like to take a whip to Azual! No! He slashed down again, gritting his teeth and refusing to voice a cry. Better. Maybe if he'd flogged his students more, then he wouldn't be lost in the wilderness right now. Spare the rod and spoil the child. It was Jillan who was to blame, that evil and bewitched boy. In fact, the boy was so despicable that he was probably not even human – yes, he was no doubt some doppelgänger creature of the Chaos. And his parents had lived in that cesspit lair of the Chaos, New Sanctuary, until the holy Saint had come and cleansed the place. The mother must have fornicated with demons and devils in some pagan ritual or other – yes, he could see it now. How weak the flesh! He slashed down on his forearm again, hardly feeling the pain now, now that his faith had revealed the schemes of the Chaos to him so that he would be able to resist its corrupt influence and blandishments.

The holy Saint was as wise and merciful with the People as he was terrible and unforgiving with the Chaos. The holy one had seen that Jillan, rather than the dutiful Minister, was to blame for all that had happened. He had also seen that one as faithful as the Minister was wasted in a backwater like Godsend and that the Minister was ready to be put on the path to sainthood, for this is what the journey to the mountains was. On this final journey as a Minister he would cleanse his mind and body entirely, so that he was ready to be a vessel for the divine will of the blessed Saviours. At the same time he would cleanse the mountains of the pagans or the pagans of their corruption. The Empire would be enlarged for the good of all and the further glory of the blessed Saviours.

Now he welcomed the bite and pain of the crop, for it brought him closer to purity and divinity. The pain was a joy instead, a religious ecstasy of revelation and enlightenment. And the bony back of the mule was no longer a punishment; rather, it was a sweet scourge to the area of his flesh that was most vulnerable to temptation and the wanton whisperings of the Chaos. He must not allow his body to control him, lest it compromise his faith; rather, his faith must control his body.

Yet will your faith feed you now that most of your food is gone? Silence! He slashed down hard with the crop, opening up the flesh and making blood run into his white shirt. Just as his congregation had fed, housed and clothed him in Godsend, as was their duty, so his faith would see to it that he had food here in the wild. He'd seen winter berries and mushrooms several times already on his journey. *You do not know which ones are poisonous and you dare not try them on the mule.*

He slashed harder and deeper than before, neither flinching nor wincing. Faith did not demand answers and guarantees. If anything, faith rejected such demands, for they were born of the Chaos and sought to ensure cooperation through second-guessing, fear and intimidation. 'Sacrifice and duty safeguard the People against the Chaos,' he said to himself, quoting from the Book of Saviours. Besides, it did not do well to overindulge the body in case it became used to and demanding of such indulgence, self-pitying when it did not receive it and then too weak to suffer even divinely inspired and correct punishment without complaint.

Smiling to himself, the Minister put his forearm to his mouth and sucked at the oozing blood. He patted the mule as well, not that the stupid brute showed any sign of noticing it. There was no chastising or encouraging certain creatures. Like Jillan, they could not be successfully taught or censured. Like the Chaos, they were corrupt in their essential nature and could only be dealt with in one way: by way of total destruction.

The Peculiar never rested, could never find rest, as much and for as long as he had craved it. The life and thoughts of other beings constantly niggled and tore at the edges of his being. The more the Geas had grown, the worse it had become, and so the Peculiar had welcomed the arrival of the elseworlders and the brutal curtailing of the Geas. He'd even aided them in toppling those childish godlings Sinisar, Wayfar, Gar and Akwar, although he had stopped short of helping the elseworlders seize the Geas and all the power of this world. After all, he didn't want the elseworlders becoming too powerful, for then they would think to turn on him in order to force his secrets from him. If the power of this world was going to belong to anyone, it was going to belong to him, and if he couldn't have it then he would have to see it destroyed so that it did not fall into the wrong hands.

He'd always kept his motivation from the elseworlders, for he did not want them understanding him and being able to predict his actions. His initial cooperation had bemused them, and he had refused to give them his name, so they had always referred to him as the Peculiar instead. Sharing his name with them would have enabled them to apprehend something of his nature, and he certainly didn't want that.

There was an uneasy alliance between himself and the elseworlders. They had no reason to trust him, and from what he'd seen the elseworlders didn't even trust each other. In some ways he was surprised that they'd managed to become any sort of force in the cosmos. Still, there it was.

The elseworlders came to him every now and then with some request or other. Sometimes he would indulge them – if he judged it to be in his own interests or if he judged it harmless and wanted to surprise them – sometimes he would dismiss them disdainfully or with feigned sorrow. In payment, he demanded they build him a chamber of sun-metal, and then another chamber around that, and then another, and so on, so that he had somewhere the life and thoughts of the other beings of this world would struggle to reach, somewhere the roaring agony of their existence was reduced to a whispering irritation, somewhere he was not always on the brink of insanity.

The chamber was his only refuge, but now someone banged on the outermost surface. Someone was coming in! He quickly shifted into a grey nondescript humanoid form, for he did not want the elseworlders knowing his true form and origin, and waited for the visitor to enter his inner sanctum.

The visitor banged on the wall of each chamber as it came so that the Peculiar would have ample warning of its arrival. Six crashing sounds in all and then the small, final door began to open. A willowy elseworlder bent almost double to come inside and then unfolded to stand at full height, which was almost to the ceiling. The elseworlder shadowed its eyes with its hand, the brilliant light from the sun-metal clearly causing it some discomfort.

'Which one are you then?' the Peculiar asked in an untroubled voice. 'You all look the same to me.'

The elseworlder gently nodded its elegantly sculpted head, a gesture the Peculiar didn't really understand but took for some sort of etiquette. 'I am Thraal, the one who has spoken to you on the last three occasions. They say the planes of my cheeks are wider and more angled than most of my kind.'

'Do they? I suppose it doesn't really matter which one you are anyway, does it?' the Peculiar asked without inflection.

'As you say, Peculiar. I represent my entire kind with this visit, so indeed it does not matter.'

'For reference, how long has passed since your last visit?'

'Some three hundred years, give or take.'

'Is the world much changed? How fares your Empire? It can't be faring too well if you're having to visit me.'

'On the contrary,' the elseworlder replied smoothly. 'And perhaps you will soon see for yourself. But I am curious. What have you been doing for the last three centuries? What is it you do here in this chamber on your own? What sustains you? Does not the sun-metal stop almost all energy from entering?'

The Peculiar stifled a yawn. 'Didn't you ask me these questions during your last visit, and the ones before that? I keep myself busy, you know. I sleep a bit, meditate a bit, compose terrible verse, you know, the usual sort of thing, much like *you* do, I imagine. As to how I sustain myself, well, anticipation of your next delightful visit, Thraal, is all I need to keep me going. But enough of my impure thoughts of you. What is it I can do for you?'

The elseworlder blinked slowly, as if committing each word the Peculiar had said to memory or as if silently sharing the words with others of its kind. 'We wish you to deliver a particular boy to us. He has the sorts of powers at his disposal we have not seen among the People in a long time. We wish you to end the plague that has begun in the southern region. We suspect there is a connection between the boy and the plague.'

'Fancy that! An old-fashioned bringer of plagues and curses.' The Peculiar smiled with an air of nostalgia.

'There is a third thing that we wish.'

'Oh, sorry if I interrupted. I'm not good at standing on ceremony, you know. I get backache, you see, and that then brings on my piles. Terrible trouble they give me. Blood and everything. Had some turn septic once. *Very* nasty. Do you ever get 'em? Piles, I mean?'

'We wish you to deliver a woman of stone to us. She broke out of a mine in the north. She was last seen heading towards Old Fort. This way.'

'Don't want much, do you?'

'Explain please, Peculiar. I do not understand your words and manner.'

'Are your kind incapable of dealing with such apparently trivial matters? You have a whole Empire at your disposal, complete with Saints, Heroes, Ministers and slaves to clean your cesspits, do you not?'

'We will build you a seventh chamber although it will use up the Empire's entire reserves.'

'Do you know, Thraal, if I didn't know better, I'd say you sounded desperate. Tell me, why has the mad one begun to scream again?'

Thraal hesitated. Then he said evenly, 'We believe the Geas has finally begun to move.'

'Well, why didn't you say so before? That's put a different spin on things. All right, I'll do it. Two conditions, however.'

'What are your conditions, Peculiar?'

'First, I want the seventh chamber built even if I complete only two of the three tasks, and second, I want a helmet fashioned entirely of sun-metal provided to me before I set out.'

'Then a binding bargain is struck between us.'

'And I want you wearing something nice for my return, Thraal. Those stiff and dowdy robes of yours really do you no favours at all. Have you thought of something with a bit of colour? Red, maybe, although that might make your face look even more washed out. Green, perhaps. Just what colour are your eyes?'

'We need the tasks to be completed as soon as possible.'

The Peculiar released an exaggerated sigh. 'You really are no fun, are you? Very well. I will go out into the world as soon as my helmet is delivered to me. Make it a large size so I can grow into it. And no scrimping! I know what you lot are like. I'm sure the walls of the sixth chamber are thinner than the others. Make sure the metal in the helmet is good and thick.'

'. . . and his wife made him sleep in the dog's kennel every day after that for the rest of his life,' Jacob finished.

Aspin laughed loudly. He must have heard a tale about everyone in Godsend by now, yet the trader showed no signs of running out. 'Tell me something about Saviours' Paradise then. I've only been there once before, and that was when I was younger.'

Jacob's busy eyebrows beetled up the expanse of his forehead. 'Indeed? Well, I heard some people spend their whole lives without stepping foot beyond the walls of their own town. Why, old Yulia in Godsend reckons she's not had cause to venture beyond her own veranda in the last ten years, what with a strapping son like—'

'What about Saviours' Paradise though?'

'What? Oh yes, Saviours' Paradise. Well, see, the trees are now giving way to open fields. All the land as far as the eye can see belongs to the town. It's a large place, bigger than Godsend and Heroes' Brook combined, by my reckoning, prosperous too. But for all its wealth, the people are renowned for being very particular with their coin, if you take my meaning. I'm not one to speak ill of a neighbour, mind, but there's some I've heard describe them as mean and miserly. Not sure I'd say as much myself, but they certainly drive a hard bargain when it comes to trade – I guess that's how they've become so rich, eh? They like to dicker plenty, see, so if you want a good price for your skins, young Aspin, be prepared to wrangle till sundown or even the next day, if you have the time. There's some that will leave you dangling till the end of the market so that you'll take whatever price is offered in desperation.'

Jacob finally took a breath then continued. 'The problem is that Saviours' Paradise has so many people coming to it, their traders can afford to walk away from a deal if they don't like a particular price, and can buy from somebody else instead. Worse, the traders of Saviours' Paradise are well organised. They have a Chief Trader, see, called John Largeson, and he's large by name and large by nature. You can't miss his girth. If Chief Trader John lets it be known none of the traders in Saviours' Paradise is to pay beyond a particular price for your skins, say, then no one will pay beyond that price. So stay on his good side if you should run into him. You may need to give him a free sample, if you take my meaning. Then there's the issue of the traders from other towns having to buy a permit if they're to set out a stall and start selling in the town's marketplace. Eight silvers the permit costs, can you believe, though the permit is good for a year. So traders from other towns have to charge more for their goods to cover the cost of the permit, which means they're usually more expensive than traders from Saviours' Paradise, see?'

'But I don't have eight silvers,' Aspin objected.

'Hmm. Well, you can just walk around carrying your wares and someone will come up and whisper a price to you. If it's to your liking you might then follow them to a quiet place to make an exchange, but there are risks with that. Sometimes, you'll find that someone has the local guard standing by to have you arrested for trading without a permit. Your goods will of course be confiscated and you'll never see them again – that's the best that will happen, if they don't decide to make a bloody example of you, see? Otherwise, you can try selling direct to traders from Saviours' Paradise outside the walls, but you won't get much of a price there, and there are plenty of guards around to ensure traders from other towns aren't all doing deals with each other and all but setting up a rival market. Worst comes to the worst, young Aspin, I'll let you sell your wares off my stall once I've set it up. I'll only take a copper a skin off you for the privilege – it's the least I can do for the good company you've shared with me on our journey here.'

Aspin smiled. He didn't need to be a soul-reader to know this man: Jacob was largely honest but still a trader at heart. The offer was a fair one. Jacob would be as good as his word and Aspin understood enough to know he needed to secure some of the coin of this Empire if he was ever going to survive in it. 'Thank you, good man Jacob. I will accept your offer if I may.'

'Of course, young Aspin. Here, let's shake on it. All well and good. I will need to stop outside the walls for a while, to renew certain acquaintances, find out any news about traders in Saviours' Paradise and so forth. You can wait on me if you like or look around the town and find my stall later.'

Aspin knew that once Jacob got gossiping with the other traders he might be more than just *a while*. 'I'll take the chance to look around the town if you don't mind, get a sense of the people and their wealth, and so forth.'

Jacob nodded approvingly. 'Smart thing to do. Why, I remember—'

'Just one more thing, good man Jacob, while we're on the topic of Saviours' Paradise. Are the people particularly . . . religious? Do they quickly bend the knee to their betters?'

For once Jacob struggled for words. 'Well, I . . . That is . . . Yes, of course! I dare say they're as faithful to the Saviours as any other townsfolk. I hope I didn't give you the wrong impression about them with my talk of their appetites when it comes to trade. The traders of Saviours' Paradise greatly benefit all the communities! Why, I happen to know that Chief Trader John is an extremely generous benefactor of Minister Baxal and always pays more than the necessary tithe at the temple. Don't dare speculate otherwise, young Aspin, for we would not want to cause the traders of Saviours' Paradise unnecessary trouble with the holy Saint, now would we?' Then Jacob gasped and looked queasy.

'Does something ail you, good man Jacob?'

In a faint voice the trader replied, 'The holy Saint always knows. He will have heard us. O Saviours, forgive our jealous and impure thoughts! Young Aspin, join me in a prayer of repentance.'

Aspin murmured nonsense to play along. It appeared that the lowlanders referred to the others as the Saviours, and prayed to them. It was clear that Jacob believed the Saviours had the sorts of powers gods would have, but how could that be? The others were normal beings, or so his people had always thought. Yet how could normal beings have toppled the old gods? How could a man defeat his own god? It was preposterous, wasn't it? *Why* would a man even want to defeat his own god?

He scratched his head. Perhaps a man would want to ascend to the place of the god, as the Saviours had done. Perhaps a man would simply want to be free of the god. Both reasons made sense. Now he thought on it, he was not sure just why he would want to find and help restore the old gods anyway. Wasn't he simply being manipulated by Torpeth? Why would he actually want to raise a new authority over himself? Besides, who was to say the Saviours weren't actually an improvement on the old gods? From all that Jacob had told him, the lowlanders were happy in their Empire, prosperous and relatively free to live their own lives. Could it be that Aspin's people might actually be better off in the Empire?

He sighed, remembering something of his revelation from the sacred grove of yews. It always came back to the Geas. The old gods had been protectors of the Geas, the life force of the world. In replacing those gods and creating an Empire in which they ruled over the majority of the people in this world, the Saviours were close to having the Geas at their command. If it were not for the likes of Aspin's own people eluding them, the rule of the Saviours would be all but absolute. Then it depended upon the intentions of the Saviours towards the Geas. If their intentions were entirely selfish, then there would be no will or meaning except as prescribed by the Saviours. There would be no freedom or escape, ever! Of course, if they were well disposed towards the Geas, everyone would lead fulfilled lives and live happily ever after.

Happily ever after? Aspin couldn't imagine what that would involve. Life never worked like that, because there were always jealous and selfish people like Braggar, whose version of happily ever after tended to be at the expense of someone like Aspin. More than that, it was clear that Jacob was scared whenever he mentioned the Saint. Apparently, the People of the Empire had something to fear from their Saviours.

'Don't worry, good man Jacob. If the holy Saint always knows, he will know that we allowed speculation to get the better of us but were quick to repent once we realised our fault. Surely the holy Saint is understanding and forgiving of our imperfection.'

'Err . . . yes, of course he is! That's right, the holy one will know we meant no harm. He is . . . f-f-forgiving. Yes, he is forgiving. Even so, we should be sure to pray long and hard tonight.'

'Does the Saint answer such prayers?'

Jacob's jolly smile and relaxed attitude were now entirely gone. He looked at Aspin in horror. 'Why would you ask that, young Aspin?' he whispered. 'Are you seeking to bring divine retribution down on our heads?'

'I was just—'

'No, young Aspin, not another word!' Jacob interrupted, bringing Tilly and Floss to a sharp stop. 'I do not know what Minister Stixis tolerates in Heroes' Brook, but where I come from it does not do well to question the holy work of the representative of the blessed Saviours. Their wisdom is infinite compared to our own and far beyond our simple understanding. Look, we are not far from the town now. I suggest you step down here and go the rest of the way on your own. I have enjoyed your company, but I now have other business to which I must attend. I wish you luck in the market and good day, young Aspin of Heroes' Brook.'

So he had found a topic that could silence Jacob the trader. A mixed blessing perhaps. Aspin could foresee that Jacob would say nothing of their conversation to anyone else but that there was also nothing Aspin could now say by way of apology or to rescue the situation. Resolving to be more careful the next time he ventured to talk to a lowlander about the Saviours, Aspin reached back for his weapon and pack and climbed down from the wagon. He waved as Jacob moved off, but the trader did not look back or otherwise acknowledge him.

The path here – which Jacob had referred to as a road – was smooth and even, so Aspin set himself a good pace, although he made sure not to go so quickly that he caught back up to Jacob's wagon. The sky was a flat greyish silver and the wind constantly rose and fell, but the weather was pretty much dry and he did not smell any rain or snow coming either. For the time of year, this would pass for very good weather in the mountains. Plus, anyone going any sort of distance in the mountains would invariably find themselves out of breath as they ascended or holding their breath as they picked their way downwards. All in all, then, the lowlands were easy and comfortable, and Jacob's tales had certainly painted a picture of a similarly soft and self-indulgent people. No wonder the others had taken these lands and its people with relative ease. He must not let himself be drawn in by the ready smiles and friendliness of the people, lest he forget himself and become too much like them.

After a short while the road rose in a slight gradient, although nothing to trouble him. In the far distance, however, he saw that the road took on a significant slope and the fields gave way to heather and rockier ground. He could just make out the top of a wall running the length of a ridge of higher ground. The closer he got, the higher and longer he realised the wall was. How big was the place and how many must make their home inside? How could his people ever hope to stand against the multitudes of the Empire, especially when the Empire had the power to construct a place like this? He revised his opinion of the lowlanders yet again.

He climbed the slope and found himself on an immense apron of ground before walls that were far longer than he'd ever seen in his life – perhaps even two miles – and at least six times more than his height. The place had to have been built by giants! His mouth hung open in wonder and fear, but he was soon blinking and looking around in equal wonder at the countless number of wagons covering the ground. Most were stacked with sacks, barrels, boxes and cages. An area of the apron had also been given over for animal pens. Surely there were enough beasts to both carry and feed an army! The din was terrible, as men and women shouted greetings, shared news and haggled over prices; chickens squawked; dogs snarled and barked at each other; horses whinnied and stamped; children screamed as they chased each other through the crowd; donkeys brayed; and hulking guards in brown leather yelled at people that they needed a permit to trade and that any further transgressions would result in broken heads. The place was terrifying, but at the same time thrilling.

'Paradise it ain't, eh?' A passing stranger smiled, seeing his face and disappearing before Aspin could think of a reply.

'Talon of Heroes' Brook!' called a familiar voice somewhere. 'Well, I'll be! I didn't think to see you here. I'd heard the road of your town was still flooded. No? Someone I was travelling with said . . .'

Aspin realised it was Jacob's voice and headed in another direction before he could be seen. He was bumped and jostled several times and someone cursed at him. People were beginning to look at him and he felt exposed even though he was in the thick of humanity. With no other obvious direction to go in, he made his way towards the long queue of people waiting to enter the gates of the town.

There were six guards manning the gates. They looked people up and down, checked permits carefully and asked questions. Aspin told himself he had nothing to worry about – no one knew he was from the mountains so he shouldn't have a problem, should he? Yet the queue of people was restless, for individuals kept craning their necks and leaning out to see what was going on up at the front. Apparently, this sort of delay was not usual.

'Here, what's the hold-up?' a woman standing behind Aspin called out. 'Keep us waiting much longer and my pies'll go stale. Who'll want them then, eh? And I'm getting old standing here. Who'll want *me* then, eh?'

There were a few chuckles from others in the queue. Aspin glanced back at the woman. She was middle-aged and wore a low-cut red dress that didn't leave much to the imagination. Aspin guessed that the cloth must have been expensive, for he'd never seen such a colour before, but no one in the mountains would ever wear such a revealing dress – in part because it was too cold to do so.

The woman caught him looking and plumped her hair. 'Like what you see, dearie? I have a field that needs ploughing.' She grinned invitingly at him, revealing two rows of brown teeth with gaps in them.

Aspin blushed and turned away, a few bystanders laughing knowingly as he did so.

'Quiet, woman!' the man in front of Aspin said back over his shoulder. 'Don't you know who that is in the darker leather with the gold trim? That's Skathis, the holy one's Captain himself.'

'Really?' The woman smiled. 'Maybe he's heard I'm coming to market and can't wait to see me.'

More laughs. Aspin looked for the man called Skathis and saw him standing with arms folded and forearms on display towards the back of the guards. His dark hair was cropped close to his head, not that all the white scars across his scalp would have allowed much hair to grow anyway. His face was similarly frightening, with most of the skin pulled tight or out of place by the way old cuts and injuries had healed. He must have seen countless fights, Aspin reasoned, and was a man to be feared given that he had survived them all. Strength and skill alone in combat could not be enough either – the man must also be charmed with good luck or a quick intelligence. Skathis silently watched and listened as people passed one by one through the gates.

Aspin tried to read more of the man, but could glean nothing. Was something blocking his reading or did the man just have very little soul to be read? He couldn't help feeling nervous now. Was it really possible for him to pass under such intense scrutiny undetected? What had Jacob meant when he said the Saint always knew? He chewed the inside of his cheek and wondered whether he should just leave this place and find another town or village. Wouldn't he find the same there, though? And if he stepped out of the line now, wouldn't he serve to attract the attention he was trying to avoid? Despite the chill air, he felt himself sweating under his armpits.

'What is it with all the questions then?' the woman asked over Aspin's head. 'Are they asking after me?'

'Hang on,' said the man in front of Aspin as he asked the man ahead of him. Less than a minute later the man muttered back to them, 'Asking where people are from, whether they've met anyone unusual on the road, anyone from Godsend.'

The woman snorted. 'Everyone from Godsend is unusual! They live too close to the wilds, eh? They say the babes of the townsfolk are taken in the night by dark spirits and replaced with changelings. Knew a man from there once. Terrible appetites he had, and thick hair all over his back. Eyebrows met in the middle too.'

'Nothing wrong with a bit of hair on a man's back,' a matron a few places further back in the queue answered. 'It's only manly and gives you something to hang onto. They don't half complain if you have to hold them by the ears instead. And most men are animals given half a chance.'

Cackles, nudged elbows, agreeing nods or, from the more respectable, disapproving scowls. The queue edged forward and then it was Aspin's turn. Four guards stood around him. Had the man Skathis just taken a half-step towards him? Were his eyes narrowed?

'Where you from?' asked a guard who had a flat nose and smelt overpoweringly of body odour.

Aspin licked his lips. 'Heroes' Brook. The road out of the town is no longer flooded. My name's Aspin Longstep.'

'Didn't ask your name,' the guard said, suspicion evident on his face. 'And you're short. Why would they call you Longstep?'

'Err . . . it's some sort of joke.'

The guard grunted. 'Anyone else here can speak for you and confirm you're from Heroes' Brook?'

Aspin hesitated, thinking desperately. 'Wait a second . . . Er . . . yes, Talon of Heroes' Brook. Talon the trader. His wagon's over there. He said I could sell my skins from his wagon in the marketplace later. He said he'd only take a copper a skin for the privilege.' He tried not to swallow too obviously and carefully avoided the gaze of the man called Skathis.

'Here to sell goatskins?' the guard frowned. 'Everyone's got goatskins. Why would you come so far to sell goatskins?'

Why else would he come to a market? 'It's not just for the skins. I heard that there might be maidens who weren't yet spoken for in a place as big as Saviours' Paradise. All those in Heroes' Brook seem to be taken.' He managed a convincing blush and tone of embarrassment that made one of the guards grin for a moment until he noticed none of his fellows was smiling.

'Meet anyone on the road?' the flat-nosed guard asked, beginning to lose interest.

Aspin nodded with wide-eyed innocence. 'Of course. Lots of people coming for the market.'

'Anyone unusual? From Godsend? Wearing armour with lots of gold patterns on it perhaps?'

He could read that the guard now believed him and intended to let him through. He was just asking these last questions because he'd been told to and because the man called Skathis was listening. 'Ha! Everyone from Godsend is unusual, I heard.'

''Sright!' said the woman in the red dress behind Aspin.

Flatnose looked up at the woman and interest flickered in his dull eyes. He waved Aspin through, already forgetting him.

Aspin kept his eyes down and hurried forward. He kept his senses sharp. At the last moment he read that Skathis was coming for him. He dodged left but something heavy caught him across the back of the neck and stopped him in his tracks.

Everything went dark. He felt a rough fabric against his forehead and cheeks and a soporific herb filled his nostrils. They'd hooded him as if he were some untamed animal.

'Move, you wretches!' barked a razor-blade voice that could only be Skathis. 'It's him! He fits the description. Get that iron around his wrists and ankles. Quickly! He's dangerous. No! Wrists pulled round behind him, dolt! Foot to the back of his knee. Get him down.'

Two men pinned Aspin to the ground. How could this be happening? He'd only met Jacob since he'd entered the lowlands and the trader wouldn't yet have had a chance to betray him, even if it were unwittingly. How had these men known to be waiting for him here when he hadn't even known himself he'd end up coming to Saviours' Paradise?

'Here, what are you doing to him?' cried the voice of the woman in the red dress. 'He's only a boy. It doesn't need all of you like that. No need to be so heavy-handed!'

Skathis ignored her. 'Got the gag? Pull his head back.'

The material over his face pulled tight and his neck was bent back up off the ground.

'Now.'

The hood came off. He blinked, disorientated. A fist came out of nowhere and punched him hard in the face. His top lip split and a tooth broke. His jaw hung loose. A balled piece of cloth was crammed into his mouth and he was tied with a gag.

His vision blurred and then focused on the pitiless face of Skathis.

'Still conscious despite the herbs, eh? Tough little beggar.' Skathis gave a small nod to a guard standing off to the side. Another punch caught Aspin on cheek and chin and sent him spinning into darkness.

'Brutes!'

'You two get him to the punishment chamber and I'll inform the holy one of our success. And someone shut that woman up.'

Jillan watched in horror from the back of the queue as the Heroes dragged the innocent youth away. He exchanged glances with Ash.

'You don't think—'

'Best not to think – out loud at any rate,' Ash murmured. 'All right, follow my lead now. Ready? Jillan, pay attention!'

'What? Yes, okay.'

'Stay close now. Let's go.'

The woodsman drifted forward as the line of people moved left and right to get a better view of the excitement. Jillan stuck close behind him and found that they were steadily getting closer to the gates. There were fewer guards now, and they were struggling to deal in any sort of orderly fashion with the number of people trying to get into the town.

Ash seemed to have an instinct for when anyone ahead of him was going to move left or right, for he would step with perfect timing into any gap they left. Their progress was so smooth and effortless that it was almost as if the crowd was parting before them. They were right up near the gates in next to no time.

'Stay close. Wait here for a second. Wait. Now we go.'

They stepped forward just as the guard before them leapt to steady a precarious stack of egg trays carried by a young girl. Ash turned side on, apparently to give the guard room, at the same time easing past him.

'Thanks,' the guard said distractedly as he caught his breath.

'No problem,' Ash mumbled as he led Jillan into the town.

They were on a cobbled street that led straight towards the centre of town and presumably the marketplace. It was wide enough for two wagons to pass each other, although all the traffic was heading into town at that moment. Everything was at a standstill, however, as a wagon had lost a wheel, spilling cages of chickens onto the cobbles and allowing a good number of hysterical birds to escape. A few pedestrians stood and watched the entertainment and a few tried to herd the chickens back towards the red-faced wagon-driver, while other drivers behind him either shouted in anger or rolled up their sleeves to help him get the wheel back on.

'Who needs the Chaos, eh?' Ash winked at Jillan. 'People are more than capable of making trouble for themselves. Come on, let's head down here.'

Ash led him into a narrow street on the left and down a little. The wooden buildings to either side were mostly two storeys high and leaned over the street so that any rain or garbage coming from above landed well away from front doors. The gutters along the street were near to full with rotting vegetables, fruit, clumps of hair and worse. A mangy-looking dog was eating something unidentifiable and an aggrieved rat was squeaking at it. A naked toddler with snot running from its nose sat on a doorstep whacking at the dead body of a rodent with a stick.

'By the Saviours, it stinks!' Jillan gagged, his eyes watering.

'Oh, you get used to it and it puts hairs on your chest,' Ash replied merrily. 'It's not the richest part of town, to be sure, and it could do with some fresh pitch in places, but it's where you get the cheapest ale.'

'We're here for ale?' Jillan asked loudly, coming to a stop.

'What?' Ash replied as a woman came out of her door with a babe suckling on one of her large bared teats. She smiled at Ash and then pouted as if the babe gave her both pleasure and pain. 'I . . . er . . .' Ash blinked and dragged his attention back to Jillan. 'Look, there are a couple of inns down here,' he said, lowering his voice, 'where we can ask around for this Thomas friend of yours and have people keep an eye out for your parents without drawing the notice of the town's Heroes. One of the innkeepers is fond of my wood carvings too, and will usually accept them in exchange for a good few flagons, unless you're carrying silver with which we can buy information or the ale we need to loosen tongues. Well, got much silver about you?'

Jillan shook his head with a frown. 'What about that boy the Heroes attacked and took away?'

'What about him?' Ash replied absently.

'Well, it was my fault he was taken. Shouldn't we see what we can do to help him or something?'

Ash stopped with hands on hips. 'Are you mad? Just what is it you think we can do when the town's Heroes have got him?'

'Well, I don't know,' Jillan was forced to concede. 'But we can find out where they've taken him, can't we?'

'Look,' Ash said with an air of exaggerated patience, 'we don't know for sure that they did think he was you. He may be wanted for theft or something. And if they have got it wrong, they'll soon realise their mistake and let him go, won't they? He'll be fine. Stop worrying about other people, Jillan, when you'd be far better off worrying about yourself. You've got enough on your plate as it is, don't you think? Now come along.'

Jillan followed along, not entirely happy with how Ash was deciding everything for them, but not immediately able to gainsay his logic either. Besides, Jillan didn't have any plan of his own as to how to go about finding Thomas Ironshoe or his parents in a place as big as Saviours' Paradise. He didn't know anyone here and he didn't know how things worked either. Having little choice but to stick with Ash for the time being, therefore, he resolved to make the most of it. Anyway, he was curious about what an inn would actually prove to be like, for he'd never been allowed in one in Godsend. Inns were places where adults talked freely about the sorts of things they usually lowered their voices for when children were around. They were places where people sang and played at dice in front of a bright warm fire on a winter's night. They were places where men and women drank themselves merry and where forbidden assignations took place. They were dangerous and exciting places.

'Here we are,' Ash announced in front of a door at the end of a row.

'How do you know it's an inn?' Jillan asked.

'All the sign you need is the state of the street just here, no?'

'I suppose.' Jillan nodded, catching a stronger whiff of urine and vomit here than elsewhere in the street.

'Don't worry. It'll be better inside. Let me do the talking in here though, agreed?'

The inn was one big room with tables and benches set out, a serving bar in one corner and a narrow staircase leading to the floor above. The windows were small, making the place gloomy even though it was early afternoon and even though there were a few candles burning feebly on several tables. In contrast to the street outside, however, the place was relatively crowded. A group of four traders talked loudly and toasted each other enthusiastically as if they were old friends who hadn't met in a long time. A hopeful-looking but largely ignored youth sat in one corner strumming tunelessly on a lute. Several old men sat alone, nursing their drinks and surreptitiously eyeing up a bored harlot. Two men were arguing about the price of some goods or other, and a spare surly looking fellow sat cleaning his fingernails with the tip of his knife while idly watching everyone else.

A serving girl moved as lazily through the place as the flies did, but it was the owner himself who came bustling over as Ash and Jillan found a small table for themselves against the wall and near the stairs. The owner was a smallish man – a good head shorter than Ash – but he had thick arms and a barrel chest. He did not return Ash's ever-present smile, but there was no obvious enmity in his voice when he spoke.

'Last two carvings sold no trouble. Can even let you have a drink on the house, woodsman.'

'It's good to see you too, Tapmaster Brimful. How have you been?'

'None of your nonsense now or I'll have my bladesman put you out,' the innkeeper said with a curt gesture towards the surly man cleaning his nails. 'I take it you have no coin.'

'Not as yet, but—'

'Then you'll show me what you've got; we'll agree a price; you'll have a drink on the house and then be on your way before you can go upsetting my customers like you did last time.'

'Now, hang on, that wasn't my fault! That muttonhead—'

'I don't want to hear it!' the innkeeper cut in harshly. 'Just think yourself lucky I'm prepared to tolerate one of the Unclean under my roof, especially when the holy Saint's in town. Don't go abusing my generous nature by causing me any trouble, hear?'

Ash's smile faltered, but he managed a stiff nod of agreement.

'The Saint's here?' Jillan asked faintly, but the two men ignored him.

'So what is it that you have brought me?' the innkeeper urged. 'Did you remember to carve benevolent spirits of the trees and nature like I told you? The Saviours forgive the People of this town, but such depictions are always popular. Or animal totems? Or a wooden phallus or two for fertility?'

Ash searched in his leather bag and pulled out a number of objects wrapped in cloth. The first was a carving of the black wolf, its skin stained with charcoal.

'Fine. Well observed. It'll sell. Make it look wilder next time, though, with more teeth showing.'

The next was a beautiful maiden with hair like a waterfall.

'I think I'm in love. Do you see such women in your mind, woodsman? You must get lonely out there, eh?'

The third was a fairly ordinary toadstool.

'What on earth is that? People can get the real thing whenever they like. Ridiculous. Leave it here as a candleholder and I'll give you a second drink.'

And the last was a strange confusion and tangle of snakes, stemmed flowers, eels, curling ivy, salamanders and buzzing bees. They'd been rendered so faithfully that the mass looked to be moving in the candlelight.

The innkeeper took an involuntary step backwards. 'By the Saviours, what have you done, woodsman?' he breathed. 'There's no doubting your skill but why use it for this? It's wrong. I don't know how or why, but it's wrong. Cover it up, quickly, before someone else sees it and word gets out to Minister Baxal or something.' His words tumbled over themselves just as the chaos of life in the carving had done. The innkeeper was left panting and with a sheen of perspiration on his brow.

'S-sorry,' Ash mumbled. 'I don't know what made me carve it. I wasn't really thinking of anything at the time.'

'Well, I don't want to see anything so monstrous again, if you please,' the innkeeper insisted, his breathing coming more easily now that the carving had disappeared back into Ash's bag. 'So, let's see. For the wolf and the maid, four silvers. A flagon for the toadstool. And one on the house.'

'They're worth twice that,' Ash said hopelessly.

'Well, try your luck with others then. Take it or leave it, but I may not have four silvers to spare later. Come on, that'll be enough to buy your monthly supplies, as long as you don't go spending it all on ale.'

'Throw in another drink for the rareness of the maid's beauty?'

The innkeeper hesitated, then relented. He spat in his palm and shook Ash's hand. 'That's three ales then. You want the first now?'

Ash kept hold of the man's hand. 'Actually, I was hoping for some information as well. Nothing much, just some local news – why the holy one is here so late in the year, where I might find a man called Thomas, things like that.'

The innkeeper pulled his hand free and wiped it on his apron. 'I have a business to run. I don't have time for idle gossip, woodsman. Besides, such talk only seems to attract trouble, if you catch my drift.'

Ash gave him a pained expression. 'You're right of course, good Tapmaster, but if I can find this man Thomas, he might put some coin my way, coin that I will of course look to spend or invest with those who have helped me previously.'

The innkeeper hesitated, like everyone in Saviours' Paradise never too quick to pass up the chance of extra coin. 'Why don't you invite my bladesman to join you? He's more familiar with those who come and go. I'll get that ale for you, and a light beer for the boy. This is Spiro.'

At a signal from the innkeeper, Spiro brought a chair over to Ash and Jillan and sat down with a nod. He had tanned skin and the sort of dark looks which were more common in the eastern region of the Empire, the region that saw the most unrest, and where a man lived by his wits and strength. Spiro was probably not a man to be trifled with. He waited in silence.

'Er . . . may I offer you a drink?' Ash ventured.

'That would be welcome,' Spiro said with a lilt that was not local. 'What is it you want?'

'They say the holy one is here. It is an *unexpected* blessing for the town.'

Spiro stilled and his eyes flicked appraisingly over Ash and Jillan for a second time. 'Indeed. It demonstrates the benevolence and righteousness of the blessed Saviours that they ensure benefit for the People even when trouble is afoot.'

'Praise the Saviours! Does this trouble originate in Saviours' Paradise then that the holy one should come here?'

'Indeed it does not, from what I hear. There has been foul murder in Godsend. The killer is said to be on his way here, perhaps wearing unusual leathers.' Spiro's eyes drifted to Jillan. 'I'm sorry but I did not catch your names.'

The innkeeper returned and placed two foaming flagons and a half measure on the table. Jillan resisted the temptation to adjust the cloak that concealed his armour. He kept his expression as natural and neutral as he was able, but he was not sure how convincing he was. If only the bladesman would stop watching him like that.

Ash raised his flagon, acknowledged Spiro and Jillan with it and then took several large swallows before wiping the foam off his top lip. 'Ah, that's good! I am Ash and—'

'I have heard of you.'

'—a-and this is my cousin Owain from Heroes' Brook.'

'An unusual name, Owain,' Spiro observed, still watching Jillan.

Ash laughed. 'His parents have always had aspirations for the boy. He's come to meet the daughter of a good family here in Saviours' Paradise. They have great hopes for him, and Owain has great hopes of the daughter, eh, Owain?'

Jillan nodded mutely. He coughed and said weakly, 'I don't feel so good.'

'You do look a bit green. He's due to meet the girl for the first time in a few hours,' Ash confided to the bladesman. 'Why don't you get some air while I talk to Spiro here? In fact, take a turn round the market and I'll see you back here later.'

'Y-yes, I think that might be a good idea,' Jillan said and excused himself.

The woodsman's a drunk and a waste of space, whispered the taint. *Did you see the pathetic way he all but begged the innkeeper to buy his carvings? The woodsman's Unclean. He has neither friends nor influence here in Saviours' Paradise, but he's desperate to be accepted. Once he's into his cups, he'll betray you to Spiro for the price of an ale. Forget him!*

Jillan stepped out of the inn with a sigh of relief. The air cooled his hot cheeks and helped him get his nerves under control. The Saint was closer now than ever. The holy one always knew! Heroes could be heading for the inn even now.

He looked up and down the street, but all seemed quiet. He headed back the way they'd originally come and joined the press of people and wagons on the main thoroughfare. Movement was slow but at least no one would find him too easily in all this.

After a good while edging forward, Jillan found that the street he was on opened out as it met other thoroughfares, and then suddenly he was into the ordered mayhem of the market proper. Most of the wagons and stalls were set around the edges of the town's vast Gathering Place – Godsend's own centre would have fitted four or five times over in this place – but several dozen had prime position in the middle, with what looked like permanent display tables.

It seemed that everyone in Saviours' Paradise had turned out for the market, for he couldn't move more than a few paces without colliding with another body. Most wore the sort of finery that was only ever seen on temple days in Godsend. Those not rich enough to possess any sort of finery found a place from which they could ogle others, begged for coins or picked pockets.

The swell carried Jillan into the middle and he found himself standing before the stall of a giant man who could only be a blacksmith. Displayed on his table were gleaming knives, swords and axes of all shapes and size. These were far from being tools for mere farmers.

There was something hypnotic about the weapons and their shining surfaces. Jillan wanted to pick one up, heft it in his hand and feel its balance, but at the same time he feared the potential of the sharp, hungry edges. He needed a real blade with which to defend himself, he knew: the confrontation with Valor had proved that.

'You won't find better,' the giant announced in a voice so deep that it was felt as much as it was heard.

Jillan blinked slowly and nodded.

'Expensive, of course. I'd need to see gold, even for one of the smaller blades . . . or something valuable you might have in exchange.'

Jillan stared at his reflection in a long two-edged knife. The eyes that looked back at him saw right into his heart and held him in place.

'Learned my craft in the east,' the giant rumbled softly, 'where they temper and cool their blades in the blood of their enemies. They say such blades give the owner the strength, knowledge and skill of any whose life and blood were lost so that the blade could be forged.'

Jillan had one item in his pack that the blacksmith might accept in exchange. *Give him Samnir's blade, whispered the taint. It's a dull and clumsy ceremonial thing, no use in a fight. Coming from the Great Temple, though, it's probably valuable. The blacksmith could melt it down for something else.* He began to fumble for the chunky blade, which of course had inconveniently found its way to the bottom of his pack. He found an edge and traced along it to find the hilt. His hand brushed against several of the stones from his collection, which he'd forgotten about till now. Gripping the so-called weapon, he tugged on it, but it was caught on something and refused to come free.

'Stupid—'

'You, boy!' called a familiar voice. 'Over here!'

'What have you got there?' asked the blacksmith curiously as he glimpsed burnished metal. He loomed closer.

Jillan looked round. His annoyance was replaced by shock as he saw Jacob the trader waving at him from a stall along the side of the Gathering Place. Should he run? No, he'd only attract attention and the blacksmith was already bearing down on him.

He turned back and met the giant's eye. 'I'll be back in a minute. Save the long knife for me, will you?'

The blacksmith looked from Jillan to Jacob and back again. 'Very well,' he said gruffly and retreated. 'Don't be long, though. I'm not about to deny another willing customer when I've seen no down payment from you.'

Jillan nodded and trotted over to Jacob's stall. He kept a few paces back, however, in case the trader intended to grab him.

'I'm glad to see you. Are you well?' Jacob said with a broken smile. Then he added more quietly, 'I did not shout out your name, did I?'

'I am well, sir, thank you.' Jillan smiled, happier to see the trader's familiar careworn face than he would ever have expected. 'Hella isn't . . . here with you, is she?'

'I'm sorry, no. Yet she is well, particularly now the Minister has been banished. Come, pretend to examine my paltry wares and we will be less conspicuous.'

Judging it safe, Jillan stood closer. 'What of my parents? Have they travelled with you?'

Jacob's face fell. He looked around briefly, to be sure they were not overheard. 'The Saint took them away in chains. It may be for the best, though, for there is plague in Godsend.'

'What?' Jillan's mind reeled. 'If the Saint is here, then so are my parents. I must find them.'

'Wait!' Jacob said, pulling him back. 'There is something else you should know. Samnir . . . Samnir was cruelly punished by the holy one. He lives still, but his mind is gone and he sits all day in his own filth in the Gathering Place of Godsend. I know the two of you were close. I will do my best to look after him when I return, but I don't know how much I can really do for him.' He paused. 'Jillan . . . Jillan, have you thought of handing yourself in? It might be for the best.'

Jillan began to back away. Jacob followed him solicitously.

'Stay back!'

Several people glanced towards them curiously.

We could kill all of them. These people only want to betray, use or sell you.

'Jillan, I only . . .'

'Stay back! That's not my name! I'm Irkarl! I'm Owain!'

'Here, what's going on?' the blacksmith called. 'The boy's got something I want to see.'

Jillan moved away more quickly, his cloak flapping open.

'What's that you've got on underneath, boy? Hey, I think it's him! The one they're looking for! Stop him, someone!'

Jillan ran for all he was worth.

CHAPTER 7:
Or what we once were

'Stupid mule! May the Saviours curse your stubborn hide. Chaos beast! Must I perform an exorcism on you before you will take another step? Are you some devil transformed into animal shape? Must I bear the burden of our journey myself? Would you have *me* carry *you* upon my back before we may proceed? Do you not know I am on a holy mission?'

Minister Praxis yanked and hauled on the mule's reins, but it would not take a single step further across the snow-covered slope. It brayed at the Minister.

'You laugh at me, do you? Then truly you are bewitched or possessed by dark forces seeking to subvert the will of the blessed Saviours. I am soon to be Saint Praxis of the Mountains. How dare you heap such indignity upon me, you hirsute heathen!'

The Minister dropped the reins and went round behind the mule. He slapped its rump and it flicked its tail in annoyance. Then the Minister bent his knees, put his shoulder to it and heaved. A hoof kicked out and caught him painfully on the shin.

The Minister shrieked and collapsed to the ground clutching his leg.

'How dare you attack a holy servant of the blessed Saviours, you pestilential and maniacal miscreant! To think I feed you, you miserable ingrate, when I would surely do myself a kindness were I to carve you up for my cook pot. Yet even boiled your flesh would no doubt be as tough and intolerable as you are alive. Nay, it would poison me! Do your evil designs and conspiracies against me know no bounds?'

The mule began to urinate, the steaming yellow torrent not quite managing to splash the prone Minister.

'You foul creature!' the Minister howled. 'Must you corrupt the earth with your filth also? Truly, you are a pagan suited to these parts. Those that dwell in these mountains will no doubt welcome you then, perhaps setting you as a king or god over them. They will seek to emulate you and befoul themselves, their beds and their own salvation. So it is that the Chaos and its pagan horde ultimately undoes itself and proves the righteousness and sanctity of the blessed Saviours. I will not tolerate your blasphemy against my cause, presence and person a moment longer. You will desist, you hear, you misbegotten and malevolent malacant!'

The mule now lifted its tail and began to defecate. The Minister's sobs and outrage echoed across the peaks.

'There, there,' a voice breezed down from the top of a cottage-sized boulder not much further up the slope. 'You're probably just a bit light-headed because the air up here is thinner. Some have visions because of it when they go very high up. They think that Wayfar speaks to them at such times, and that's why the youth do it, you see.'

The Minister's head jerked up. 'What new devil is this come to taunt me in my distress?'

Torpeth put his head on his side as he considered the Minister. 'Or perhaps you haven't been eating enough. You're very thin, and those small bags atop Dobbin do not look as if they carry too much.'

'Devilish inquisitor, begone! I will tell you nothing, lest you twist it and seek to lure me to my doom. Begone, terrible trickster! Begone, I say!'

'Hmm. It's neither visions nor light-headedness then. You are feeble-minded, are you not?'

'I will not be led astray by you. I will not be diverted from my path or holy mission.'

'Listen.' Torpeth frowned. 'If you do not step off your path, you will tumble into that chasm concealed by the snow directly before you. Your neck will be properly broken, spindly as it is. Why do you think Dobbin has remained unmoving? Dumb Dobbin has more sense than you yourself do, lowlander. Is that why you trespass here? Have your own people realised you are so weak-minded and dangerous that they have thrown you out?'

'You are a creature of forbidden and corrupting magicks to know such things!' the Minister gurgled. 'Yet whatever spells and illusions you seek to cast over my eyes and mind, my faith allows me to see you for what you truly are – a small and hairy homunculus sat unnaturally naked and uncaring of the cold.'

Torpeth scratched his behind and shrugged. 'You get used to the cold after a few years, especially once your hair starts to grow thicker. I'd advise you to grow a beard, lowlander, lest you be mistaken for a woman – albeit an ugly one – by one of the rougher warriors hereabouts. Otherwise, they might not allow you out of the darkness of their homes until you have borne them a child.'

'What is it you say, consort of the Chaos? You speak of unnatural things. Do you think to tempt me like this? My faith is too strong. I will not be suborned.'

Torpeth sighed and shook his head. 'Truly, you are crazier than me, lowlander, and I am so crazy that my people call me holy. Yet I do not mix nature, chaos and order as you do. Perhaps then you are holier still. I have half a mind not to turn you away, although I turned away all those who came before you. I have half a mind not to bring down the mist to disorientate you or send you back to the lowlands. I cannot protect my people forever, can I, not when the gods are long since broken, payment is due and the balance is ended? The others cannot be turned away forever. Indeed, perhaps they should not be. Perhaps it is best if you come to my dwelling place tonight and I take you to the chief's village in the morning.' Torpeth brightened. 'Do you like pine nuts?'

'And so the unholy creature must capitulate before my faith and the righteous will of the Saviours.' The Minister nodded.

Torpeth rolled his eyes and looked to the gathering sky. 'Utterly crazy. I would get more sense from Dobbin there.'

'The mule is your familiar then, man-witch!'

Torpeth poked his tongue out at the Minister. 'The only one who's been speaking to poor Dobbin there is you, lowlander. I heard you rail at him as if expecting him to answer. But who am I to judge, eh? Perhaps you hear him answer. Do you hear his voice in your head?

They say magic-users in the past used to be able to commune with animals. Do you hear other voices too? There was a time when I thought I heard the voices of the old gods, but that was long ago now. They have either fallen silent or I am not as crazy as I once was. Or they have just decided to talk to someone else instead. They're somewhat fickle and easily bored, you know. It wouldn't be so surprising if they had started talking to others, for these days I'm mostly occupied with harassing goats, haranguing youth, gathering pine nuts and examining the colour of my bodily expulsions. You wouldn't want to watch and discuss such things for long, would you?'

'Absolutely not, lurid devil!'

Torpeth looked disappointed. 'In which case, we'll spend just the one night in each other's captivating company, eh? Besides, I suspect Dobbin wants to see you delivered to your destination as soon as possible.'

'Impudent imp!'

'Keep this up, lowlander, and I won't even let you have any pine nuts.'

'The Saviours will provide, prating pagan!'

Saint Azual waited in the darkness of the imposing edifice that was the temple of Saviours' Paradise. This place was no less draughty, damp or uncomfortable than the temples of his other communities, but there was a sense of escape and quiet reverence here – set back from the hubbub of the marketplace as the temple was – where there was only silence and emptiness in the other places of worship. Here, when he meditated, he fancied he could sense the vast and overshadowing intellects of the Saviours. Here he was close to communing with them, close to becoming one with them. How fitting then that his pursuit of the boy would end here and he, Azual, would finally have the power he needed to ascend.

His eye flared open and lit up the dark. They had him! The Saint leapt to his feet, all dynamic action and force now. Now was the moment of his will.

He quickly left the temple and brushed his guards aside as his intent carved a path through the town. The People scattered as he rushed on, his thoughts compelling them to throw themselves aside. A young child was suddenly directly in front of him. It was too young to have been Drawn, so was unconnected and unaware of its ruler's silent command to the People. It sat with small arms raised, bawling for its mother. Azual paid the filthy urchin little mind – he was certainly not about to deviate from his course because of it. He dashed past, his heel clipping its temple and knocking it on its back. It screamed as he left it in his wake.

My touch has blessed it! his mind told the People in the vicinity.

'Thank you, holy one!' a woman cried out.

Azual stormed across the town. A disorientated drunk could not get out of the way in time and was thrown to the floor by other people scrambling to move. 'Forgive me!' the old sot blubbed from where he lay. Azual's foot came down on the man's throat and crushed his windpipe. The Saint passed on. People standing nearby nodded and gave thanks for the object lesson provided by the holy one.

He overturned a wagon in his way, ignoring the terrified screams of the horse toppled and trapped in its traces. He crashed through a potter's stall and entered the street that led to the punishment chambers next to the barracks of the town's Heroes. Within a hand of seconds he was through the small stone square where the town pillory and gibbet were set up and was descending the stairs into the rock beneath Saviours' Paradise. Captain Skathis was waiting for him. The officer signalled to a guard to unlock a cell and then bowed as the Saint passed by without a word.

Azual bent his head and stepped into the small bare cell. Manacled to the wall and hanging by his arms was the fair-haired boy who'd led them such a dance. The light wasn't good, for there was only a smoking torch on the wall outside the cell by which to see.

'Remove his gag.'

Captain Skathis hurried to obey. The boy coughed, gasped and then vomited down his front and onto the holy one's feet.

The Saint slowly turned a baleful eye on the Captain. 'This is not him,' he seethed.

The Captain knew better than to attempt excuses. He lowered his head and eyes, ready to accept the death-blow his incompetence deserved. The silence stretched.

'This is not the face his parents see in their minds. This one is older than the one we want, the one called Jillan, or Irkarl as he calls himself. Yet there is something strange here. This one has not been Drawn. How is that possible in one his age? Who are you?'

The Saint grabbed the boy's chin. 'Answer me!'

The boy coughed, saliva stringing from his mouth. 'A-aspin Longstep from Heroes' Brook . . . h-holy one?'

The Saint's eye became unfocused for a second or two. 'There are none that think that name in Heroes' Brook. Why have you not been Drawn?'

'I-I do not know, holy one.' A hesitation. 'Minister Staxis keeps saying I'm not ready.'

'How has this happened?' Azual asked tightly, turning on his Captain again. 'I can see this Jillan entering the town!' An image of a line of people waiting for the guards to question everyone. The one called Jillan in a cloak, standing with a woodsman.

'Once we took this one and brought him here—' the Captain began.

'Silence, you oaf!' More images floated past his mind's eye as he sorted through the jumble of thoughts and memories of the People. Jillan in the marketplace, pursued by several stallholders. Jillan at an inn near the town's main gates. 'Send men to all the inns near the main gates. There's a woodsman called Ash and a bladesman called Spiro in one. They know the boy. And I want regular patrols through the marketplace. Move, Captain, for if I do not have him this very day, I promise you that the next sunrise will be your last.'

'At once, holy one.' The Captain bowed. 'Holy one, should we now release this one here?'

The Saint considered Aspin for a moment. 'No, there is something strange here that I will return to later. I suspect that it is no coincidence this one is here to distract us. There are all the signs that the Chaos is seeking to exert its influence and keep the boy from me. I *must* have him, Captain! The enemies of the People must be hunted down and exterminated. No more delay.'

Jillan darted through the crowds, his small size meaning he could slip through gaps and change direction quickly where the blacksmith could not. He lowered his bow to his side so that it would not flag his whereabouts and then raised his hood to hide his hair. After a minute or so he slowed to a stroll and disappeared into a side street to catch his breath and regain his self-control.

The taint had been muttering in his head the whole time. *Ridiculous that we should have to run from those treacherous thieves. They deserved short shrift and you know it! Word's bound to get to the Heroes and Saint soon enough. We'd better not hang around here too long.*

He pushed off the wall he'd been resting against and began to head back in the direction of the main gates.

Are you mad? You're not really going back to that inn, are you? I thought we were going to find your parents or at least that youth they mistook for you. The woodsman will be paralytic by now, stretched out asleep under a table, lying in a puddle of piss. He's unreliable at best, not to be trusted at worst. It's too dangerous. And the further we stay from that wolf of his when we leave this place, the safer we'll be.

'Ash may have discovered where we can find this Thomas Ironshoe. And we'll need Ash and maybe Thomas to help get my parents,' Jillan muttered.

The taint harrumphed but finally subsided. Head clearer now, Jillan negotiated his way through the crowds and streets of the town. All around there were rich smells in the air that made his mouth water. He realised he was ravenously hungry. He reached into his pack and pulled out a handful of fragments of the dried biscuits, broken and smashed among the other contents of his pack. He sighed and crammed them into his mouth. They were tasteless and hard to swallow, so he had to sluice them down with a swallow of water. If only he'd had a few coppers with him to buy a pastry or something. He decided to ask Ash if he could borrow some coin.

He reached the inn, pushed the door open and stuck his head round. The main room was even more crowded than before. Hard-eyed men in brown leather armour. The scarred man Skathis handing a purse of coins to Ash. Ash hiccuping and reaching for it, looking up and seeing Jillan.

Told you! crowed the taint. *See the guilt in his eye. Maybe you'll listen to me next time, if we live long enough for a next time. Well, better get running again, Jillan, m'lad!*

'Oh no! Owain! It's not how it looksh! I . . .' Ash slurred plaintively.

'After him, halfwits!' Skathis rasped, his voice like a blade leaving a scabbard.

Half a dozen Heroes turned and saw Jillan at the door. Everything froze for the briefest and longest of seconds. Then the room exploded as men scrambled towards him and patrons unintentionally got in their way, particularly the harlot, who wailed like the restless spirit of one of the dead.

'Alive! We need him alive!'

Well that's something at least, the taint commented as Jillan sprinted away from the door. *They're not trying to kill us. Having said that, I hate to think what the Saint has in store if he requires us alive. Bound to be unpleasant. It's not too late to kill yourself, you know – might be the lesser of the two evils.*

'You're not helping!' Jillan replied. He headed away from the main thoroughfare this time: he wouldn't be able to lose himself among the People of Saviours' Paradise with Heroes shouting after him; if anything, the People would want to help the Heroes and would catch him in seconds.

Well there's gratitude for you. And after I'd given you a timely warning to ensure you approached the inn cautiously instead of just bursting in there like some thirsty yokel. I think I'll keep my own counsel from now on. See if I care!

'If only you would!'

Jillan careered round the corner on which the inn stood, having to push away from the wall to keep from colliding with it. He ran hard, ignoring all turnings to the left, for they would either dead-end against the town walls or lead him to other Heroes on guard duty. He flashed past an alley to the right before he even noticed it but managed to throw himself into the next one just as the first of the Heroes came charging round the corner of the inn. He tore down the alley, his feet splashing in puddles of muck and spattering him with filth. Several times he almost slipped on slime and waste, but the walls to either side just about kept him up.

Just as he was reaching the end of the long passage and about to enter a walled and cobbled courtyard, a voice behind him echoed, 'Down here!'

He dashed across the square and through an archway. He found himself in a near-identical courtyard to the previous one, but this one had linen pegged on washing lines across the way, and an outhouse in one corner with roses growing around the door.

Oo! A pretty pair of bloomers!

'I thought you were going to keep your own counsel.'

That wasn't counsel I just gave you. It was a comment on the lady's undergarments. Now you've done it – it's a dead end. Quick, put on the bloomers and other female finery and the guards might not recognise you.

Jillan heard the booted feet of the Heroes coming closer. He ducked under the washing lines and ran to the back door of one of the well-appointed houses ahead of him. It was unlocked. He went inside and found himself in a small room full of buckets and scrubbing boards. Then he went through into a large kitchen beyond.

A woman was lounging in a wooden tub of soapy water in front of a wide fireplace. 'Who are you?' she asked dreamily, making no effort to hide her modesty. 'Bit young for this sort of place, aren't you? Not surprised you use the back door.'

'I am no one, ma'am,' he replied, blushing furiously as he hurried across the kitchen.

'Ah, that's nice, calling me ma'am.'

What's the rush, Jillan? She seems friendly. Hmm. She'll slow down those Heroes for us if we're lucky.

Jillan barged his way out of the kitchen and into a dim corridor, off which there appeared to be large reception rooms. Glancing into one, he saw expensive padded benches and other items of furniture on which beautifully scented women in bright dresses either perched prettily or lolled seductively. There were murmurs and whispers on the air, an occasional male voice rumbling an enquiry and tinkling female laughter.

'You! What are you doing loitering in my back passage?' shouted a large harridan who'd emerged out of one of the rooms near the front door. She had thick face paint on like a street entertainer, but a voice harsh with age and overuse.

'I . . .'

Think quickly, m'lad. The guards won't be far behind. Perhaps you'd like my counsel now, eh? I can get you out of this fix if you like.

'Shut up!'

'What did you say?' the harridan asked slowly, her voice rising a notch and her brows drawing together.

The taint laughed.

'Sorry, not you, ma'am! I . . . I . . . Damn! All right, go on then.' The taint smoothly took over Jillan's voice and facial expression. 'I've come to warn you, ma'am. Spiro sent me.'

'Spiro? I don't know any Spiro. The Saviours take you, boy, what are you blathering about?'

Oops. She doesn't know Spiro. Never mind. The taint raised Jillan's eyebrows as high as they would go, made his eyes widely innocent and tearful and put a frantic quaver in his voice. 'Heroes, ma'am! They're coming here right now!'

'What? But I've paid Chief Trader John already this month!' the harridan protested as she glanced towards the unsecured bolts of the front door.

'Ma'am! They're coming through the back way. Do you have any guests who might be embarrassed to be found—'

There was a sudden scream from the kitchen.

'There are Heroes here to arrest us!' the harridan roared.

Jillan squeezed past the harridan as she came barrelling down the corridor towards the kitchen. *Hopefully, she'll wedge her bulk in the door and block our pursuers.* He made it to the front door just as people in various states of undress came pouring out of the salon rooms. There were screams of alarm and demands to be allowed out first. He was nearly trampled as he opened the front door and they all spilled out onto the street.

I'm beginning to enjoy this.

With several others, Jillan jogged away from the house. What with the earlier chase in the marketplace as well, he was close to exhaustion.

Don't look now.

He looked back.

I told you not to look!

A single Hero had made it out onto the street. He spotted Jillan looking back and started to give chase. Groaning, Jillan tried to run faster but knew he wouldn't be able to keep it up for long.

Dogged and determined, this one. He's a trained soldier. You won't be able to outrun him. There's only one choice.

'No.'

Look, if you don't have the stomach for it, then I'll do it for you, as I did in the house of pleasure back there. I won't even expect you to thank me, ingrate that you are.

'No! I will not let you kill him. He's done nothing wrong.'

And I will not let you give yourself up to them. I've worked too hard just to let you petulantly throw it all away now. Your parents spoiled you, you know. It's time to stop acting like a child, Jillan, if you want to live long enough to be worthy of a woman like Hella. Now stop whingeing and do what you must. It's kill or be killed. Let me *do it.*

'Skathis said they were to take me alive!' Jillan said through gritted teeth.

Are you simple? That's just until the Saint's got his hands on you. Once he's used you for his own designs, there'll be nothing left of you.

'There'll be nothing left of *you*, you mean!' Jillan shouted angrily. 'The holy one will purge me and then I'll finally be rid of you. I'll be free of this evil curse!'

A man without any hose or trews who was running near Jillan overheard the outburst. He glanced nervously at the disturbed boy and decided to put a good distance between them.

The taint did not respond. In fact, it seemed to have gone completely.

Jillan stepped into a doorway and readied himself. He counted to ten and stepped back out, raising his bow as he did so. The Hero slid to a halt, presenting an unmoving target. The arrow buried itself deep in the top of the soldier's thigh. The man cried out and just managed to keep his feet.

Jillan nocked another arrow.

'No! Please!'

'Get down! On the floor! Don't move, you hear? Stay there and I won't have to kill you. And throw me your purse. Quickly!'

Jillan picked up the purse and slowly backed down the street, his weapon trained on the soldier, who had now sensibly turned all his attention to staunching the potentially fatal flow of blood from his leg. Then Jillan turned away and disappeared into the rapidly darkening streets of Saviours' Paradise.

*

The Old Fort stood on a high promontory formed by a fork in a river. Behind the fort, on the far side from the fork, was a sprawling, higgledy-piggledy town where the People who serviced the fort and its large force of Heroes lived. The mean buildings in which the People lived were nowhere near as old or durable as the fort itself, for its defensive walls had been built, it was said, by ancient sorcerers even before the time of the Empire. The dark and massive stones of the walls fitted so perfectly together that all agreed magic had to have been used in their construction. It was commonly believed that should a Chaos-inspired force ever besiege the fort and launch rocks from catapults, then the walls would magically repel the missiles before they even landed. Of course, it was blasphemy to suggest that there had been any sort of meaningful life before the arrival of the Saviours, so everyone also agreed that the ancient sorcerers responsible for the fort had fought jealously among themselves and destroyed each other, thus leaving an empty shell for the Saviours to come and fill with new life and wisdom. The only other trace of the ancient sorcerers ever having existed was the strange patterns carved above certain doors and on particular walls, presumably as some form of decoration, but decoration that never seemed to wear away in the wind.

Freda stayed safely beneath the ground as she followed the two wagons on their way between the overground chambers of the town. It was becoming increasingly difficult not to lose track of those she followed, however, as other wagons crossed their path and the vibrations of so many people walking above drowned out almost everything else. With a sigh, she realised she'd need to go above ground, so found a quiet place and climbed up and out.

It was bright – *early*, as the Captain had called it – but the large orb of sun-metal did not seem to be in evidence. Through the gauze of the bandage she wore over her eyes she could discern the outline of the trundling wagons quite well.

Trying to stick to the shadows, and staying as far from people as she could, she followed along. Even so, she caught mutters like 'Poor soul!' 'Saviours-cursed freak!' and 'Pagan monster!' as a good number of folks noticed her.

The wagons climbed steadily past all the overground chambers and she realised they had to be heading for the dark place at the top. Yes, even above ground and at this distance she could feel the vibration of all the heavy men in that place. She had promised Norfred, though, and it seemed that this was the place to which Jan had probably been brought.

Freda went back beneath the ground for the remaining journey to the dark place, since there was now virtually no cover and she didn't want the Captain or any of his men seeing and trying to catch her. Once or twice she thought the Captain had glanced back in her direction, but her eyesight wasn't good enough to be sure.

The rock beneath the dark place wasn't like any she'd encountered before. It tingled when she passed through it, not unpleasantly but as if she were being *touched*. It was like when Norfred had used to stroke and talk softly to her in order to calm one of her bouts of frustration or rage. There was some sort of feeling in the rock here, but it wasn't a bad feeling of evil intent as she might have expected of this dark place; rather, it was a feeling of *sadness*. She wondered how rock could feel sad. Did the rock not like the heavy men? No, that could not be it, for the heavy men didn't really have any effect on the rock, did they?

She sensed an unoccupied gap beneath the dark place and stepped into it. There was absolute darkness here, so she could sense her surroundings quite clearly. There was no way in or out of the chamber, for the likes of the heavy men anyway, who could not move through rock. There may once have been a door out at the top of some stairs, but there was now a heavy slab of stone sealing it off. The slab emitted a high-pitched whine almost beyond her hearing and she decided that even she might have trouble passing through it.

The chamber was empty except for four large rocks or crystals in the middle. One she recognised as being of the same stone as the jade dragon she'd seen in her dream, but the others were types of stone she had not encountered before. People like Norfred would have described them by their colours – green, red, yellow and blue – but to her each one had a different resonance or feel. Like the slab over the door, each of the four stones emitted a whine or buzz, their different pitches creating a harmony of sorts.

The drone, or music, of the four stones relaxed her, and her eyes became heavy. Before she knew it, she was entering some sort of trance or sleep. She dreamed, but whether it was her dream or the ancient memories of the stones, she did not know. She saw people in simple clothing visiting this chamber and asking questions of the stones or praying. An old man wearing a jade amulet round his neck, a yellow stone at his forehead and a red and blue stone at each wrist seemed to be leading and guiding the people, like some sort of Overseer. No, the people knew him as a priest of Gar of the Still Stone. This was his temple. The priest helped the People commune with the stones, and through them commune with . . . the rock god, and through the rock god commune with . . . commune with . . . the Geas! The glorious Geas that was the communion of all living things in this world! Through the Geas, one person was connected to everyone else. Through the Geas, a person was truly one of the People and truly at one with the People. Without it, there was no *People*, only eternal isolation and selfishness, eternal loneliness and despair, the eternal void and desolation. Without it, there was only the desire for oblivion and nothingness.

Now, through the shared memories, Freda could read some of the patterns and symbols on the walls of the temple. They seemed to be telling her where to find Haven and the Geas! Yet she could not understand all the instructions, for many of the symbols still did not make sense.

'I don't understand!' she cried.

The priest turned to her with a kindly smile, but there was a haunted and ominous look about his eyes. 'You must find and free the other three temples. Commune with and free Wayfar, Akwar and Sinisar. Their shared knowledge will interpret the symbols for you and help you find Haven, but be quick, child of the rock god!'

There was a rumbling sound and the temple shook. People fell to the floor and cried out for help. There were terrible screams outside the temple as children and adults alike were slaughtered. The priest pitched forward and split his brow on one of the four stones. Blood poured down his face.

'What is happening?' Freda wailed.

'They are coming!' The priest grimaced as he used his power to begin dragging the horizontal stone slab across the door to the subterranean temple. 'They seek to possess the Geas for themselves. You must be quick, child of the rock god, for they are hunting you now. You must not let yourself be diverted from the path or taken by them, for time is short. They are almost upon you!'

As the slab closed across the doorway, the light and the dream began to fade.

'Wait!' Freda begged. 'Don't leave me on my own!'

The priest smiled at her with pity as his eyes became blackened and empty hollows. His skin wasted away as he said with his last breath, 'Simply know that you are no monster, child of the rock god. You are a part of the Geas. There are others you may find if you are lucky, but those you know as the Overlords have corrupted almost all of them. We are so few, so few. Beware, for the Overlords are always watching and miss nothing. Stay hidden, child of the rock god, or all will be lost.'

The slab finally slammed home and all was darkness once more.

The pain in Aspin's shoulders was excruciating. He'd been chained and hung by his arms for hours, and now he could feel them slowly being pulled out of their sockets. His torso had also been stretched by his own body weight, so that it was harder and harder to breathe.

'Dying,' he croaked. 'Help!'

'Quiet down there!' called a voice. 'Or we'll gag you again.'

'Dying. The holy one won't be happy. Wants to question me.'

There was no immediate response as the guards debated whether they could be bothered to leave their warm brazier to come down and check on him. Aspin prayed that their fear of the Saint was greater than the desire to keep warm. After all, the Saint was a terrifying being.

When the Saint had entered the cell earlier that day Aspin had naturally sought to read his soul. His mind had recoiled so violently from the twisted vileness he found that he'd been unable to prevent himself vomiting down his front and onto the holy one's feet. Children murdered, sharp metal inserted into their flesh. Mothers holding new-born babes burned for crimes that were merely imagined. A boy abused by his father using a wooden rod-like doll. Old men coming to watch, becoming aroused, then wanting to take a turn. Unspeakable acts. Degradation, humiliation and then hatred. White-hot molten hatred that spilled out of his mouth, eyes, nose, ears and other parts. Becoming nothing but that hatred – a creature intent on doing whatever was necessary to see its hatred visited upon those responsible and then any who did not submit to its will. Bowing without a care to the Saviours so that it would have even greater power to visit its hatred on others. Slaughter. Raping others of their power so that its hatred could become greater than any other's. Becoming stronger and hungrier with every horrific act. A hunger so great now that it wanted to devour the world, crunch on its bones and suck its marrow dry. It would sodomise and then destroy the Geas, singing softly in its ear all the while, as its father had sometimes done when using the wooden doll. But the boy had escaped! Jillan had escaped! He must be found before the acts of hatred could be exposed or betrayed to the Saviours. The boy had to be found so that he could be abused in the dark again. The only thing that could still terrify the hatred was the boy being free. The boy! The boy!

There was a heavy footstep on the stairs and Aspin gasped in fear.

Jillan crouched in the darkness listening to the two Heroes talking by the brazier. Their breath clouded in the cold air as they spoke.

'. . . as strong as an ox, he was, but collapsed on the ground, unable to get up and as weak as a babe. Lot of his hair come out though he were young. Teeth too, rotted before my own eyes. Tears of blood. No one would go near him. Blacksmith he was, in the marketplace.'

'Plague, then?' whispered the other, making the pagan sign – which was forbidden but used by everyone – against the evil eye.

'Aye, they say so. Just like in Godsend.'

'Shh! Keep your voice down. That's not to be spoken of. The wind and darkness will hear you.'

'Huh! That's just an old pagan superstition,' replied the first, although he prudently lowered his voice.

'Whichever, the holy one always knows, and he don't want us talking of it.'

The first sighed in frustration. 'All I'm saying is we pulled the short straw coming here after all. There was some of us laughing at the half-dozen that was chosen by the Captain to accompany the parents to Hyvan's Cross, while we was all getting excited about coming to Saviours' Paradise to see the dancing girls. And see what happens! We end up freezing our noses and burning our balls guarding some puking peasant in a town awash with plague.'

The second shrugged fatalistically. 'As we's always told – the blessed

Saviours will find a way to punish those not thinking firstly of their proper duty and sacrifice.'

The first spat out a breath. 'S'pose so at that. Just had a bad thought, though, entered my head. Think it's more punishment for me, 'tis.'

'What is it then?' the second asked with obvious trepidation.

'Mayhap I shouldn't tell it, as then it'll be punishment for you too. It'll spread from me to you, just like a plague, see. Saviours help me, but it's already too late.'

'What? What is it?'

'Don't you see? The plague! I just told it. What if the puking peasant we's guarding is puking precisely because he has the plague? With the unhealthy air and spirits hereabouts, the foul vapours that must cling to yonder stocks and gibbet, is it any surprise that the peasant has the contagion? By my thinking, it's now done for us as well, Saviours protect us!'

'Listen!' squeaked the second in fright. 'What's that?'

'Dying,' moaned a disembodied voice. 'Help!'

The second's jaw moved up and down but no sound came out, so great was his terror. The first chuckled. 'Calm down. I was just giving you a turn with all that talk. Wait till I tell the others.' He sniffed and smiled. 'Peed yourself too, I reckon. It's just the puking peasant, nothing more.' Then he raised his voice. 'Quiet down there or we'll gag you again.'

'Dying. Holy one won't be happy. Wants to question me,' came the voice from below.

'What think you?' The first sighed. 'Best one of us go down there to see he's not puking himself to death.'

'But the contagion.'

'Hmm. If we were gonna get it, then I reckon we already have, coming to this cursed town and all. Tell you what, I'll toss you for it.'

'Don't bother,' replied the second. 'My luck's so bad I already know I've lost, especially when it's you tossing the coin.'

Jillan crept away, having heard all he needed. It seemed his parents had been taken to Hyvan's Cross, of all places, where the Saint's main temple was located. It would be a long and dangerous journey and even harder to get inside undetected, but what other choice did he have? He wasn't about to let his parents die in a punishment chamber like the youth, not without trying to save them. And it was completely wrong that they should be locked up for his crimes. They were innocent. It was his fault, all his fault. Even if it cost him his life, he was determined to make it up to them.

The youth was his fault too. And dying. How many people would he be responsible for killing before it was over? Despite his insistence to the taint that he wouldn't kill anyone who was innocent, he would be doing just that if he didn't try to set the youth free. It was of course risky, but it seemed that the Saint wanted something from the youth, just like he wanted something from Jillan. If Jillan could deny the Saint the youth, then . . . then what? No, he wouldn't exchange the youth for his parents. So? He wasn't sure. It would certainly frustrate the Saint and perhaps cause the holy one to make a mistake, just like Haal, Elder Corin's son, would always make the mistake of rushing blindly at Jillan when teased. If the Saint made a mistake, then maybe it would be easier to free his parents. Maybe.

The wind carried another of the youth's cries to his ears.

Freda lay in the bedrock beneath the dark place, wondering at the strangeness of her existence. What did she know of gods and old temples? What was the Geas really? Strange words and ideas, none of which had helped her when she'd needed help in her life.

Why were the Overlords chasing her? It wasn't fair! She felt guilty as she remembered that she'd killed men, but she hadn't meant to, and they'd forced her to do it. And they'd killed Norfred! Well, it wasn't exactly the men she'd killed who'd done for Norfred; that had been Darus. Maybe she'd done wrong after all.

But they kept confusing her with their threats and orders. Darus had told her what to do, and now so did the rock god. Both had threatened her. She was tempted just to avoid others for the rest of her days, but they hunted her, even in her dreams. Why wouldn't they leave her alone?

The only one who hadn't told her what to do was Norfred. He'd told her she deserved more than cruel treatment. She deserved to be free of people like Darus and the frightening jade dragon of the rock god's fabulous will. Norfred hadn't ordered her to find Jan – he'd only asked that if she happened to see him she should tell Jan that Norfred had loved him. And so she would find Jan for Norfred and then worry about everything else.

She felt and listened to all the comings and goings above her. Heavy men marched backwards and forwards, shaking the ground with their intent and orders. The children from the wagon she'd been following were inspected by one of the heavy men. Half the children were sent to put on dead skin and become heavy, while the others, mainly the lighter females, were told to get back in the wagon.

Before putting on the dead skin, the children that were to become heavy visited a woman who asked them questions and checked that they were well. She sounded kind and reminded her of Mistress Widders. Freda moved closer.

When the woman was finally alone in her overground chamber, Freda climbed out of the ground behind her.

'I am Freda,' she said in her lightest tone, making her throat hurt.

The woman stifled a scream and whirled round. 'Oh! You startled me! Where did you . . . Saviours preserve us, but I've never seen the condition so bad or advanced. Are you in pain? Would you like me to give you something for it?'

Freda blinked as she tried to decipher the woman's sounds and questions. Her voice reminded Freda of one of the caged birds that the miners had used to check for invisible gas. Perhaps the woman had such a bird inside her now checking for gas. No, that would be silly. The feathers would tickle too much. 'It hurt when a shining spear went in me here,' Freda said slowly, pointing to the shoulder where Overseer Altor's weapon had impaled her.

The woman frowned and stood on tiptoe to peer at the wound. 'I . . . er . . . It seems to be healing well enough. But the rock blight, dear one, it must be affecting your movement and speed of thought, no? You are slow, yes?'

'I'm no slower than anyone else, I don't think,' Freda rumbled after some serious thought. 'I am looking for Jan. Have you seen him? Did he come here? I want to find Jan for Norfred. Norfred is Jan's father.'

The woman listened carefully and nodded her understanding. 'I see. Jan, is it? I don't recall a Jan, but there are many that come through here and don't spend more than a week or two. They are given some basic training with swords, pila, javelins and the like, and are then usually sent out east. They say that no amount of training can compare to the real thing, you see. I suppose they're right, but it breaks my heart to see so many of our young people going out to face those awful barbarians. Oh, and then there are some I don't even get to see, for they are sent straight to the Great Temple. Good-looking is he, this Jan? If so, chances are that he'll have been lucky enough to be selected to serve in the Great Temple itself.'

Good-looking? Freda couldn't really answer because she hadn't seen Jan. Besides, she didn't know how to judge such things. Had Norfred been good-looking? She didn't know. He'd been kind, but that had to be different because it was a different word. What she did know was that she herself was ugly. Everyone said so. 'He isn't like me,' Freda mumbled.

The woman nodded. 'Look, why don't you go and ask the Selecting Officer? He'll know if this Jan has gone east or south. They keep records, you see, in case anyone goes missing when they shouldn't. It's important to know how many leave here and how many arrive somewhere, so that no one can run off without people knowing, you see. And they record names, what a body looks like and places of origin so that a person's easier to find if they do run off. Come on, I'll take you to the Selecting Officer if you like.'

Freda hung back.

'Come on then. Don't be scared. No one will hurt you when you're under my care. Don't worry, the men jump when I tell them to. I've treated nearly all of them at one time or another, when they've been seeing the painted women in the town and picked up some infection or other. The things I could tell you! Every now and then, one of them comes to me with hands a-wringing and crying that they've got some woman with child and that they need some brew to stop the child ever being born. These Heroes aren't allowed families on any account, you see, and the punishment for disobedience terrifies them witless. They've all heard of the men that's been gelded. Nothing to laugh at, eh?' she chortled. 'The smart ones, of course, come to me before they visit the painted women in the town. I give them a brew to make sure they never get a child on some woman in the first place. If they want to keep getting their brew, then they stay on the right side of me, you see, if they're smart, as I've already said. So come along, Freda.'

For once, Freda was glad she had a stony face so that the heat and crimson embarrassment she felt at the woman's words wouldn't shame her. She hadn't understood everything, but she'd understood enough to know that the woman had spoken of intimate things that went on between a man and woman when nobody else was around or when everyone knew not to notice or talk about what was happening. People weren't meant to talk about such things! They were forbidden, wrong somehow.

The woman took Freda gently by the hand and led her out into the dark place.

Saint Goza drooled in anticipation. Saliva dribbled from the corners of his generous mouth, around his wide chin and down onto his straining tunic. It had been a long while since his personal cook had been able to buy a newborn, and the taste and exquisite experience simply could not compare. The flesh and magical potency of older children, even children just a few weeks older, was tragically bland by comparison and only served to increase his all-consuming desire for a newborn.

For the unfathomable magic of the mother and the near-miraculous energies of creation still clung to a babe several hours after its birth. Such power consumed the Saint as much as he consumed such power. It was beyond intoxication, beyond the high of the strongest narcotic, beyond insatiable appetite, beyond religious ecstasy: simply *beyond*. It was now essential to his being and definition. It was his every waking and sleeping thought, fantasy and motivation to act. He only moved if it was to feed or to bring him closer to his desired source of physical, emotional and spiritual food.

He consumed such volumes and was now so large that he could only move through the use of the magic he absorbed from the People he owned, bred and dined upon. He was proud of his size, though, for the bigger he was, the more he could consume at a single sitting, the closer he could get to satisfying his ever-demanding hunger and the greater his power to realise eventually the goal of the eternal, unending feast. He would consume this world and its Geas. He would gorge himself on the cosmos. He would . . .

His mighty nostrils twitched. *Ah, the meat was roasting now and close to done.* He preferred it rare, of course, although he tended to get stomach trouble when it was too bloody. The sauce the cook was preparing was intriguing too – shallots, a splash of red wine, wine from the east if his olfactory powers weren't mistaken, and something else. It was a game Goza and the cook liked to play: seeing if the Saint could identify every ingredient. If the Saint failed to guess correctly, the cook could make any request he desired of his liege lord. However, if the Saint did guess correctly, the cook would decant a mug of blood from his puny arm and offer it to the Saint to wash his meal down with. In the thirty years or so that the cook had been with Goza, the Saint had never once been wrong. Yet today's sauce was more of a challenge than he'd had in a while.

The Saint was about to tuck his outsized napkin under his chin when something else caught his attention. *What was this? Oh, not now!* The timing was dreadful. It would simply have to wait – otherwise, the meat would become overdone or cold while he attended to this irritating matter.

Yet the matter intruded and he knew that if he did not deal with it first he would not be able to enjoy his meal fully. Cursing vilely, he threw the napkin down with one hand and thumped the table with the other, cracking the wood. He snorted to herald his intention to speak. The Saint's revolting manservant – a creature so thin and covered in cankers, he wasn't worth eating – hurried inside the tent to wait on his liege lord's wisdom and command.

'Yes, holy one? Should I fetch buckets to catch your divine excrement?'

The Saint grunted as he summoned the power to draw enough breath to say, 'No, you overeager lickspittle! Sell it, do you, my effluence? Or do you dine on it yourself, hoping to gain whatever meagre energies might still remain within it?' Goza wheezed with suspicion. 'Is that it? You hope to become as powerful as your master? You think to challenge me and become the Saint of this region?' He drew on more of his power to unleash a gargantuan roar: 'Well?'

The manservant grovelled low, his fright causing several of his cankers to start oozing pus at the same moment. 'Holy one, I see to it that your largesse is freely shared with the faithful hereabouts. The local farmers joyfully spread your benevolence on their fields, for it increases the yield of their crops tenfold. Truly, it is a miracle that sees all the People rejoice and declare they only live by your grace.'

'You are smooth-tongued,' Goza responded accusingly. In his mind's eye he'd seen the man do as he claimed, but he still did not believe him. Goza did not trust any who might one day be his lunch. 'Indeed, it is probably the only worthwhile part of you. I would have it boiled and served with quails eggs if I did not need you for tedious day-to-day details. Tell the cook that he should slow the cooking by half a clock. If the roasting meat dries out too much, tell him, I'll have his skin peeled off and his body immersed in pickling fluid.'

'At once, holy one,' the manservant replied as he hurried out.

With a burp and fart that extinguished a few candles, Goza heaved himself onto his wide split feet and pounded his way out of the tent, lifting his bright war hammer as he went. The weapon was far too large and heavy for any ordinary man, but it had become small in his hands of late. Perhaps it was time to have a new one forged. After all, sufficient sun-metal had been pulled from the ground recently to allow him a new weapon without the Saviours having to suffer any fall-off in their normal supply.

Cooking pots on the campfires of his personal guard rattled and jumped as he paced up to his Captain. 'Bring the cage!' he blew at him and turned away without waiting for a reply. The Saint started to make for the fortified walls just beyond his camp.

A stray dog whined and rolled onto its back submissively as the Saint passed it. He would have grabbed it by the scruff of the neck and bitten its head off by way of a light repast to keep him going, but the thing looked emaciated and was probably riddled with burrowing worms. Goza had had an infestation of worms in his back once and it had itched terribly. On another occasion he'd even lost weight, which had been truly worrying.

Even though there was very little sun in evidence in the white sky, sweat had already begun to lather his magnificent physique. The exertion required to keep such a formidable bulk moving could have easily toppled these moss-covered walls, no matter how long the Old Fort was said to have stood. The People had no true idea of strength and eternity, no genuine understanding of how lucky they were to have him among them and watching over them. After all, how could they?

They were little more than another type of burrowing worm really. They made him itch.

He powered onto the training ground inside the walls, and several hundred new recruits and Heroes abased themselves before him. He moved to the centre of the wide space and came to a stop. The soldiers would continue to lie on their faces until he instructed them otherwise. He settled in to wait, knowing it wouldn't be long. He started to daydream about the meal waiting for him. Just what was that other ingredient in the sauce? Its smell reminded him of a particularly red and toxic berry found only along the shore of a hidden lake in the far north. Surely the cook didn't have the inspiration and wherewithal to procure an item so rare, did he? Goza smiled. Perhaps he did, at that, given he'd been told money was no object and he might use the holy one's name as necessary.

The Saint dribbled freely as he thought of the dressing for the meat. He was now so long-lived and of such a size that he did not need to fear any sort of poison. If anything, the hallucinatory effects of poisons brought whole new dimensions that were beyond the physical to his gourmand delights. They gifted him with visions and vistas far beyond this world of anaemic worms. They transported him beyond the tawdry limits of this world and its thin range of tastes and flavours. They spread his will across the reaches of the cosmos, where he would feed on new and greater energies and begin to expand, until even the furthest corners of existence were his.

He blinked slowly and stepped out of the puddle that had formed around his feet. She was coming. Being led by the hand. Bandages over her sensitive eyes, the only part of her that was at all soft. Perhaps when he peeled off that hard shell, though, he would find moist and tender flesh below, as with a crab or lobster, and hopefully as tasty.

'Oh my! The holy one is here,' the woman exclaimed with equal surprise and excitement and threw herself to the ground.

Freda gazed through her bandages at the shadowy figure blocking out half the sky-cave. She was confronted by something as big as the rock god, but it was all wobbling rolls of flesh instead of chiselled granite. Was the figure a god of the soft people, then? Should she bow to it, even if just to be polite? It must at least be an Overlord, and that meant she would be in trouble for escaping from the mine. She couldn't help feeling guilty.

The huge hammer of sun-metal that the god – or Overlord – held was painful to look upon and she had to shield her eyes with one of her hands. It was like the orb that sometimes shone high in the sky-cave. Had the god or Overlord of the soft people dragged it down from on high so that he could use it as a weapon against her? Now she felt afraid.

'I am very angry with you!' the giant roared, his voice making the walls around them and her stony skin ring painfully.

Instinctively, she hunkered closer to the ground. 'Don't be angry! Don't send me back to the mine and Gang-leader Darus!' she begged.

'Silence!' he bellowed, the sound threatening to crack her open. 'You have not been given leave to speak in the presence of holy Saint Goza. You are young and ignorant, for you have not yet been Drawn, but I cannot forgive your other crimes. I sheltered you in the mine, allowing you life, and this is how you repay me. You not only defy your Gang-leader, but also your Overseer! Then you escape the mine and sow division among a squad of Heroes. Worst of all, however, you pull me from my breakfast to deal with you. I might well suffer indigestion later because of this inconvenience. Is there no end to your wilful blasphemy? You even presume to tell me how I should not punish you. Tell me then: how should you be sanctioned?'

'I cannot return to the mine. I will not! There is something I must do for Norfred.'

'Incredible. Would you now defy *me*? Would you topple *me*, as if I were something less glorious than the very mountains?' the Saint asked in outraged disbelief. 'Would you then defy the blessed Saviours, those who have given life and protection to all the People including yourself? Topple the Empire, would you? You are ungrateful and undeserving of the Saviours' gifts then. Your utter self-obsession has warped and twisted your mind as much as your body. You are truly corrupted by the Chaos both without and within. There can be no salvation for one such as you, for there is no longer anything left of what you may once have been. There is only one sentence I can pass – your existence is forfeit. Our judgement and justice will swallow you up and break you down until you are nothing more than a stinking slurry to be fed to the pigs or spread on the fields.'

The Saint smiled and licked his lips. 'To be honest, I do not think I have ever tasted one with the rock blight. Does it lend a particular flavour to the meat, I wonder? I suspect the crackling will be a bit tough, though, eh?'

He meant to eat her! It was unimaginable. She felt sick. She dived for the ground and ploughed it up in her haste.

'Where do you think you're going? Surely you know there is no hiding place from the will and might of the Saviours and their apostates! All realms and matter are theirs to command. Still, it can be an interesting eating experience to devour something while it's still struggling for life. Yes, catching you will serve to whet my appetite all the more.'

The Saint raised his hammer high above his head and slammed it into the ground in front of him. The concussion waves that spread out bounced Freda up out of the ground and left her flopping and flailing like a fish out of water. She desperately tried to submerge herself once more, but the hammer smote the ground again, blasting a crater in it and causing fissures in both the ground and her skin. Screaming, a number of people tumbled into the yawning earth and were slowly ground into nothing. Rocks the size of cabbages rained down on others, crushing limbs and skulls.

The Saint moved down into the crater, where Freda lay in the bottom. The sun-metal rang on and on, hammering a nail through her head just as the rock god had been pinned and left helpless so long before. She couldn't think, see or hear anything. She lost her sense of place entirely.

A swollen fist wrapped itself around one of her ankles and began to drag her up and out of the crater. She lashed out, striking folds of flesh savagely.

'Oo, that tickles!' Saint Goza laughed.

Freda heaved herself up so that she could reach her ankle. She smashed down on one of the Saint's shell-like fingernails and was relieved to see it crumple and start to bleed.

'Ow! You bitch!' he cried, releasing her. 'You'll pay for that!'

She managed to get several feet into the earth before he caught her with a looping swing of his hammer, which lifted her and threw her a dozen feet through the air. She landed on a soldier, crushing him. She was badly injured herself – the Saint's blow had caught her in the stomach and chest. She thought her ribs were shattered and it felt like her guts had been torn out. She wanted to be sick but her body seemed too broken to even manage a gag.

The Saint lumbered towards her, smearing several of his own men underfoot. 'Out of my way, everyone!'

At last having permission to move, the recruits and Heroes rolled away or leapt up and scattered in panic. One unfortunate was disorientated and staggered across the Saint's path. He collided with the prodigious holy personage, was knocked to the ground and crushed. The smell of blood, sweat, ozone and fear pervading the air was overwhelming.

Saint Goza reached down for one of her wrists and hauled her up into the air. Separated from the ground, she was weakened even further. The Saint placed one of her fingers in his vast mouth of tombstone teeth and bit down. She squealed in shock and terror. He chewed thoughtfully for a second and swallowed.

'Hmm. Not the best. Even with plenty of salt, I'm not sure I'd bother with any of your other fingers. I don't really know where they've been, do I? Still, it serves as a lesson to you for the fingernail, does it not?' He shook her and yelled into her face. 'Does it not?'

Freda whimpered. 'Please, no more! I'll go back to the mine. I'll apologise to Gang-leader Darus.'

He shook her again. 'You're just not getting it. It's too late for the mine. Now, must I repeat myself? It serves as a lesson, does . . . it . . . not?'

'Yes!' she choked.

'Really, you should be thanking me for wasting my valuable time on teaching you, but it's all too boring. Besides, I need to get back to my tent to replenish myself. I feel like I'm wasting away out here. In fact, if you think about it, every moment I'm not eating, I'm using and losing energy and getting thinner. Now, just hold still and we can get this over with, without any more fuss.'

Holding her with one hand, he dropped his hammer and reached inside his voluminous tunic with his other. He pulled out a pair of manacles made of sun-metal. He clapped one manacle around her wrist.

'It burns!' she moaned quietly, tears running down her face as wisps of smoke rose into her eyes.

He ignored her, lowered her to the ground and put the other manacle on her. He let her go. She didn't even try sinking into the earth, knowing her sizzling bracelets would prevent her from travelling any distance.

'Captain, where are you? Ah, there. The cage if you please. Have one of your men hurry to the cook and tell him to serve me in my tent in a hand of minutes from now. And have a large cauldron obtained from the town. I will have this creature boiled in it for my evening meal.'

A swarthy Hero with no trace of emotion on his face signalled two men to bring a gleaming cage over to Freda. It was made of rods of sun-metal so thin that they were almost a net.

'Inside!' the Captain ordered and she crawled into the small space. 'I wouldn't struggle to get out if I were you, for sun-metal is far stronger than it looks. If you fight, you will end up wrapping it more and more tightly around you, and as you have discovered, it burns something fierce.'

'See that she doesn't struggle then, Captain,' the Saint rumbled. 'I don't want my meat too seared, now do I? You know how I get if a meal is spoiled. In my upset I might just have you for dessert.'

'Yes, holy one, as is your will.'

Wearing a delivery cap and crisp white shirt he'd liberated from a washing line, and carrying a firkin of ale under each arm, Jillan whistled jauntily as he made his way through the dark. As he passed the gibbet, he spat over his shoulder, as was the custom, to keep restless spirits away from him.

'Halt! Who goes there?' called one of the Heroes gruffly.

'Smiddy from the Recalcitrance Inn, that's who,' Jillan replied musically.

'What do you want, Smiddy from the Recalcitrance Inn, eh? Don't you know we've got dangerous criminals down here?'

'It's not a matter of what I be wanting, sir, but a matter of what your good Captain orders and a matter to which ye may be partial.'

'Speak plainly, boy,' the same Hero advised, although his voice became softer as his eyes alighted on the two firkins.

'Well then, sir, your good Captain plainly ordered that I should bring'e a nightcap, see, if that be plain enough for'e. He further ordered, plain as ye like, that ye should drink this here nightcap which ye can plainly see here, even if it be a darkish night.'

'He did?' the second Hero asked in wonderment, clearly struggling to believe their luck. 'Not like the Captain. Call it an indulgence, he would, and indulgence makes you soft, he says.'

'I wouldn't know much about that, sir.' Jillan shrugged. 'If ye like, I can return this best brewed ale and tell the good Captain ye refuse his orders . . . or, for a small consideration, I can make the ale disappear and tell him ye gratefully received it.' He put the firkins down, coughed and put out a palm.

The first Hero would have none of it. 'Be off with you, you cheeky rapscallion. Enough of your *plain* this and *plain* that, and your *ye* may and *ye* might. Think to blackmail the Saint's own guard, would you? That would be a terrible sin, wouldn't it, Jack?'

'Certainly would.' His comrade nodded.

'So, Smiddy from the Recalcitrance Inn, just leave the ale here, where it will be well looked after, and be on your way, see?'

Smiddy gave a tired soldier's salute and a 'Yessir, sir! Yes! Sir!' Then he jumped away as the Hero tried to put his boot to his backside. Smiddy stuck his tongue out and disappeared into the night.

'Kids today, eh, Jack? In need of a thrashing or three to help them respect their elders.'

'Say, this ale ain't half bad, though.'

Jillan returned half a clock later to find both guards soundly asleep. The herbs he had bought from a physicker woman had more than done their job, judging by how loud and deep the men's snoring was. He took the ring of keys from the first Hero's belt and then crept down the stairs to the punishment chambers below.

'Who's there?' whispered a thin voice from one of the cells. It was the youth Jillan had seen arrested at the main gate. He was slumped against a grimy wall and looked the worse for wear. He was wearing manacles secured to the ends of two long adjustable chains that passed up through a metal hoop in the roof before reaching an attachment on the far wall.

'Is there anyone else here?' Jillan asked quietly.

'No. Just me. I'm Aspin. Who are you?'

'Oh, don't worry about that.'

Aspin gritted his teeth. 'What do you want? How did you get past the guards? Bribe them, did you, just so you could have a look at me and tell all your friends. Honestly, you people . . .'

'No, no! I'm here to get you out. Look, I have the keys.'

Aspin was silent for a few seconds. 'You have? Why?' His voice was thick with suspicion. 'Some trick, is it? We'll escape together and then, overcome by gratitude, I'll tell you everything, is that it?'

'What are you talking about?' Jillan asked in confusion. 'I thought they'd arrested you because they thought you were someone else.' He hesitated. 'So what sort of things do you think I want you to tell me?' Now he thought about it, once the Heroes had spoken to Ash and spotted Jillan at the inn, why hadn't they realised the youth was innocent and released him? Perhaps the youth *wasn't* innocent. Perhaps it wasn't a case of mistaken identity after all. Perhaps this Aspin was dangerous. Jillan backed away from the bars to the cell.

'Why the hell should I trust you?' Aspin spat.

'Because I was the one who was going to free you, although I have to tell you I'm having doubts about it now. Quite frankly, I couldn't give a prickly fig if you do trust me or not. Some thanks wouldn't hurt, though, now would it?'

'Keep your voice down,' came back a surly voice. 'All right, sorry. I'm tired and hungry and my arms are killing me. I hate this place, I hate that damned Saint of yours and I hate you stupid lowlanders! But thank you anyway. There, are you satisfied?'

'You should keep your voice down too. You called me a . . . low-lander, was it? Does that mean you're from th-the . . .'

'The mountains? Yes.'

'B-but that means you're a-a pagan!'

'So you lowlanders call us, but we're just the same as you. Not exactly the same, of course, but . . . well, you know what I mean.'

'But if you're a pagan, surely you have magic and can get yourself out of here?'

'Magic? Pah! I don't know where you got that from, but if we all had magic, we wouldn't have been murdered in such numbers and driven out of our lands, now would we? Your Saint has far more magic than any of my people, that's for sure. I've been told I'm a soul-reader, but all that means is I have an instinct about people's characters, whether I can trust them, that sort of thing. It's never been much use to me, though. It didn't stop me getting thrown out of my village. And it's not helping me get out of this cell any faster.'

'So what does your magic tell you about me?' Jillan asked warily.

Aspin frowned and squinted, as if having trouble. 'One moment it tells me to trust you, and the next it says I shouldn't. It's like there're two of you or something. See, I told you it wasn't much use.'

Jillan recoiled. The taint! The youth knew.

It's hardly a secret, is it? Everyone knows you're a twisted killer. If you killed everyone who knew that, there'd be no one left alive, now would there? Let him out. He might be useful to us. And if a bit of panic is sown about a pagan being on the loose, that can only work in our favour. The more confusion there is, the easier it'll be for us to avoid capture.

He couldn't let the youth out. He was a pagan! Dangerous.

Aren't you forgetting that you're now a pagan as well? Aren't you forgetting that you're the one who's used dangerous and forbidden magic? You're just the same as he is. Worse, probably.

No. It was an accident. I can't be a pagan. They're evil. Besides, the youth said his people didn't have much magic. The Saint has magic.

Nothing made sense any more. If the pagans didn't have magic, then was everything Minister Praxis had told him untrue? Was the Book of Saviours untrue? How could that be? It would mean nothing in his entire life had been true. It would mean nothing in the world was true. Impossible. There was only emptiness and lies. Just a whisper on the wind. Just a shattered reflection on water. A shadow cast by flame. Just ashes on the earth. Just the void. Nothing.

Heart hammering, unable to breathe, Jillan sat on the floor and put his head between his knees.

'Are you all right?' Aspin asked curiously.

Dizzy. There had to be something that was true, something that was real. His parents were true. Their love for him was real. They'd been happy in their little home in Godsend. He wanted to go back there.

No. Godsend is not your home. You know your parents were from New Sanctuary, a place that no longer exists thanks to the Saint. They never told you either, did they? You had to overhear it. They were never truthful with you about where you came from or about what they once were. You can't even picture them any more, can you, eh?

Shut up! Samnir's affection had been true. His steely gaze and unflinching silhouette as he stood against the wilderness. A lone sentinel who would never yield and would always keep the borders of the Empire safe and intact.

He's broken now, thanks to the Saint. Sits in his own shit and piss while people laugh and throw things. Where're your Hero and Empire now, eh?

Stop it! Hella's blue eyes were true. Their friendship was real. She'd stood up for him when no one else had. She'd smiled at him when everyone else had sneered.

The taint sighed with what sounded like genuine sorrow. *The Saint has no doubt Drawn her by now. Her eyes no longer shine as they once did. Her smile is no longer quite so magical and affecting. Her father wants you to give up and turn yourself in. He wants it all to end. No more pain and struggle, just the peace of letting go and fading away. No more fighting for life and meaning. No more.*

Tears trickled down his face. He cursed the Saint for what he'd done to all the innocent people in his life. He now knew that if any of them was ever to have any sort of life with meaning, then he would have to start fighting rather than be forever running and hiding. If he constantly fled from danger and sought non-existent places of safety, then he would be just like Jacob – he would be meekly letting go of any life and character in return for long years of grey monotony and a gentle passage into death.

He was tired and numb, but at last had some sort of resolve, some sort of direction. He would fight the Saint, even if he ultimately died for it. He would release Aspin simply because the Saint wanted him imprisoned. In that sense, Aspin and Jillan were the same, for the Saint wanted Jillan captured and imprisoned too. In many ways, Jillan had always been a prisoner to the law and will of the Saviours and their Saint. The Empire was a prison – albeit a large one – for life, the mind and the soul. Just as he'd accused Ash of being a prisoner, so he was one also. Perhaps he'd been unfair on Ash. What choice had the woodsman had really? He had no freedom to speak of, no freedom to choose or exercise his own will. Well, now, Jillan intended to do what he could to fight his way free. He wasn't afraid to die. He didn't have anything left to lose anyway, since he didn't have any life worth living as it was.

Jillan wiped his face and got shakily to his feet. 'I'm fine,' he said to Aspin and unlocked the door to the cell. He moved inside and tried the different keys on the manacles as Aspin held them up.

'Oh no! None of them fit. But these were all the keys the guards had.'

Aspin sighed despondently. 'Thank you for trying. I think the other guard, the Captain, had the key for these.'

Jillan followed the chains from the manacles to the far wall, where they were securely affixed. 'Hold on, let me try this.' He pulled Samnir's blunt short sword out from inside his shirt and fitted its rounded point into the loop sunk in the wall. Then he put his weight on the hilt to try and prise the loop free, praying the sword wouldn't just bend or snap.

The point slipped. 'Gah!' Jillan hit his forehead against the wall and clattered with the weapon to the stone floor.

'Careful! You all right?'

There was blood on the blade. As Jillan gazed stupidly at it, the blood was absorbed by the metal and its dull surface began to gleam. Brighter and brighter.

'Ye gods! How it shines. 'Tis like the sun!' Aspin said in awe.

'I think it's sun-metal,' Jillan replied in amazement. 'It's very valuable. Here, let me try it on the manacles now.'

The sun-metal cut through the iron as if it wasn't even there.

Jillan couldn't take his eyes off the sword. It sang to him. And Samnir had given it to him! The old soldier had given away the one thing that might have successfully defended him against the Saint. Samnir had given Jillan his life! He felt elated, guilty, responsible, grateful and awful all at once.

There was the scuff of a footstep at the top of the stairs. Jillan's heart leapt into his mouth.

Thought you were ready to die? Looks like it's going to happen a bit sooner than you reckoned.

'There's someone coming,' Aspin hissed unnecessarily, trying to get up, but his arms refused to work. He rolled awkwardly onto his knees like a beggar who'd been deliberately crippled so that he could make a better living.

'Stay back!' Jillan challenged.

Oo, brave! Bet that scared 'em.

The footsteps did not stop coming. Darkest shadow engulfed the stairwell. A red eye blazed malevolently upon them.

'Did you think I would not know, Jillan?' scraped a voice from his nightmares. 'The Saint *always* knows. At last you are mine!'

CHAPTER 8:

Life therefore being a prison

'I feel sick,' Aspin muttered as the monster stared menacingly down at them.

Jillan waggled his sword at the Saint, the air shimmering around the blade.

'Where did you get that, boy? It's no child's toy. You stole it, did you not?'

'It's mine by right,' Jillan said fiercely. 'Come closer and see if I'm playing.'

'Put it down now and I might not kill you.'

'He lies!' Aspin gulped with difficulty. 'I can read it. He wants you alive for some reason.'

'Silence!' the Saint thundered at Aspin, his voice deafening them in the enclosed space.

The boys clapped their hands over their ears in agony, Jillan having to juggle his weapon. Blood trickled between the fingers of one of Aspin's hands.

'How does it feel to have someone know what *you're* thinking, eh?' Jillan retorted, although his voice sounded small and whining even to his own ears. 'Not very nice is it, h-holy one?'

'He cannot know what I think,' the Saint denied. 'My thoughts are far beyond his understanding. Jillan, enough of this pretence. I am your holy Saint. You know better than to disobey me. You should be bowing to me. The incident in Godsend was . . . unfortunate, an accident, was it not? You have not been served well by those around you, for it has brought you to this blasphemy. They should not have encouraged and helped you to escape. If the matter had been dealt with correctly in the first instance, far less harm would have been done. You do know that the boy Karl did not die, don't you?'

Jillan's jaw dropped.

'Yes, he only suffered a few burns, that's all. All is well in Godsend. I will purge the taint from you and you can go home.'

'He lies,' Aspin asserted. 'The boy is dead. Jillan, keep the point of your sword up. He intends to rush you.'

'Wretched pagan!' Azual roared, shaking the chamber and making rock dust fill the air.

They all ended up coughing, the Saint included.

'Th-then he is dead?'

'Jillan.' The Saint had to work hard to make his voice reasonable. 'Jillan, I merely sought to spare you guilt and grief. I know it was an accident beyond your control. In some ways, it was my fault for not having Drawn you sooner. I know how you have suffered in this. You are a victim of the accident too. The innkeeper got what he deserved, though. You did well. I am pleased.'

Jillan blinked. He so wanted to believe the holy Saint Azual. He wanted everything to be all right again. He wanted the taint out of him. It was all the taint's fault Karl had died anyway.

Well, there's gratitude for you. Those bullies would have probably killed you.

He was tired and wanted to go home, to find his mother cooking broth and smiling at one of his father's jokes. He wanted Jed to ruffle his hair, clap him on the shoulder and give him a new stone for his collection. He wanted to see Hella, desperately wanted to see Hella. It hurt just to think of her and how he'd ruined everything.

'Y-you have taken my parents.'

With exaggerated patience and a flickering smile, the Saint explained, 'I put them under guard for their own protection. You know what Minister Praxis and the elders of Godsend are like. They are simple folk who too quickly look to blame others. It's not surprising really, given how close they are to the wilderness and the dark influence of the Chaos. The Minister and Elder Corin had them all stirred up and ready to lynch your parents for having come from New Sanctuary. You knew they were from that town originally, yes?'

Jillan nodded.

'He's lying again.'

Azual's nostrils flared in anger but he did not raise his voice this time. Instead, he shone his eye fully on Jillan and said with soft sibilance, 'You know you can't trust a pagan. They are corrupt, they are liars by nature. Through dark manipulation, they seek to bring down the Empire. You know this, Jillan. It is part of scripture. Do not let yourself fall under his spell. He says the opposite of my holy word and has you believing him. Resist him, Jillan. Put the sword down. I will purge you and all will be well again. I will talk to the elders of Godsend and they will allow your parents to live among them once more. Do you not want to see Hella again?'

'Get back! Look out!' Aspin shouted.

Jillan had stopped blinking as the Saint asked the question at the heart of things: he had found Jillan's sacred heart and spoken directly to it. 'I-I . . .' he stammered. He started at Aspin's warning and saw that the Saint had sidled closer.

Jillan tried to get his blade up and put some distance between himself and the Saint, but it was already too late. Azual swept forward, slapped the sword out of Jillan's hand and kicked it behind him. Then he curled long thick fingers around Jillan's neck and pulled him off the floor. Aspin ran forward, but the Saint was ready for him, planted a foot in the middle of the youth's chest and propelled him back across the cell. The young warrior crunched into the wall and collapsed.

Azual drew Jillan's face close to his own. Jillan could see his blood-red reflection and the pulsing veins in the Saint's livid eye. The all but permanent snarl on Azual's face gave him a feral, animal look. His hot breath smelt of old blood and rotting things.

'What do you have to say for yourself now, boy? I gave you a chance to repent, but you would prefer to betray everyone that's ever cared for you or provided you with shelter than see your selfish desires thwarted, would you not? You would prefer to side with the jealous enemies of the Empire, would you not? What is it they promised you, eh? What price your faith and duty? No, don't deny it! I have caught you red-handed consorting with a miserable pagan. There's not a single community in the Empire that would spare you the rope for that. What will Hella think when she hears, eh? She will feel ashamed, sullied and dirty for ever having known you. She will be reviled for some years for the friendship she afforded you. Thus are the innocent preyed upon by the Chaos and its minions. Well, boy, out of words suddenly, or does your guilt make you choke on your answer?'

He couldn't breathe and had to use both hands to ease the pressure of just one of the Saint's fingers on his throat. He desperately gulped down a lungful of air. 'I—'

The Saint stuffed a glass phial into Jillan's mouth and forced his jaws to close on it. The glass shattered, lacerated his lips and spiked into the soft palate at the top of his mouth. The Saint's wide thumb stroked down the front of Jillan's neck and triggered the swallowing reflex. Jillan tasted blood, most of it his own, but then a liquid that moved like an eel slithered down his gullet as well. He wanted to retch, but too quickly it was squirming all through him, as if seeking something. Mercifully, he managed to avoid taking down any of the glass and spat it free of his lips.

'And in return for my blood, I will now have yours. As your Saint, it is mine by right. *You* are mine by right. I own the People of this region, body and mind. None are permitted magic other than by my say-so and good grace. Yet you are a traitor. For the safety of the Empire, your life and magic are forfeit,' Azual said with satisfaction and raised a thin tube of sun-metal. He held it like a knife, pulled it back and prepared to stab it into the base of Jillan's neck. Jillan experienced a flashback as he saw the Empire's emissary stab down with a knife into the neck of the pagan chieftain.

He will bleed you until there's not a drop left. You're just going to let this happen, are you, after all the efforts I've made?

No! He did not want it to end like this, with this meaningless horror. He could not let it end like this. What would happen to his parents, or to Samnir and Hella? Would they be next? He reached desperately for some sort of power, any sort of power. It was slow to respond, torpid and sluggish. The Saint's blood in him fought against his attempts, coating, dampening and muffling his magic. Come on! It rose reluctantly.

Why are you struggling then, Jillan? Didn't you say you wanted rid of this taint, you wanted it gone, you wanted it out of you? Well, your Saint will give you precisely that. You must decide once and for all what it is you want. You must truly decide if you will give yourself to me once and for all. If you truly wish to fight the Saint and the insidious, paralysing negation he represents, it is the only way. Here is your final moment of choice, warrior. Choose! Will you give yourself over to me?

I can't!

Choose!

With a sob that racked his entire being, he gave himself to the magic. It poured from him as a coruscating liquid fire, sweeping through the chamber, washing along the Saint's arms and over his head. Red lava boiled from Jillan's mouth and eyes and he spat it at the detestable creature in front of him.

The Saint howled and staggered back, frantically trying to scrub the magic from his face. Aspin registered the danger he was in, but had no strength to get out of its path. There was nothing high enough off the ground to save him. Magic licked up his clothes and set him alight. He screamed.

The Saint lurched away from Jillan, clearing the path out of the cell. His skin bubbled and the smell of sizzling pork filled the room.

Get the sword!

Jillan took a faltering step forward, the magic stuttering for a moment. With determination, he drew more power from the core of his being and took long strides towards his weapon. His vision began to swim and the magic abruptly snuffed out. One more step and the wall was tilting through ninety degrees. He realised, as if from a long way away, that he was lying on his side. The sword was only a few feet from his nose, but his arms wouldn't obey him.

Somewhere Aspin groaned, put his back against a wall and pushed with his legs until he was standing.

Then came a chilling voice. A charred and hairless Saint emerged out of the darkness near the lower punishment chambers. 'Stupid child!' he sneered. 'Did you really think my blood that is in you would let you kill me? Did you really think your bastardised pagan magicks could stand against the will and power of the blessed Saviours?'

'Jillan, get up!' Aspin begged.

Jillan flailed for the hilt of the sword, found it, but his fingers had no strength. The Saint's foot came down on his hand and ground it against the floor. Pain and adrenalin gave him a few seconds of focus as he cried out. Aspin hopped over to them and kicked at the Saint's knee, bringing all his weight down against the joint in a direction in which it was not designed to bend. As strong as the Saint was, he could not stay on his feet as his leg buckled. Azual shouted in anger as his wide seven-foot frame fell awkwardly against the stone floor.

Aspin hopped forward on one leg and kicked the Saint hard beneath the chin with his other foot, the mountain warrior keeping perfect balance the whole time. The Saint's head went back and his throat was exposed. Aspin stamped down with his kicking leg, intent on crushing his loathsome enemy's windpipe.

A large hand shot out and caught the base of Aspin's foot. The hand twisted his leg savagely. 'I don't think so, little pagan!' Then Aspin was hurled aside as the Saint rose.

Azual lifted the tapping tube of sun-metal again. 'You see, my moment of transformation cannot be denied. It has an inevitability that can only be destiny. And I created that destiny. My will is my destiny. Events and timelines align around my organising power, a power that owns, dictates and decides your individual existence, the existence of the communities and the existence of the People. It was *I* who brought them into the Empire, it was *I* who Drew them to the Saviours, it is *I* who provides them with their entire meaning. Behold the moment of ascension and godhead, paltry and eternally unworthy beings!'

The tube plunged down towards Jillan's heart. He bucked and magic flared brightly across his chest, burning his white shirt away and revealing the armour below. The symbols over his heart glowed and the strength of Azual's blow rebounded back at the smouldering Saint, flinging the holy one back. The Saint slid unceremoniously across the stone floor, charred skin tearing off him in long strips.

The sun-metal sword had been dragged away in the struggle, and was beyond Jillan's reach. 'Aspin?' he whispered, but there was no response or sound. Azual slowly began to stir.

Breathing hard, Jillan struggled into a seated position and reached a hand beneath his armour to pull out a handful of the stones he had brought with him for luck and strength. His fumbling fingers dropped all of them save one. The rest scattered and skittered across the floor.

The Saint rolled over noiselessly and got his arms under him. He levered himself up. His terrible eye swung towards Jillan. 'The armour! It is the same armour, is it not? Ha. You cannot know.'

'I know,' Jillan panted, having to work his jaw. 'I was there!'

'Impossible!' the Saint hissed. 'None survived. None!'

'It is not just the Saint who always knows. You are *not* special! You are nothing, you hear me? You believe in nothing, give nothing to the People and turn the lives of everyone into nothing!'

'Enough!' the Saint shouted, but his voice lacked the devastating power of before. 'You are ignorant of the ways of power. You *know* nothing! You prattle like one of the simple-minded folk they usually throw down a well.'

'You're wrong! I know plenty. Plenty about you.'

'What are you talking about?'

Jillan took a deliberate breath, stealing moments where he could to recover. The problem was, the Saint would also be recovering. 'Haven't you read all the Book of Saviours? Some Saint you are! There's a whole chapter about you in it. Everyone knows what your father did to you, but you don't need to take it out on everyone else!'

'You will not mention . . . him!'

'Ha! Just because he was cruel, humiliated you and took your freedom away doesn't mean you can then do the same to everyone else. I saw what you did to the pagans before Godsend ever existed. You stole their land. You burned their homes. You killed them. You took away the freedom of others. There's nothing holy about you whatsoever!'

'Blasphemy!' the Saint seethed, slapping the floor. 'Evil child!' He moved towards Jillan again. 'You have never seen the Saviours. You cannot know their glory. They have brought peace and prosperity to all. Within their Empire none can behave like my father once did. They have brought us their divine salvation, even though most are unworthy. And the unworthy refuse to understand, refuse to acknowledge the wonder of the Saviours, refuse to bow to them, refuse to perform the duty and sacrifice requested of them, although it is in their own interest and the interest of all the People. For the good of all, the unworthy must be corralled, controlled and forced to their knees in prayer.'

'Stay back, murderer! I'm warning you!'

But the Saint was no longer listening. He made noises of inchoate rage as he came. His eye burned the air with uncontrolled power. A fierce heat radiated from him and smoke rose from his head.

Jillan gulped and tried to still the shaking in his hands. He waited until the last possible moment and then threw his stone straight at the Saint's eye.

A screech piercing body and mind. The Saint arching backwards. Blood spurting and spraying. Limbs lashing and head thrashing. Blinded.

Bile and fear in his throat, Jillan shunted back as far as he could. He had to get up.

'Here, get on my back!' A ragged Aspin coughed and bent down to him.

Jillan pulled himself up. 'Wait! The sword!'

Aspin carried him over to the weapon and bent again so that Jillan could lean for it.

The Saint slashed the air with arms outstretched and fingers formed into talons. Aspin kept low and stayed out of reach. The Saint suddenly stilled, listening for movement. 'I can hear you breathing,' he sang, his voice turned to madness. 'I can smell you!' His tongue slavered. 'I can taste you on the air. Come here. To me.'

'Go, go!' Jillan urged.

Aspin half limped and half danced to the steps, and then they were climbing free, cool air filling their lungs as if it were their first breath in many minutes.

'Come back here!' the Saint cooed. 'Jillan, I have your parents in Hyvan's Cross. I will have them executed when I arrive there, unless you deliver yourself to me before then. Come here. Their deaths will be ugly and lingering.' A moment of pause. Then an explosive command that echoed off the sky: 'Heroes, awake! The punishment chambers! Captain, raise the men! Guard the gates!'

'Quickly, down there,' Jillan said in Aspin's ear.

'Ow! I can't hear you. Use the other ear.'

'Sorry . . . Down there. To the wagon and horse.' Jillan gulped air.

'You'll have to drive it for us. To the end of the street and left to the smaller western gate.'

'But the guards, Jillan . . .'

'We are the blacksmith's sons. He's in the back of the wagon there, with plague . . . I found him at the physicker-woman's when I went to buy a sleeping draught from her for the guards. We've been told to get him out of town before he can infect anyone else . . . They'll let us out quick enough, you'll see. But the Saint will see through the eyes of the guards and know which way we've gone, so we'll have to get the horse moving as fast as we can once we're outside, and get the wagon off the road when we can.'

'D-does he really have plague?'

'Oh, aye!' Jillan laughed, tiredness and relief making him giddy.

'Oh, good. I was worried things were about to get boring.'

'Well, you're a new visitor to the Empire, aren't you? It's only polite to show you some entertainment. Come on! Can't you go any faster?'

'I think there's something wrong with the air down here in the stinking lowlands.'

'Doesn't seem to stop you speaking.'

'Well, your gabble makes me wish I was deaf in both ears.'

'Carry on, and you might just get your wish.'

'Hmm. Maybe I'll just leave you for the Saint.'

'What, when we're having so much fun?' Jillan giggled and then cried with tiredness. His eyes closed and he knew no more.

Minister Praxis clung to Torpeth, trying not to breathe. The pagan holy man smelt worse than the mule upon which they rode. The holy man's nakedness and filth were exactly what the Minister would expect of the uncivilised pagans, but actually having to come into contact with them was surely far beyond the worst suffering any Saint in the entire history of the Empire could ever have had to endure.

When Torpeth had insisted on riding the Minister's mule with him, the Minister had naturally refused point blank – only those of a higher station within civilisation were accorded the right to travel upon the backs of lesser creatures or beings. But the treacherous mule had refused to move an inch from Torpeth's home until the holy man's skinny buttocks were perched on the beast's shoulder blades and he had made a clicking noise with his tongue to tell the mule it was all right to proceed. Here was further proof, were it needed, of the base nature of the pagans, for it was clear the man and the beast had conspired together. They were of a similar mind and lesser nature. The pagan was a witch-man with savage beasts as his familiars.

The Minister cringed away from Torpeth's back, which was directly in front of his nose, but he only succeeded in making his seat on the mule dangerously precarious. If he were to become dislodged, his fall probably wouldn't stop until he was at the bottom of the vertiginous slope they were climbing. His head would be split open on a rock and there would be little even the Saviours could do for him. Ugh! Were there things moving in Torpeth's matted hair? The man was infested with lice, blood-fleas, maggots no doubt, and all the creatures of corruption. He was a living embodiment of the Chaos! There was no way the Minister could hold close to him, even if it cost him his life. He prayed ardently.

Almost immediately he began to itch all over. The creatures of the Chaos had inevitably attacked him now that his sacred prayers had disturbed them. Ah, how he suffered! But he had to endure, had to remain strong in faith, else fear and doubt would topple him from his seat and undo him. Ah, but the Chaos was subtle and cunning in its ways. It inveigled itself into even mundane tasks like riding a mule up a mountain. He would not yield! He would ascend this mountain of challenge, he would prove the transcendence of his faith and the will of the blessed Saviours, he would ascend to Sainthood. He would become the more enlightened and powerful being who was Saint Praxis of the Mountains!

'What are you muttering to yourself now, lowlander?' Torpeth asked, hawking and spitting into the wind, only to have it blown back into his beard, not that he seemed to care. 'You know you muttered the whole night through, do you not? Troubled dreams?'

Disgusting, soiled creature! Because he would not succumb to the skittering, jumping, biting Chaos creatures that infested them, the pagan now sought to attack his mind and self-belief. 'I pray even in my sleep,' the Minister replied calmly. 'My every thought, word and deed are described by my faith.'

'They are none of you, then? There is nothing of your own character and volition within them? Surely it is not faith then, is it? It is slavery of body, mind and spirit. How is it you ever know to loosen your bowels, for surely your so-called faith does not circumscribe your bowels, does it? Yet your body needs free will if it is to evacuate itself, does it not?'

The mule hiccuped and snorted as if to join in the pagan's scatological attempt at mockery. Yet the Minister knew the conversation had naught to do with humour; rather, it was an attempt to demean and undermine his faith.

'Wait, I have it!' the pagan continued with glee. 'You never loosen your bowels then! You never evacuate yourself! You are always full of it. No wonder you would have none of my pine nuts last night. No wonder you always have a pained expression on your face.'

The Minister remained stoical. He endured with fortitude. He would not be troubled by this devil. 'My faith feeds me. It is all I require.'

'But you do eat? Shame, I was hoping you were some sort of miracle from which I could learn. Your faith feeds you, you say. Does it also wipe your arse?'

Again, the pagan obsession with basic bodily functions, as if he were a young child who still had to learn not to soil himself. Minister Praxis responded with serene equanimity, 'My faith has brought me to this place to wipe the arse-end of the Empire, my tiresome and talkative friend.'

'Has it indeed?' Torpeth nodded, biting on his thumb for a moment. 'I see. Your faith and Empire occupy themselves with curious concerns then, concerns that are not entirely lofty, eh, even though you are now in the mountains? Still, your concerns would never be lofty given you are a *low*lander, hmm?'

Maybe I should throw this wretch down the mountain. No, for then the mule would rebel. And the Minister needed the wretch to guide him for a while longer. 'Word games, like in a school yard, pagan?'

'Look out! Beware!' Torpeth cried.

Minister Praxis twisted his head back and forth, suddenly scared.

Torpeth's behind trumpeted loudly.

'You odious ogre!' the Minister gagged, too late burying his nose in his sleeve. Tears came to his eyes.

'Your faith didn't see that coming then? I'm surprised – it seemed a bit of a know-it-all just before. And did you not have fair warning? Are you all right back there? Surely my lofty mountain wind has not unmanned you and shaken your faith, has it? Yet while you're back there, you did say you'd come to wipe the arse-end of the Empire, did you not? Well, wipe away! Be gentle, though, for I am quite attached to it, troublesome though it might sometimes be. Wipe away, I say! Come, lowlander, it is your holy mission, is it not? It would be blasphemous not to do it, would it not?'

Minister Praxis pulled a letter-opener from inside his long black coat and stabbed it with feeling and venom into Torpeth's bare backside.

'Aiee!' screamed the mountain man and leapt high over the mule's head. He danced around on the slope clutching his brutalised behind. 'Ye gods, but how you have pricked me, lowlander! Your faith is such a pain in my posterior. I did not know you had such a prick about you and that you were prepared to be so free with it! Is nothing sacred to you then? Was it not your sacred mission to wipe my holy arse? What crimes have you instead committed against it, then? Will you not beg forgiveness of my holy arse, for it is red raw with righteous rage! Look, see!'

Torpeth bent over as if the Minister cared for a better look at his livid behind. The Minister turned his face away and nudged the mule onwards. For once, the animal obeyed him, although that was probably because Torpeth hadn't told it to stop.

The holy man skipped alongside them, rubbing furiously at his tender flesh every now and then. He ran ahead, sat in some snow and shouted back at them, 'There is a lesson in all this. Your faith is cruel and unapologetic. It is not to be tangled with. It will inflict itself on others in whichever manner it chooses, no matter how those others might be harmed. It cannot bear to be questioned or laughed at. It—'

'And your faith is grotesque and reductive!' the Minister spat back. 'It prances about and flaunts itself. It lacks decency and decorum. It is utterly offensive, completely ill-mannered. It disgusts where it should seek to deserve. It is ignorant of reserve and deliberation, and far too familiar with filth and farting. It makes animals of men, while making men of animals. It—'

'It is honest and joyful, were you not blind and insensitive to it! It does not force itself on others and dictate to them. It does not give itself power while taking power from others through clothes, convention and circumscription. It does not imprison or end lives; rather, it explores and encourages life. It—'

'It is meaningless! It bows to no one or thing.'

'Not true! It deifies the Geas!'

'Prostitutes itself, rather! I know what lewd acts constitute your pagan rituals, and that you perform them in the hope of some power in return. You are a bestial, beaten and broken race.'

'The only thing that is beaten and broken round here is my arse! The only bestial act that has gone on is your attack on that very same arse. Yours is a faith that seeks to bestialise, beat and break any that will not enslave themselves to it. You cannot know otherwise, as it will not allow you thoughts of your own. Ack! I should have left you lost in the snow. I was a fool even to talk to you. Even if you were to hear, you would not listen. Even if you were to listen, you would not understand. The lower village deserves you, I reckon.'

The Minister smiled. 'Do you not get on with the lower village, pagan? Is not all well within even this small community? Tell me, what is wrong? Maybe I can help. Maybe the ways of the Empire and the blessed Saviours can help.'

Torpeth glowered at the Minister but did not reply. From thereon he stayed well ahead and away from the Minister and the mule. He did not even look at them as he led them to the lower village. The new travelling arrangements more than suited the Minister, as now he had clean air in his lungs, although he still needed to scratch himself intermittently, and he was now so hungry he felt light-headed enough to fly the rest of the way.

The youth was so handsome of face that he bewitched men, women and children alike. His eyes were large and soft, as green and lush as pasture one second and as blue and clear as the purest waters the next. His nose had a strong profile but gentle curves. His lips were full with promise yet firm of purpose. His chin was carved yet delicate. In short, he was so quixotically perfect that he should not have been able to exist. People were entranced to the point of stupidity when they looked upon him, but doubted their own memories when no longer in his presence. Surely the youth was some sort of dream or fantasy.

'Is he one of the blessed Saviours?' asked one of the younger Heroes in a hushed voice as they followed in the beautiful youth's wake.

'Is that a halo around his head? It's brighter than the heavens.'

'It's a helmet, I think.'

'Sun-metal p'raps. Must be worth a fortune.'

'But if any head is worthy of it, 'tis that one.'

The Peculiar walked slowly through Saint Goza's camp, his hands held out so that all could touch him. Whenever he adopted this form, the people flocked to him and sought some sort of contact, as if they could thereby receive a blessing. He indulged their simple ways, as it only increased their fervour and compliance.

It had been strange to see the walls of the Old Fort again. They had once been near-living things, radiant with power and faith. Now, they stood a tarnished and silent vigil, bearing witness to the slow decline of the people. They'd had such potential in the early days, led by their brave young gods, but had inevitably overreached themselves and been their own undoing. They'd become twisted, stunted and self-absorbed, easy prey for the elseworlders when they'd arrived. Now they were hardly recognisable compared to what they had once been. Surely it was only a matter of time before their demise was complete, given that even their Geas had run mad. Perhaps it would be kinder if he put them out of their misery once and for all. Perhaps.

They came to the large cauldron in the middle of the camp. The rock woman was already sat inside it, miserable in her chains of sun-metal. There was water up to her neck, and a roaring fire beneath. The water was close to boiling. Presumably the rock woman had been in the water from when it was cold, so that her body would not be able to perceive the steady rise in temperature; otherwise she would have been thrashing about already. There were probably worse ways to die, the Peculiar reflected, for this was perhaps like going to sleep in a warm bath. Of course the thought that someone would soon be eating you wasn't particularly pleasant, but a disciplined mind should be able to ignore that.

He cleared his throat and in a honeyed voice ordered the Heroes following him, 'Dowse the fire. Remove her from the cauldron. Release her chains.'

Like sleepwalkers or as if in a trance, a dozen or so of the Heroes moved to obey him. Steps were brought, and it took six of them to haul Freda's dead weight up and out of the bowl. Her sun-metal manacles fell to the ground with a soft thud, and she collapsed on top of them when the men stopped supporting her. The Peculiar crouched down near her.

'Freda, can you hear me? I have come to free you. I am your friend. Nod if you understand.'

She did so groggily.

'It is important that you do not go to sleep. Can you stay awake for me?'

Another nod.

'Get me a blanket soaked in cold water,' he directed the men.

The ground began to tremble. Several of the men blinked as they came back to themselves. They looked around in confusion and consternation. One of them slapped a comrade round the face to bring him back to full consciousness.

The Peculiar arched one of his perfectly expressive eyebrows. 'His Pigginess awakes! Prepare a trough and a bucket of slops.' The Heroes still under his spell tittered.

'Who dares disturb my camp?' a large voice echoed around them, blowing open the small hill that was the Saint's tent.

'Did someone hear something? Sounded like flatulence. Oo, be so good as to bring me a wagon, would you? I think it will be a while before my friend here is able to walk properly.'

Saint Goza emerged with his hammer of sun-metal and powered towards them, casting a shadow over all. 'Where do you think you're going with my dinner? Captain, what is the meaning of this?'

The Captain, who still stared raptly at the Peculiar, only managed an incoherent mumble. He dribbled from both corners of his mouth.

'I think he's in love.' The Peculiar beamed at the Saint. He fluttered his eyelids winsomely. 'My, you're a big one! Surely you have more than enough to spare. You do not need the rock woman.' He made his voice resonate with a full range of coercive and sympathetic tones.

The Saint shook his head as if troubled by flies. '*I* rule here! Guards, seize him!'

The Peculiar raised a forbidding hand and the Heroes around him froze. Now he used more discordant and strident vibrations to instil fear in the Saint. 'You *will* release her to me! It is the will of your Saviours! You must bow to that will!'

The Saint sounded like he'd all but lost the ability to speak. 'I . . . represent . . . their . . . will . . . here.'

Then the sweet and seductive song of compulsion: 'Come, dear one, you must know who I am. You know it would be futile to oppose me. It would only end in heartache and grief. You would be risking everything, for what? Just this harmless blighted woman, who is surely very far from a tasty morsel? You are merciful, magnanimous and enlightened. You will give her to me, knowing that the Saviours will reward you for your loyalty and faith. You will become prime among the Saints and all regions will hearken to your word and will. Come, nod your beauteous brow, dear one.'

Goza let his head fall forward as he said woodenly, 'Yes, I give her to you, to show my generosity and greatness. Take her.'

'Thank you, holy one. You are as wise as you are fat. Oh, just one thing before I go.' The Peculiar's voice became flat and deep to imprint itself on their minds and memories. 'You might want to think about bathing a bit more. There must be a lake big enough somewhere in this region, no? Or would that cause a drought? Someone your size must sweat constantly, I imagine, which creates quite a body odour, so most people no doubt smell you long before they see or hear you coming. I wouldn't be surprised if your Saviours in the Great Temple could smell you even from this distance. And maybe bits of food get caught in your folds of flesh and then rot. Just how many chins do you have? Lost any attendants recently? Maybe they got trapped in one of your folds or chins and found themselves unable to fight their way free. Or perhaps you sat down too hastily one time and your crack swallowed . . . Anyway, you get the idea. Time I was off, I'm afraid, good people. Now, don't cry. Busy, busy, you know how it is. Build a shrine to me or something if you really are going to miss me that much. That's it. Get my friend up into the wagon there. That's it. Well done. A fond farewell to you all. Come on, you're all big soldiers. No weeping and wailing now. Bye, bye! Bye, bye! That's it, wave. You'll feel better.'

Heroes sobbed in each other's arms. The Saint blew his nose on his sleeve, the strength of the blast knocking his manservant over and splattering him with mucus. Some cheered as he left, others groaned as if they must surely die because they were so heartbroken. One sensitive soul tried to compose an impromptu ode to the wondrous stranger and ran after them, declaiming it loudly.

The Peculiar flicked the reins to increase their pace. 'We'd best get out of here before someone with brains about them questions what happened here. Once one of them starts having doubts and suspicions, it quickly spreads and the shared illusion is shattered. If they were to chase us, things would get extremely tedious, not to mention messy.'

'Thhhank you,' Freda enunciated carefully, her tongue and the rest of her so swollen that she did not feel like she was in her own body. 'I am Fffreda. What is your name?'

The Peculiar gave her his sunniest and most loving smile. 'You're welcome, Fffreda. In return for saving you, I want nothing but your friendship. I say nothing, yet such friendship would be of great, great value to me. I try to do good things to make good friends, you see. It doesn't often work, but you seem nice.'

'I do?' the rock woman asked with shy happiness. 'I would like to be your friend. I don't have any other friends in the sky-cave of the Overlords, you see.'

'That's good then.'

'But what is your name, friend?'

He grinned, wondering which name it was safest to give her. One of his few strictures was that he might not invent a name for himself. 'Many have called me Anupal. How about that, Freda?'

'A-nu-pal,' she repeated, trying it out.

'That's it. Now, in return for my name, Freda, will you promise not to run away and leave me alone in this scary . . . sky-cave?'

She didn't hesitate. 'Of course, Anupal. I don't want to be alone here either. I promise.'

'Oh, thank you, dear Freda. You don't know what that means to me. And, tell me, do you think I'm handsome?'

Now she did hesitate. 'Er . . . of course, Anupal.' She sounded like she was being polite or didn't want to upset him. He did not like that, not one little bit. This one would need watching, very careful watching.

'Why don't you get some rest, dear Freda? You must be quite exhausted after all you've been through. I will keep us heading south, although the clever horse seems to know where I want it to take us.'

At his suggestion, her eyes began to droop. She yawned, 'What does *south* mean, Anupal?'

'Hmm. It's like *down*, Freda, whereas *north* is like *up*, if you see.'

She tried to frown, but couldn't hang on to it as she was dragged into sleep. 'I probably like south far more than north then. Explain it more to me later though, Anupal, when . . . when . . .'

Jillan wandered through the ruined landscape, searching for signs of life, anything. All that remained of the trees were burned-out hulks or drifting piles of ash. The sky was one continuous pall of black smoke, precious little light getting through from above. Superheated rocks and smouldering remains glowed enough for him to see by, although he was not sure what there was left to look at and how much more of this devastation he really wanted to see. It was stifling hot and the air was thick with cinders and dust.

He coughed and staggered over the next rise, kicking up plumes of ash with each step. Ahead of him was a large green hill. On the top grew fruit trees and cattle were grazing. Clear air and sunlight surrounded the heights. A sea of desperate people surged up the slopes, but they broke against an unyielding line of Heroes who stabbed down with spears tipped with sun-metal. On the very crest of the hill was a large throne on which basked the one-eyed Saint Azual.

The Saint immediately saw Jillan. 'What are you doing in my dream, pagan?' he roared across the gulf separating them.

'Are these your thoughts?' Jillan asked, sickened.

'Get out of my head!' Azual howled, leaping from his throne and across the divide, landing ten yards short of Jillan. 'How dare you presume to judge me? All this is far beyond your understanding.'

'What's to understand? Is this all you desire? Or is it some nightmare?'

'Your intrusion is destroying its beauty,' Azual asserted and ran at Jillan, delivering him a glancing blow to the head.

Jillan blinked and looked up at a blue sky. He breathed clean air and was relieved to see healthy trees passing on each side. There was another jolt and he realised he was in the back of a moving wagon.

'Sorry about that.' Aspin smiled back at him. 'This road isn't as smooth as the one from the main gate out of Saviours' Paradise. Lot of loose stones. How're you feeling? They don't appear to be chasing us, but I thought it wise to put some distance between ourselves and the town rather than waiting for you to wake up. We've been travelling all night.'

'Water?'

Aspin passed him a leather water bag and Jillan sluiced the phantom ash from his mouth.

'That's better. Thanks.' Jillan picked his way past the unconscious blacksmith and joined Aspin on the top board. Feeling a bit woozy, he asked, 'Got anything to eat?'

Aspin passed him a small slightly shrivelled apple. Jillan swallowed it in a few bites. It would do until they stopped and ate something more substantial.

'He hasn't woken up at all then?'

Aspin shook his head. 'Hasn't even moved. And he looks awfully pale. I haven't gone too close to him, obviously, but he's clearly in a bad way. Nearly all his hair has fallen out now, and there's blood on his lips and around his nose. Unless we can get him to eat something, he'll only get weaker and weaker, and then he'll die. But I don't want to touch him, so we can't feed him either.'

Jillan rubbed at his forehead, a stabbing headache between his eyes making it hard to think. 'If he comes round, the Saint will be able to see us through his eyes too. He'll know everything we say and do, where we're going, everything.'

'That settles it then,' Aspin said through tight lips.

'What does?'

'We'll have to leave him somewhere.'

'What? We can't just leave him!'

Aspin looked at the younger boy as if he was crazy. 'Of course we can. It's not our fault he's got the plague. There's nothing we can do to help him. And the longer we keep him, the greater the chance we'll catch it too.'

If only he didn't have this headache. 'Look, it's just not right. Don't you understand? We took him from the town just so we could escape. If we'd left him with the physicker-woman, she might have cured him.

We're responsible. We can't just leave him by the road, knowing that will kill him.'

'Everything dies, Jillan,' Aspin replied flatly. 'It's just his time, that's all. Perhaps you're too young to understand. Or just squeamish. Have you ever seen a dead person before?'

'I didn't hear you saying I was too young when I rescued you! And of course I've seen dead people. I've *killed* people! I bet you haven't.'

Aspin's face became scornful. 'I'm a warrior and a hunter. I understand fighting and killing better than other types of people. And, anyway, I'd have escaped without your help.'

'You liar!'

'I am no liar. You'd better not be insulting my honour. You'd better be careful.'

'Honour?' Jillan sneered. 'How is leaving a man to die by the road honourable? You're just a murdering pagan!'

'Take that back!' Aspin snarled, putting his hand to his knife. 'I'm warning you.'

Jillan drew on his magic, the headache exploding through his mind. Seeing only red, he flung Aspin off the wagon. He saw the warrior's heart beating in his chest, saw how easy it would be to burst it. Yet that would be too quick and not at all satisfying. He would make the pagan suffer first, pouring more and more into him. He felt so strong, so *right*, when he burned with power like this. Surely now he would become one with the Saviours and ascend to godhead. At last, he would rule all the People of this pathetic world.

I will not let you destroy me like this, the taint rattled, trying to deny Jillan its magic.

'Yes!' Jillan belched in the Saint's voice. 'My will is all powerful. *I* rule here!'

Jillan felt himself being torn apart as the taint and the power of the Saint's blood warred for control; as his magic demanded release, the Saint sought to kill and his mind begged him to save Aspin. He was going to die like this!

'Jillan, stop!' Aspin pleaded from where he lay on the road, lightning arcing and crackling wildly around him. 'I'm sorry! We'll take the blacksmith with us.'

The blacksmith! Jillan turned towards the dying man and deliberately unleashed the pent-up fury within him. With that energy gone, the energy that had sustained him as much as it had poisoned him, Jillan was left helpless. He pitched off the wagon and onto the road next to Aspin.

'Wow, that's some temper you have,' the mountain warrior observed. 'Remind me never to get into an argument with you again, eh? Jillan? Jillan?'

Children and villagers alike chased along behind Minister Praxis as Torpeth led him up through the lower village of the mountain people. Most wore furs or goatskins, the warriors tending to go bare-armed and bare-legged. They were full of curiosity, the women stretching to feel the material of his coat, the children shouting questions at him and the men deliberately standing in his path to see if he would challenge or step around them. Nearly all of them had wide flat faces, blunt noses and heavy brows.

Inbred savages, the Minister thought to himself, slapping away a few of the hands that pawed at him, causing general merriment among the crowd. How could such people even be worth saving? Surely they could add nothing of value to the Empire except, perhaps, as slave labour. Yet even then they looked too clumsy and unruly to be worth the trouble of supervision. How could such vermin actually be a threat to the Empire? Ah, but the Chaos was subtle and cunning. Appearances were always deceptive when it came to the ancient enemy. Simple they might look, but that was sure to be some disguise for their devious and divisive nature. These people had secrets, secrets that he must discover for the Empire. How else could they have resisted and survived for so long?

There didn't seem to be a level path anywhere. A twisted and crooked place, just like its people. His calf muscles were soon sore and burning, but he refused to stop amid this rabble. He kept his head above them, where the air was no doubt cleaner. At least he and Torpeth had divested themselves of the mule upon entering the village, so the moody beast was no longer around to add to the Minister's vexation and torment. With luck, one of the savages would make a stew of it, boil its bones down for glue, or some other suitable punishment.

Between the stone hovels in which the savages lived the Minister spied an occasional area of roughly turned and raked ground. Very little grew here in the cold and among the stones, however. *Even the earth is loath to support these corrupt creatures*, the Minister decided. Nothing of beauty could ever grow here. On the slopes above the village some terraces had apparently been cut, but they seemed abandoned. He looked more closely at some of the people. They seemed well fed nonetheless. There didn't appear to be enough goats around to feed them all, and surely there wasn't much game to be found in this inhospitable environment. It was plain to him, therefore, that the pagans either regularly descended into the Empire to steal food or consumed their young. After all, did the Chaos not multiply wherever and whenever it could? These mountains would have been buried in pagans were it not for their apparent cannibalism. Furthermore, did not scripture say that all corruption ultimately consumed itself?

Evil, unholy creatures. How could they laugh and smile, knowing what they'd done? Grinning ghouls. Perhaps they were eyeing him up even now for their cooking pots. Trying to get a measure of the length of spit they'd need to roast him. Blessed Saviours preserve him. Was there no end to their shamefulness?

'Torpeth, wait for me!' he called, lifting his long legs in as spritely a manner as his cramping calves would allow.

This caused the villagers much hilarity and they all tried to mimic his ungainly gait. Torpeth stopped to watch, twining his beard through his fingers. 'Perhaps you have hidden talents, lowlander. For all your strange aloofness, it seems they like you. Share some of your magic with me and I'll rethink that curse I'd intended for you.'

'You would think to lay a curse on me?' the Minister asked in outrage. 'How dare you! My faith need have no fear of you or your curses.' Then he considered for a moment. 'Yet I will share some of my . . . magic with you in return for your secrets.'

Torpeth stuck a finger in his ear and waggled it about vigorously. Examining the end of it, he tasted it experimentally and mumbled, 'I'll think on it. You want to taste some of this? It's good, although not as good as pine nuts. Suit yourself. This way then.'

They moved up through the village to the large hovel at the end. It seemed to sit across the path that wound up into the peaks.

Torpeth tried to drag his fingers through his hair and only succeeded in getting his hands caught. He jumped and skipped as he tried to yank them out. At last they came free, but with clumps of hair ripped from his scalp. Next he spat in his hands and wiped his hair as flat as it would go, which wasn't flat at all. Finally he grabbed an old piece of rope from somewhere and tied it around his waist, the ends dangling between his legs and almost covering his manhood.

'How do I look?' he asked the Minister anxiously.

'Er . . . like a haystack?'

Torpeth nodded. 'Good, good. What's a haystack? I can't remember. Never mind, it sounds exotic.' He tapped the side of his nose. 'Always does well to look one's best for the headwoman, if you know what I mean.'

The Minister nodded.

'But don't get any ideas, you hear!' Torpeth added fiercely, waving his dirty finger beneath the Minister's pinched nose. 'I've been wooing her for decades. I saw her first. I've known her since she was a child. I won't have any outsider coming in here with his fancy ways and sweeping her off her feet. And don't go using any of your magicks to befuddle and infatuate her, neither.'

'My friend, how could I ever be a rival to one such as you, you being such a fine example of manhood and all?'

This seemed to mollify the pagan. 'True enough. Not everyone seems to have your clarity of vision, for some reason.'

'Well, they're self-deluded fools, my friend, self-deluded fools. You should pity them. Yet there is a problem I foresee.'

'There is? Where?' Torpeth asked, looking all around, inside men's tunics, under women's long dresses and into children's hats, scaring most of the villagers away.

'Come here and listen. If this headwoman has captured the heart of such a fine man as yourself, then surely she must be a wondrous beauty.'

'Oh aye, she is.'

'Well, then, it will surely be hard to keep my wits about me to resist her charms, no? I suspect you are asking a very great deal of me.'

'Ah, I see. Yes, perhaps I am. Would it be easier for you if I removed your head? Or blindfolded you? Or both?'

'It would be a shame to kill me when you are still desirous of my magicks, would it not? And surely a blindfold would not work when her voice is no doubt as beautiful as her visage.'

'Then should I break your ears? A few stabs with a long needle would do it.' Torpeth nodded. Then dubiously, 'Or cut out the headwoman's tongue?'

'No, that would be messy and unsightly. You do not want to drip blood in the headwoman's home, do you? No, there is only one way. Listen, my friend. With the proper motivation, I am sure I could find a way to resist her. I will make my determination central to my character and faith. But the motivation must be great indeed and therefore help me with my holy task, a task that defines me. You must agree to share your secrets with me so that I may better fulfil my task.'

Torpeth looked troubled. He jumped from one foot to the other. 'There is no other way? Either I tell you my secrets or she is lost to me? Ah, the gods are yet cruel! Why must they still test and punish me like this? Am I not already a naked warrior? But my crime was so great there could never be a punishment great enough. At last I understand why the gods brought you here, lowlander. It is to see to my further punishment. And my people continue to suffer for it so that I must witness the ongoing consequences of what I have done. That is why you have come – to create division, visit pain and heap misery on us – is it not? That is your holy task, I now see.'

'I regret to say it is so, my friend, although it grieves me.'

'Ah, payment is ever due!'

'Yes, payment is due.'

'I knew it!' Tears left clean tracks down his cheeks, probably the first water they'd seen in a good while. 'Very well, you will have my secrets, as long as you leave me my love. She is all that is left to me, all that I have . . . except for my pine nuts, and no one seems to want those anyway. Come then, lowlander.'

They passed over the sill of the headwoman's large stone dwelling, stepping into a smoky interior. Minister Praxis thought he saw shadowy figures before them, but the smoke shifted and they were gone. He was immediately on guard. If this was a place of unholy spirits and demons, then they would by no means find him easy prey. The headwoman was likely to be a witch. How else would a female have risen to any sort of position of power? Who else would be able to command the naked and noisome pagan at his side? Yes, a place of pestilence and perversion. After all, it was outside the Empire. It was probably the gaping maw of the very Chaos itself.

The Minister licked his dry lips, feeling more than a little trepidation despite the strength of his faith. Sweat trickled from his brow and he tugged at his collar. He was infernally hot one moment and cold to the marrow the next. The laws of nature and order did not operate here. Perhaps the smoke was the breath of the Chaos. It was filling his lungs even now, seeking to take hold.

'We've entered the mouth of a dragon!' He shuddered.

'Don't be daft, lowlander,' Torpeth coughed. 'Whoever heard of such a thing? Sal puts herbs on her fire upon occasion to help with her visions and that. It's probably run away with you is all.' Then he shouted, 'Beloved, I'm here!'

'Who's that?' croaked a voice that sounded anything but human. 'Some old goat who should know better that's got curious and wandered in from outside?'

Torpeth cackled as if it were the funniest thing he'd ever heard. 'Beloved, here is a lowlander come to bring us great suffering. Will he be admitted to the higher village?'

'And why exactly would I permit such a thing, eh?'

Torpeth pulled Minister Praxis towards the sound of the toad somewhere in the rolling smoke. If it was able to speak, the toad had to be a Chaos creature that had swallowed down some unfortunate wanderer. Perhaps he was next! The pagan was leading him towards a hungry, wide-mouthed monster. Once it had devoured him, it would be able to speak in many tongues, in many voices. It was legion! An impossibly long and sticky tongue was about to come snaking out of the gloom, wrap itself around his neck and drag him into its insatiable bottomless maw. He would fall, and fall, and fall, forever! Spinning through the eternal void and emptiness that was the Chaos.

'Blessed Saviours preserve me!' he shrieked, staggering as the heathen floor tripped him. He fell to his knees and began a shaky prayer.

'It is the will of the gods, beloved. Sinisar of the Shining Path lit his way here. Gar of the Still Stone did not trap his feet, Akwar of the Wandering Waters did not block his way with rain and snow, and Wayfar of the Warring Winds did not batter him back with a tempest.'

Torpeth dragged the kneeling Minister into the presence of a wizened old woman whose skin was as lined and dark as an ancient oak. Her eyes, though, were a startling blue, and as clear as any child's.

'What's he doing?' she creaked. 'I do not usually ask that visitors pray to me, although I must say it suits him well.'

'Beloved, there are many strange things about these lowlanders that I do not understand.'

'But you do understand that they are our enemies, do you not, you muddled old goat? How could you not? You were there when our people lived upon the lower lands. You were there when the others drove them out. Why then do you bring their vassal before me and speak on his behalf?'

'Beloved, I do not know that the lowlanders are our enemies. The events of the past are continuous with the events of today. The lowlanders that we were are continuous with the lowlanders of today. We are all one with the Geas.'

'Careful, old goat. It was your thinking in the past that caused so much trouble. Your thinking of today might well keep that trouble continuous. You cannot dispute that the others are our enemies. They seek to make the Geas their own – you know this. They will destroy our way of life. They will destroy all life.'

Torpeth nodded. 'Who is to say our way of life should continue forever? All life ends, beloved.'

'To be reborn again! The others would bring an absolute end, however. Who am I to say they should not be permitted to bring that end? Just an old woman who cannot stand the cold any more. Yet it is not for the others to decide they have the right to do so either. The right belongs to the Geas alone, and none other.'

'P'raps so, p'raps so, beloved. But, as we are, we can do nothing to prevent the others. Something needs to change. This lowlander will change things, I know it. He has a magic of sorts. Who is to say he does not do the work of the Geas, even if it is unwitting on his part?'

The headwoman sighed. 'And if you are wrong, you condemn us all. Still playing with all our lives then, unrepentant and unlearning Torpeth? Perhaps it is you who still needs to change. It is you who still needs to be punished and sees us punished. Here is my decision then, old goat. I will let you take this one to the higher village, but still I refuse to be yours.'

Torpeth's face became tragic, his shoulders hung dejectedly, and he looked down as if in shame. His whisper was hoarse. 'Thank you, beloved, for seeing me again.'

'Go now, old goat, for there is nothing more for you here. Yet do not tarry in the higher village overlong, for you know well that the warriors near the peak are neither gentle nor as forgiving of you as those of the lower village. There are several who have pledged themselves to Wayfar, and he was ever quick, tempestuous and slow to abate.'

D'Zel, organising intellect of the northern region, had long considered D'Selle of the western region a fool. As a corollary, the north was run efficiently and had a Saint in Goza who understood the value of things in terms of how they added to both his own and the Empire's strength, while the west was decadent and had the self-beautifying and profligate Izat as Saint. A flawed Saint was nothing new, of course, as they were of a far lesser race, but a foolhardy Saviour simply could not be tolerated, lest they threaten to bring down the whole. Imagine confronting one as young and inexperienced as D'Shaa like that! Every Saviour in the Great Temple had sensed the echoes of the encounter and effectively witnessed what had gone on. D'Selle simply could not resist gloating over the Saviour of the south, could he, but how much triumph was there in catching out the newest of the organising intellects? More than that, it had been extremely incautious of him to show his hand and let others know where he'd been directing all of his energies.

It was just incredible that D'Selle had managed to survive so long with such clumsy plotting. Fortune favoured the brave, true, but it just as quickly saw to the downfall and demise of the foolish. D'Zel pondered that, wondering if D'Selle might actually be more subtle than he appeared. No, surely not. He could not have foreseen that D'Shaa would have approached Elder Thraal in desperation and secured the release of the Peculiar. As a consequence, however, the imbecile had placed the entire Empire in an unstable and unpredictable position. What had D'Selle been thinking, to attack D'Shaa instead of waiting several more centuries in order to assess fully her style of operation? He should have known better than to attack an unknown quantity.

If D'Zel had been in Elder Thraal's position, he would have had D'Selle undone immediately for erring so badly. Not only was D'Selle utterly humiliated, but he had also exposed himself badly. Such negligence could not go unpunished. Did the elders expect D'Selle to undo himself because of lost honour or overwhelming shame? Well, they'd be waiting a long time, for he had already shown he was completely without shame or honour.

D'Zel wondered at Elder Thraal's lack of action in the matter. He also had to wonder at the precipitous decision to unleash the Peculiar. Was the elder's judgement everything it should be? It was not unknown for the minds of some of the most ancient to become lost on the Great Voyage. Their intellects would become all but entirely detached from reality or too tightly bound up with it. They were no longer able to retain focus and individuality in the waking dream. Everything would lose meaning or everything would take on immediate meaning and overwhelm them. Was there an opportunity here, then, to supplant the elder? Imagine what it would be like to join the vastness of the elders, to see and reach across time and the cosmos. But how did one supplant an elder? What mechanisms could there possibly be to effect it? Hmm. He could seek an audience with Elder Thraal as D'Shaa had done, could he not? The precedent had been set. Yes, it was a beginning, and a beginning was often a means to an end.

In the meantime, the north now demanded his immediate attention. His region had been well in hand – Goza had managed to get off his substantial rear and subdue the rock woman with little trouble. He'd been about to consume her and learn whatever secrets she held concerning the Geas, but then the Peculiar had intervened and taken her beyond his control or influence. Damn that D'Selle – and D'Shaa, come to that. If the rock woman caused trouble elsewhere in the Empire, then he would look negligent in some part himself. He would no longer be able to accuse D'Selle from an unassailable position. D'Selle would be able to share the appearance of negligence around all the organising intellects of the same rank, as if it were a contagion of sorts, and the elders would find it almost impossible to single him out for punishment.

Again, he had to wonder if D'Selle was more cunning than he realised. Could it be that the Saviour of the western region had spies in the north, had learned of the rock woman, understood her likely connection to the Geas and then triggered a series of events that would wrest the rock woman from D'Zel's clutches? Was it possible, incredible as it might seem? Surely no Saviour had such foresight! Unless they had sources of information and assistance about which D'Zel knew nothing.

Either way, D'Zel now knew he would have to take action against D'Selle himself. His hand was being forced. That made him hesitate. Was there an intellect looking to make him act, hoping to bring him out into the open, where he would inevitably be more vulnerable? *Perhaps an alliance with D'Shaa would be advantageous, then, although she is flighty and unpredictable. At the same time, she is inspired and has shown great ability to survive under adverse conditions. I could do far worse than align myself with such as her. I might even make a Declaration for her, although that might tie me too much to her, and make it impossible to be rid of her should she become a liability. Yet I need to attach her to me if I am to be sure of having some part of the boy being used by the Geas. The Empire has become unstable, but an alliance would bring some stability to my position.*

How best to be rid of D'Selle then? A number of ways presented themselves, but none of them seemed quite elegant or poetic enough. D'Selle needed to suffer before being undone, not because of anything as absurd as irony, revenge or justice, but simply because D'Zel enjoyed causing others' suffering. It was his one vice, but why else would he consent to remain on this primitive world unless it was to create suffering? What else was there to keep him entertained while the life was inexorably Drawn from the Geas over millennia? Suffering was the nature of existence and eternity, but he who imposed it on others was closer to absolute rule than anyone else.

Yes, if D'Selle was to suffer, then D'Selle's region – the western region – would first need to be destabilised. It was time to give Goza a little more exercise, and to use the spy he had planted in the west. Then would come the culling. Ah, the delicious culling!

CHAPTER 9:

To punish and protect us

The wind was like a cold blade scraped across his throat. Minister Praxis raised his collar against it. The wind became angry and threatened to pluck him off the narrow path, which was more suited to a giddy mountain goat than any sort of sensible or civilised man. Needless to say, ahead of him Torpeth was having no trouble making prodigious leaps and finding purchase on the treacherous shoulders of the mountain. The Minister would have paid more attention to the handholds and footholds the pagan used, if it weren't for the fact that looking upon Torpeth meant having to view his unsightly naked behind. The Minister was sure that the pagan had deliberately stopped on a couple of occasions just to see if he could get the Minister's refined nose up his unwashed arse.

'This is intolerable,' the Minister declared, standing up straight. 'What sane creatures would live up here? None. Only the madness of the Chaos could bring your people here. It is further proof of your corruption.'

Torpeth crouched and adroitly turned on one ankle to survey his charge. 'Careful how you speak, lowlander,' he half reprimanded and half beseeched. 'These slopes are sacred to all of the gods, but particularly Wayfar of the Warring Winds, for at these heights nothing can be hidden from him. Here, Gar of the Still Stone has raised the earth so that we may have a privileged view of the world. Here, the freezing bite of Akwar of the Wandering Waters is felt more keenly than anywhere else. Here, Sinisar of the Shining Path is brighter and illuminates all.

The air is clearer than any crystal mined by the upper village; there are rocks stronger than any man's ability to break; the water is so pure and sustaining that it must be the food of the gods; and fires burn here without wood or any other fuel.'

'Ha! I care not for these demons you pagans call gods,' the Minister shouted back, although the wind all but stole his breath and words away. 'I am not interested in their nonsense or mummery.'

'Lowlander, be careful, please. Broken though our gods are, they are stronger here than anywhere else. None can defy Wayfar and expect to live. The warriors of the upper village only live to learn and serve his will. He will pick you up and throw you down from this mountain.'

'Balderdash!' the Minister yelled as the wind whipped higher and forced him to bend low or lose his place.

'See, lowlander! The warring winds force even the proud to bow their heads.'

'What poppycock! You pagans are just ignorant savages. By what simple-mindedness do you worship the fickle forces of nature? By what delusion do you see omens in every oddly shaped cloud, in the way leaves fall out of trees and in the manner of your bowels shifting of a morning? In the Empire nature is commanded by the Saviours and their People. We bend nature to our will so that our eternal civilisation can be ordered and built. We are not governed by silly superstition and the tired tales of your windbag of a demon.'

Torpeth leapt from his rock and threw himself down at the Minister.

'Do your worst, pagan!' the Minister screeched, bracing himself against the onslaught of the wind and the oncoming pagan. But his coat flared up around him and the air all but lifted him from the ground. The balls of his feet dragged against the path as he was pulled backwards towards empty space. Now he was on his toes, teetering on the edge. First his heart was in his mouth, then his stomach. If his feet followed, there would be nothing left of him. He screamed for the Saviours to intercede and preserve his life.

Torpeth collided with the Minister's legs and wrapped his arms tightly around them. 'Mighty Wayfar, forgive him! He does not know what he says. He is from a different world to our own. His mind has been moulded by an arrogant Empire that has wrested the People from the Geas! Killing him will show and teach him nothing.'

'Unhand me, you snivelling pagan! I need no forgiveness from your demons. My faith will sustain me. Wayfar, you say, pagan? Better he be called Whatfor!'

The howling wind blasted them against the earth, and then ripped them away again, hurling them high into the air. The Minister landed in ungainly fashion on top of Torpeth, who was winded as the air was crushed out of him. The wind smote the Minister again, flattening him cruelly and whacking his elbow into Torpeth's ribs.

'Arghh! Ask for forgiveness, you fool, or it'll be the death of both of us!' Torpeth coughed in agony. 'I can't take much more of this! Who cares whether he is god or demon! Can't you see Wayfar's strength?'

'What, should I pray to some passing squall?' the Minister cried above the keening wind. 'It is naught but coincidence it should blow up when we are speaking of the manifestations of the Chaos.' He grabbed another breath. 'In fact, such weather is no doubt common here, so it is quite predictable it should occur during our ascent.'

'Stubborn man!' Torpeth wailed. 'If you know it to be naught of Wayfar, then you know any words you recite asking for forgiveness will be as empty as the wind. Nothing will be lost, nothing will be betrayed, and much might be gained.'

'Nothing will be betrayed, save my principles! Nothing will be betrayed, save my faith!'

'I don't give a rutting goat for your principles! Empty words are not so much to ask when they are exchanged for our lives.'

'The only words that are empty are those spoken by pagans. There are no empty words in the Empire. Words that may be empty when spoken by a pagan take on weight and moment when spoken by one of the People of the Empire.'

Torpeth was slightly relieved that the wind was now so loud it had drowned out most of the Minister's mindless rhetoric, but panicked again as the lowlander was tugged off him towards a precipice. Clouds began to come together and build. Torpeth lunged for the Minister and missed.

The Minister was rolled onto his front and dragged across the face of a boulder, the skin torn from his hands and cheek. His legs hung over the drop and his hips slid away from him.

'Help! My friend, help me!' the Minister gibbered.

Torpeth lunged again, nearly overshooting, and caught the scruff of the Minister's coat. The Minister grabbed Torpeth's beard and yanked hard.

'Arggh! Let go so I can move back and haul you by your hands and arms!'

'Help me, help me, help me!' the Minister cried hysterically, his legs kicking wildly.

'Let go! You'll kill us both!'

The wind shrieked in delight, buffeting them and almost succeeding in somersaulting Torpeth over the top of the Minister and down into the valley far below.

'Don't let me drop! All right, all right! If I have offended the wind, then I ask its forgiveness!'

There was an instant lull and Torpeth managed to scrabble backwards. Then, hand over hand, he pulled the Minister up by the back of his coat. The Minister shunted his way onto the boulder and rolled onto his back, his chest heaving.

'Come, lowlander. We must move from here before the whimsical wind changes its mind. There is a small cave up ahead where we can rest. Up! Come, I'll help you.'

'Saviours be praised!' Minister Praxis muttered under his breath, watching the lowering sky carefully.

The cave was cramped but furnished with a stock of dry wood, flint and striking metal. Torpeth got a small fire going and watched as the Minister shivered. 'I don't suppose you are persuaded, are you?'

'Pah! Persuaded by the changeable weather? What sort of man would I be if I changed my faith with the seasons?' the Minister answered haughtily, although the effect was spoiled by his chattering teeth. 'I would better ask why you insist on your pagan worship of the weather's vagaries. It keeps you stunted and ignorant. You study nothing beyond it. You wilfully limit your potential and deny yourself enlightenment. You live within a dark cave of corruption.'

Torpeth's brows beetled down and he brooded for long moments, looking into the insubstantial flames in front of them. Then he sighed. 'I promised you secrets, lowlander, did I not? Know then that I honour the gods not out of baseless fear and a witless belief in the stories told by my people, but because I have long known the gods. I was once their favourite son, long, long ago. Before the others came, those you know as your Saviours, I led all the people in their worship of the gods and the Geas.'

'What fantasy is this?' the Minister laughed. 'There was nothing of meaning before the coming of the Saviours.'

'Torpeth the Great, they called me.'

'You will have had mad visions and demonic visitations to create this alternative history of the Empire. I will not be so easily misled.'

Torpeth's eyes became distant. 'Through all those years of warring and conquest, I was convinced my cause was righteous and that I would create an eternal holy empire. I was sure I could create a perfect immortal race. The gods were against it, of course, and tried to warn me, but in my arrogance I thought they were simply jealous of their power over the people. I now understand that immortality is not within the nature of the Geas. I was deluded.'

'Indeed you were. You still are, pagan.'

Torpeth's eyes now misted. 'Perhaps. And so the collapse of all I'd fought for was inevitable. The harm I did to the people is beyond imagining.' His voice began to shake. 'To think of the numbers who died under my tyranny. I broke the people, I broke the gods, I broke the land!' He let go an inarticulate cry of anguish. Tears spilled down his cheeks. 'It was I who made it so easy for the others. I have tried and tried, but have been unable to recover anything. I have only hastened the end for my people!'

'Haunted dreams is all, pagan. You cannot be so old. Only the Saviours are eternal.'

Torpeth nodded. 'In many ways I am still not old in understanding. I am a mere child. But it is true that I have existed since before the others. It is my punishment to do so, to witness the fall of everything I had striven for, the fall of the gods, the subjugation of my people by the others, and our slow decline here in the mountains. The Geas has decided I am unworthy of death and renewal. The gods have turned their faces away from me. *Holy man* my people may sometimes call me, but they revere me only as much as they hate, mock and pity me. They know what I am. They know my shame, for the manner of their lives has been decided by it. Even the goats shun my presence.'

'But do you not see, pagan? You only succeed in keeping your original error alive. That is why the decline continues. That is why your corruption does not end. You are the holy man of your people, around whom their false beliefs and stories are organised. It is because of you that their worship of these false gods continues. Was it you or one like you who originally brought them to these mountains, denying them the opportunity to join the glorious Empire of the Saviours? Do you not see you are still that flawed and arrogant individual who caused all the trouble? Do you not see that you still cause such trouble for your people? Why must they live difficult and empty lives here in the mountains, when they could instead be welcomed into the civilisation of the Empire?'

Torpeth bleakly met the Minister's eyes. 'Perhaps the gods have sent you here to show me my error, lowlander. At the same time, they would also wish you to learn from it. Can you not see that these Saviours of yours seek to build an eternal holy empire in exactly the same way as I did? It can only end in failure again. It is a tyranny that takes freedom and lives from the people. But there will be no escape to the mountains this time, no chance of redemption. If your Saviours are not prevented, then they will see an absolute end to the gods, the people and the Geas. All will be destroyed!'

'I will not listen to this blasphemy. Oh, but the twisting guile of the Chaos knows no limit. It matches itself to that which it envies, mimicking it so that the listener becomes confused and mistaken, and then perverts their belief and understanding. You seek to appropriate the history of the Saviours' Empire so that you may then redefine it.'

'Lowlander, heed my warning before it is too late. Do not make my mistake, I beg you!'

'Ah, but you are cunning, pagan. How else is it that you still survive? But we will see, pagan, what your people say. We will see if they still wish to cling to their desperate and miserable lives here once I have told them of the bounty and forgiveness that awaits them in the Empire. You said that they despise you, did you not? Are you surprised when your error and selfishness has imprisoned them in this wintry fastness? Given a choice; do you really think they will want to remain here, or is it more likely that they will have me lead them out of this self-imposed hell and into the promised lands of the Empire? You will finally be left here on your own, pagan, with nothing but the wind and the echo of your self-tormenting soul for company. You know it is true!'

More tears trickled from Torpeth's eyes. 'It grieves me that I cannot make you understand, lowlander, but perhaps you're right. I should not be their jailer. Perhaps it is time I finally put my faith in my people and allowed them to choose for themselves. After all, just making a declared decision is a change of sorts, and something needs to change if we are ever to be free of this slow decline and the Geas is ever to flourish again. We will see then, lowlander. Yes, we will see. Just be careful not to mention the chief's nose. He's very sensitive about it.'

In his stupor Jillan found himself at the bottom of the large green hill. Above him, people frenziedly fought their way up the slopes. Many were trampled underfoot, none stopping to help them. People bit at each other, pulled at hair, gouged at eyes, tore at mouths, punched, elbowed and throttled. All to get beyond their neighbour or past those in front of them. All to get to the waiting line of Heroes, with their deadly sun-metal-tipped spears.

Sickened, Jillan turned his face away. To his right and left there were fissures and cracks in the base of the hill from which steam and noxious gases poured. The crack nearest him looked to be dormant, however, and wide enough for him to squeeze into if he went side on. Azual would be unable to follow him through the narrow opening, so it would be a good place to hide until he could wake up and escape this nightmare.

His armour protected him front and back as he squeezed into the crevice. He knew there was a distinct danger he would become wedged fast, but he decided that would still be better than having to face the Saint or his Heroes. He pushed deeper and deeper into the heart of the hill. The earth became soft and then ribbed and fleshy, like the brains of the hunted animals his father sometimes brought home.

He stepped into the core, a large echoing cavern. At the centre was a curiously lit statue. It was grey and unmoving, as most statues were meant to be, but the limbs of the figure were unusually thin and there was a floating feeling about it completely at odds with any statue he'd seen before. Its large head was only supported by a spindly neck, which meant that the stone of which it was made had to be impossibly strong.

The figure's face was relatively featureless, with just slits where its eyes, nostrils, mouth and ears should be. The top of the head was wider than the rest of it, even though it had been carved without hair.

Black orbs watched him, and he jumped back as he realised the eyes had opened. The living statue had not otherwise moved.

How dare you, you disgusting mite! hissed a voice out of the air.

'I-I-I'm sorry,' Jillan blurted.

How did you come here, into this space of the waking dream? Tell me quickly!

'I-I don't know,'

We know who you are! You cannot hide from us!

'I didn't mean any harm.'

Mean? Your meaning is not for you to decide. We decide everything!

'Who are you?'

How dare you ask a question of us, cursed creature? We are the infinite. Cower before us!

Jillan's knees shook and threatened to prostrate him before what could only be one of the blessed Saviours. It was a thing beyond his limited comprehension, just as he'd always been taught. He was as privileged as he was cursed to be here in the divine presence. His every fear and inadequacy were made clear to him, his crimes and blasphemies laid bare. He felt once more the guilt he always used to experience in front of Minister Praxis.

'I-I did not mean to hurt anyone,' he confessed. 'I have consorted with the Chaos. I beg for forgiveness, unworthy as I am and will always be. Guide me, blessed Saviour!'

Forgiveness! the voice chided him. *Your very existence is the presumption that begs forgiveness. Yet you take another breath, and another, committing the offence over and over. Your repentance is made false by it. There is only one path to forgiveness.*

'Tell me!' he pleaded.

Find and reveal the Geas to us. Then there will be a final end to the presumption and offence. Then forgiveness will be allowed for your despicable kind. You will find and reveal the Geas to us, do you understand?

He nodded dumbly.

Then you are committed. Fail us again and we will eat you alive. The statue began to stir, first slowly and then with increasing speed. *We will eat you in this space now so that you know what awaits you should you fail.*

Jillan screamed and suddenly came awake. He was drenched with sweat and realised it must be because he'd been close to a fire. Someone had also placed a blanket over him.

'He's awake,' called a deep voice he didn't recognise.

'Ah, there you are.' Aspin smiled as he came into view. 'You had us worried.'

Jillan craned his neck and found the blacksmith sitting on a log. He'd lost most of the dark curls from his head and there were a few conspicuous gaps in his teeth, but there was a touch of colour in his cheeks and his eyes were clear. He appeared miraculously recovered from the plague.

'Here's some water,' Aspin said as he proffered Jillan a beaker. Then he whispered as he came close, 'It's all right, he's trustworthy . . . or he's as good as his word, at least.'

Just as there's many a killer as good as their word.

Jillan took a drink and then quickly looked about the campfire. 'Where's my sword?'

The blacksmith nudged a scabbard with his foot. 'Here. Still interested in selling?'

'No. It's not for sale.'

'You sure? You're a bit young for a blade like that. I'll give you a good price for it.'

'Leave it alone. It's mine!' Jillan replied more fiercely than he'd intended.

The blacksmith raised his hands. 'All right, all right! Sun-metal, isn't it? Where did you get it?'

Don't trust him. You've no reason to, after all.

'None of your business.'

The blacksmith nodded slowly. 'You're right, it ain't. And it's said I've you to thank for bringing me back from death's door, Jillan.'

Jillan glared at Aspin. 'What do you think you're doing telling him my real name? You had no right! There are things I could tell him about you too.'

'He already knew who you were,' Aspin protested.

He's a spy for the Saint!

'Look, I didn't have to be the smartest of men to work it out, now did I?' the blacksmith reasoned. 'Everyone in Saviours' Paradise knew to be on the lookout for a fair-haired boy of your age. I'd also had word of a boy called Jillan being involved in a killing in Godsend, the place they say the plague started.'

'How could you know these things unless you were working for the Saint? He's watching us through your eyes right now, isn't he?' Jillan challenged him, throwing off his blanket.

Quick as thought, Aspin took up a thick branch from the woodpile and stood watching the blacksmith tensely. Clearly, the mountain warrior had read something in the blacksmith's possible response that he didn't like.

The blacksmith's eyes slid between Jillan and Aspin. He rolled his head on his corded neck and flexed forearms as wide as Jillan's thighs. Then he made his hands into mallet-sized fists and squeezed them until his knuckles cracked. Aspin adjusted his grip on the branch.

Suddenly the blacksmith laughed heartily, his strong voice reverberating around the clearing where the wagon had been drawn up. 'I'm just joshing with you, lads! You're right to be cautious, but if I meant you harm you'd have already had it and no mistaking. Young Aspin, that branch of yours would do little more than tickle my bonce, and yon wizard is too spent to be helping you any. It'll take more than you two ragamuffins to get the jump on Thomas Ironshoe.'

Jillan's mouth fell open in surprise. 'You're Thomas Ironshoe?'

'Aye, wizard, I am. Heard of me, have ye?'

'I'm no wizard,' Jillan said.

'Why, sure ye are! Come now, there's no shame in it. Indeed, one of my best friends is a wizard, but don't go telling him I called him friend. Don't want him getting too big for his britches or thinking I'll start doing him any favours, do I? Tricksy sorts these wizards, if you take my meaning, no offence to your good self, Jillan.'

Aspin nodded. 'I've had similar trouble with them too. That's how I ended up here, and I've been imprisoned and had to fight for my life along the way.'

'You know other wizards?' Jillan asked the blacksmith. 'Then, are you a-a . . .'

'Pagan? A demon-worshipper? A consort of the Chaos? A dark corruptor of innocence? Some would say so, and those people would say precisely the same of you, wizard, would they not? Jillan, I'm just an ordinary man, with a family, hopes, dreams and fears, like everyone else. There's a hamlet of similar folk not far from here if you'd like me to take you there? And to answer your earlier question, no, the Saint is not watching you through my eyes right now. There are ways of clouding the mind that mean he can glean very little when at some distance. I can show you the trick if you like. The least I can do, I'd say. Or have you been fortunate enough to avoid being Drawn?'

Jillan nodded slowly. Why did he still not trust this apparently affable man? After all, his parents had told him to find him Thomas Ironshoe, and Aspin seemed comfortable with him, didn't he? 'I'm not sure if we have time to go to your hamlet. I seek Haven, and then I have to get to Hyvan's Cross, which is a long way from here.'

Thomas stilled. 'What do you know of Haven? Where did you hear that name?'

'My mother, Maria.'

'And what is your father's name?'

'Jed – Jedadiah.'

Thomas's eyes widened in recognition. 'Maria and Jedadiah from New Sanctuary? Did they end up in Godsend then? I'd always wondered what happened to them. You do not know what it means to hear they are well. They were sensible to disappear – dark days back then. And you're their lad, are ye? Figures. It all makes a bit more sense now. Well met, Jillan of Godsend! It's an honour. But you're not from Godsend, are you, Aspin, judging by your accent?'

Aspin shook his head. 'I'm from close by, though.'

'Well, Aspin-from-close-by, it is also an honour. Praise the gods that they have brought us together.'

Jillan shifted uncomfortably at this open lauding of the pagan gods, while Aspin nodded in agreement with the blacksmith. Thomas did not miss the difference in their reactions and smiled to himself.

'What is Haven?' Jillan asked, to distract him.

Thomas gave him an assessing look. After a moment he said, 'Haven is here,' placing his hand over his heart, 'here,' touching his head, 'and here,' touching his stomach. 'It is the home of the Geas, our life energy. It is the energy we all share, the thing all life shares. It is that which keeps us quick, keeps us animated. You need not seek it, for it is here, all around us, Jillan.'

He's not telling you everything. The Saviour was sure it was a place that could be found. You're right not to trust him.

Aspin threw the branch he was holding onto the fire and moved between the two of them. 'As Jillan says, we need to be moving along. We cannot afford the time to visit your hamlet with you, Thomas, unless it will see us equipped with horses.'

'Of course, Aspin-from-close-by! The way I see it, I owe you two my life, so two horses are the least I can do. My wife would not have it otherwise. She will also insist on making you the best home-cooked meal you've ever had, I'll be bound. She will insist, and I can't see the two of you refusing, judging by how famished you look.'

Aspin nodded and turned to Jillan. 'What do you think? The horses will buy us valuable time,' he whispered.

'It's good you thought of that,' Jillan replied gratefully, more pleased than he could say that Aspin had not sided with Thomas, and had apparently decided to travel to Hyvan's Cross with him. It was like having a friend again, although no one could ever take Hella's place. It meant he wasn't on his own any more. It made him feel braver, stronger. 'Why didn't you tell him you were from the mountains? I thought—'

'I know, I know, but I sense you have doubts about him. He's as good as his word, I'm sure of that, but I get strange flashes from him every now and then. They're so quick, though, that I don't catch them properly, as if he's deliberately smothered them before I can read them. I'm happy to follow your lead, Jillan, as I was when you got me out of that cell and out of the town safely. I'm sorry about before . . . you know, when I said you were too young and all that. It wasn't right. And you were right about not just leaving Thomas to die by the roadside.'

Jillan couldn't help smiling. 'And I'm sorry I called you a . . . a murdering pagan.'

You're not really sorry, though, are you?

'Well, I would have been, were it not for you.'

'You were just doing what you thought best. And who's to say you were definitely wrong? We'll only know if we get through this without any more trouble. A home-cooked meal does sound good, though, doesn't it? If I never have to look at dried meat and hard biscuits again, it'll be too soon.'

'If you're still worried about lost time,' Thomas called over, 'I'll show you shortcuts and secret ways through these woods. I'll get you to Hyvan's Cross in next to no time. Come, Jillan, and meet our wizard. He may be of help to you. Moreover, on our way I'll tell you tales of when your parents were young and you were but a twinkle in your father's eye.'

Laying it on a bit thick, isn't he?

'All right, we'll come along, but we will need to leave tomorrow morning,' Jillan consented as he tested his weight on his legs. 'In the meantime I'll have my sword back, thank you, Thomas Ironshoe.'

In desperation, she'd thrown everything to the winds, and now she found she could foresee nothing. What hope was there for an organising intellect that could not anticipate events in order to manipulate and control the outcome? Yes, she'd temporarily thwarted D'Selle and she'd won herself a stay of execution in persuading Elder Thraal to unleash the Peculiar, but now all the others had scented blood and were circling her. D'Shaa was not fooled for a second that D'Zel's offer of an alliance would secure her power or position in any way. His Declaration for her was more surprising and promising, and had probably caused consternation among the other organising intellects, but from what she'd read none of the Declarations among her kind through the ages had ever ended happily. Invariably, one of the parties to the Declaration became Dominant and undid the Lesser. Certain Lessers had survived for millennia before capitulating, but in the end the result had always been the same. D'Shaa was in no doubt that D'Zel would quickly wish to become the Dominant party to their Declaration, so that everything she was and that she organised would become his.

Not only was she unable to anticipate and pre-empt the others of her rank: now she could not even pre-empt those under her sway in her own region. She'd been far too indulgent of Azual for far too long, she decided. He was impulsive, wilful and erratic. She should have had him put down immediately after the episode in New Sanctuary. Why hadn't she? Because she was the most inexperienced of the organising intellects and had feared to undermine her position further at the time. Now look where that initial lack of confidence and foresight had got her. Now look at what it had resulted in: a lackadaisical Saint leaving a boy Undrawn for far too long; meaning the boy's magic became manifest; meaning that the boy had the power to frustrate and overcome the Saint; meaning that the boy had learned to use the Saint's own nature against him; meaning that the boy had now found access to her in the waking dream through the Saint. It was beyond belief. The boy was an abomination. Just contact with him had been so abhorrent and unsettling to her that she found it hard to maintain the mental discipline required to remain within the waking dream. See how close it was to destroying her! If she was absent from the dream for too long, Elder Thraal would immediately be aware of it. He would see how the magic of the Geas had spread like a virus through her region and her own organising intellect, and he would have no choice but to destroy her before the virus could spread further through the rest of the hierarchy. What if it had already spread to D'Zel as a result of the Declaration?

With panic beginning to eat away at her mind, she performed drill after drill, as if she were a novice again, just to retain her sense of self. The calm centre which is both the self and the absence of self. Enter the waking dream. Become infinite once more. The demands of the physical vessel disappear, for it is no longer the vessel. Yes, she had lost control of her region and yes, she had allowed the Geas a foothold, but she had also begun to expose the Geas and bend the boy to her will. Azual held the parents hostage and unexpectedly seemed to be making progress in the mountains. And the Peculiar was in play. All the mechanisms of her will and control of the region were still in place; it was now a matter of exerting that will more forcefully, of imprinting her desires on the thoughts of the People and thereby even the most simple of day-to-day events, of seeing herself writ large across the entire history and definition of this world and its energies.

'Azual!' she projected through the waking dream.

Holy one, came back the surprised and nervous thought. *What is your will? Command me!*

'You have failed thus far.'

Hesitation. Fear. *Yes, holy one. There is no excuse.*

'You are inadequate, Damon, unworthy of Sainthood.'

Mortification. Anguish. Self-hatred. *Yes, holy one.*

'The fault must also be mine for ever having raised you up.'

No, holy one! Forgive me, but I must have deceived you in some way in the beginning.

'Silence!' D'Shaa had to admit that she admired his devotion, however. In that, he had never been lacking. 'Your deception aside, how has this happened? There must be traitors working against us, or innocents being used against us without their understanding. Who or what has been using the boy? As you do not yet know, then your search has been neither subtle nor exacting enough.'

Doubt. Irritation. Suspicion. *Holy one, I am neither wise nor skilled in divining the truth of the past, but the boy has definitely been aided by strange agencies of which I cannot identify the origin. His parents were of New Sanctuary, but what was the origin of the force that was using them? I eradicated most of those that the force used, but I now believe I did not eradicate the force itself. Through me, you will have seen the guard Samnir and heard he was Drawn by another. Perhaps he was an agent of another Saint. Also, there was the strange warrior who was captured in Saviours' Paradise and freed by the boy. I did not recognise the warrior and do not know from where he came. How can he have any connection with the boy when it is the boy's first time beyond Godsend? Then there is the plague, which muddles things even further.*

'There is a range of forces arrayed against us,' D'Shaa decided. 'All operate through and around the boy. He is a powerful organising focus for them. Yet he is still within the web of my region and will, and I shall instruct you so that he remains so. Before that, however, there is something which you should know. I have unleashed the Peculiar, and he will soon enter my region. He is our ultimate guarantee that forces that depend on the boy will ultimately fall to the Saviours, even if it is not directly to you and me.'

Surprise. Uncertainty. Dread. *The Peculiar exists?*

'By the definition of this world, it must.'

I have only read fragments and subsumed half-memories of him. I assumed he was just a pagan myth. If he truly exists—

'Enough, Azual. You will not dwell upon such things, for it is beyond your understanding, and you well know the dangers of only partial understanding. Similarly, you will avoid any encounter or confrontation with the Peculiar.'

What if he seeks to take the boy from me?

'You will ensure the boy is dead long before any such eventuality can arise, Azual. It means that you must act quickly now, however, and follow my instructions precisely. So attend well to my words. Here is what you will do in my name . . .'

'Most splendid Chief Blackwing . . .' Torpeth sonorously addressed the fat old man in the outlandish throne, who eyed them suspiciously from his seat fully ten feet off the ground.

How did he even get up there without breaking his neck? Minister Praxis wondered. *There's no ladder that I can see. Surely he didn't fly up there with that cape of feathers, did he? No, there aren't enough feathers to carry his weight.*

'I bring this lowlander to you . . .'

He may once have had hair and beard as dark as a raven, but it's all grey now. He is vain then, this pagan chieftain. Still, there's nothing vain about his men, the Minister decided as he took in the hall full of lean and undecorated warriors.

'. . . to . . . ah . . . Well, that's it really. I bring this lowlander to you.'

There were tense long moments. A warrior broader but slightly younger than the others pushed his way forward, stood at the foot of the throne and faced them. He looked the Minister up and down with obvious contempt and then asked Torpeth, 'Is this the best gift that you can bring the upper village, holy man? It is worthless to us. Is it one of your mad jokes, perhaps? No one is laughing. Or is it a deliberate insult?'

'Brave Braggar,' Torpeth declaimed theatrically, 'how have you been?'

'Answer me,' Braggar growled dangerously, whether because he didn't want to lose face in front of the stranger and the assembled warriors, or because he genuinely wanted to tear Torpeth limb from limb wasn't clear.

'It is no gift, jest or insult from me,' Torpeth replied lightly, hopping from one foot to the other. 'It is a lowlander the gods have allowed to come here. It may be gift, jest or insult from them, therefore. I suggest you take your issue up with the gods, brave Braggar.'

'Do you mock me?' Braggar growled, but his voice broke just before the end and the word *me* came out in a squeak.

Torpeth froze mid-hop, one foot level with his knee, his testicles slapping down against his thigh. He tilted his head. 'I thought I heard a bird. Have you been stealing them from their nests and devouring them, Braggar, thinking that it will give you the power to ride the wind and come closer to holy Wayfar?'

Rage darkened Braggar's face and he raised a clenched fist, but Chief Blackwing now spoke in harsh tones. 'Enough, troll! You have only been here moments and you have already outstayed your welcome. I thought I warned you last time that if you ever returned to the upper village we would throw you from the highest peak to see just how dear you were to the gods, and whether holy Wayfar would allow his winds to break your fall.'

Torpeth stifled a giggle. 'I thought your words were mere wind born of poor digestion and a diet too rich. Maybe you should try pine nuts instead. I swear by them. They keep me quite regular. I suspect your sour moods and grudges are born of a backed-up bowel, great Chief. Not even your feathers tickle you loose and put a smile on your face, no?'

'This is not wise, pagan,' Minister Praxis sighed.

'Seize the troll!' the chieftain bellowed to the dozens of lithe warriors in the hall, some of whom had already begun to move towards Torpeth.

The holy man continued his strange hopping dance, skipping over a warrior who had dived low, and then jumping behind the Minister to avoid another. He bumped into the Minister so that he fell forwards with a squawk.

'That's it, lowlander! Wayfar is also known as the Screaming God!' Torpeth nodded as he leapt to stand momentarily on the Minister's bent back. 'So now I will begin a prayer to him. Wayfaaaaaa . . .' He began ululating and kicked off the Minister's back to meet the chins of two warriors with the hard soles of his feet.

'. . . aaaaaaa . . .'

Torpeth landed nimbly and instantly bounced high, allowing two more warriors to collide together in the space directly below him. He landed on top of them, a foot on each of their backs, smacking their foreheads against the compacted floor.

'. . . aaaaaaaa . . .'

'Catch him, you sluggards!' the chieftain spat, almost toppling from his perch, so angry was he.

'. . . aaaaaaaaa . . .'

Four warriors rushed at Torpeth from the sides, front and back. There was surely no escape. The small naked man waited for the backs of the warriors beneath him to flex and heave and then sprang at the warrior directly ahead, landing hands on his shoulders and vaulting over his head. The four warriors tumbled to the ground on top of each other.

'Use your weapons, you stoneheads!' Chief Blackwing cried in red-faced apoplexy. 'Kill him!'

'. . . aaaaaaaaaa . . .'

Braggar picked his moment and moved with deadly speed for the holy man's back. Torpeth nodded as if he felt the breeze of Braggar's movement and approved. He darted forward between warriors to the hall door and flung it open, letting in an icy blast that staggered the chief's son and unbalanced all those nearby.

'. . . aaaaaaaarr . . .'

Torpeth put his back to the wind and flew with it into the faces of those still coming for him. His loose hands whipped into eyes and throats; a hard heel thudded into a solar plexus; his feet climbed into the air, and he was over the heads of the warriors as they cowered behind upraised arms to protect themselves.

He is a veritable imp of mischief, a devilish elemental! How these pagans like to cause trouble, as much for themselves as for any other.

'. . . rrrrrr . . .'

'For the love of the gods,' Chief Blackwing pleaded, 'someone grab or stab him!'

The wind circled round the hall, faster and faster, torches guttering and the air around Torpeth seeming to blur the eye. A vortex wove and danced towards the rocking throne.

'. . . rrrrrrrRR . . .' the ululation deepened until it was a grinding and clashing storm over the mountains.

A warrior managed to loose a wobbly arrow, but it was hurled wide of its mark to clatter into the wall. Overwhelmed and in fear of his life, Minister Praxis went to his knees, bent low and put his hands over his ears. Were those feet upon his back once more, lifting off straight towards the chieftain?

'. . . RRRRR!!'

Then came a shriek, the creak and crack of breaking wood, and a heavy thump as Chief Blackwing unceremoniously came back down to earth.

There was a sudden silence and pained stillness. Men feared to start breathing again lest they attract the attention of the spirit that had chosen to punish them. All feared to move lest they discover they had died as part of the righteous vengeance. At best, bruised and broken bodies awaited them. The chieftain groaned.

'That was by way of introduction to the lowlander,' Torpeth said mildly, 'for he has been sent to test us all. Remember that when you hear his words in the days ahead. Remember that the greatest warriors of the upper village were defeated without difficulty by an unarmed naked warrior. Remember that they were undone by just an old man, and a dirty one at that. Think on it when you wonder if you have the strength to take on the Empire. Think on it again so that you may know whether it is true faith or mere vanity that urges and inclines you to fight. Ask yourselves if it is better to die gloriously or live with the inner peace of the Geas. And if you find an answer to that last one, let me know, would you?'

And then he was gone, so the warriors of the upper village could start breathing and moving again.

Hella pulled her cloak closed and hurried through the pale light of the dawn to the Gathering Place. She found him sat there, as always, staring vacantly at the ground just before his feet.

There was no one else around, of course, because it was so early. Added to that, the town had been in a subdued and sluggish mood ever since the incident, the visit of the holy Saint and the spread of the plague. People seemed to seek the shadows whenever they moved through the town, and seemed to have less reason to seek out their neighbours than in the past. There were fewer disputes than usual, less cause to approach the council of elders and a general unspoken agreement that the season had turned, that there was little to be gained from sending workers out into the fields, and that most right-minded individuals would spend their days by the fire at home. Hella didn't even see her classmates any more, for no replacement Minister had yet arrived from Hyvan's Cross.

'Hello, Samnir, it's me again, Hella,' she said gently. 'How are you today? I hope it wasn't too cold last night. Are the blankets I brought you warm enough? Does the lean-to keep most of the wind out?'

Samnir didn't respond. She waited. After a minute his red eyes ran and he managed an autonomic blink.

'That's good. Papa got back from Saviours' Paradise last night. Guess what!' She lowered her voice and whispered excitedly: 'He saw Jillan! Spoke to him! The Heroes and the Saint chased him, but he escaped. Isn't that incredible?'

A lone bird twittered once or twice and then gave up. A cold breeze pulled at their hair. Hella turned her face away while Samnir remained as he was.

'Anyway, there's me going on when you're probably hungry. Broth again, I'm afraid. Sorry, but it seems to be the only thing you like.'

She took the lid off the small brown-glazed pot she'd brought with her and dipped a small wooden spoon into the thick contents.

'Smells good, huh? I found some wild garlic, so it should be flavoursome.'

She gently pushed Samnir's head back and then pulled on his chin so that his mouth opened. She checked the broth wasn't too hot and then spooned some between his lips. After several spoonfuls, the gentle pressure of the food caused his body to swallow.

'That's good,' she said, as always. 'Want some more? Here you go.'

'How is he?' asked a quiet voice.

Hella gasped and came to her feet, hiding the spoon behind her back as she whirled round. Haal stood watching her from a dozen or so yards away. His eyes remained on her for a few moments and then fixed on Samnir, who still sat with his head back, looking at the sky.

'What do *you* want?' she demanded scornfully. 'What are you doing, spying on people?'

His eyes went to his feet. 'Didn't mean to spy,' he mumbled. 'I was just passing is all.'

'Going to go tell on me, are you, Haal Corinson?' she accused, hands going to hips. 'Going to tell your father and all the other elders, are you? I hen't done anything wrong. Just showing some care for a neighbour is all.'

Haal nodded, his cheeks flushing. 'You're doing it for *him*, aren't you?'

He meant Jillan, but she refused to be embarrassed, even though heat was also coming to her cheeks. 'I en't! And what's it to you even if I was? Anyway, what are you doing just passing at this time of the morning? Does Elder Corin know you've sneaked out of bed? You'll be in a heap of trouble if you do anything as stupid as tell him you saw me here.'

He looked at her with a strange expression on his face that brought her up short.

'What is it then? What's wrong, Haal?'

'Pa's sick, Hella. Frightful sick! Ma's sent me to fetch the physicker.'

'Is it . . . the . . . you know?'

He refused to nod in case that would make it true. His eyes glistened and he bit at his lip worriedly. 'Don't know. None of the rest of us has got it. Ma said it's best not to tell anyone 'bout it lest it cause panic and make people not want to help us. Don't tell anyone, will you? I won't tell about Samnir, promise.'

She didn't want to feel sorry for him. He was stupid, boasted about how important his father was all the time and pushed the other kids around because he was bigger and better fed than they were. She knew he liked her, but she didn't want him to. She strongly suspected he'd always picked on Jillan because she liked Jillan and not him. It only made her dislike him even more. It had almost made her glad when Haal's friend Karl had died, not that she was ever glad when someone or something died. It almost made her glad Elder Corin was ill. She didn't want to feel sorry for Haal, because it felt like she was betraying Jillan. But she did anyway. Just like she felt sorry for Samnir, even though he was a blasphemer and a traitor to the Empire. Why were things so difficult?

She sighed. 'Course I won't tell. My father's just back from Saviours'

Paradise. If there's anything the physicker needs, maybe my father can help. But I'm sure your pa will be okay. You know what it's like: the cold weather always brings its share of shakes and shivers, and it's colder this year than most.'

'You think?' Haal asked with forced optimism. Then his face fell. 'They're saying it's the cold wind that carries the corruption of the Chaos out of the mountains. They say that the plague in Godsend is because the Chaos has got stronger of late, and the People of the town need punishing if they're to mend their ways. The Saint came because we needed punishing.'

She nearly became angry with him again, but knew it wasn't his fault he wasn't as smart as everyone else. 'And did your pa need punishing?'

He frowned. 'No.'

'Well, there are you are then!'

He nodded slowly, looking confused.

'It shows it's not the Chaos, Haal. It shows it's just people saying things. It's just a plague is all, nothing to do with the Chaos, nothing to do with people being punished or people having done anything bad. See?'

He nodded more vigorously. 'Yes, yes! Thanks, Hella. I owe you one. If you ever need . . .' He tailed off.

She nodded her own understanding. 'Course. Thanks. I hope your pa gets well soon, Haal.'

He'd heard a tale once of an old man who had been buried alive. Of course, everyone had thought him dead when in fact he'd probably only been asleep. Feeble as he'd been, however, none had been able to feel the whisper of any breath escaping his mouth or nostrils or the flutter of any pulse in his wrist when checking to see if he'd passed on. It being a hot summer, and the old man's sons being eager for their inheritance, the man had been hastily placed in his coffin and the lid promptly nailed down. The funeral service had taken place that very same day with no one the wiser.

It was only when the gravedigger had all but finished filling in the grave that evening, when everyone else had gone home, that the muffled cries for help from the trapped man were heard. At first the gravedigger thought himself haunted and ran back to the town to find an inn, some bright company and strong drink to calm his nerves. Once he had himself under control, his more rational side began to assert itself and caused him to venture back to the graveyard.

All was quiet as he began to dig out the grave once more. 'Hellooo!' he shouted whenever he needed to rest in between his bouts of increasingly frantic digging. There was no word of reply.

The gravedigger spared no effort as he worked down to the coffin and feverishly levered open the lid. Blank eyes stared back at him accusingly. The old man's clawed hands were raised and bloodied from where he'd been trying to fight his way free. The inside of the coffin lid bore scratch marks and one torn fingernail from his struggles. The gravedigger stood for a moment and then gently replaced the lid. He'd filled the grave and returned to the inn, but the company was no longer bright enough to lift the shadows from his brows nor the drink strong enough, nor in sufficient quantity, to calm his nerves.

Samnir felt like the old man from the tale, except that rather than being trapped in a coffin, he was trapped in his own body. His mind tried to claw its way free but it was becoming weaker and weaker. Perhaps more like a stone, which no one knows has awareness, stuck at the bottom of a well. One of the people might throw a bucket in and it might land near him, but he lacked the wherewithal to climb into it.

'Hello, Samnir, it's me again, Hella. How are you today? I hope it wasn't too cold last night. Are the blankets I brought you warm enough? Does the lean-to keep most of the wind out?'

I hardly feel the cold or the wind, child. I hardly feel anything. You trouble yourself for nothing. Perhaps it's best if you leave me be. Be like the gravedigger and just gently replace the lid.

'That's good. Papa got back from Saviours' Paradise last night. Guess what! He saw Jillan! Spoke to him! The Heroes and the Saint chased him, but he escaped. Isn't that incredible?'

Ha! Jillan! He outwitted the Saint, eh? Heh, heh. It's good that I have not given up my life for nothing.

Even if Jillan had been captured, punished and Drawn, Samnir still wouldn't have regretted trying to help him. He'd regretted just about everything else in his life, but not this one act. He'd given Jillan a chance at the life he had himself given up far too easily when young. He'd been a different person back then, of course, proud and repentant of nothing. He'd never erred in his life and owed nothing to anyone. If anything, the People owed him for the hard work he did protecting them as a Hero and his fair-mindedness when settling disputes. Yet the People never showed him gratitude and caused him nothing but trouble with their petty and selfish ways. He'd had to become far harder and start knocking heads together before they started to understand what civilised behaviour was all about and that they needed to obey the rules for their own good. He'd quickly earned a reputation as an uncompromising and ambitious individual. He'd been sent to the Great Temple for officer training and then out into the deserts of the eastern region to pit his wits against the savage pagans and barbarians who still resisted the Empire. Years of slaughter had followed. He'd turned the white and gold sands of the region red. He'd poisoned the blue and green waters of every oasis he could find and burned every tree and bush. Yet it hadn't been enough, and nothing had really changed in the eastern region, despite his best efforts. No, that wasn't true. Nothing had really changed except himself. He'd become frustrated and dissatisfied, manic even, as if he was searching for something he couldn't find. The more brutal, bloodthirsty and successful as a soldier of the Empire he'd become, the worse the black moods became. His superiors had begun to look at him with fear, distaste and horror in their eyes. None of his superiors were weak men, either, but it was clear that in their eyes he'd gone wrong and become the sort of monster they were meant to be fighting against. The only one of them who'd treated him differently was General Thormodius, whose reaction was the worst of all, for his gaze had held pity. It was the General who'd decided Samnir had served in the east long enough and he should return to the Great Temple. Samnir had been furious and railed against the General, who'd then had no choice but to have his officer subdued and removed from the east in chains.

Samnir had then begun long years of service within the labyrinthine Great Temple. The other Heroes there were always courteous when dealing with him, but none had ever offered him friendship. And his black moods hadn't disappeared either; if anything they'd become worse without the outlet of battle that he'd had in the east. He'd become withdrawn and difficult and then started to say out loud whatever came into his head, whether there was anyone around to hear him or not. He'd uttered a good number of blasphemies and battered most of his comrades in fights before he was finally put out of the Great Temple.

He'd been sent further and further from the sacred heart of the Empire, until he'd ended up serving Saint Azual, whom they called the mad Saint because of what had happened at New Sanctuary. Yet even the Saint had considered Samnir too rabid to be of use, and sent him to Godsend, where he'd begun his lonely vigil on the southern gate. He wasn't exactly sure what he watched for, but the isolation had slowly begun to deaden his moods and give him a sort of peace. And then the boy had come, the boy he'd once been, the boy who was precisely the opposite of the monster Samnir had become.

'Anyway, there's me going on when you're probably hungry. Broth again, I'm afraid. Sorry, but it seems to be the only thing you like. Smells good, huh? I found some wild garlic, so it should be flavoursome.'

I can't smell or taste it, child. In many ways I don't want it, because it keeps me alive in this coffin. Can't you just leave me be? I know it might be ungrateful of me, but you're only prolonging my suffering. Bless you, child, for you cannot know. You think all life is sacred, don't you, that it should be preserved at all costs? I'm sorry, but it's not. It saddens me that you will all too quickly grow up to find that out, if the plague spares you that long. If you catch the illness, please bring it to me so that I will finally be free. And perhaps it would be for the best for you if you caught it, child, as then your innocence will not be cruelly destroyed by this life and you will not be turned into any sort of monster.

Saint Izat watched and listened to the girl through the soldier Samnir, whom Izat had Drawn to the Saviours decades before. The Saint congratulated herself on all the plotting and hard work she'd originally done to turn the young Samnir into the driven and merciless man who would first get selected by the Great Temple and then be sent out east. It had been tricky and Izat had had to use a number of valuable resources to ensure that Samnir had survived his desert tour of duty and had been recalled to the Great Temple. After that, it had been relatively easy to see to it that Samnir was sent into the rival southern region. Izat had been delighted when she'd been able to spy directly on Azual and help bring about the destruction of New Sanctuary. Such a joy to watch Azual descend into madness and commit such slaughter. Just a pity Azual had thus far survived the episode.

Once Samnir had been banished from Hyvan's Cross Izat had largely lost interest in the soldier and given him little further thought until the night of the incident with Jillan. Izat had had to use every shred of magical power at her disposal to reach from her western region all the way to Godsend to convince Samnir's mind that he should help the boy escape, but now look at how the effort was repaying her! Not only was the boy still at large and causing Azual no end of trouble, but it now seemed some sort of plague had also resulted – unless it was just happy coincidence – so that traders from other regions were now reluctant to deal with the south. The south's economy was beginning to collapse. Soon the People would begin to complain that Azual was not doing enough to help them, and then Azual would be facing a proper uprising, particularly if Izat were to use her other resources in the south judiciously. Whether Azual managed to quell the uprising or not, the blessed Saviours would not forgive him for having allowed the instability to begin in the first place. The Saviours would look for another Saint to oversee the south, and there was none better suited than Izat, whose own region had always been peaceful and prosperous. Saint Dionan in the east always had his hands full with the pagan and barbarian tribes of the desert, and Saint Goza in the north was too far removed and indolent to be able to rule the two regions at once. There were other lesser Saints scattered across the Empire, to be sure, but none could be a serious challenge to Izat.

Soon both west and south would be hers. Then she would turn her attention elsewhere. She'd always fancied having a sun-metal mine, for the wealth and power it could bring were considerable.

Something caught her attention. What was this? She rolled the naked youths off her, her interest in them long gone. They were too delirious to protest and probably would not recover from being Drawn for several days, some perhaps never. The orgasmic bliss of being Drawn by her was too much for some, but for those who survived the heady passion it was something they would remember and lust after for the rest of their lives. It was her gift to them, not that she didn't take pleasure from it herself, but in recent centuries it had become, well, a bit monotonous, a bit limited. She'd experimented extensively, of course, but there was only so much that could be done to and with the physical forms of the People. That was why she'd become more and more voracious in terms of trade and politics, always looking to extend her dominion so that she might uncover something new, always looking to have more so that she could delight in new senses and experiences.

She wrapped a robe around her svelte golden figure just as a young body-slave hurtled in to prostrate himself before the Saint. From the way the boy was breathing it appeared he had been running, which was most unseemly, although it had brought an attractive blush to the boy's cheeks.

'What is it, Julian?' Izat yawned and gracefully raised a manicured hand to her mouth. She preferred to be surrounded by those who had not been Drawn, because she found it titillating to be served by those who still had some mystery about them.

'Resplendent one, Saint Goza of the north approaches the border.'

Saint Izat almost lost her famous poise and bearing. 'What did you say?'

'Resplendent one, Saint—'

'Yes, Julian, dear, that was rhetorical. But this is unprecedented. No other Saint has entered this region since, well, ever! How dare he do so without my invitation! I haven't had time to bathe, do my hair or anything. Julian, have water drawn for me immediately and my finest robes laid out. The dark blue would be best, don't you think? How has he even come so far? I didn't think that stinking gutbucket could even walk any more. I must be sure to stay downwind of him, eh, Julian? I'd hate to have to hold my nose the whole time.'

'Resplendent one, Saint Goza comes in a wheeled throne larger than any wagon and it is drawn by six horses.'

'Does he indeed? And how many men does he have with him?'

'Fifty, resplendent one.'

'Very good. Tell Captain Tyrius to have my prettiest thousand lined up on our side with bows that are both decorative and lethal. Should one person set foot in this region without my permission, even if it is Saint Goza, sweet Tyrius is to fire, even though it is sure to create quite a mess. Do you understand, dearest Julian?'

'As well as I may, resplendent one.'

'Very good. Then run along while I decide whether to go with curls or ringlets. Curls have more gravitas, while ringlets more artistry. Oh dear, let's go with wavy hair instead. Far more nonchalant, far less threatened.'

An hour later and Saint Izat was ready to face her visitor across the boundary between their two regions. She sat on her largest body-slave, giving Saint Goza her most coquettish look. 'My, my, it appears size is everything with you, no? Or are you compensating for something, do you think? Did you have a troubled childhood, dear Goza? Come, you can tell me.'

'I did not come all this way to suffer your insolence, Izat,' Saint Goza puffed from his prone position in his wheeled throne.

'That is immaterial, dear Goza.' Izat smiled as she folded her smooth hands in her lap. 'What else did you expect when you have thus far failed to compliment me on my wardrobe? I'll have you know I've gone to quite some effort for you. What is it? Were the canapés I provided not substantial enough? Is that why you're in a grump?'

Saint Goza ran one of his large hands back through his greasy hair as he struggled for calm. 'Izat, no more if you please. Yes, you look lovely. You always do. It is a given. Forgive my error in not mentioning it previously. I was overcome by your elegance and was mentally . . . confused for a while. Etcetera. Now will that not do you, Izat?'

Saint Izat preened herself for a moment, deliberately running a fingertip over one of her eyebrows in case one of the hairs should be out of place. She smiled radiantly at her fellow Saint. 'There now; that wasn't so difficult, was it? Goza, the People follow our lead and example, so we should always be mindful of our manners, should we not? How else can we expect them to improve themselves? Well, now that we have observed the formalities and shown ourselves to be paragons of proper protocol, just what is it that I can do for you, pray tell?'

Saint Goza's eyes swept over the Heroes to either side of them. 'Perhaps we should talk somewhere more private.'

Saint Izat gave an insouciant shrug. 'I will simply remove all memory of our meeting from the minds of my People. There are none in my retinue who have not been Drawn by me. Surely you can do the same with your guard, no, Goza?'

'Err . . . yes, of course. Very well. What do you know of the affairs of the south?'

Saint Izat touched a finger to her full bottom lip to show she was thinking. 'Why, absolutely nothing. You?'

Saint Goza grunted. 'I should have expected you to be coy. It matters not. You should know that there is rampant plague in the south.'

Saint Izat put her hands to her cheeks to express calamity. 'Surely not! Those poor People. And Azual is such a darling.'

'Look, I have posted guards on my southern border to turn back any traders and refugees from the south who have come through the central region. I suggest you similarly guard your borders with the southern and central regions. If you do not, there is a risk southerners will travel through your region and into mine through the border between west and north. I do not have enough guards to cover both my southern and western borders effectively, particularly as I permanently have to guard my eastern border against incursions from pagans and barbarians as well. Therefore, I am proposing that we coordinate our forces to ensure the security of our own regions, but also the safety of the wider Empire.'

'Why, Goza, that sounds like a perfectly splendid idea. You are such a clever fellow, really you are. But of course I would like to coordinate my force with your force. It would be a beautiful thing, the coming together of your strength and my splendour. A marriage to inspire the very cosmos!' She fluttered her eyelashes. 'We can start straight away if you like.'

Saint Goza nodded, frowned, shook his head and then rolled his eyes. 'I'll take that as a yes, Izat. That is all I wished to agree with you, so unless there is anything else, I'll be leaving.'

'Such a short honeymoon? But I hardly noticed it. And now you are leaving? Woe is me.' Saint Izat waved languorously. 'But such is the way with marriages. All too quickly the initial bloom of love fades and withers, leaving only thorns and toughness for the once ardent admirer. Still, as long as we can remain civil with each other, then our lives together should not be too onerous. Adieu, cruel Goza, adieu!'

D'Selle watched and listened to Goza through the senses of his Saint, Izat. So, D'Zel was warning him to have nothing to do with the south, was he? D'Zel no doubt considered himself as having the right to insult him in such a manner, now that D'Zel had made a Declaration for that witch D'Shaa.

He couldn't believe that she'd managed to survive so long, but surely these were her final death throes. As Izat had rightly deduced, the south would not survive as it was for much longer. It would fall to plague, uprising or the reprisals of the Peculiar soon enough. The question then was, who would succeed D'Shaa as organising intellect for the south? Surely the elders would not allow D'Zel to succeed D'Shaa, for through his Declaration for her he would share the shame of D'Shaa's downfall. Instead, the elders were sure to favour D'Selle himself, weren't they? Once the south fell, he could no longer be embarrassed by or frowned upon for his public and failed attempt to cause D'Shaa's immediate downfall.

D'Zel must know all this, so just what gambit was he playing in first making a Declaration for D'Shaa and then warning D'Selle off the south? D'Zel had never been arrogant or overly aggressive, so he could not just be trying to defend the south and the other party to his Declaration. Surely D'Zel did not think the south and D'Shaa could survive, did he? No, ridiculous. D'Zel's own ambitions would not want to see the south survive, rally and potentially become a threat to his own interests in the future.

What was it then? What was D'Zel's goal? It just wasn't possible for D'Zel to become the next organising intellect of the region, given that the south was soon to fall and shame both parties to the Declaration.

Ahhh! Then D'Zel's goal had to be something else. D'Zel was not looking to become the organising intellect of the south; he was looking for . . . what?

Ha, ha! Of course. If D'Selle hadn't been in the waking dream, he would have been tempted to dance with glee, although it would have threatened to snap his limbs. *Ha, ha! I have it. There is none as subtle and incisive as me. I know what it is you scheme for, my overambitious D'Zel! It is the boy, the boy! You think he will find and reveal the Geas for you, do you not? Ha, ha! I see you. Truly I am your better, your superior. The playing out of events will show the inevitable truth of it, and that my being, nature and essence are those of the next elder! Foolish, limited D'Zel! I will enjoy your demise even more than D'Shaa's, for she is inexperienced and a slip of a thing, whereas you are the eldest of our rank and a far greater prize. But my wile and guile are greater.* I *am the greater!*

His mind became momentarily giddy, and then he began to school and discipline himself so that his thoughts would become more ordered. It was vital that he reach the boy.

'Izat, can you hear me?'

Yes, divinity. Your voice is in my mind, came back his underling's voice, no primping or posturing now.

'It is about the boy. He must be brought under my sway. You will keep your border with the south open and put word out to the southerners that the west offers them sanctuary. The boy may be brought to us by the exodus. Do you understand?'

Yes, divinity. I have agents in the south whom I will also task with locating Jillan and bringing him west.

'If your agents cannot bring the boy from the south, then they must not hesitate to kill him. Do you understand?'

Yes, divinity.

'Yet time is short and the Peculiar heads into the south. If he finds the boy first, your agents will be powerless to strike at him. Only you might be able to do so, Izat. Therefore, you will enter the southern region immediately and seize or kill the boy. Do you understand?'

The Peculiar is let loose? Izat asked queasily. *Then it will be as you say, divinity. Should mad Azual learn that I have entered his region without his permission, he will be within his rights to seek to kill me. Do I have your permission to kill this Saint before he has the chance to make any such attempt, divinity?*

'You do, Izat,' D'Selle replied with serene magnanimity. 'And the more and the longer the mad one suffers before he dies, the better.'

As you will it, divinity, as you will it!

Many of the sky warriors had been for slitting Minister Praxis's throat right there and then. They'd hit him with quick flicks and punches which, although light, were precisely delivered and immediately had him doubled up and unable to breathe. Then there was a razor-sharp blade pressed against his neck so that he dared not swallow for fear of moving his Adam's apple and killing himself.

Another chair had been brought for Chief Blackwing and placed in front of the ruins of his previous seat, but the chieftain ignored it and paced angrily back and forth in front of the Minister. The chieftain's raised hand had halted the knife so that all present would first hear him speak and be forced to recognise the reassertion of his affronted authority.

'I will have your blood let like some animal's. A cowardly lowlander like you should not be allowed the honour of dying in combat,' the pagan fumed, his breath sour with alcohol. 'Come as a test, have you? From the gods? The gods would not sully their hands with a lying, thieving lowlander. I will not allow you to speak. It offends me that you breathe the sacred air of the upper village. Every moment that you live up here contaminates the air and my people. The words of the crazed one are meaningless at the best of times. He cannot be believed or trusted. Therefore—'

'And what would have persuaded the headwoman to let him pass in the first place?' interjected one of the oldest warriors present, a man with hair like snow although there was little else to mark him as being of some age except for a few lines around his eyes. His body was as whip-like as that of all the others.

Chief Blackwing checked himself, the old warrior's words clearly carrying some weight in the hall. 'Yes, Slavin, a right question. All know she indulges the crazed one too much, and that he is not incapable of tricking her. If the lowlander is a test for us, the test must be whether we are foolish enough to allow him to speak. Are we so full of self-doubt that we would even need to hear him?'

'Or are we so full of self-doubt that we would fear his words?' Slavin responded evenly, eliciting a few nods from others present.

The chieftain glared at the warrior and a bristling Braggar came to his father's side. Apparently thrown by his son's move and how it made him look in need of support, Chief Blackwing tried to wave Braggar away. 'No, Slavin. None of the upper village knows fear of words or lowlanders. We are the favoured of Wayfar and all need fear us! The lowlander will cry for mercy and puke that fear over us so that it is plain for all to see. Then he will be made an instant sacrifice to Wayfar.'

Slavin nodded slightly and turned his eyes expectantly towards the Minister. Chief Blackwing had no choice but to signal to the warrior holding the knife to the Minister's neck to lower his weapon.

'Speak, snivelling lowlander,' commanded Chief Blackwing.

What indignities, degradation and deprivation I have suffered for my faith. None of the Saints in the holy book suffered one whit as much as me. I will be the greatest of the Saints, the most holy and the most revered. I will be a shining example to every student in every town of the Empire, Minister Praxis told himself. *Yet first I must undo the Chaos that ensnares these pagans. I must do whatever is required to see to their ultimate Salvation, whether they come through that Salvation alive or not. I must find a way to lie and manipulate, although it is against the fundamental integrity and honesty of my nature. Ah, none have been so tortured by the world as I! The hardest and coldest of warriors would cry were they but to hear the tale of my plight and woe. Whole nations would collapse. The earth would crumble and fall into the sea. The skies would fall. The cosmos itself will tremble with pity when it learns of what I withstand here. I am the living will of the Saviours. I am the holy book made flesh. Nothing I say, do or describe can be wrong.*

From where he knelt, the Minister met the fat pagan's eye. He did not allow his voice to shake as he said, 'I have come for revenge on the lowlands, Chief Blackwing!'

The Chief peered blearily at the Minister, as if seeing him for the first time and not quite sure what to make of him. Warriors muttered to themselves and each other.

'Revenge because I was exiled by my own ignorant and jealous people!' the Minister bit, finding that he did not need to fake his anger. *It's not that far from the truth, after all.* 'I can lead your warriors to the town of Godsend and show them how to take it from the Empire. Then you will have some revenge for how the Empire originally took the lowlands from you.'

The murmurings among the warriors became louder. Chief Blackwing swayed back a step and his eyes went round the hall. His head swung back to the Minister and he curled his top lip. 'You would turn on your own people? You would expect us to agree to be led by such a creature? The people of the mountains are not as lowly as your own kind. You sicken me. I have heard enough.'

The chieftain looked towards the warrior with the bared blade.

'It is not I who is cowardly, Chief Blackwing,' the Minister said quickly. 'It is not I who would hide from dying in combat. I would not be content with growing fat and old while my enemy made free with my lands and cattle. And what are you chief of anyway? A few barren rocks? Do those rocks really need your protection?'

The warrior with the knife hesitated as discontent and mocking laughter were heard among the warriors. Braggar bumped the warrior and the man dropped his knife. The eyes of the chief's son were alive with emotion, but whether with anger or something else, the Minister could not tell. The air was thick with the threat of violence. Jostling began among the warriors and a number pushed forward. Someone fell to the floor with a curse.

With a roar, Chief Blackwing bulled his way forward. 'Wayfar guide us!' he yelled in the middle of the crowd, raising his arms high and spreading the colourful underside of his winged cape wide. 'We pray to you, holy Wayfar!' Half of the warriors in the hall went to their knees and those who remained standing looked around uncertainly. 'We are not proud when we stand or kneel before you.' The chieftain's voice echoed back from the high roof space. Half of those standing now lowered their heads and began to pray silently. The rest looked to Slavin or Braggar, but it was clear the chieftain had stolen the momentum. 'We are not proud when we ask for the gift of your wisdom. We will listen to the high winds through day and night before raising a blade in your name!'

Chief Blackwing stared straight at Slavin as he spoke, nodding at him meaningfully until the snow-haired warrior finally capitulated and returned a resigned nod.

'It is well that we seek his divine wisdom now. Surely we have just passed through the first part of his test and not been found wanting. Take the lowlander to the place of high meditation, for he will spend the day and night there so that he too may be tested. You two, take him. Now!'

Two wiry warriors caught the Minister under his armpits and hauled him to his feet. They dragged him out of the hall, shaking or cuffing him whenever he tried to ask anything, and up a slippery shale path. At the edge of an overhanging precipice was a small stone shelter. They led him inside and secured a rope around his waist.

'Down there!' one of them ordered curtly.

'Saviours preserve me, what unholy place is this! A pagan garderobe! It is the stench of the Chaos itself!'

'Move, lowlander,' coughed the other and showed a length of his knife. 'Down the hole!'

The Minister approached the hole in the floor where the pagans of the upper village disposed of their waste. The giddy drop below made his stomach lurch and he tried to back away, but the pagan devils were right behind him, pushing him forward, wrestling him down the hole.

He screamed and screamed until his lungs gave out. Then he was being lowered as the wind taunted and twisted him. He was a thousand feet high! Tears of terror froze on his cheeks.

His feet made contact with a pillar of rock that rose hundreds of feet from the slope of the mountain and ended a dozen or so feet below the overhang and garderobe. The pillar had a flattish top about four feet across, and it was onto this that the Minister was deposited. The rope dropped down, lashing his head and left shoulder as it came. He just about caught it without overbalancing.

He was stranded in the void. The wind nudged him and he was convinced he was falling. He saw the detail of the valley floor as it rushed up towards him. The sky sailed past him. *Don't look at the clouds! They're moving and will take your balance! Don't look down! Close your eyes. No, don't! The pillar's swaying in the wind.*

'Holy Saint Azual preserve me! Master, where are you? Help me!'

Praxis, you must endure. You must persevere, replied a voice from everywhere and nowhere, but he did not know if it was the Saint or just his own mind speaking out loud.

He shuffled his feet back under his bottom and then further back until he could lower himself forward flat on his stomach. He now presented less of a target for the wind at least.

Liquid spattered down on him from above and the two pagans laughed evilly.

'. . . until Bess made the mistake of fluttering her eyelashes at Jed. Your mother was not about to let anything even get started, so it came as no surprise to any of us when Bess suddenly broke out in an ugly rash all over her face and had a terrible itch in all the wrong places. Well, none of the men of New Sanctuary wanted to know then, did they, lest they catch something? Bess started screaming that your mother was a witch and the elders became right discomfited, for it's one thing within the Empire for a woman to know herbs and remedies, but quite another for her to conjure with spells and curses. Well, next thing you know, Bess loses her voice so that she can't be complaining no more and your mother says to her for all to hear, "And you'll be losing a lot more than that, Brazen Bess, if you don't take yourself and your wickedness off to some other town. Next time, you'd better think twice before trying to turn the eyes and mind of a good man like my Jedadiah, you hear? Now be off with you, for my patience and the indulgence of this town are all used up." And Brazen Bess ran out of the town's gates and was never heard from again!'

Thomas finished relating his story as he guided the horse pulling their wagon onto a near-invisible side road. Aspin laughed and slapped his thigh. The blacksmith's yarns had worked their charm all afternoon, helping the mountain warrior to relax and forget his aches and pains, completely winning him over.

Jillan remained quiet. At first he'd been enthralled by the tales of his parents in New Sanctuary, but his unease had increased with each anecdote. He couldn't put his finger on it exactly, but there was something about the stories that just didn't feel right. It felt like Thomas was criticising his parents, although Jillan couldn't remember anything specific he'd said. As Aspin had hooted louder and louder, Jillan had withdrawn into himself more and more.

Thomas suddenly stopped and looked all around, anger flickering in his eyes. 'We're being followed.'

Aspin also looked around and groped behind him for his bow. 'How do you know? I haven't seen or heard anything.'

'It's what we haven't heard. I know these woods. They're too quiet. There's some hunter out there. I can lose them, though,' Thomas replied, and flicked the reins.

'How can we possibly lose them?' Aspin wondered.

'My people know the hidden paths of the woods. There are the roads everyone can see, but then there are other routes and ways. Otherwise, the Saint and his Heroes would have found our hamlet long ago.'

'Is it magic?' Aspin asked with raised eyebrows.

'Yes and no. It's to do with all life energy somehow being connected, but our wizard, Bion, can explain it better than me. Have your bow strung nonetheless, warrior.'

Aspin worked quickly and had an arrow nocked and his weapon raised before Jillan had even begun to wonder whether he should be doing the same. He watched everything as if in a dream. He was detached from it all somehow. There was no sense of danger as far as he could tell.

A large shadow blocked the route ahead. The blacksmith cursed vilely, dropped his reins and produced wicked shimmering blades out of nowhere. 'Shoot it, warrior!'

Aspin raised his bow.

Jillan blinked. 'No, Aspin, do not.'

The mountain warrior hesitated, blinking himself and half shaking his head.

'Shoot it!' Thomas grated.

'Do not! It is my friend. You will not shoot, Aspin. All is well.'

A huge black wolf sat in their path. Its orange eyes watched them carefully. The horse reared and shied and Thomas had to scramble for the reins again. 'Woah! Woah! Damn it!'

A woodsman stepped from the trees and smiled apologetically at them. His hands were empty and he held them out from his sides. 'I am sorry if my friend startled you. He did not know how else to present himself, you see.'

'Ash!' Jillan grinned.

'Jillan, hello! Fancy meeting you here like this.'

'It is no coincidence,' Thomas sneered, causing the wolf to growl softly and the horse to roll its eyes and whinny in terror. 'None can chance upon this path unless they have deliberately bent their will to it. You have been stalking us. You do not speak the truth. Aspin, keep your bow trained on them.'

Ash wobbled his head this way and that. 'What can I say? Not much escapes my friend the wolf. He was concerned for Jillan and I simply followed him here.'

'Aspin, it's all right,' Jillan ventured.

Aspin shook his head again as if troubled by invisible buzzing things. 'This man cannot be trusted. He is . . . inconsistent. I can read that he will one day betray you.'

Ash's ready smile slipped slightly.

After all, he has already betrayed me once. But how can Aspin know Ash will betray me again? Surely the future isn't already written, is it? If it is, then I fear all will happen as the Book of Saviours says. Are we all doomed? Me, my parents, Samnir, dear Hella, Aspin himself? Should I just give up?

Jillan, remember yourself, sighed the taint. *Ash may have betrayed you before, but he had no choice in the matter. You know that. It might happen again in the same way. So what? Who are you to judge betrayal, eh, when you betrayed your town, the Empire and everyone who loved you? There is one person you still have not betrayed though, isn't there? Yourself, Jillan! Betray yourself and then it will truly all be over. Still, at least I wouldn't then have to point out the obvious to you every five seconds. Look, let Ash come along with us even if it's just to put that blacksmith's nose out of joint. Besides, who wouldn't want a big black wolf at their side? That creature would make even the mad Saint hesitate.*

'Aspin, is it Ash's *intention* to betray me?'

Good boy. For once he listens.

'No, probably not.'

'Then he comes with us. I assume that's what you want, Ash?'

'More fun than staying in that shack, or prison as you call it, on my own. The wolf gets bored just eating squirrel skewers by the fire and I can't stand his bilious guts. You know how he gets.'

'No!' Thomas said vehemently. 'I will not risk him coming to the hamlet. The decision is not yours, Jillan. The Saint will know.'

'Ash is Unclean, Thomas. He has never been Drawn. The Saint will *not* know. Either Ash and the wolf come with us or Aspin and I will be leaving you right now.'

The blacksmith's brow became an anvil, but he had no choice but to agree. He gestured furiously at Ash to climb into the back of the wagon and then lashed the sidling horse forward with the reins. The wolf had already disappeared.

Minister Praxis moaned in the darkness as he clung to the top of the pillar. His fingers were so numb he could feel nothing. For all he knew, he was clutching at thin air and spinning through the eternal void. His teeth chattered a prayer to anything that could hear him or would listen. He hardly knew his own name any more.

Something slapped him in the middle of the back and he screamed like he'd been crucified.

'Pssst! Grab the rope, lowlander. Put the loop round you.'

Ever so slowly, he unclenched himself and dragged elbow and knees in. He did not know if his body had the strength to support even its own weight any more. It was a dead thing to him. Was he rising or falling? He travelled on the wind. Free at last! But he became tangled in the rope. He flailed at it but it drew tighter around him and trapped him. It yanked him back into the world of hardship and suffering.

'No!'

'What are you doing, lowlander? Have you lost your mind? Be still, curse you!' the voice shouted, the stone shelter amplifying it. 'Mind your head.'

'Argggh!'

'I warned you! Up now. Like being born again, isn't it? The hole is a cunny of sorts, they say. The cunny of the gods. Here you are. Drink this,' boomed the voice in his face, all but overwhelming him.

A mug was roughly pushed into his hands. Its contents were warm but smelt awful, like goats or something equally unclean.

'I . . . cannot.'

'Then you have lost all sense and I may as well throw you to your death right now. It's fermented goat's milk. It will restore you. You are nothing but bones. I had no trouble pulling you up on my own. Do you not eat? Drink it or I'll stuff you back down the hole and you'll end up broken at the bottom of the mountain. Then you'll never have your revenge, will you?'

Praxis, you must endure.

The Minister tentatively sipped at the foul substance. He blinked and finally took in his rescuer. 'You are the chief's son,' he said slowly, gazing at the brute's bullish face and hefty young shoulders.

'Tell me of this revenge you plan,' Braggar insisted. 'And drink!'

Several sips. 'I-I will see them all die for what they have done to me. Every last one of them will die.'

'Yes!' Braggar said eagerly. 'But my father is a coward. He will not fight. He shames me and all the warriors of the upper village. How can he claim to be faithful to Wayfar of the Warring Winds when he will have no war? Even you, a mere lowlander, seem to have more courage than he. Yet he refuses to step aside to let a real man lead the people. He will not be persuaded.'

A larger sip this time. He was feeling a little better. *Endure!* 'I see, I see. Then he must be . . . removed, for the good of all, so that the desire of your gods can be carried out. If you do not do as the gods will it, they will turn against you and put an end to your people. Do you not see that if you love your people and the gods, Chief Blackwing must be removed? If you love your father's good name and hope to be able to honour his memory one day, then he must be removed before he can shame himself in front of all your warriors tomorrow.'

'Yes, yes! It must be done tonight. You will do it, lowlander.'

A gulp of liquid that was too hot. '*I*?'

'Yes. Or I have no more use for you and you can go back down the hole.'

See how corrupt and conniving these pagans are. To think that a son would condone the killing of his own father! How typical then that the son should lack the courage and conviction to commit the deed himself. Yet what was the life of a pagan to him? Less than nothing. Every pagan that lived was an offence to the Saviours. Every pagan that died represented a weakening of the Chaos. It would not be murder. It would be Salvation. 'How must it be done?'

'My father scales the peak with the coming of every dawn, to see the world born anew and to greet storm, sun and rain. Of late he has drunk through the night before making the climb. I pray that he never slips, but if the gods should will it then so be it, for I am ever *their* faithful son.'

'It will be done.'

'Then I will go see him one last time and raise a toast in his name.' Braggar laughed.

With satisfaction, Elder Thraal watched through the waking dream as the organising intellects of the regions schemed and fought among themselves. He'd always known that D'Selle of the west and D'Zel of the north had designs on challenging him and becoming elders. That was precisely why he'd persuaded the council to endorse his promotion of one as young and inexperienced as D'Shaa to the rank of organising intellect. Just as Elder Thraal had known would happen, the ambitious

D'Selle had been unable to resist attacking D'Shaa. Elder Thraal had then held off punishing D'Selle's failure so that D'Zel would be drawn into the conflict. Thus distracted, none would have the capacity or resources to plot against him.

All had gone just as he'd planned and knew it would. His indirect but deliberate destabilisation of the southern region was also beginning to succeed in drawing out the pagans and the Geas. If he could secure the Geas on behalf of the Declension, then the glory would be his rather than the Great Saviour's. Surely the Declension would then consider having him replace the Great Saviour of this world.

Elder Thraal congratulated himself on having had the extreme foresight to put himself forwards as Watcher of the elders millennia ago, when his kind had first arrived on this world. In his role he was often awake, in regular close contact with the organising intellects and capable of influencing them and events in their regions directly. By contrast, the other elders and the Great Saviour himself were all but permanently asleep, influencing affairs in this realm only indirectly as they communed with their kind and the cosmos beyond this world. Yes, he aged faster than them as a consequence, but the final victory would ultimately be his alone.

Chief Blackwing stood upon the edge of eternity and spread his arms wide as he welcomed the rising sun. How it burned his eyes! Such was the cost of gazing upon the light of the divine. The wind numbed his face and he let his cape drop to the ground so that he was naked save for his necklace of gemstones. If he stood like this for the time it took the sun to rise, he would die of exposure. Such was the cost of being embraced by the air of the divine. Blood trickled between his toes. The sharp stones of the mountain peak had cut the bared soles of his feet as he'd made his dawn pilgrimage. Such was the cost of walking on the ground of the divine. The clouds around the peak made his skin wet and the rocks wet. If he was not careful, he would slip and break open his head. Such was the cost of sharing the life-giving waters of the divine. Death was the cost to a mortal who approached too close to the divine. Yet no mortal could exist without the divine or resist its call either. That was why death always came, he knew. That was how he could be so accepting of it.

He was prepared. He was ready as he heard death moving up behind him. He'd said goodbye to his son, a son whose eyes showed him that now was his time. Chief Blackwing did not regret the life he'd led, nor did he regret the death he would have. How could he? It was what his warriors needed of him and he'd always tried his best to give them what they needed. He just hoped that it would not be they who regretted it.

'Have faith, my people, have faith!'

A stone skittered behind him and he turned.

Chief Blackwing smiled. 'You bring death to my people, do you not?'

'Yes, I do,' Minister Praxis replied as he pushed the pagan off the peak.

CHAPTER 10:

For and from the sin of being

'Ah, you're awake, dear one. You slept a good number of hours. How do you feel?'

'I am well, friend Anupal, thank you,' Freda replied, shading her eyes against the bright sky. 'Where are we?'

'Heading south. Would you be able to run, do you think? We would make better time that way. The world never stops or waits for anyone, you see, not even me. If we do not get to where we need to be on time, it might not even be there any more, and we might never find it, for places are people as well as rocks, trees and buildings. Places are moments in time. Do you understand what I mean, dear one?'

She stuck her tongue out in concentration. 'So if I went back to the mine now, it wouldn't be the same place?'

'Precisely.' He smiled approvingly. 'Some of the same rocks would still be there, but others wouldn't. Some of the same people would be there, but some wouldn't and there'd probably be new ones. Certainly it wouldn't be an entirely different place, but it would be different enough in very important ways.'

She could see that. Without Norfred there, the mine would never be the same place for her. 'So a place can only ever be visited once? There's no going back to it . . . in time? That's strange. And also very sad, Anupal.'

Her observation slightly caught him out. He'd never thought of it like that before. Yes, it was sad really. The wonderful places he'd known but would never see again. They could not be recovered. Such a shame that the mortals of this world had such short lives, like leaves on a tree waiting to fall. He forced the corners of his mouth up. 'But let us not be melancholic or downhearted, dear one, for we are in a good place now. We have each other, yes?'

'Yes, Anupal.' She nodded, mimicking his smile, although it made her cheeks grind. 'I have a question, though. If we do not know if a place will be there when we get there, how do we know where we're going in the first place?'

'Ah! And here is the nature of the will. Your will must decide what it wants or needs and then create that place by travelling there on time. With most places, there isn't much need to rush, but with others you are tested to your limits. And some places are impossible to find, just fantasy.'

'I see. What is it your will wants or needs then, Anupal?'

'Why, I have been told there are people in the south who might also become my friends if I arrive there in time to do things for them. Do you remember I said I try to do good things to make good friends? That is enough for me. What is it you want or need, dear one?'

Freda hesitated. He'd told her what he wanted, so it only seemed right she told him the same. And he was her friend. 'Well, I need to find someone called Jan, who either went east or south, although I don't know what east is. And I need to . . . to . . .'

'Is that a stutter you have? Be not afraid to tell me, dear one,' the Peculiar said and touched her injured hand.

His touch sent a sparkling thrill through her. Other than Torpeth, he was the only person ever to touch her in a way that wasn't hurtful. He didn't feel as warm and firm as Torpeth – in fact, his light fingers felt like a spider that had scuttled over her once – but it excited her nevertheless. In a rush, she said, 'I need to find three lost temples so that I can then find Haven.'

His head jerked up and back as if she'd punched him. She was suddenly worried she'd upset him, but then his lips took on their habitual smile. 'Do you indeed, dear one? Curious places to need to visit, and they may well test us to our limits, but I will help you find them if you help me make these new friends and promise to go with me to the Great Temple one day.'

'What is the Great Temple? Is it one of the lost temples?'

'Nothing quite so interesting, I'm afraid. It sounds far grander than it really is. It's just my home, that's all. I need to go there to rest sometimes, but I could not bear to be parted from you, my friend.'

'I will go there if it makes you happy, Anupal.'

'That's good. We are agreed and now of one mind and will. We are one, Freda.'

'We are one,' she echoed. It sounded nice, if a little strange.

'Then let us run together, Freda! I will race you. First to the horizon, that line in the distance.'

Exhilarated by the idea, she dived off the wagon and into the ground. The road here was paved, so there weren't too many tree roots in the ground to slow her down. She came back up and coursed forward, her flesh intermingling and speeding through the road's substance.

'Hey, not fair!' the Peculiar yelled as he leapt to set the horse free, giving it a mental command to follow on behind them. Then he lengthened his perfect limbs and began to sprint after her. He skimmed over the ground, only lightly touching it every ten metres or so. He quickly overtook her and then created a cape for himself so that he could soar and swoop at even greater speeds.

Behind him, Freda came on like an earthquake, deliberately shaking his flighted stride whenever he was forced to touch down. The Peculiar laughed like a delighted child, though he hardly had the breath for it. He inevitably slowed and Freda managed to draw level with him.

What an amazing creature she was. Part of the reason the Peculiar had suggested they run was so that he could test her. The fact she could keep up was amazing in itself, but over a longer distance, with her relentless and stone-based stamina, she might even be able to overhaul him, for he would eventually tire. No wonder the elseworlders wanted her for themselves.

Yet that fool Goza had simply intended to have her for a snack. Did that mean the elseworlders weren't actually aware of her potential? That would mean they were also likely to be unaware of her quest for the lost temples, the old gods and Haven. All the better for him then. Could it be that this simple golem would finally deliver him the Geas where all else had failed? Incredible if it were so, but tellingly ironic. Where his scheming and manipulation were too often frustrated, faith and innocence found a way. And he had never met one as innocent as her. He found that she charmed him as much as his nature despised her. In some ways it would be a shame to reach that moment when all her illusions were shattered and she was thereby destroyed. But it was the way of things, the essence of his being and the nature of his will. As it had always been, so it would always be, and getting there still gave him pleasure.

Thomas guided their wagon out of the trees and onto a route that passed through a cluster of small dimly lit buildings just as it was getting dark. 'Welcome to Linder's Drop! May not be much to look at, but there are a few outlying farms too and a meeting house yonder. My forge is just beyond the stream there.'

'It's quiet,' Jillan said, looking around owlishly.

'There are people watching us though,' Ash said, rubbing the back of his neck as if it prickled.

'The people here are shy and gentle,' Thomas said softly. 'They are rightly suspicious of strangers. Some of the other forest communities are far more belligerent than we are. But the people will all come to say hello in the morning, you'll see, once Bion has had a chance to size you up and has given the all-clear.'

'Bion is your wizard, yes?' Aspin nodded. 'Is he your holy man?'

Thomas chewed on his answer for a moment or two. 'In a manner of speaking. People will ask him to explain things from time to time, and he'll choose either to answer them or not. It's not always clear if he's giving an answer or avoiding it, though. Once I asked him something quite simple and he remained silent. I thought he was refusing to answer and left him sitting on his rock. But he found me the next day and spoke the answer, explaining that he'd been so busy working it out that he hadn't even noticed me leave. He says strange things quite a lot that I'm sure are responses to things he's been asked years before. But is he holy? We don't worship him and he doesn't lead us in worship, if that's what you mean. Each of us chooses our own relationship with the Geas, making observances to the gods as we also choose.'

'Does he have matted hair, walk around naked and eat pine nuts all the time?' Aspin asked.

'Er . . . no. He is hunched, well dressed, constantly smokes a pipe and eats more than any ten men put together without ever getting any bigger. Suffice to say, he doesn't get invited to dinner by anyone any more.'

'Sounds as bad as my wolf friend, although the wolf doesn't usually wait to be invited. When I'm having dinner, he tends to be of the opinion that I've stolen the food from the forest, and since the forest belongs to him I've stolen it from him. He therefore has no qualms about taking it back if he chooses.'

'Then I pray Bion and the wolf do not meet, lest the wolf give the wizard ideas.'

They all laughed, although Jillan had long since tired of the back and forth between Thomas and Ash. He needed to get to Hyvan's Cross to free his parents. Everything else was an unwelcome distraction at best and a dangerous loss of time at worst. He understood Aspin's argument that coming to Linder's Drop might be a useful means to an end, but he was finding it hard to have faith in anyone or anything any more.

Well, it was your parents who told you to find this Thomas Ironshoe in the first place, remember? the taint observed.

'Do *you* trust him then?' Jillan asked silently.

Me? Ha! I don't trust anyone, do I? I hardly trust myself sometimes.

'Precisely.'

That would mean your parents were wrong then, wouldn't it?

'I suppose,' Jillan conceded.

Parents make mistakes all the time, I imagine. Thomas said he hadn't seen them in how long? Perhaps he's changed in that time.

'Changed how?'

How do I know? You've *changed in just the short time you've been away from Godsend, haven't you? People change. It doesn't mean it's impossible to have faith in anyone or anything though.*

'I haven't changed.'

Of course you have.

'How?'

You've become far more annoying and you ask far more stupid questions than before.

'Not true. Minister Praxis said I always asked too many ignorant questions too.'

Yes, and it was your questions that started all this in the first place. Have you learned nothing by asking them? Why can't you just stay quiet and behave yourself like everyone else? Why can't you just do as everyone tells you, eh?

'Because then nothing would ever change. The bad things would last forever.'

Precisely. Nothing would ever change, and where would we be then, eh? It's important you remember that and have faith in it from hereon in.

'What do you mean? Taint, answer me! Why is it important I remember that? Taint, please. Is it to do with Thomas? Is it to do with freeing my parents?'

But there was only silence and now they were pulling up to a long two-storey wood-beamed building with lime-washed plaster between the pillars and cross-beams. Lanterns shone from behind half-closed shutters and a coal fire glowed invitingly deep within. There was the tantalising smell of freshly baked bread and the air was rich with stewed meat and vegetables. Adjoining the main house was a large shed containing a brute of an anvil and a full range of buckets, pincers, hammers, some surely taller than a man, and other tools.

'This is your home?' Aspin asked in awe.

'Giants must have built it,' Ash whispered.

Thomas smiled with some pride. 'Honest hard work – and the help of my neighbours and the wizard, of course. But I need such a place to contain my good wife and our three girls, for verily they are forces of nature, as you will soon see for yourselves. What say you, Jillan? Was it worth the visit?'

Jillan was spared the need to answer as a gale of shrieks and excitement assailed them.

'Papa! Papa!'

'Papa is home!'

'And he has brought visitors, Mama!'

'Did you bring us ribbons, Papa?' called the youngest of the voices. 'You promised me a yellow one!'

Thomas looked at his companions ruefully. 'Some say I spoil them, but I am powerless before them.' Then he jumped down from the wagon and spread his arms wide as three girls burst from the house and threw themselves at him all at once. Large as Thomas was, they almost bowled him over. Fluttering eyes looked over their father's shoulder and around the side of him at Jillan, Aspin and Ash.

'Look at that one, Betha! He's your age.'

'No, Ausa, he's older. Too old for me. Yuck!'

'Not that one. That one!'

'Oo, yes!'

Only the youngest noticed her father's loss of hair.

'Don't worry, it'll grow back once Bion's found a magic cowpat large enough to cover my head,' he said, and she giggled. 'Now, Stara, may I introduce you to my good friend Jillan. Stara, Jillan saved my life.'

Stara stared and stared. Then she became bashful and hid behind her father, until he dragged her back out and forced her to face Jillan. She suddenly thrust her hand out and an embarrassed Jillan had to clamber down and shake it. Stara then wouldn't let his hand go and pulled him after her and up the several stairs into the house.

'Mama!' Stara called. 'This is Jillan and he saved Papa's life!'

'Then he shall have pride of place at the table and will be toasted by us all. Stara, lay extra places. Maybe Jillan will help.'

Wooden bowls and spoons were thrust into Jillan's hands as Stara directed him towards a large dining table. He'd hardly managed a nod to the homely looking woman in the kitchen area. She wore a startlingly white dress, like all her daughters. *How on earth did they manage to keep them clean?* He looked down at his soiled and torn clothes guiltily. His mother would have told him off at length for coming home like this.

'Here, slow-snail, I'll do it,' Stara said energetically and whipped the bowls back out of his hands.

He dropped several spoons.

'Clumsy claws!' she giggled and swept them up before he could bend down.

Ash and Aspin entered, each with one of Thomas's daughters on his arm. Ash was with Ausa, a tall china-skinned brunette, while Aspin escorted Betha, a dimpled auburn. Stara was suddenly before Jillan again with twinkling eyes and rosy cheeks. 'Come sit next to me,' she breathed, her breath smelling of cinnamon, which was also the colour of her hair. She put her hands to his shoulders and pushed him round the table to the top chair. Thomas's other daughters peeled away to help their mother bring through piled trenchers of food, while Thomas poured beakers of ale from a keg and waved Aspin and Ash over to seats at the table.

In moments all were seated and staring longingly at the bread, vegetables and cheeses. Thomas's wife ladled an aromatic stew into bowls, which were passed quickly round the table.

Thomas stood with his beaker of ale in hand. 'I know it is a terrible test to ask you to hold your appetites in check for a minute longer, but the stew is piping hot and will only burn the hasty eater. I'd like to welcome Ash and Aspin to our table, and also Jillan, to whom this family is indebted. I'd therefore like to ask you all to raise your cups in a toast to him. The ale is my best and as restorative as my wife Sabella's fare is hearty. So, the toast is to Jillan and new friends!'

Everyone repeated the toast and drank from their cups, Ash draining his in one and only then realising that everyone else had sipped theirs. 'Sorry,' he said with a cheeky smile. 'I think there was less in mine than everyone else's.' There were giggles from the girls and Thomas tapped him another generous measure. The blacksmith then looked at Jillan expectantly.

Jillan squirmed slightly and blushed. 'I . . . Well, it was nothing, you know. I don't know what else to say really.'

Sat next to him, Stara beamed proudly as if he'd spoken with inspirational grace and wonder. 'Can we eat now, Papa?' she asked, saving an immensely grateful Jillan from further embarrassment.

Thomas chuckled fondly. 'Of course, daughter.'

And anything else he would have said was lost in the hubbub of requests for trenchers to be passed, arms stretching, the clatter of cups and serving spoons, and excitement. Aspin wasted no time tearing off a large piece of bread for himself, heaping stew onto it and then cramming too much into his mouth.

'He eats with more alacrity than my wolf,' Ash declared, winning the attention of all three girls at once as they gasped, cooed and begged to hear about the beast.

Aspin didn't mind one bit as he grinned at Jillan with bulging cheeks, juice running down his chin. Jillan had to smile to see his friend so happy. Then Jillan turned his attention to his own bowl and realised he was hungry beyond sense or description. He shovelled food into his mouth, swallowed and felt dizzy for a second. He took another spoonful. He'd had a sick emptiness in his gut since he'd left Godsend but the well-seasoned stew was already doing much to put an end to that. As he ate, his spirits began to lift and he felt a strange mix of emotions: giddy relief, guilty pleasure, happy discomfort and the quelling of fears. He finished his ale and Stara refilled his beaker.

'I don't mind telling you we never had anything this good in the mountains,' Aspin said as he cut into a crumbly white cheese.

'You're from the mountains!' Betha sighed, hanging on his every word. 'I knew there was something special about you. They must be beautiful. I'd love to see them one day.'

So Aspin regaled them with tales of the mountains and a comical holy man called Torpeth who wandered around naked and worried the goats. The mountain warrior enjoyed being the centre of attention for a while and none begrudged him it. Thomas listened attentively to everything that was said, smiling and nodding with the rest. Jillan recalled that when they'd been travelling in the woods, Aspin had avoided saying he was from the mountains, but now it didn't seem to matter. What difference could it make anyway?

Jillan smiled winningly as Stara offered him another beaker. He felt a twinge of conscience as Hella came into his mind for the first time since they'd arrived in Linder's Drop, but he suppressed any feelings of guilt. *I haven't done anything wrong*, he told himself, *and her eyes are nothing like Hella's.*

In the dark his helmet shone so brightly it was hard for her to look at him. It lit the nearby water he called a *stream* and the hollow among the trees where they'd stopped to rest for what he called the *night*. There were white twinkling things up high, which she took to be large diamonds embedded in the roof of the sky-cave, and a silver crescent, which looked like some sort of hook. Maybe the Overlords ran chains over the hook to lift heavy objects. Maybe the silver metal was particularly strong, but she couldn't sense anything from it.

'Anupal, doesn't the sun-metal hurt your head? It would burn me.'

He blinked at her. 'Actually, my head would hurt even more without it. Yes, it burns a little, but I use some of my strength to restore my skin. It's a constant drain on my power, of course, and the only reason I didn't thrash you more easily in the race.'

'I let you win.'

His mouth dropped open in surprise and then he frowned. 'You did not! You're teasing me.'

She made the air boom within her chest to show she was amused.

'I knew it. You minx!'

She boomed again and then stilled. 'The sun-metal helps you then?'

'Yes,' he replied. 'It protects me from all sorts of things.'

'I'm glad it can be used for protection too. I thought its only use was weapons.'

'I know what you mean. Let me tell you about the essential nature of sun-metal then. It is the distilled and counteracting force to omnipotence. Were it not for sun-metal, the gods would be omnipotent, but that would be impossible. If they were omnipotent, of course, there'd be no other life on this world, meaning that its gods couldn't exist either. Thus, the existence of the gods demands the existence of sun-metal, to which they are vulnerable. In fact, I suspect sun-metal wouldn't exist without the gods either, although I might be wrong there. Sun-metal is inert as far as I'm aware, which stops it from being omnipotent as well. Do you see?'

'No.'

'Oh. Well, hmm. Let's see. To stop any of the gods becoming all-powerful, we have sun-metal. Imagine if one of the gods went mad and started destroying everything. That would be terrible, wouldn't it? How could they be stopped? Well, we have sun-metal to do that. How about that?'

It made a sense of sorts. 'Yes. So sun-metal is good?'

The Peculiar scratched his head, which turned out to be his helmet. 'Only problem with this thing,' he muttered, picked up a thin stick, inserted it between brow and helmet, and then waggled it about vigorously. 'Ah, that's better! What were you saying? Oh yes. Is it good? Well, it's inert – dead – so it's neither good nor bad really. It's good it exists, I suppose, as otherwise nothing would exist. Hang on, is that right? Yes, probably. But forget that. Sun-metal is a weapon and a defence. It is neither good nor bad in itself. Only the things that people do with it are good or bad. Only people are good or bad, but it's usually very, very difficult to know what's good or bad. What one person thinks is good, another often thinks is bad, and vice versa.'

Freda pondered that for some time while the Peculiar watched the moths dancing around his helmet, touching it and then flaring as they died. 'But you said you like to do good things to make good friends. Would some people think the things you do are bad?'

Oops. I've underestimated her again. That'll teach me to run away with my mouth. Always was a weakness of mine, that. What do you expect when I haven't spoken to anyone except those dusty old elseworlders for millennia? Of course, my vanity doesn't help me keep quiet either. But I'm so beautiful, how could I not be so vain? Blithely, the Peculiar answered, 'Why, you're right, I suppose, friend Freda. Do you think the things I do are bad?'

She shook her head. 'Of course not. You saved me.'

'Well, there you are. It's only when people agree like that that they can be friends, yes?'

'Yes,' she said happily. 'So would me getting you more sun-metal help you do good things?'

What's this now? 'Why, I should think so. It is a powerful substance, after all. Why, do you think you could find me some?'

'Oh yes. It's easy to find. It vibrates in a particular way, you see.'

It does? Amazing! 'Well, if it's easy to find, I'd be grateful. Lot of it around is there?'

'Not so much really, but there are areas of it. The Overlords had exhausted most of it in the mine. I'll get some when we come close to more.'

The elseworlders are running out in the north then? That's worrying. If they don't have a breakthrough in the east soon, then we'll all have problems. Still, if you can find more for me, I won't have to deal with them any more. In fact, I might keep you for myself rather than hand you over to them. 'That's good, dear one. You must be tired, though. Time you slept, for we will have a trying day tomorrow as we pass through the central region. We could go around it, but we'd lose too much time. The central region is overseen by a minor functionary, one Saint Virulus. He's in charge of very little because there are no towns, fields or mines in the region. The Overlords don't want anyone coming too near them in their Great Temple, or sacred heart as they call it, you see. They struggle to tolerate even their attendant slaves – retainers, they call them – at the best of times. The region's largely rocky crags, lichens and moss. There are small forts, of course, but they're manned by the army's undesirables, because no one else wants a posting to that barren place. Most Heroes would prefer a tour in the east than the central region.'

'Why will it be trying, friend Anupal?'

The Peculiar picked at a seam on his tunic, avoiding her eyes. 'Well, I may have been a bit rude to the Saint on the way to find you before. I may have called him a jumped-up little jobsworth. Can you believe he demanded to see my papers or some such, as if a piece of paper could prove my identity? I, Anupal, Lord of . . . Well, anyway, it was insupportable! I was so irked by the manner of the creature that I couldn't remain as handsome as I usually am, which meant I couldn't completely charm him. Then the little runt ordered some of his louts to arrest me because I didn't have a piece of paper. Well, I was having none of that and ended up causing quite a fracas – or ruckus, whichever. They'll be on the lookout when we pass through again. We'll be able to elude the senses of the Heroes without trouble, of course, for you can pass below them and I can pass way overhead, but these Saints are unpredictable, and Virulus may be better prepared to marshal a troubling power against me this time. I'll annihilate him as necessary, of course, but it would be inconveniencing, eh, and the Overlords might then start complaining and I'll get no peace whatsoever. I'll never hear the end of it, as they never forget, these Overlords, and they *do* like to hold a grudge. Quite tiresome, they can be.'

'Anupal, you said the Overlords are in the Great Temple in the central region, yes? Is not the Great Temple also your home? Why would you live in such a barren place with the Overlords?'

The Peculiar pulled a face. 'Well, it's complicated and a long story. Meanwhile, the night is getting short.' He dropped his voice an octave and made it thrum soothingly. 'Enough questions for now, dear one. Go to sleep and have sweet dreams.'

Her lids became heavy and she yawned. 'Yes, friend Anupal.'

Jillan jolted awake, disorientated. Where was he? He was in a room he'd never seen before. There was no one else there. Full daylight came through a pair of shutters, and not the harsh light of a new morning either. It felt closer to the middle of the day. How could that be?

His head hurt. The room was small and golden-beamed. He lay on a raised bed covered in linen. It was strange to sleep so high off the ground. He pushed over-piled pillows away from him so he could move more freely.

'Taint, are you there? What happened last night?'

The only reply was from birds twittering beyond the shutters. Their song sounded flat.

He put his feet on the floor and realised he was only wearing his underclothes. Where were his other clothes? A floorboard creaked beneath his foot and he heard movement in response some distance below. Footsteps on stairs, coming closer. *My clothes, where are they?* The door to the room began to open.

'Are you awake, dear?' came Sabella's voice as the blacksmith's wife entered. 'I brought you your clothes. Cleaned and mended.'

'Th-Thank you . . . ma'am,' Jillan replied, his tongue feeling thick in his mouth.

'There's bread and honey below with which you can break your fast. You do like bread and honey, don't you?'

'Y-yes. It's my favourite,' Jillan said with a pang, suddenly missing home. Sabella almost looked like his mother. And she was kind and caring. 'I'll be down immediately. I'll just get dressed.'

'Very good, dear. I'll set some tea to steeping.' She smiled gently and bustled out.

He wasted no time and was soon down in the eating area. Stara sat waiting for him.

'There you are, sleepyhead. Mama said you drank too much ale.'

'Where are Ash and Aspin?' he asked, for want of anything else.

'They left.'

'Left!' he panicked. 'Left for Hyvan's Cross?'

'No, silly. Left to see Bion. Betha and Ausa wouldn't just let them leave for Hyvan's Cross, would they? You don't like bread and honey, do you? I can have yours if you don't.'

'Hey, that's mine!' exclaimed Jillan, leaping to grab the thick piece of bread just before it got to her mouth. He was starving again.

'Greedy guts!' she grumped.

'Come now, Stara,' Sabella chided as she came in with tea. 'You had several helpings this morning.'

'I'm a growing girl. You say it all the time.'

'Go and hunt for something in the woods if you're that hungry. Jillan is a guest.'

'The wolf's out there. It's not safe.'

'Oh, the wolf wouldn't attack people,' Jillan said between mouthfuls. 'I don't think so anyway.'

'There you are,' Sabella said with her arms folded, giving her daughter a hard stare.

'Oh, all right,' Stara sighed melodramatically. 'But I'll never grow up at this rate. I'll take Jillan to see Bion. Maybe the wizard will give me some honeycomb.'

'Maybe,' Sabella acknowledged.

'Come on, Jillan. Haven't you finished yet?'

'Finished,' he said with a smack of his lips and a slurp of the tea. 'Thank you, Mrs Ironshoe.'

'You're welcome, dear. Hurry along now, or the sun will have set before you get back.'

He looked out through a pair of shutters. The sun was already past its zenith. He pushed back his chair and went after Stara as quickly as he could. They ran past the forge, which was all clanging, hissing, steam and smoke.

Stara stopped for a moment to watch. 'That's Papa fighting a dragon. The clanging is his hammer hitting the dragon's metal scales. They fight like this all the time. Papa will win and the dragon will be scared for a while, but it doesn't have a very good memory and will then want to fight him again as if he were a completely different person. Come on then!'

She ran off, her hair streaming behind her like a comet, and he had to run hard just to keep her in sight. She flitted across the stepping stones of a stream that was so clear its chuckling waters were almost ghostly. They then zigzagged down through a copse of trees, jumping their playful roots. And through a wild meadow of snaring brambles, sleep-filled blossoms and insects and small creatures playing hide and seek. The sun warmed and dazzled them. *How can this be winter?* he wondered. *This place is magical.*

There were standing stones at the end of the meadow, from behind which clouds of smoke were drifting. Snatches of voices came to him on the wind.

'. . . not so easily persuaded . . .' Was that Ash?

'. . . listen to reason?' He didn't know who that was. '. . . think, Aspin?'

'. . . sure . . . convinced myself, to be honest.'

Stara reached the stones, Jillan some seconds after. Stara didn't even appear out of breath, but Jillan had to lean over with his hands on his knees. There was a long grassy drop straight ahead of him, and he suddenly felt so unsteady on his feet that he let his knees fold so that he could sit on the ground.

'Oof!' he puffed, taking in the incredible view over which they sat. The land rolled down and down like a swathe of tailor's cloth, all the way to the distant shears of the horizon.

'Here he is,' Aspin said, with something like relief in his voice, and passed a long-stemmed pipe to a gnome of a man – whom Jillian took to be Bion – crouched on one of the stones, which lay flat and provided a perfect seat from which to take in the landscape.

'Amazing, isn't it, Jillan?' Ash said dreamily as he followed Jillan's gaze out over the land. The captivated woodsman accepted the pipe from the gnome and took a large draw, exhaling slowly.

Jillan waved the perfumed smoke out of his face and coughed. 'Yes, nice hills.'

'How are you, Stara?' Bion breezed.

'Hungry, of course.'

'Of course. Here's some honeycomb then. And you'll find strawberries in the meadow there when you take Aspin and Ash back to the impatient Betha and Ausa. I bet they're unhappy with me for stealing their suitors away, though it has been for but a handful of moments.'

'Yes, I promised Betha I wouldn't be long,' a lazy-lidded Aspin mused, although he showed no sign of wanting to move immediately.

'And Ausa said she might not remember me if I took too long,' an entranced Ash mumbled, the pipe becoming loose in his hand.

Bion stretched a hand out and grabbed the pipe before it could fall. He clenched it between his teeth and clapped his hands smartly, making them all start a little. 'Best be running along then. I'll see you later. I need to have a talk with Jillan here. Stara, help them up.'

The girl pulled on Ash and Aspin until they got to their feet, and then they were stumbling after her. Aspin only remembered at the last moment to turn and give Jillan a clumsy wave. Then they disappeared beyond the stones.

The gnome's face was gnarled and nobbled like wood, but was natural and characterful rather than ugly. He had a hunched back, long spatulate fingers and was dressed in leathers of unusually bright red and green. Jillan realised he was probably staring at the man.

'Sorry,' he said.

Creases appeared at the corners of Bion's eyes as he scrunched his face into a smile. 'Quite all right. Better to take a straight and honest look rather than steal a sly and sideways glance. So, you're a wizard, are you?'

Had Ash and Aspin told Bion everything? 'Not really.'

'Oh. A pity. I was hoping to meet a fellow wizard. Can be lonely being the only wizard in a place.'

Jillan hesitated. 'Well, certain things have happened, but I wouldn't say I'm a wizard.'

'Hmm. Have you had any training?'

'No.'

'Pity. I was hoping you might be able to train me some. Oh well. Want a puff on my pipe?'

'No, thanks,' Jillan replied politely.

''Sall right. It was only by way of friendship.'

Jillan remained silent and began to feel awkward. He looked out at the view again. It hadn't changed. He felt Bion's eyes on him and shifted uncomfortably. What was he doing here? If they didn't leave soon . . .

'So what is it you want to know, Jillan?' Bion suddenly asked, interrupting his thoughts. 'Ask me about magic. I know all sorts of things.'

Jillan stole a glance at the gnome. 'Well, I . . . Magic is dangerous, isn't it?'

'Oh yes, very dangerous. Even when the intention behind it is good, all too often innocent people get hurt.'

Like Karl. 'But can't it be controlled?' he asked, trying to keep desperation from his voice.

Bion sighed. 'If only, if only. You see, the magic-wielder draws on the life energy around them and then channels it. But the act of drawing requires them first to use some of their own life energy from their core. The greater the work of magic undertaken, the more the magic-wielder must use of themselves. Their core is essentially lessened by the use of magic. If you've used magic at all, you'll have experienced a terrible tiredness afterwards, no doubt? Yes. The core then demands life energy be drawn to replace that which has been lost. It's like a hunger or craving. The more a wizard uses magic, the more they are essentially lessened and the greater the hunger becomes. Most tell themselves they can control the hunger, but the hunger becomes greater and greater until eventually it is the hunger that controls the magic-wielder. You asked me if magic can be controlled. When you are young and strong, yes, but ultimately no. Magic ultimately turns all wizards into unthinking, ravening beasts. They lose all feeling and do not care for friends or loved ones. There is only the magic and the need to consume more, even though it is themselves who are being consumed. Fortunately, by the time magic takes control, the wizard's core has become so lessened that they are weak, twisted and old long before their time. They either simply fade away or they go out in one final blaze of glory. Don't believe me? Just look at me, Jillan! I was once a strapping and handsome six-foot man.'

Jillan's eyes became as large as wagon wheels as he stared at Bion. He *did* believe him. Hadn't the taint already taken control of him on several occasions?

'Heh, heh. Well, maybe I wasn't as tall and handsome as all that. But I was much stronger and straighter.'

'S-so I shouldn't use magic at all?'

Bion nodded. 'Precisely. I hardly use it at all any more myself. I want to enjoy as many days as I can among the good people of Linder's Drop, smoking my pipe here on my thinking stone and taking in the wonder of the Geas. What better life could there be? It is safe here and I am never forced into using magic. Thomas is a friend to all and his daughters delight the soul, do they not?'

'Yes,' Jillan replied numbly. He wanted to call on the taint but dared not. It might try to take control of him again.

'Are you sure you don't want a puff? You look a bit overwhelmed, Jillan. The smoke will calm you and help you see things more clearly.'

The pipe was pushed into his hand and he held it limply, staring out on the scene in a reverie. Magic was dangerous. It hurt innocent people. It made him into a monster who didn't care about anyone or anything. It would only make things worse if he tried to help anyone by using it. It would be better if he did nothing and avoided places where he'd be tempted or forced to use his magic. Perhaps it would be better if he stayed in a place like Linder's Drop instead.

As the sun touched the horizon, its light refracted momentarily and made him blink. How long had he been sitting here? The pipe had gone out. He thrust it back at Bion.

'I have to go,' he said urgently. 'If we don't leave before its dark—'

'But we didn't finish our chat about magic, Jillan,' the gnome reproved him.

'I have to save my parents in Hyvan's Cross.'

'But they would not want you to risk yourself, Jillan. They helped you escape knowing what it would mean. If you go to Hyvan's Cross, their sacrifice will have been in vain. And you can't use magic to free them. They sent you to find Thomas because they wanted him to bring you to Linder's Drop so that you could be safe, and perhaps happy one day.'

'Who told you about them? Neither Ash nor Aspin knew those things.'

'Why, you yourself did, Jillan,' Bion said in surprise. 'We've been sitting here talking about all sorts of things. Maybe the smoke was stronger than I realised. It can cause people to forget things sometimes, particularly if they're not used to it.'

He hadn't told the wizard about his parents, had he? He couldn't remember. His head was in a muddle. He needed to sit down and think properly, but there was no time.

'Don't worry. If you need to get to Hyvan's Cross, I can show you a secret and direct path. You'll be there almost before you leave. Trust me, it'll be fine. How long before you need to be there?'

He was on his feet, dithering. 'I'm not sure. I've lost track. Ten days maybe.'

'Well then, there's nothing to worry about, is there?'

'I-I need to find Ash and Aspin. Bye bye, thank you.'

'Wait! I thought you wanted to know about Haven?'

But he wrenched himself away and raced back across the meadow.

Where had he originally entered it from? He didn't recognise the trees now that their shadows had lengthened. He heard the stream off to his right and ran towards it. There were no stepping stones here but he knew he needed to be on the other side. He splashed through and followed the far bank, relying on it to take him to where he'd crossed earlier. But after a while it began to bend further to the right and lead him in a direction all his instincts told him was wrong. The stream then ended in a dramatic waterfall down the wooded side of the drop. He turned around to follow the stream all the way back to where he'd come from.

He told himself he was an idiot for not paying better attention in the first place. Now he came to a place where another stream joined his, and he realised he must have been following the wrong stream all along. He opted to follow the new one and was soon in a thick and dark part of the woods he didn't recognise. *Don't panic! Think!* He made his way back to where the streams met and wondered what he should now do. Dare he just strike out into the woods in a direction he guessed was correct, leaving the streams behind him, or would that only get him into an even worse mess?

'Helloooo! Can anyone hear me? Ash! Aspin! Stara! Hello? I'm lost.'

Freda trammelled through the ground. It was so much nicer to be travelling through proper rock, rather than the thin sludge everyone called mud. Hard rock scraped her clean and left her feeling fresh. It removed all the mites and beetles that liked to lurk and nest in the cracks of her skin. She could kill them herself, of course, by squeezing the cracks closed, but the resulting ooze inside her joints felt distinctly unpleasant. Plus bits of insect body got trapped inside, grated, and caused her irritation.

The rock here was particularly dense too, making it feel more real than most places in the world of the Overlords. There was a great strength and power here, which presumably originated from the Great Temple, as if it were some centre of gravity separate from the rest of the world. She thrilled at the feeling of the central region, but at the same time it made her nervous. It was probably best if she got through this place as quickly as possible.

She powered onward and then became aware of a distant vibration. It was not the natural and inherent vibration of the rock itself; rather, the rock was carrying the sound and movement of something trapped deep below. Trapped? What made her think the source of the vibration was trapped? She moved closer. Screams. High-pitched and unpleasant, then low and animalistic. What monster could make such sounds? How terrible must its suffering be?

She knew she should ignore it because there was no time to do otherwise. She didn't want to disappoint friend Anupal, after all. She'd promised she would go with him to the place where they could do good things to make good friends; and that place would only be there if they got there in time. Yet her heart wouldn't let her just leave the screamer, monster or otherwise, in such distress. She would see what she could do and make up the time afterwards, carrying friend Anupal through the night if necessary so that he could get the rest he needed.

Closer still and she felt a more sinister vibration beneath the screaming. Sun-metal! The screamer was trapped inside a cube of it. She was appalled. Who would be so cruel as to do this to another being? It was the worst of tortures, eternal diminishment and a stripping away of being. No wonder the creature screamed constantly. It must have been driven mad by its imprisonment. It must yearn for death.

'I see you!' it resonated, and capered about in the cube, first on the ceiling, then it crouched in a corner. 'Come to taunt me? Gar sent you, didn't he? Told me not to overreach, didn't he? What do you expect of Gar of the Still Stone? Inertia. No ictus for dynamic change. No catalyst. Nothing! What sort of god is that?' A moment's hesitation. 'But what sort of gods are there any more? None. Leave me! You depress me. Leave me!'

Its demand was so strident that it was painful to listen to. She backed away, at a loss as to how she could help anyway. She was powerless against the sun-metal.

'Leave me, leave me, LEAVE ME!'

Agony. The screamer's. Her own. The rock's. Her mind rattling and fracturing. Fragmentation. She had to get away before it shattered her. She vomited dust and debris, the rock around her becoming a deluge. She ran and swam and fought her way up, refusing to let it sweep her away into the bottomless pit of eternity, where the punishing Underlords awaited the fall of the world. She hardened, solidified, became immovable bedrock and faced the tearing torrent. She would not let it drown her.

It finally began to abate, as the mad screamer's mind wandered and forgot itself once more. Exhausted, she hauled her way up to safety and for once welcomed the light of the sky-cave on her skin.

'Net her,' ordered a tight little voice.

There was a blur of red and gold as a gossamer web of sun-metal was cast over her and pulled closed. It began to eat into her.

'No, please!' she begged. 'I haven't done anything wrong!'

'That's not for you to judge,' disagreed the voice. 'I am the authority here. I bet you haven't got any papers either, have you? Honestly, this Empire would completely fall apart if I weren't here to detect unauthorised intrusions, pick up the pieces when proper procedure wasn't observed, and so forth. There'd be absolutely no order or organisation if we all came and went as we pleased. It would be chaos. Nothing would ever get done, would it? I'll ask you again. Do you have any papers?'

'Noo!' she groaned.

'Then how am I to know who you are? How am I to know if you're a threat or not, hmm? After all, you're quite odd and dangerous-looking, aren't you? If anyone needed papers, it would be someone like you. So what am I going to do with you, hmm?'

Through the spots and stars of her vision she made out a prim figure who was all straight lines and uniformity. Even his face had a perfect and unremarkable symmetry about it. By contrast, the half-dozen heavy men with him were all slouched and scuffed, straps on their armour hanging loose, their hair dishevelled, dirt on their faces, lopsided expressions, and so on.

'What? Let you loose in the wider Empire to cause who knows what trouble? I don't think so. That would be quite negligent of me. And how can you expect to cross a border into another region when you have no papers? No, I'm going to have to detain you until you can prove who you are to my satisfaction.'

'But how can I prove who I am without papers?'

'Well, you should have thought of that before you decided to come storming through here without manners, invitation or permission, shouldn't you? Don't worry, because you'll have plenty of time to think about how you can prove who you are in your holding cell. All the time in the world, in fact. Take her away.'

'Yes, holy one,' the heavy men responded as three of them took hold of the net and proceeded to drag her off.

The well-ordered authority looked up at the sky. 'And prepare a second cell, as we will soon have another unauthorised arrival. This one's a repeat offender, so I'll have to come down hard or we'll just end up with a free-for-all.'

The Peculiar chased the eagle up into the clouds, widened his mouth to ridiculous proportions and then swallowed it whole. He burped. The eagle struggled inside him, pushing his stomach out in the shape of head and beak, and then talons.

'Oo! That tickles. It's your feathers. Ouch! That hurt.'

He coughed and spat the bird back out. It plummeted a good distance before it managed to right itself and slow its fall. It landed heavily but looked like it would survive – if delayed shock didn't kill it, that was.

'Never liked the taste of eagles anyway,' the Peculiar grouched. 'Taste like frogs, which taste like chicken, which taste like carp, which eat pooh and mud off the bottom of rivers. Far too primitive a life form ever to taste good. Ah, how I wish wyverns still graced the skies. Now *they* were a challenge. Sneaky too. Tasted almost as good as people, in fact, if not better than some. Whatever happened to the wyverns, I wonder? Bet Goza ate them all. Doesn't leave much that's new these days. The world's in decline, of course, the power of the Geas slowly drained by the elseworlders. Yes, the disappearance of certain species is no doubt connected to the dwindling of the Geas. Still, I wonder what elseworlders taste like. Look a bit bony. Hmm. Something to mull.'

He hit a still pocket of air and the wind went out from under him. He plummeted much as the eagle had just done.

'Oops. Too much mulling. Should have looked where I was going.'

Next he was caught in a downdraught and hurled towards the earth. He decided against wasting any power to halt the fall because he was more interested in getting to earth as quickly as possible. He'd just about had enough of this meddlesome Saint. It was time to deal with him once and for all.

'This is going to hurt,' he said to himself.

His body punched into the ground, throwing up a shower of pebbles and stones. After a minute or so of reknitting his limbs and flesh, he pulled himself out of the deep depression he had made. He slowly pushed his right shoulder and then his left shoulder back, sighing as his spine cracked back into place.

'Ahh! That's got it.'

'Well, well! Just look who's dropped in for another visit,' simpered the voice of Saint Virulus.

'Don't you know who I am, you witless cock-a-mouth? I can't believe you've never heard of the Peculiar, otherwise known as the Lord of Mayhem, the Great—'

'I don't care who you think you are!' Saint Virulus shouted from atop a rock that made him appear taller than his henchmen. 'This is my region, and I intend to see to it that order is instilled in everyone and everything. It is the only way to pre-empt the Chaos and ensure eternity.'

'I don't know how you managed to alter the air up there, but if you think you've got any chance of instilling order in the Lord of May—'

'Silence! I control the very elements of this region. Control, control, control. Not even the air flows without my say-so. None are capable of breath or speech without my permission. Silence, I say!'

A gag of air had been forced into the Peculiar's mouth to stop him speaking. He spat it out furiously. 'That does it! I will spread you like manure across this region. The soil could do with it after all. Rejoice that for once in your uninspired life you will be of some passing use!'

'And you will be brought to heel,' the Saint sniffed. 'Enough of your wayward words and rabid ranting, you . . . you . . . vagabond. Net him!'

A gossamer web of sun-metal was thrown over the Peculiar. He shrugged it off and laughed softly. 'To think I actually hesitated to kill you before, in case your Saviours got their knickers in a twist. I now realise I'll be doing them a favour. And I have my reputation to think of. If I were to let this pass and word spread, then every insipid Saint I came across would take it upon themselves to interfere with me.' He took a pace towards the Saint.

'Net him! Net him!' Saint Virulus urged. 'I *will* have order!'

Two nets were thrown at the same time. The Peculiar became a liquid and ran between them, his helmet of sun-metal carried through on the stream.

'And now what will you do?' the Peculiar asked.

The Saint raised his hands above his head, palms facing inwards as if he held a block of stone. He hurled the air at the Peculiar. The Peculiar became a ghost and the force passed straight through him, although his helmet slipped askew.

'And now what will you do?' he asked, righting the helmet and taking a step closer.

'Attack him!' the Saint called to his six men. 'For the Empire!'

'Stay where you are!' the Peculiar compelled them with a snatch of song and a lover's sigh. He took another step closer. 'And now what will you do? Your orders have foundered; your attempts to control matter are limited and limiting. Now what will you do, vapid little Saint? Will you accept that just as there is order, there must be disorder? Will you accept that nothing can be all-controlling and all-powerful if this world is to exist? Will you accept that your Saviours are *not* eternal?'

'Anarchist!' the Saint gnashed, unleashing spirals of flame from his hands to engulf the Peculiar.

'Silly of me,' the Peculiar said. 'Of course you won't accept it. It's just too great an admission of error, false belief and inadequacy for you. Such a self-deluding creature is man. Such a self-defeating conception and philosophy. Fancy thinking that you can impose yourself on the world which created you, and that you can take absolute command of it. So circular, so flawed! Do you not see that it is the very attempt that always undoes you? But I know why your kind does it. I am not without understanding, not without compassion even. It's because you feel so alone and lost in the universe, isn't it? Come, let me hold you.'

The fiery figure burned all the colours of the rainbow as it stepped up onto the rock and embraced the Saint.

'Nooo!' The coiffured man screamed as his hair caught alight, his skin began to melt and his uniform burned away. The aroma of cooked meat filled the air.

'There, there. It's all right. I'm here now.'

The Saint's flesh blackened and crisped. His dying moan became one sound with the roar of the inferno. His limbs remained for a moment as thin and twisted wicks for the spectral flames and were then nothing but ash on the wind. The fire suddenly snuffed out as if the Saint had never been.

The Peculiar stepped down from the rock, dusting off his hands and adopting his previous form of a painfully beautiful youth. 'I did warn him. You heard me warn him, right?'

The six staring Heroes nodded.

'Friend Anupal!' called a voice. 'I am imprisoned down here.'

The Peculiar's brows drew down in sultry displeasure. 'You curs have incarcerated my friend? That is no way to treat a lady!'

'Monster, you mean,' responded a hatchet-faced Hero, who appeared to be shaking off the glamour.

'Take your sword and cut out your tongue. Good, good. Now swallow your blade with your words.'

The other five watched in helpless horror.

'You!' the Peculiar said to one who had wet himself. 'Release my friend.'

The Hero took a tentative step forward, his knees knocking. The Peculiar tutted and touched the soldier on the shoulder. The man fell dead, a look of surprise on his face.

'Too slow. I'm busy, busy! I have places to be. You! Release my friend.'

The next Hero wasted no time and made it to the first stair to the punishment chambers before the Peculiar yawned and clicked his fingers. The man tripped and fell down the stairs. The sudden silence from below told the remaining three that their fellow had broken his neck.

'You!'

The fourth man was already moving.

'Good presence of mind and initiative.'

The remaining two sighed with relief. The Peculiar turned his eyes towards them.

'Unlike you two.'

One threw himself to his knees and clasped his hands before him. 'Mercy, holy one!'

The Peculiar touched him on the forehead as if in blessing. 'Very well. I will make it quick and painless for you.' Then he turned to the last of the Heroes. 'Well?'

'I-I . . .' He shrugged. 'I'm sorry?'

The Peculiar gave him a severe smile. 'Good try, but what use is being sorry after the event, eh? You need to be sorry before the event, so that the event never occurs.' He stroked the soldier's cheek. 'Remember that if the Geas deigns to allow you another lifetime.' He caught the man as he fell and laid him gently on the ground.

The fourth of the Heroes now returned with Freda. He looked down at his dead comrades and swallowed fearfully.

'Ah, there you are, dear one. Are you well?'

'Yes, friend Anupal.'

'That's good. Then let us leave this unpleasantness and be on our way.' He took her by the hand and they walked away, leaving the Hero behind.

'I'm glad you didn't kill all of them,' Freda murmured despairingly.

'But of course not, dear one. I'm not a monster. I seek to do good things where I can, to make good friends. It saddens me when I cannot do so.'

Besides, I need one left alive so that the story can be told to the current generation of this world. My reputation needs to be re-established.

Jillan jolted awake, disorientated. Where was he? A small golden-beamed room. There was no one else there. Full daylight came through a pair of shutters, not the harsh light of a new morning either. It felt closer to the middle of the day. How could that be? He'd lost something but didn't quite know what. He felt nauseous with déjà vu.

His head hurt. He was tempted to call on the taint to ask what had happened the night before, but Bion had warned against any sort of magic. That was it: he'd been talking to Bion and then got lost on his way back to the smithy and Thomas's house. Stara had eventually found him and led him home, but it had been fully dark by the time they'd got there. He'd gratefully allowed the welcoming faces and warmth of the fire to soothe away his distress, and willingly joined the revelry and cheer. Hadn't he stood on the table at one point to sing them all a song? He felt slightly embarrassed to remember it now, but it had pleased Stara.

He frowned. Another evening lost. He pushed the over-piled pillows away from him so that he could move more freely. He put his feet on the floor and realised he was only wearing his underclothes. Where were his other clothes? With relief, he saw them draped over a chair and quickly put them on. Where was his pack? What had happened to his armour? Was it magical and therefore something to be avoided? No, it had saved his life on more than one occasion and he wanted it back. Added to that, he'd only really borrowed it from the pagan chieftain, so he should try and take good care of it. He dared not lose it. Oh no! Where was his sun-metal sword, the one Samnir had given up even though he'd known it was all he had to defend himself against Saint Azual? Thomas had always been interested in it. Had he taken it?

Jillan crossed the room and pushed the door open. Stara was waiting for him, blocking his path.

'There you are, Jillan. I've missed you since last night.' She blushed prettily. 'Do you want to come pick mushrooms with me for breakfast?'

He took her by the upper arms and gently moved her aside. 'First I need to find my pack, and then Aspin and Ash.'

He went down the stairs and Sabella came bustling up to him. 'There you are, Jillan. Too many ales again last night.' She winked knowingly. 'You'll be wanting some bread and honey. It's your favourite. It's all laid out for you there.'

He gave her a small smile and then looked carefully around the large open room. Everything gleamed and competed for the eye's attention: the polished oak chairs, the shining surface of the leaf-carved table, the brasses around the newly swept ever-burning fireplace, the light reflecting off delicate china plates and through jars of preserved fruit, the glare off cutlery, Stara's sparkling eyes and white dress, Sabella's bright cheeks, the sun flooding in through the open door and shutters.

He looked for the shadows, where things would be hidden. Ah, there. He moved to the small space under the stairs. Pushed to the back were his armour and sword. He pulled them out and began to put them on. Then he saw his pack and the two bows he'd stowed in the wagon before rescuing Aspin from Saviours' Paradise. These he also took.

Sabella's smile faltered. 'Why, Jillan, are you going out, dear? You should have something before you go. How about just some tea? I have some steeping. I'd never forgive myself if you left without something to keep your strength up.'

He cinched the last buckle on his armour, immediately feeling more like his old self. The gold symbols on his breastplate glinted and he thought he heard something in the distance. Was that a howl? Now he thought on it, the wolf had been calling for quite some time, hadn't it? He just hadn't seemed to notice before.

'I'll go with you,' Stara insisted and followed him out of the door, 'so you don't get lost again.' She gave an affectionate laugh, but became downcast when he didn't share it. 'Do you want me to take you to Aspin first? Judging by the mood Betha was in earlier, I think he's with Bion again.'

Jillan nodded and let her lead him past the forge, where Thomas battled his dragon, across the stream, down through the copse and out across the wild meadow. Off to the side of the path he heard Ash whispering and Ausa squeaking in delight.

Jillan put a finger to his lips and he and Stara crept closer to the voices.

'So your father won't mind us being together?' Ash mumbled where he lay in the tall grasses next to Ausa.

'I've already told you. He lets us choose for ourselves. You're nothing like the other boys and men round here, Ash. You're different, special. You will stay here with me, though, won't you? You won't go away?'

'Of course I'll stay. Forever and ever! How could I not when my heart is here?'

'O, Ash, that's wonderful!' she exclaimed, throwing her arms around him. Then she drew back. 'But won't Jillan mind?'

'Why would he mind? He'll understand, I'm sure.'

'Maybe you could convince him to stay too.'

'Well, I don't know about tha—' He broke off as she pushed her lips urgently against his and groaned with pleasure and desire.

'Say you'll convince him, my beloved Ash. I couldn't bear to see Stara's heart broken, and it would be better for him if he stayed, anyway. He'd be happy here. We'll all be friends together. Say you'll convince him. For me.'

'Anything for you.'

Jillan stalked away, not needing to hear any more. Startled, Stara ran to overtake him. He reached the stones at the same moment as she did.

'Ah, Jillan, join us,' Bion drawled. 'Here, have a puff.'

'Aspin, I need to talk to you,' Jillan said to the woozy-looking mountain warrior. 'Over here.'

'Whatever you sure Jillan say,' Aspin mumbled. 'Sure. Whatever you say . . . Jillan.' He got to his feet at the second attempt and stumbled after Jillan as he retreated behind the stones.

Stara hovered nearby, watching and listening anxiously. Jillan looked at her and did his best to smile reassuringly. 'Go back to the house, Stara. Don't worry. I won't get lost this time. I need to learn the way on my own if I'm going to stay here with you.'

'Really?' she squeaked and clapped her hands together.

'Really. Why don't you run and tell your parents the good news?'

'Oh, yes! They'll be so happy!' the girl cried and ran off through the butterflies and drifting dandelion seeds.

Jillan took his friend by the elbow and began to lead him across the meadow. He checked the position of the sun, which had raced further across the sky than it should have done. Jillan had no doubt that by the time they got to the other side of the meadow, dusk would be upon them. Time passed too quickly here. The weather was too good. The setting was too perfect. It was all wrong, and all designed to discourage them from leaving.

'Come on!' Jillan urged as he tugged Aspin along. 'Pick your feet up.'

'What's the rush, hmm? Where are we going? Aren't we staying?'

'Here, take your bow. We're leaving.'

'Oh, okay. What about Betha?'

Jillan didn't reply.

'I should say goodbye to her, shouldn't I?' Aspin asked dopily.

Jillan kept on pulling as the sky darkened behind them. 'We have to get to the stables. We need horses.'

'Where's Ash then? Isn't he coming?'

'He'll catch up with us, like he did before. Can't you hear the wolf?'

Aspin blinked drowsily. 'Wolf? What wolf?'

'You know, Ash's black wolf. You saw it on the trip in, remember? It was hard to miss. It's howling in the distance now. Can't you hear it?'

'I . . . Not really. Are you sure? Bion said you were trau . . . Now what was it? Oh yes, traumatised.'

'Forget what he said. Come on! Do you think you can run?'

'Run? Run where?'

'Just follow me. That's it.'

They jogged through the copse. At one point Aspin seemed to lose concentration and stopped. Jillan went back for him and pushed him on. Jillan hopped across the stepping stones, but Aspin's reactions were too slow to manage them, so he had to splash through the stream. It was now full night.

Jillan led them round the back of the smithy and the house, keeping them in among the trees so that they remained out of sight of anybody inside. The stables were on the far side. They crept further round.

Inside the house a girl passed a pair of the open shutters, silhouetted by the light behind her. Aspin stepped forwards. 'Be—'

Jillan clapped a hand over Aspin's mouth and with some difficulty dragged him back among the trees. The silhouette hesitated and leaned out for a second. Then she shook her head and disappeared from view.

Jillan released the breath he'd been holding. It was fortunate that Aspin hadn't struggled too much.

'I don't understand,' Aspin complained. 'It's dark and cold out here. I want to go in where it's warm and we have friends and family. I want some ale and some home-cooked food.'

'So do I, Aspin, but none of it's real.'

'Eh? Of course it's real. I want it to be real.'

'Precisely. It's everything you've ever wanted, everything I've ever wanted. That's how I know it can't be real.'

Aspin rubbed at his temples as if his head hurt. His brow furrowed.

There was the sound of footsteps on wooden stairs from the front of the house. 'Jillan! Aspin! It's time to come in now,' Stara called.

The wolf's howl began to sound more frantic. Jillan put his finger to his lips, warning Aspin to remain silent. He pulled his friend round the corner of the house, across the yard and into the stables. There were two mares inside – a bay and a dapple – who snorted at them curiously.

'Get saddles on them,' Jillan instructed Aspin, who now moved with a bit more coordination than before.

A minute later they had the horses out of the stables. Jillan mounted the dapple and looked across at Aspin. 'Ready? We'll need to ride back through the hamlet to find a road that we know. We'll have to ride hard.'

'Ready.' Aspin nodded tiredly. 'Don't feel so good though. Like I haven't slept or eaten in days.'

'I know. And you probably haven't either. Come on then. Yah!'

They kicked their horses into a gallop and came round the front of the house. Thomas came bursting out of the front door.

'Come back!' he roared. 'I will show you the secret paths to Hyvan's Cross.'

But Jillan wasn't about to stop. He leaned into his mare's neck and pushed her to greater speed, only looking back once to check Aspin was still with him.

They flashed through the hamlet, riding down the pale figures that came out of the houses to block the road. A mother clutching a babe to her chest wailed in front of them.

'Don't stop!' Jillan shouted at Aspin, spurring forward through the phantasm. 'Head for the sound of the wolf!'

They passed the last building of Linder's Drop and entered the pitch black beneath the canopy of the woods, the moonlight only able to penetrate in a few places. Aspin slowed his horse.

'Jillan, it's too dangerous at such speed. The horses will catch a root or we'll hit low-hanging branches.'

'No! It's not real. Trust me!'

Aspin kicked on after Jillan with a devil-may-care shout. They drummed through the woods for a hand of miles and then they saw a lighter grey area beyond the trees.

'The road. At last!'

They slowed as they came closer and turned onto the compacted surface. It didn't seem right somehow.

'We're back in the yard!'

They'd come full circle. The stables stood to the right and Thomas's house to the left.

'But how can that be?'

'I'm not sure, but we're not staying here,' Jillan said determinedly, heeling his horse. The dapple refused to take another step.

The dark outlines of a giant and a dwarf came around the corner of the house. The giant hefted a hammer as tall as Jillan in his hands. Red light from a pipe lit Bion's face.

'Those horses know who they belong to. They won't be moving. They're home and not about to let themselves be stolen by two sneak-in-the-nights!' Thomas snorted.

Hands shaking, Jillan raised his bow and got an arrow to the string. 'Stay back! You promised me those horses, Thomas Ironshoe, aren't you forgetting? You can't stop us leaving. I won't be kept a prisoner here.'

'Is that any way to be talking to someone who's invited you into his home, offered you his hospitality, not to mention his best ale, and allowed you to court his daughter? Taking off in the night without so much as a thank you or goodbye? It's just not decent manners. You should be ashamed of yourself, boy.'

'Now, now,' Bion said calmingly. 'It's late and we're all tired. We're just trying to do right by you is all, after what you've done for Thomas here. It's the least we can do. And we hope you would be doing right by us too. We don't think it wise for you to be heading for Hyvan's Cross, but if you really insist on going then you are free to do so. As we promised, we will show you the quickest path there.'

'Good. We're leaving then, for Hyvan's Cross. Just point us the right way and we'll be off.'

Bion took a meditative puff on his pipe. 'Very well, we will do so in the morning. But there is something you should know. Aspin doesn't think it's a very good idea to go to Hyvan's Cross, do you, Aspin? He doesn't believe you two boys have any chance against the thousands of Heroes stationed there, not to mention the Saint, who of course always knows. Aspin thinks you're deluding yourself. And Aspin actually wants to stay. He promised Betha he would, didn't you, Aspin? Well, go ahead, tell Jillan.'

Aspin dropped his eyes guiltily. 'Jillan, I—'

'It's all right. Don't say anything. Stay on your horse!' Jillan said through gritted teeth, refusing to look at his friend. 'Last chance, Bion. Point us the right way.'

'I don't like your tone, boy!' Thomas advanced towards them.

'Peace, good Thomas, peace,' Bion waved him back. 'Jillan, if you must leave, at least consider heading west. The plague is rampant in this region. Saint Izat has let it be known that fleeing southerners are welcome in her western region, however. And you know your parents would not want you risking yourself. You're just too important. Will you at least think about it, Jillan?'

Aspin looked across at Jillan. 'Maybe we should think about it.'

Self-doubt screamed at Jillan from one side; temptation whispered from the other. There was nowhere to turn. What about this, Jillan? What about that, Jillan? You didn't think about this, that or the other, did you? Just stop for a moment and it'll be all right. Even his friend, his only friend, thought he should stop. But then nothing would change.

'The right way, Bion! Now!' Jillan quavered.

'Very well. We will show you in the morning, once we've all rested properly. It's too dark now. We'll go inside, eat, sleep, say our goodbyes and then set out early.'

It was completely reasonable. Indecision deafened him. He couldn't think. He was so tired. He couldn't hear anything any more except his own heartbeat, the blood roaring in his ears and the howling, howling madness in his head. The ravening, eternally restless beast, the violent and terrible wolf. *The wolf! Why couldn't they hear it?*

He moved the trembling line of his sight and let fly with his arrow. It zinged through the air and shattered Bion's pipe, throwing burning cinders up into the gnome's face and across the yard. Thomas bellowed, raised his hammer over his head and charged at Jillan. As the gnome fell back with a cry, for a moment so brief that it seemed the eye tricked the mind, the house and stables became ruins.

Jillan yanked hard on his reins and the dapple reared, its flying hooves keeping Thomas at bay. As the blacksmith came forward again, Aspin's turning horse blocked him for a second. Jillan made his horse rear again, but Thomas was now at his side. He felt himself slipping backwards off his saddle and tried to grab the horse's mane, but it slipped through his fingers and he was suddenly airborne. The fall kept him out of the blacksmith's reach for moments longer, but the impact with the ground drove all the wind out of Jillan and he curled then arched with pain.

'Don't kill him, Thomas,' Bion commanded. 'Restrain him. Knock him out if you must.'

The voice helped Jillan orient himself, and he rolled away from Thomas. Hooves stamped down to either side of him, one missing his head by the width of a piece of straw. He rolled again, desperately trying to draw magic, but there was nothing.

Nothing but the howling wolf. 'I can't find you! Where are you? Can't you come to me? Come to me!'

At last! howled the taint joyously. *At last he thinks to invite us in!*

The embers floating in the air grew into glowing eyes. The darkness came alive, and a wolf as tall at the shoulder as the horses, but twice as broad, leapt into the centre of the yard. With a single swipe, it hurled the dapple away from Jillan. Thomas flung himself out of the mare's path, dropping his formidable hammer. The wolf now stalked the blacksmith.

Magic flooded Jillan, red light blazing from his eyes and in his hands. He hurled it at the gnome.

'Mistress, I have failed you!' screamed the twisted creature as he was bathed in terrible radiation. His nose drooped. His eyelids ran into his eyeballs. He opened his mouth to scream again, but his face slid down into his throat and he swallowed himself. His body liquefied, becoming a steaming puddle, and then evaporated into the night.

'Noooo!' Thomas wept, his anguish tearing the air in two.

The house and stables collapsed into decay. Four white mice scurried out of the shell of the dream house and ran towards Thomas. The wolf leapt . . .

'Please! Have mercy!'

. . . and snapped all the mice up in one go.

Broken, the giant blacksmith hugged the ground and sobbed.

'What just happened?' Aspin asked as if waking up.

A befuddled Ash kicked mouldering boards out of his way and climbed through what had been the side wall of Thomas's house. Joining them, the woodsman sighed, 'Should have known it was too good to be true. She was a mouse then, was she? I suppose it would never have worked.' He eyed the wolf. 'And you don't need to look so smug either. It's not funny.'

CHAPTER 11:

Repentance always coming after

The blind Saint beckoned the criminal out of the corner of the cell. The young Hero through whose eyes Azual saw everything stood silently watching by the door, just as he'd been commanded. If he dared turn his eyes away when the Drawing happened, his life would be forfeit and the Saint would find himself another pair of eyes. The Hero had to watch everything, no matter how distasteful he found it, so that the holy representative of the Saviours could see how and where to move.

This was the last of the criminals left in the punishment chambers of Hyvan's Cross. All the others had been drained until they were dead.

'Come over here!' the Saint demanded.

The criminal came reluctantly, head bowed low. The wretch had probably realised all the other cells were now silent and feared what was to come. Azual could hardly stand the brief moments of delay caused by the creature's slow progress across the floor. He needed to Draw more power than ever before if he was to restore his eyesight. He ground his teeth and his hands twitched impatiently.

'You are guilty of a crime against the People and the Empire,' the Saint said quickly. 'Your soul is corrupted. However, you have a chance to redeem yourself if you repent and give yourself willingly to me. Tell me that you wish for Salvation.'

It was always easier to Draw one of the People when they were willing. He could overcome any resistance they put up, of course, but that usually required him to use up almost as much energy as he gained from them, pretty much making it a waste of time. True, a life would be lost as well, but these criminals had proved themselves lacking in faith so the People were better off without them. It was like removing an animal born with a deformity from a flock or herd. Such creatures were generally short-lived anyway, so what did it matter if they died now or a while later?

The criminal – whose face was younger and more angelic than any of the others Azual had seen today – was now right before him and looking up expectantly. Had it spoken?

'What?' Azual snapped.

'Holy one, forgive me, but I said I did not commit any crime. The baker said it was me who stole the bread, but I didn't, honest.'

'Whether you did or not,' the Saint growled in irritation, 'there can be no doubt that you have had thoughts of stealing, jealous thoughts of possessing something that was not yours to possess. You cannot deny it unless you are willing to commit the sin of doing so.'

Tears pricked the corners of the youth's eyes. 'It is true, holy one. I have thought of having pastries my family cannot afford. It is difficult when the baker puts his wares out on display, not that I make any excuse! But the smells make my mouth water, and I . . . I . . . am weak! But only of thoughts – I never stole anything! Holy one, I repent, truly I do! I give myself to you willingly and wish for Salvation.'

'Good. I will cleanse your soul.' Azual took the youth by the neck to hold him steady and then plunged his tapping tube of sun-metal into the jugular. Blood arced out of the end of the tube and into Azual's mouth. The Saint stirred the traces of the magically imbued blood that still existed in the youth from an initial Drawing several years before. He called to it and it came, bringing the youth's own life energy with it.

Azual swallowed and swallowed. Ah! So strong, so puissant! The flow of blood eventually slowed to a trickle and then a drip. He wiped his chin and let the youth's empty body drop to the floor. He felt a flutter of revulsion from the Hero, but chose to excuse his attendant's lack of understanding.

Azual concentrated the power brimming within him and directed it towards his ruined eyes. He demanded that they be repaired, but his magic merely washed around his eyes without changing them in any way. He strained and cried out in frustration, for he could not create new nerves and flesh, no matter how he tried. A voice inside him whispered that the magic he'd Drawn from the People was the corruption of the Chaos and therefore only capable of destruction, but he didn't want to hear it. There had to be a way. He just wasn't powerful enough yet.

He came up out of the punishment chambers and emerged into the moaning winds that always circulated around Hyvan's Cross and its unusual sandstone formations. He mentally called to Captain Skathis and told him to come to the temple at the top of the sculpted crag upon which the town was built. Azual had captured the place from the pagans centuries before and made the ancient temple his home. Like most of the other original buildings, it had been hollowed out of the soft rock. There were no straight lines or flat surfaces to be seen on it because the harsh winds moulded the rock into smooth curves and strange fluid shapes. By rights, he should have had this place of pagan worship and power demolished, but there was something about it that relaxed him. While the wind was droning or haunting around most of the town, its sound here, as it funnelled through circular openings and yawning arches, was soothing and almost melodic. He found it easy to meditate in the temple, whereas elsewhere his thoughts would interrupt each other, snarl and fight.

And he seemed to see better when he allowed the temple to calm his mind. Indeed, he imagined he could now see far more than he had when his eyes had been working. It was almost as if his eyes had held him back from seeing properly. Now that he saw exclusively through others, there was no primary vision forcing others out. Now he usually saw every object and event from multiple perspectives at once, meaning that he also understood them in a more complex manner than before. His consciousness had expanded. Was this what it was to be a Saviour, to be a god?

Perhaps he did not need to restore his eyes, then. He could manage without them. Yet he chafed against having to be dependent on others – lesser beings at that! – for what he saw. Yes, he'd developed his skills to the point whereby he could see simultaneously through the eyes of every being in Hyvan's Cross and not miss a single detail, but it was a constant drain on his power. He never had enough power, whether it was to restore his eyes or maintain his expanded consciousness. He had to have more. Nothing else mattered. He had to have the boy! The boy would give him everything he needed, whether he was willing or not. And once Azual had drained every last vestige of power from Jillan, *then* he would wreak his full and bloody revenge on the boy.

As Azual reclined on his temple throne, the attendant Hero blinked wearily. Azual's immediate view of himself bobbed and weaved, without his ability to correct it. He felt queasy seeing himself in his own mind as if through a broken mirror. He would never get used to this, could never accept it. It was humiliating to be tied to such a gross lumpen creature as this soldier.

'Get out of my sight!' the Saint seethed. 'Send a replacement.'

As the soldier hurried out, Azual switched his view so that he saw through the eyes of the arriving Captain Skathis instead. Azual watched himself lean forward in his throne and appear to glare down at the man.

'Neither hide nor hair has been found, Captain. Nothing!'

Azual was suddenly looking at the floor in front of Skathis's feet. He realised that the damnable fool had bowed to him.

'Well, what have you got to say for yourself, Captain? Got some explanation as to the spectacular failure of your men, hmm? Better make it good.'

'Holy one, Saint Izat has invited all southerners wishing to flee the plague to enter the western region,' the Captain replied impassively. 'It could be that the warrior and the boy—'

'What?' Azual hissed. 'How dare she! It is an outrage! I cannot believe . . . Wait. Have extra guards sent from Saviours' Paradise to close the border on our side.'

'I have already done so, holy one.'

'Excellent, Captain. I can see I chose well when appointing you.'

'We are patrolling the border in good numbers, holy one. Unless the fugitives chose to head into the west immediately upon leaving Saviours' Paradise, they will not have escaped. They will be found.'

'I doubt they will have headed west so quickly. Why would they? I still have the boy's loving parents. He knows he has but one week left to present himself here. Yet, to be on the safe side, I will lay an aegis on the minds of all the People in the region to watch for the fugitives and immediately report any sighting. I will plant an image of the fugitives in the minds of everyone. It will tire me, though, so see to it that the punishment chambers are full of new criminals by tomorrow morning, Captain. And have all children who have not yet been Drawn brought to me at the temple, no matter their age.'

'As is your will, holy one.' The Captain bowed, giving Azual a moment of motion sickness.

'Jillan must not be killed, do you understand? I would prefer the warrior taken alive also, but if that is not possible then so be it.'

'Of course, holy one.'

'Good. Only leaving the issue of the plague. I know it is rife in both Godsend and Saviours' Paradise. I will instruct the Captains there to prevent any from leaving and all from entering. Hyvan's Cross is still unaffected, however. Hmm. Captain, it would be a dreadful shame for the west if some of the plague victims were to find their way through our border guards, wouldn't it?'

'Very much so, holy one,' the Captain replied, for once allowing himself a smile, a small ugly thing.

'Have any victims that still walk rounded up. Saint Izat may yet come to regret her generous invitation, eh?'

'As you will it, holy one.'

Azual's replacement pair of eyes arrived, allowing him to switch his view and regard both himself and the Captain at once. Azual nodded and rose. 'Then I must now see the mother.'

Maria sent out as strong a call as she could manage, but there was no reply. Either there were none of her people nearby, or the strength of the Saint's power in this place blocked all her projections. She gave up. She'd been trying for days now and was exhausted. If she didn't rest, then she'd have no strength to take advantage of any real opportunity that presented itself.

She'd been kept in a small empty chamber carved into the solid rock. There was no window. There was a single blanket, an unyielding floor, a metal door and that was it. It was devoid of anything she could use to scry for Jillan, Jedadiah or any others who might help her. She would have used the cups of water that were brought with her morning and evening meals, but one of the guards always stood over her while she ate and then took everything away. She'd urinated into her cupped hands at one point, but – as she had feared would be the case – was unable to scry the outside world using her own bodily fluids. No, this was a prison that not even her magic could free her from.

She fretted for her dear Jedadiah, who had never been able to control that temper of his, even when it was in his own best interests. She didn't think any less of him for it, for he was a man of strong passion and principles – qualities for which she could only love him, even when it got them into trouble. He was a fine man and a fine father. There was much of him in Jillan.

And how she fretted for their beloved son. More than fretted. Her nerves were shredded. She now feared she'd been wrong to hide him from the world. Perhaps she should have encouraged magic in him when he was younger, so that he would now have control of it. She thought she'd been oh-so-wise to flee New Sanctuary and make for the more remote and less noteworthy town of Godsend with her young family. She thought they would be able to remain relatively anonymous and have a semblance of happiness. Now she wondered if she'd been more cowardly than wise. And the life they'd led in Godsend had been a constant trial, always watching over their shoulders, guarding every word they said, keeping potential friends at arm's length. It had limited them in ways she'd failed to anticipate, cruelly confining Jedadiah's free spirit and harming Jillan's development. And all for what? Where had it got them? Jillan accused of murder and a fugitive. Jedadiah and herself imprisoned by an increasingly suspicious and deranged Saint. If the Saviours' vassal decided they knew more than he'd so far gleaned and chose to break them, then the consequences didn't bear thinking about. More than just her precious family would be lost. The entire world!

It began to occur to Maria that it might have been better if they'd all died in New Sanctuary after all. Death was not to be feared, she knew, for the Geas continually remade life. She feared it anyway, because it meant leaving behind and forgetting her sweet husband and innocent son. And it was that fear, that weakness, that had ultimately led her here and might still prove to be the undoing of everything.

'No, Maria, you are not wise. You are a coward,' she told herself.

Tears ran down her cheeks. If she twisted the blanket or tore it into strips, she would have a rope she could tie around the bars of the small grille at the top of the metal door. If she used her weight just so, she could snap her neck before—

There was a scrape in the lock and the door squealed as it was dragged open. A huge frame ducked into the cell. She backed away from the grotesque and looming figure, who had to be nearly twice her height. Too late! She'd delayed too long, agonised self-indulgently during the precious seconds she should have used to end her life. *What have I done? Geas forgive me! I am unworthy, have always been so. Do not receive my spirit! End it instead. Strike me down here and now so that I may not betray you to the insatiable and parasitic Saviours. End me! I beg you, Geas! Please!*

But there was no reply, just silence, as silence had greeted all the projections she'd attempted in the last few days. The Saint's wide nostrils quivered as he scented the air to locate her. He moved towards her, hearing her shift to press against the back wall of the cell. Then he suddenly seemed able to see her. He came closer, his shadow casting her into darkness, and then his face was an inch from hers, smelling her fear and dribbling in anticipation. His hot breath smelt of death, the bloody pits where his eyes had been oozed pus and bloody tears. Surely this creature of nightmare had never been human? There was a greenish tint to his skin that spoke of poisons so lethal they could have no place in the life and nature of this world. Her flesh crawled at the sight and closeness of him. Her lungs spasmed in terror. Her mind teetered.

'Are they treating you well?' the ghastly thing whispered.

She wanted to be sick. She couldn't nod because she couldn't stand the idea of coming into contact with his loathsome flesh. He was anathema to everything she knew and believed in. Her throat was constricted. She couldn't speak.

'Ahh, but you are afraid. I do not mean to scare you.' He grinned, tilting his sightless head and taking a step back. 'I apologise. I imagine I am not looking my best. This has all been quite . . . unfortunate, as difficult for me as for you and your husband. I wish it had not come to this, truly. You feel the same, yes, Maria?'

She finally managed to prise her head away from the wall and nod weakly. The word escaped her: 'Yes.'

He went down on his haunches, his head all but level with hers now. There was an air of sadness about him. No, she would not feel sorry for this insane monster, not after the things he had done. But his magic was influencing her, appealing to her maternal and nurturing capabilities.

She tried to shore up her mental defences, but she'd drained herself in the last few days and had hardly slept. To her unending shame, although rationally she knew none of the fault was hers, she'd been Drawn by him when she was young. He was inside her and could not be denied if he became violent and determined.

'I have not come seeking your forgiveness, woman, understand that. I am a holy Saint, remember. You owe me your faith and allegiance. You are in debt to me for your life.'

'Yes, holy one. You have my faith and allegiance. I recognise my debt,' she replied glibly, trying to convince herself she was deceiving him.

'It is not your place to forgive me, but I will admit to you that circumstances have forced me to do things of which I am not entirely proud.'

'I am sure they were unavoidable, holy one.' *You have a tongue so forked I cannot believe it does not end up in knots.*

'Indeed, they were. I wish to restore your family to you, Maria.'

No, you devil, do not say so. Anything but that! I could resist any temptation or torture more easily than that. 'I pray that it can be so.'

'I hold no grudge against Jillan, you must understand. Like all of us, he has suffered circumstances that, as with me, forced him to do things of which he may not have been proud, but things that were unavoidable nonetheless. How can I condemn him while behaving in the same way? I cannot, Maria. Like me, Jillan has a special gift, a gift that is often a responsibility, a gift that is often a burden and a gift that is sometimes . . . is sometimes a curse. Do you understand what I say, Maria?'

'Yes.' *I do not want to!*

'Jillan and I are the same in that respect.'

She shook her head, eyes wide and blurring.

'I know your faith fears to elevate your son to my position, but I say it is true and therefore your faith must accept it. He will be a Saint one day, a protector of the People, holy within the Empire, a divine representative of the blessed Saviours themselves.'

Never! He is nothing like you. He will never become the monster you are. The killing was an accident. He was defending himself.

'And I will give him back to you. I am having him brought to this place, Maria. In return, though, I must ask you to honour your debt to me. Will you pay your debt to me?'

No! Tell him no. Do not think of Jillan returned to you. It is a lie. Do not think of holding him as a mother and keeping him safe from all harm. My sweet son, I love you! 'I will pay the debt,' she choked.

'You understand that this will become a binding aegis, an inescapable compulsion?'

'Yes.' She had not spoken the word out loud, had she? She wanted to take it back.

'Very well, then. When he comes to you, you will tell him to hand himself over to me. Reassure him that I have sworn his safety and that all will be well. He will not be able to refuse you. You know how to command him. You are his maker. Do you understand and agree, Maria?'

'You will not kill him!'

'I will not. The aegis will bind me as much as you. Is it a compact between us, for the life of your son?'

The faintest of nods. An impossibly slight zephyr. A ghostly 'Yes'.

Azual smiled. The boy would live and learn the true nature of suffering. He would yearn for death but be denied it, for death would be a kindness, and kindness was the last thing Azual intended. The boy would be made a living horror. He would be a son of sorts, the son Azual had never had.

Saint Izat picked her way carefully along the muddy road. Her grey boots were of the finest calfskin, so it would be a crime to get them dirty. She couldn't believe just how backward the south was: in her region of the west every road was properly paved and maintained. Well-kept roads meant faster transport of goods, fewer spillages, fewer accidents, more efficient trade, lower prices, greater profits, happier people and, ultimately, greater power for her region. The rutted puddles before her now were not just unsightly, but also offensive to her very philosophy and being.

'See how the land embodies the nature of its Saint! See how the mad one has made this region.'

She picked her way along a narrow strip of firm ground between the mud and trees. Her foot slipped and she screeched, frightening roosting birds up from the forest. She used her power to move at an unnatural speed to recover her balance and preserve what she could of her dignity. At this rate, she would be drained of magic before she'd travelled more than a few miles into Azual's territory. And she could not just replenish herself with any of the People she came across, as they belonged to the mad Saint, who might see her through their eyes, even if he did not sense one of his own People being drained. Izat needed to be frugal with her magic, or she would be powerless to deal with the boy when the time came. Were it not for that, she would have been able to imbue her limbs with the strength required to cross the land with prodigious leaps, and skim across the ground so quickly that it did not have time to soil her feet.

Not for the first time Izat cursed that she had not thought to bring a horse, not that she knew how to ride one, as she'd never had cause before, and not that she would have been able to tolerate it publicly defecating and urinating wherever and whenever the fancy took it. Besides, it wouldn't have been at all necessary if the blasted gnome hadn't proved himself so incompetent. Not only had Bion failed to detain the boy or persuade him to head west, but he'd also gone and got himself killed. Worse than careless! It was positively inconsiderate. Izat could not abide poor manners at the best of times, and these were very far from the best of times, what with puddles and muck all around her.

'I am holy! Divinely pristine. What an outrage it is that I must be here. And the smell is quite weakening. There aren't even any flowers here to sweeten the air. Winter would be no excuse, were they but civilised enough to have heard of mahonia, winter jasmine and box. There should be avenues of such blooms for everyone.'

Another slight slip and she had to resist the urge to draw energy again, instead grabbing a slimy tree branch to keep herself upright. She turned her hand over and flinched to see a greeny blackness on her palm. She held it out away from her as if to show and shame the world.

'Everything here is contaminating! I think the plague must be innate to all life here, so corrupted is it. None of it is worth saving. It is right that I have come to undo this region, as then a fresh start can be made. Yes, I will cleanse this region and make a beautiful garden of it, a place where people can innocently frolic, gambol and gad. I will be their holy gardener and artist. I will grow the People's sensibility and elevate them above this mud in which they grovel, as if they were still waiting to be born from the primeval ooze or primordial soup. The hold of the Geas must be broken so that the People can grow and discover potential in and of themselves. I will free them so that they can one day find their place among the stars rather than the fetid and infested bog of this region.'

The region – as it currently was – represented an assault on her very person. It would merely be an act of self-defence to drain many of the People here. Some would have to die so that the rest could live more ennobled lives. And she needed their life energy if she was to be strong enough to travel quickly, retrieve the boy, potentially fend off both Azual and the Peculiar and break the hold of the Geas. So much to do! But she had to find a way to drain the People without being detected by Azual until it was too late. Then she had an idea. It would involve a disguise.

'Oh, wonderful! I get to dress up. And I simply must have a mask for myself. How delicious! It will be just like one of my masque balls.'

But where to play out the part? The boy had told Bion he was heading for Hyvan's Cross, but that was the site of Azual's home temple, so Izat dared not attempt anything there. The next nearest town was Heroes' Brook, and Izat had an agent there who could supply her with a costume as necessary. Yes, that would be ideal.

Izat concentrated and called out, 'Stixis, can you hear me?'

Yes, holy one. One moment, came back the mental voice of the Minister of Heroes' Brook. Then: *What is your will?*

'You are wearing the headband of sun-metal? The rabid one cannot hear your thoughts?'

I wear the headband, holy one. Command me.

'I will soon be with you, adorable Stixis.'

Praise be! The Saviours are kind. What must I do to prepare for your coming?

'Gather young people together who have not yet been Drawn. Tell them you are preparing them for the day when they will be Drawn to the blessed Saviours, which might be sooner than they think. I will be with you tomorrow. Have Saintly ceremonial robes ready for my arrival, and the sort of paganesque mask that is worn by the Saints when a region is new to the Empire. It must be the visage of the Lord of Mayhem, do you understand, Stixis?'

Yes, holy one. I yearn to do your will. I yearn to see you again. It has been so long.

'Fear not, beloved. My love will be yours.'

Thank you, holy one, thank you! the Minister sobbed in gratitude through the link.

Izat smiled to herself. Heroes' Brook would provide her with the power she needed and perhaps even a young army of sorts. Yes, there was beauty and poignancy to be had from brave young Heroes giving their lives. Their deaths would be a glorious tragedy and inspiration to the rest of the People of this region, just as Jillan's death would be.

'Time I picked my feet up,' Izat announced, now free to draw on her power and lift herself up out of the grime. 'If matters can be expedited quickly in Heroes' Brook, I can be at the main crossroads to Hyvan's Cross before Jillan has passed through it. I may have everything settled and be back at home by tomorrow night. I do hope so, because I am sure the sickly air of this region seeks to play havoc with my skin. And then there's the stress of it all, not to mention missing out on sleep tonight. Honestly, I am a living and miraculous work of art to remain so divinely beautiful under such circumstances. Yet it must be done for the People. Without this form and figure to behold, they would have nothing to move them, nothing to worship and nothing to make their lives worth living. Ah, the sacrifices I make.'

The warriors of the upper village and their new chief descended into the lower village. They came in all their finery, gemstones and feathers on display, and also carried their weapons. Minister Praxis had a place of honour at Braggar's right elbow, while the white-haired Slavin stood on his left.

Sal, the old matriarch of the lower village, stood with Torpeth ahead of the assembled villagers.

'Stop fidgeting, you old goat. Do your fleas bite you?'

'They do, beloved, they do. They are agitated and fearful. Chief Blackwing is no more. A conniving lowlander stands as counsellor to the new chief, a chief who comes accoutred for war.'

'And so the gods test us, old goat.'

Torpeth scratched at his gums with his dirty fingernails, drawing blood but not noticing. 'Yes, so they test us, beloved. And the murder of Blackwing is our people's first response to that test. It was poorly done and an ill omen. I fear what is to come.'

'If we are found wanting, the punishment will be of our own making. It was ever thus, old goat.'

Torpeth sighed. 'They did not heed my warning. Yet I did not heed the warning so long ago, when I first warred on the people in the name of the gods.'

'And your punishment has been of your own making, has it not?'

'Aye, of my own making, beloved.'

'You caused great suffering and much death, old goat. Now you must live forever with great suffering, always denied the forgiveness of the gods, people and yourself. Pity will never be yours and nor will mercy, for you showed none to others. Friends, you have none. The closest you have is the lowlander, him whom you despise, for he is more similar to you than you would like. Love, you have none, for you showed none to others and I will never allow it. Grief and ashes are all you will have. Yet you have created this world for yourself, old goat, and so you must live in it forever more, or until the world is undone because of your crime.'

Tears came to Torpeth's eyes. He sniffed hard and swallowed while the headwoman remained stony-faced. 'Is there no hope then, beloved?'

'Did you allow others to hope, old goat?'

The hundred or so warriors of the upper village now came to a halt a dozen paces from them. Slavin stepped forward. 'Old Mother, send word to all the communities in the mountains that Blackwing flies no more. They should send all their warriors here, so that tomorrow they may mourn and celebrate Blackwing's passing, and then witness you placing the crown of feathers upon his son's brow the day following.'

The headwoman's eyes remained cold but she inclined her head. 'As the gods will it. And on the third day?'

'On the third day, Chief Braggar will deci—' Slavin began.

But Braggar stepped forwards and said loudly, 'On the third day, we will begin to reclaim our land from those who stole it from us!' His warriors nodded. 'We will free the people and reclaim their hearts for the gods!' They shouted in support. 'We will reclaim our pride!' They cheered and punched the air, most of the villagers joining in. 'I say that we will no longer divide ourselves as upper and lower villages!' All the villagers became enthusiastic at that, and even the headwoman's eyebrows rose. 'We will no longer divide ourselves as higher and lower peaks! We will no longer be a divided people!' They were of one voice and will as their shouts echoed across the mountains. 'An end to division and strife! Tonight, we will feast, sing the songs and tell the tales that remind us of who we are.' They danced with joy, warriors intermingling with villagers, slapping backs, shaking hands, hugging women and even sharing kisses.

The headwoman's eyes now shone as she turned to Torpeth. 'He has his father's lungs and passion, but there is more life in him than his father. Truly, he speaks with the voice of the gods, dear old goat.'

Torpeth sighed as he watched the Minister whisper into Braggar's ear. The Minister smiled and his eyes briefly met the holy man's gaze before flicking away. 'Aye, beloved, there is life in him where there is none left in Blackwing. I must speak with he who is the closest I have to a friend, he whom I so despise.'

The Minister moved away through the crowd, allowing Braggar his moment.

Presumably, the young fool can deal with his people's adoration without his hand being held. I have no intention of taking part in any debauched celebration tonight. It will no doubt become some sort of pagan orgy. I will instead tend to my prayers and find consolation in the holy book. Praxis ducked out of the crowd between two cottages, only to find the naked Torpeth blocking his path. *How did he know I would take this path? How did he get here so quickly? Dark, sneaking magic, that's how.*

'Avoiding me, lowlander?'

'Of course. You smell of goats and are unwashed, after all. I might catch something off you.'

'Or is it your conscience you seek to avoid? What have you done, lowlander?'

'Nothing that Torpeth the Great has not done in his time, from what I've heard. I have made sacrifices for my faith. My conscience is clear. How dare you accost me in this manner, you upstart! If there is aught that is not to your liking then it can only be as a result of the things you claim to have begun so long ago. You are simply paying for your crimes and corruption, that is all. Now get out of my way!'

Torpeth absently stuck the tip of his tongue up his left nostril, which had been running with snot. 'I am sorry I have not shown you better friendship, lowlander. I am sorry I have not shown you love. Is it because of that you are so twisted and murderous?'

The Minister pulled his long black coat tighter about him, buttoning up the high collar beneath his chin. 'The only love I require is the love of my faith and the divine love of the blessed Saviours for the People. You are outside that love, pagan. You do not even know what the word means. I act out of love, where you do not. I acted where you lacked the understanding and courage. I have done your people a greater service than you can fathom, for now the journey towards Salvation is begun.'

'And what would you have me do, lowlander? Does Salvation exist for one such as me?'

The Minister's long nostrils flared and his lips puckered for a moment. 'You? One who is so ignorant and mired in the Chaos? Surely you jest?' Then his eyes narrowed with suspicion. 'Or you seek to undermine me or gain advantage over me. What would I have you do, pagan? I would have you end your life . . . or, failing that, bathe and put some clothes on. Like a neglected sheep, you are in great need of shearing. You need to learn the basic manners of civilisation. It will begin to school your mind. You must discover discipline and self-sacrifice if you are to have any hope of Salvation.'

'Clothes?' Torpeth scratched at his head and pulled out a mouse that had made a nest in his hair. 'Clothes are dangerous, lowlander.'

The Minister blinked slowly. 'Just how are clothes dangerous, you weasel?'

'My clothes as a warrior were my armour. They kept me impervious from harm but also deadened feeling within me. I was free to commit greater atrocities when I wore that armour. A man is more honest when naked, lowlander. The clothes that others wear define them too much – becoming their equipment for work, deciding their contribution to the whole and defining who they are. If they are not careful, therefore, people become limited by their clothes and lose their true selves. The wondrous potential and magic allowed them by the Geas are never realised. Their clothes have murdered who they could be.'

The Minister shook his head and spoke as if to a child. 'Clothes do not murder a person, pagan. They teach a person discipline. They help a person serve their betters. They order society. They separate us from naked animals. Yes, we should be careful not to be too limited by our clothes, for we should always strive to become whatever we may to better serve the Saviours – and that is why the blessed Saviours provided us with the holy book, so that we can remind ourselves of our duty. That is why the Empire has its Ministers, Heroes and holy Saints, so that the People can be safeguarded from their own complacency, indolence and indiscipline.'

Torpeth pulled on his beard to help himself nod. His eyes were empty as he said, 'You are wise, lowlander, I see that now. There is so much to learn. Yet I do not have the necessary trappings of which you speak. And I do not have a teacher. What will I do?'

The Minister frowned. 'Well, first bathe, shear and clothe yourself. Then I will consider teaching you.'

'Truly? Oh, that would be wonderful! I fear I would have no other chance of Salvation.'

Minister Praxis afforded him an indulgent smile. 'Indeed, it is certain you would not. You are fortunate that I have come here, pagan. Nay, the holy Saint was wise to send me on this mission. Truly, your conversion would be a miracle to qualify any Minister for Sainthood.'

Torpeth's eyes became wide and staring as if he were being visited by a vision. 'Lowlander, I see it!'

'What do you see?' the Minister asked urgently. 'Is this a moment of revelation?'

'I see it, lowlander!'

'Tell me, you weevil. I command it! What do you see?'

'You . . . Oh, we are blessed! You are . . . you are a Minister no more. You are . . .'

'Yes, yes? Speak!'

'You are *Saint* Praxis!'

'Unh!' the Minister whimpered and fell to his knees, hands clasped. 'Blessed Saviours, I am your faithful servant! Praise be! Pray with me, lowly Torpeth!'

Torpeth went to his knees, mimicking the Minister.

'Not too close. You still smell. That's it.'

'And you will lead all my people to Salvation!' Torpeth cried.

'Yes, it is so!'

'You will lead me down the mountain, Saint Praxis, for you will need a servant now you have greater and Saintly duties to perform.'

'Yes, yes, it is so. You will accompany me. You will be my servant. Saviours be praised!'

The Peculiar glided down out of the air and stamped three times in the middle of the crossroads. 'Dear one, we are here!'

There was a rumbling from below and then a tremor. Small stones vibrated as the ground began to behave like a liquid and a behemoth rose up out of the depths. Freda stepped onto firmer ground, wiped dirt from her eyes and looked around.

'I can't see much, friend Anupal. This road is chalky and reflects a lot of light. And what is that white stuff on the small trees? Chalk dust?'

The Peculiar smiled. 'No, it is called snow. It is frozen water that falls from the sky.'

'It drips from the roof?'

'In a manner of speaking, yes. And the small trees are called bushes. Many bushes like this together are called hedgerows.'

'There is much alive in these hedgerows. A thing with long . . . ears?'

'A rabbit probably, or maybe a hare. Or do they hibernate at this time of year? Not sure. It could be a pixie then. Don't worry, Freda, we are safe.'

Freda peered around some more, looking down each road of the crossroads and then trying to see into the winter-brown hedgerows. 'There is flat mud behind the hedgerows. And the mud has been arranged in lines.'

'Fields, these areas of mud are called. At the moment the sun-orb is far away. That is why it's cold and there is snow. But when it is brought closer, the heat will wake things up and food plants will grow in large numbers in the fields. Plants take energy from light and warmth, you see, and they become bigger.'

'They do?' Freda wondered. 'They are very different to me then, for I don't like the light and I'm not bothered how warm or cold it is.'

The Peculiar wiped dead flies from his face, one of the hazards of flying. 'Indeed, dear one, you are different to most things. Nearly all the life of this world requires light and warmth. The miners you worked with were probably weak or ill a lot because they didn't get enough light. Apart from you, the only ones I know of who do not need light and warmth are the elseworlders, those you know as the Overlords. An interesting coincidence, if you believe in such things. It raises interesting possibilities, dear one. Do you remember your origins?'

Freda stuck the end of her tongue out and scrunched up her eyes with the effort it took to remember so far back. There were physical feelings and sounds. Screams, but she did not know whose. There hadn't been anyone there, had there? No, there hadn't been anyone until Norfred had found her – or she'd found him, anyway. How long had she been alone at the start? She had no measure. 'No, friend Anupal. I did not understand anything of it back then and still do not know how to describe it. I was in the ground. That is all.' She paused. 'But the plants start in the ground too, do they not, and then grow upwards, just as I came upwards, is that not so? Maybe I am like normal things then, a little. I would not want to be too much like the Overlords. Please don't say I'm like them!'

'All right, all right,' the Peculiar replied with an unconcerned air, stretching. 'Keep your hair on.'

Freda stuck out her bottom lip. 'Don't be mean! I don't have hair only because I don't need it to stay warm. Anyway, what are your origins, then?'

He blinked in surprise and gave her a level gaze. 'Dear one, I did not intend to be mean. What I said has a different meaning. I'm sorry I was not more careful with my words. Tricky things words, I'm sure you'll agree. As to my origins, well, it is a matter of some dispute. Many claim I was created by the Geas, and I suspect that is what the Geas also believes.'

Freda tilted her head one way and then another. The priest of the rock god had told her that she was part of the Geas but that she should also find the Geas in a place called Haven. 'Are you not then a part of the Geas, friend Anupal?'

The Peculiar pulled a face as if in pain. 'Well, I am and I'm not, you see. The Geas was necessary for me to come to this world. The Geas probably thought that the idea of creating me was her own, but I actually provided the seed of that idea. The Geas then created me here, meaning I could enter this world. See?'

'Yes. No. But you know where the Geas is?'

The Peculiar looked frustrated. 'No. As she did with the other gods, she cast me out. None of us knows where or how to return to her. She said we would find a way when she found it necessary for us to do so. Bit selfish, no? But why am I telling you this?'

Freda shrugged. 'Because you want to? Because I asked, and I am your friend?'

'Yes, I suppose,' the Peculiar nodded, slapping the side of his helmet until it made a ringing noise. 'Ah! That's better. Anyway, we have arrived where we need to be, on time. May as well make yourself comfortable. Those we need to meet will be through here soon.' He sat down in the middle of the crossroads and then lay on his back.

Freda folded herself down next to him, her limbs scraping and sliding over one another. 'How do you know this is the right place, friend Anupal? You have not met these others before, no? You are not yet friends with them, are you? And I've been wondering how you knew where to find me.'

He opened one eye and squinted up at her. 'Full of questions today, aren't we? Don't you hear all the voices on the wind? If you listen carefully, you'll hear millions of them, some quieter than others.'

She listened for long moments. 'All I hear is the wind.'

He shook his head, his shining helmet crunching gently on the road. 'The wind has no sound of its own. It is made up of all the sounds and movements of the world. Everyone talking and moving about at once creates an awful din and a very powerful draught, as you might imagine, a force that moves the clouds, can create storms, can flatten trees, and so on. If you practise long enough, you can separate out most of the sounds and listen to what everyone is saying.'

She listened again, cupping hands to her small ears. 'I hear . . . the rustling of the hedgerows.'

'And beyond that?'

'It's just a rushing noise, like water in a river.'

'Yes, it's a river of sound. Do you hear variations in the river, as if the water chatters over rocks in one place or a fish flicks its tail in another to create a plopping noise?'

She twisted her head one way and then another. 'Yes, it's slightly different in each direction, but I can't make out clear voices. It must take a lot of practice or better hearing than I have. I'm better at feeling vibrations in the ground, I think.'

'Probably. Whereas I hear far too much, partly because I can sometimes sense the energy of people's thoughts in the same way I can hear voices. All the voices in my head drive me mad sometimes and stop me sleeping. But this helmet helps with blocking a lot of it out.'

'Then you know nearly everything, friend Anupal? I can't imagine that. Is it a good thing or do you not like it so much?'

He scratched absently at his cheek. 'Hmm. You end up knowing everything and nothing really. People talk a lot of rubbish most of the time. One will espouse something with utter conviction and declare it as invaluable knowledge, but then another will espouse the exact opposite with equal conviction. My head is filled with nothing but confusion and conflict most of the time. Sometimes I lose myself and am paralysed by it. Other times I rant and rave. You would think I always knew what was about to happen and that I would then know how to act to bend things to my will, eh? Yet, more often than not, people behave at direct odds with what they have just said or have been thinking. It makes them almost impossible. Occasionally, it does all come together and I achieve exactly what I wish. At those moments I appear godlike and omniscient. That's how Wayfar of the Warring Winds and the others do it too. But most of the time the actions I take just end up adding to the general confusion and conflict. The gods are frauds in the main, which is probably why the elseworlders found it so easy to displace them.'

The gods are frauds, she pondered as she watched a beetle scrabbling along the sheer cliff of her forearm. She was worried by that, for she did not want to be following the commands of a fraud. And if she were a child of the rock god, did that make her a fraud too? She sometimes felt like one, like when that horrible fat Saint had caught her, bitten her finger off and put her in a cauldron. 'Is it never quiet and peaceful for you then, friend Anupal?' she asked, wiping a tear from her eye and dislodging the beetle. The insect fell onto the road on its back and struggled with its legs in the air.

The Peculiar stilled for a second and then one of his feet began to twitch. 'It's all relative, I suppose. It's better when I am in my home and most of the voices are shut out. But the world is never absolutely quiet and at peace, dear one, never! But you're right – I strive to bring peace and quiet to it, so that I may then have quiet and peace. Sometimes it seems it would be best if everything were dead.'

Suddenly, she feared him. She stilled her tongue at once and quieted her thoughts. She became an unmoving stone. How he must hate her!

They trundled along in silence, silence except for the trundle and rattle of the wagon and the restless rhythm of the two horses' hooves. Jillan's mind trundled and rattled and his teeth ground together. His jaw ached. He'd collapsed after the confrontation with Bion and known nothing since. Unconsciousness was a blessing of sorts, until you began to understand you were trapped inside your own thoughts. They could all too quickly become a nightmare, as they had in Linder's Drop. He desperately wanted to break free, but also feared to do so, for he knew the world he opened his eyes to was a world of ruins, plague, loss and pain.

It's not that bad! the taint argued. *Your parents are probably still alive, as are Hella and Samnir, albeit a bit worse for wear. Plus, you need to wake up to help out poor old Ash and Aspin, who just don't know what to say to that morose and brooding blacksmith. Look, I'm not going to stop nagging till you wake up, so you may as well get it over with.*

Jillan groaned.

'He's awake!'

A drinking spout was put to his lips and water trickled into his mouth. He swallowed and felt a refreshing chill spread through him. He let his eyes flicker and fall open. Aspin sat next to him in the back of Thomas's wagon.

Jillan tried to move, but the mountain warrior pushed him back down with a firm hand. 'Take a second. Drink some more water. There you go. We've made good time, apparently. We're not far from Hyvan's Cross by Ash's reckoning.'

The sky was all dark shadows and bright spots. What was he seeing? The shadows flew past far quicker than clouds usually moved.

'Where . . . What . . . ?' he murmured.

Aspin followed Jillan's eyes upwards. 'Oh, we're in some sort of sunken road. It's a tunnel of sorts, since bushes and so on have grown over it. Amazing, huh?'

'I think pagans have maintained it so that they can travel across the land in secret,' Ash called back, his voice shaking slightly with the movement of the wagon. 'Is that right, Thomas Ironshoe? No answer again. Anyway, how are you feeling, Jillan? I was quite worried when you passed out, but Aspin said it had happened before. Pretty impressive display back there, I must say. Saved our bacon, and no mistake. That's another one I owe you.'

Aspin's eyes went from the direction of Ash's voice to an adjacent point. Jillan guessed his friend was gazing at Thomas's back. Aspin gave a sad shake of his head and then looked back down at Jillan. 'Ready to sit up? You should try and eat something. We probably haven't eaten in days, remember? I think there wasn't much substance to what we ate in Linder's Drop.' He winced at his own words and his eyes flicked back to Thomas before he helped Jillan prop himself against the side of the wagon.

'Just dried meat, I'm afraid,' Ash reported glumly. 'Although there are creatures aplenty in here with us, we've been given the distinct impression by our glowering blacksmith friend here that it's not at all acceptable to kill anything that's travelling via the sunken road. You know what these pagans are like, Jillan – nature-worshipping and so forth. I suspect this thoroughfare is sacred to the gods or Geas or something. Still, the wolf was with us a while and passed a musk deer coming the other way. The wolf didn't even lick his lips, I tell you. He all but nodded respectfully to the creature instead. Strangest thing I've ever seen. You know it's not like him to hold back on his instincts and appetite, eh? If I were to relate such a tale in the inns of Saviours' Paradise, I would not be believed. They'd think it was one of my jests or that I'd gone mad living out in the woods on my own.'

Jillan accepted a piece of jerky from Aspin and began to chew on it methodically. It was so dry that it was largely tasteless and immediately made him thirsty again. He sipped more water and finally managed to swallow the hard lump. Unpleasant it might be, but he knew it would sustain him. He considered the blacksmith, who stared blankly at the road ahead, the reins loose in his hands.

'Thomas?'

The giant appeared not to have heard him. Jillan raised a questioning eyebrow at Aspin. 'What can you read?' he asked softly.

The mountain warrior looked uncomfortable. 'Well, I haven't tried really. It would have felt a bit like intruding.'

What's wrong with the pair of them? They're tiptoeing around him as if they're scared of him or something. Are they forgetting he wronged them? He knowingly tricked them and would have had them trapped serving an evil sprite for the rest of their lives if it weren't for you. Now they're letting him take you all who knows where, with no idea whether they can trust him or not, although past experience would strongly suggest trusting him is the last thing you should be doing. It would probably be safer and kinder all round if you just took one of the blades stowed here in the back of his wagon and drew it across—

'Aspin, I need to know!'

Aspin jumped but then nodded. He stared at Thomas for a long while, lines and expressions appearing and disappearing so quickly on his face that they could not be followed. He drew a steadying breath, then said awkwardly, 'Guilt and torment, great torment. He . . . can be trusted, I believe. He wants to make some amends for his part in what happened at Linder's Drop. He will do everything he can to keep us safe and help rescue your parents. Beyond that, though, he is lost and there is only darkness.' Aspin hung his head.

Jillan sighed. He got to his feet, holding onto the side of the wagon and keeping his head low so that he didn't get caught in the briars of the tunnel's roof. He edged past Aspin, tapped Ash on the shoulder and signalled that he wanted to swap places with him. The woodsman nodded gratefully and climbed back off the top board.

Jillan sat in silence next to the giant for a while. His eyes had now adjusted to the half-light and he saw movement everywhere. The road was *alive*! There was a profusion of scuttling, scurrying, scampering, buzzing, swooping and slithering life. Death's head moths flapped like suffocating dreams while bejewelled butterflies danced around them as moments of joy. Rats forged and burrowed through detritus and humus, opening paths for smaller rodents. A tawny and almost invisible wildcat slunk past them, its glowing eyes a trick of the light and the rest of it the smoke of imagination. Birds dived and flitted, playing an unending game of hide-and-seek and trilling challenges to all. Snakes and slow-worms glided and glistened, ants and spiders hitching rides on their backs. Other creatures Jillan had only heard of in stories of magic and olden times.

They travelled along one of the sacred arteries of the world; they were a part of the Geas hidden just behind and below the cold everyday earth. There was the bleak and harsh reality of the world above, a world drained of life and colour by the Saviours; but then there was this tumult of life energy beneath. Jillan felt his faith in what he was attempting restored. He was not just lost in the wilds with a ragtag group of misfits and exiles; he was on a journey to free his innocent parents and find Haven. He was not simply a murderer and fugitive from justice; he was defending himself from being drained along with the rest of the world by the Saviours. He was not just deluding himself; there was hope for him and those for whom he cared.

'Thomas, I'm sorry,' he said quietly.

The rhythm of the horses' hooves remained unbroken.

'I'm sorry for what happened back there.'

You're not really though, are you?

'You had a family in New Sanctuary, when you knew my parents, didn't you?'

Thomas's face remained empty, but he hunched his shoulders slightly, as if to defend himself from being beaten about the head. The dead exterior of the man reminded Jillan of the barren world of the Saviours. There was life beyond that world, though. There was hope within, and a power of sorts, whether it teemed or was merely a dying spark.

'Three beautiful daughters who still live within you,' Jillan whispered as gently as a leaf falling. The creatures in the tunnel slowed and there was a lull, as if time had been interrupted by the vision that now hung in the air. 'And a wife. Sabella, Ausa, Betha and sweet Stara. Dressed in white. Smiling. Welcoming. New Sanctuary fell.'

'No! Please!' Thomas suddenly begged. 'Not again! Don't make me see it!'

'The Saint came. Their white dresses were turned red, their red faces were turned white.'

'Nooo!' came Thomas's heart-rending and eviscerating cry, tears burning down his cheeks. The life in the tunnel fled. Ash and Aspin hid their faces.

Jillan hesitated. *You must do this. It is a kindness of sorts. A most terrible kindness.*

'You refused to allow it, Thomas, and would not believe it. Then Bion told you that it had not happened, didn't he? He reassured you that it had just been a bad dream and that all was well. See, here are your daughters, and wife. Still smiling. Still welcoming.'

'No! Please!' His voice was ragged and torn as if his throat were being sawn open.

'You hid them away from the world, in a place that was always bright, but the black wolf finally found their scent and came for them. Nothing has the power to hold back the shadows of time and events forever, Thomas.'

The giant's shoulders shook and his body shuddered as if he were being dismembered.

'The white mice were at last consumed by the black wolf.'

His cry was primal: man understanding death truly for the first time; a child realising its parent is not just lost on some long journey; a woman finding that what she creates is not eternal; a suffering and torment that no lie can console; the agony of existence.

Even the taint was without voice.

Could the world ever start again? The nature of being was an all-consuming desire and fear of unbeing, wasn't it?

'No!' Thomas silently mouthed.

From the core of his being Jillan brought a spark and created a brief moment of light within the tunnel. 'They live within you still, Thomas. Make that the bright place in which you keep them. Otherwise, even your memories of them will be lost and it will be as if they never existed and they were nothing but a dream that fades away with the waking of the sleeper.'

'I do not want this!' the blacksmith pleaded.

'I know, and forgive me that I am cruel. But I need you properly with us if I am to have any chance of freeing and escaping with my parents, those who were once friends of yours. I cannot allow you to remain lost in the past or in your own thoughts.'

Thomas nodded. 'But after that you will let me rest?'

'Yes,' Jillan replied sadly. 'Then you can rest.'

Ash had lowered his hands from his face. He puffed out his cheeks. 'That was scary!'

Aspin looked embarrassed. 'I think I've wet myself.'

'Don't sit near me!' complained the woodsman, slowly piecing together a smile. 'Look, you've stained that sack. It smells.'

'Are you sure you wouldn't prefer to be back at your shack in the woods?' Jillan asked tiredly, his eyelids heavy again.

'No, I am not!' Ash replied. 'Still, at least I was smart enough to bring a flask of my homebrew with me. Here, Jillan, take a pull on this. Come on, you look like you need it. No, don't be fussy. As I recall, you have quite a taste for it.'

Jillan sipped at the raw alcohol and pulled a face.

'Now you, Thomas,' Ash prompted. 'Or I'm not sure we can be friends. Might not be as smooth as your best ale, but there's plenty of fight in it.'

'Hasn't he suffered enough punishment already?' Aspin asked with a straight face.

'Well, *you're* not getting any then,' Ash sniffed. 'Especially with that weak bladder of yours.'

'Again, I am sorry, Thomas,' Jillan said.

'Hey, you!' Ash fumed. 'Thomas is a man of taste and discernment, and has a more mature palate than you, besides. Let him be the judge. I will not have you besmirching my good name and homebrew, especially when you're in no fit state to stop me putting you over my knee and tanning your young behind.'

The blacksmith raised Ash's battered flask to his lips and they all stopped. Thomas took the smallest nip and then he was choking and wheezing worse than ever. Aspin and Jillan couldn't help smiling as Ash glared at them and slapped the blacksmith on the back.

'The sooner . . . the sooner we get to Hyvan's Cross, the better.' Thomas coughed. 'Strong as I am, I'm not sure how much more of travelling with you three I can survive.'

The sunken road began to peter out. Thomas steered the horses to the right and then through the hedgerow. The foliage fit so closely together where they left the route that upon visual inspection alone none would have thought there was a way through, particularly for something as large as a wagon. The horses stepped upwards and hauled them onto a chalky compacted surface. The blacksmith made a clicking noise with his tongue, and the untroubled horses set off down the new road.

Interrupting the silent but relaxed reverie the companions had fallen into, Thomas announced, 'We must follow the normal roads the rest of the way to Hyvan's Cross, I'm afraid, for the sacred way leading from the city itself was deliberately destroyed long ago, when the people fled the Saviours' minions.'

'It is far colder without the shelter of the sunken road,' Ash said a bit peevishly, blowing on his hands.

'Yes, I would advise a blanket each. There is a crossroads not far ahead, where we will take the road that leads directly to the city. From the crossroads, it is but half a day's journey.'

As they approached the crossroads a strange sight greeted them, a statue of a big ugly woman in the centre. There was also a handsome youth wearing a sun-metal helmet who appeared to be waiting for them.

'Ah, there you are!' the youth hailed them.

As they came closer, Jillan decided the youth's eyes implied he was far older than he first appeared. Far, far older. Then he saw the statue move and he realised it was alive. How was it possible? Maybe it had a clever mechanism inside, like some of the puppets old Samuel had used to make back in Godsend.

It's rock blight, you nitwit. An illness from too much contact with stone. She's as normal as you are . . . although that's not too normal, eh? Hmm. Oh dear. If that's who I think it is, then we really are in trouble. I—

Taint? Where are you? But the taint had disappeared, or been blocked, just as it had been in Linder's Drop. More than a little concerned, Jillan whispered to Aspin, 'Can you read them?'

'I wouldn't advise it!' the youth shouted, although Jillan was not sure what the stranger was referring to. Surely the youth hadn't heard him from this distance.

Aspin concentrated. 'The grey . . . woman is . . . a good person. She means no one any ill. As for the man . . . Ouch!' His hands went to his temples. 'So many characters. Too many. It's overwhelming! Can't make it stop! Help!' The mountain warrior passed out, and it was only Ash's perfect timing that saved Aspin from falling into the road.

'Sorry. I did warn him, though. It's why I wear one of these,' the youth called, rapping his helmet with the knuckles of one hand. 'A bit of water splashed on his face and he should be all right, if a bit groggy for a while. But well met! Come closer and allow us to introduce ourselves.'

There was something seductive and compelling in the man's voice. Jillan felt as if he was meeting a long-lost friend and wanted to run to him. Even the horses seemed drawn to him, but Thomas kept them back.

'Who are you and what is it you want of us?' Thomas asked brusquely, his suspicion clear.

The man-youth spread his hands. 'Mere common courtesy. Your names perhaps. As a gesture of good faith, I am happy to give you ours, with your graceful permission and a prayer that it will satisfy you.'

'Your words are as pretty as your looks, stranger,' Ash answered as he sloshed water over Aspin's face and waved a hand in front of Jillan's eyes to break his stare. 'In fact, you are *too* pretty. Like my friend the wagon-driver here, I instinctively find I do not trust you. Your appearance seems a deception. I would prefer you more plain, or more like your companion there.'

The man-youth's smile only became bigger and harder for Jillan to resist. 'And who might you be to judge prettiness so well?'

'Me? I thought it was you who was giving the names round here. I am Unclean, if that will satisfy you. I suspect it will not, however.'

A look of distaste flickered across the man-youth's face. 'And I suspect you are Ash of the woods, while you others are Jillan Hunterson, Aspin Longstep and Thomas Ironshoe. Your fame precedes you, and it is for that reason that I have come to offer you my help. May I introduce Freda of the north, a most gifted woman and my boon companion? And I am known merely as Anupal.'

'Anupal?' Thomas repeated, as if tasting the name and finding it more than a little unpalatable. 'As in Anupal who is more often referred to as the Lord of Mayhem?'

'Well, yes,' the man-youth replied reluctantly, then hurrying to add, 'but that's really a bit of an exaggeration. There was this terrible misunderstanding between—'

'The Great Deceiver?'

'Er . . . yes, but that was just those on the losing side who called me that. Sour grapes. Those on the winning side called me—'

'The King of Lies?'

'Look, truth is a matter of opinion most of—' the Peculiar attempted to explain.

'Abbadon, He Whose Name Is a Curse?'

'That one was actually more of a joke from a drinking game I played when—'

'Malmandius, the Friendless?'

'I haven't even heard of that one. Surely a case of mistaken identity. Besides, I have lots of—'

'Morlah, the Untrustworthy?'

'Now, you see—'

'Jezziah, the Eternal Mercenary? Targ, the Devil of Durnoch. Miserath, the Traitor God,' Thomas pronounced, the names passing their own sentence.

The Peculiar took a slow deliberate breath. 'I think we got off on the wrong foot. Let's start again, shall we? I have come to offer you my help against the Saviours. On your own you can never succeed and all will end. You must know that to be true. Haven will fall. The Geas will be lost.'

'You know nothing of truth,' Thomas spat. 'You offer us your help? We would prefer you offered it to our enemies, ever-twisting demon! You share none of our concerns, for are you not also the god of chaos and endings?'

'You know where Haven is?' Jillan asked.

'I have a way to find it,' the Peculiar replied smoothly.

'Do not listen to him, Jillan!' Aspin shouted, bow raised, although he had to be held up by Ash. 'My people know of you, most evil god! He is the forbidden one, the fifth, the dark and betraying brother. Begone from here, fiendish foundling!'

The Peculiar replied through a rictus grin. 'Stupidity. You would raise a pointed stick against a god? What is this ridiculous posturing?'

'Everything has a weakness and, you never know, I might get lucky, eh?'

The Peculiar's eyes narrowed. 'And will you raise a pointed stick to the thousands of soldiers in Hyvan's Cross? To the mad Saint himself?

Or do you have a way into the city such that you can avoid them all? No? I thought not. Now, can we have an end to these tantrums? You know, I'm not actually that bad once you get to know me. Lest you forget, mountain man, I was worshipped by your people before the Saviours came. And yours, blacksmith. So enough of this. Much as it grieves me to say it, we need each other. Given that unfortunate circumstance, it would be easier all round if we could try to get along, no?'

'Shoot him, Aspin!' Thomas urged. 'Do not delay.'

'Wait,' Jillan whispered, and Aspin hesitated.

'Gah!' Thomas snarled in exasperation, knowing that the moment to act was lost.

'Anupal, how will you get us into the city? How will you find Haven?'

The Peculiar now adopted a more relaxed smile and pose. 'At last, someone with the sense to ask. Why, Freda here can pass through rock as easily as you pass through air, Jillan. She can take you straight through the city walls. And Freda has knowledge of how to find Haven.' His face became serious. 'But there is something I must have from you in return, Jillan, for payment must always be made. What I require is for your ears alone, Jillan, and you may not then let others know of the specific terms.'

'Do not listen to him, I beg you!' Thomas demanded, facing Jillan. 'We will find another way into the city.'

'Say no, Jillan,' Aspin counselled.

'Ash, what do you say?'

The woodsman blinked, suddenly the focus of everyone's attention. 'I . . . I do not know. I have never heard of Anupal. But from what you've said, would he not also be the god of fickle fate and the impossible? I . . . Well, I'll go with what everyone else thinks. But if we really were in peril, wouldn't the wolf have sensed it and, well, I don't know.'

'I will hear you out,' Jillan said to the Peculiar and climbed down from the wagon.

'Idiot!' Thomas barked at Ash. 'How could you conscience this?'

'I always knew there was some weakness in you,' Aspin sneered, pushing Ash's hands away from him. 'Would you side with the dark and betraying brother? Coward! Truly you are Unclean!'

Something in Ash snapped and he snarled back at them, 'What? Am I to be asked about conscience by one who uses his own daughters to lure strangers into the clutches of a gnomish wizard? Am I to be called coward by a pagan people who hide in the mountains, fornicating with the Chaos as they do their own mothers?'

Shouts of outrage. Hands went to weapons.

'Enough!' Jillan roared, and made the air close with his magic. 'What is wrong with you? Who needs the Lord of Mayhem with the three of you like this? If you bear me any love, you will stay at peace while I hear what he has to say, and then I will make up my mind without apology to anyone or anger on any part!'

Jillan returned to his friends and looked up at them. 'They will travel with us. All three of you were right in your own way, even Ash. Do not be angry with each other and do not worry for me, please. They *will* help us, I'm sure of it.'

'If that smug overweening worm comes near me . . .' Thomas promised, veins bulging in his neck and forearms.

'Or makes the mistake of falling asleep while I am still awake . . .' Aspin averred.

The two pagans looked at Ash, absolutely no forgiveness in their eyes, then back at Jillan, their disappointment plain. Then they turned away.

Dusk was falling. The Peculiar had chosen to make himself scarce, though no one knew where he'd gone. Jillan picked his moment to go and talk to the rock-grey woman. He crouched down next to her, barely coming up to the top of her craggy knees. Even so, she shuffled away and watched him nervously.

'Thank you for helping me,' Jillan said. 'You have not asked for anything in return.'

Mutely, she shook her head.

'I have something for you,' the boy said, holding out his hand. 'They're nothing really, but my father gave them to me. I thought you might like them.'

She tentatively held out her palm and he deposited four stones into it. She stared and stared at the stones. No one had ever given her anything before.

'To keep?' her mouth crunched.

'Of course.' The boy smiled.

Not even Norfred had given her anything for her own. *Nothing*, the boy called them! She'd never had anything so valuable in all her life. A green, a red, a blue and a yellow stone, just like the ones in the temple of the rock god. Tears came to her eyes as she set them into her skin around her neck.

'Pretty.' The boy nodded.

She gazed at him. She liked him far more than her friend Anupal, although she would never dare tell Anupal that. She hoped he would not be able to hear that thought either.

Freda's eyes drifted down to the gold symbols on the boy's armour. She couldn't decipher all of them, but the ones she could told her he was steadfast.

'I will take you to Haven if I can,' she ground out. 'Do you know anyone called Jan?'

'Sorry, no. But if I meet someone of that name, I'll tell you.'

'Thank you.'

The wind changed direction and the boy raised his head. 'Do you hear that moaning?'

'Friend Anupal says it is the city.'

'It sounds like it's in pain.'

'Yes,' she quietly agreed.

CHAPTER 12:

And always too late

They all heard Hyvan's Cross long before they saw it. Its shrieking and moaning in the wind was so loud they had to shout to hear each other.

'The air funnels up this narrow valley and plays the hollows and depressions like a flute or pipe. We get the same where I live. One of our peaks is named the singing mountain and on certain days is heard from one end of the range to the other,' Aspin told them.

Freda shook her head. 'It's more than that, I think. I hear snatches of a tortured voice on the wind. It stopped me sleeping properly last night.'

'I had strange dreams,' Aspin added. 'Fortunately, I forgot most of them as soon as I woke up, but I do remember experiencing a feeling of great relief once I was free of them. What about you others?'

Jillan shrugged, but he had to wonder what nightmares he might have had if he hadn't been wearing his armour. He looked at Thomas, but the blacksmith had had bags under his red eyes since they'd left Linder's Drop, so probably hadn't been sleeping anyway.

Ash held up his empty flask. 'I was kept entertained by my home-brew last night, which no one else seemed to want to share. Slept like a baby, though.'

The Peculiar, who'd been walking ahead of the wagon in which the rest of them travelled, dropped back a bit and shouted up to them: 'The voice is Wayfar's. When the Saviours took the city from his followers, the Saint shattered Wayfar with a blast from a terrible horn of sun-metal. Poor Wayfar was literally blown and thrown to the four winds, but still rails around Hyvan's Cross as he tries to reform himself. But his power is broken and so he must suffer this fractured existence forever more . . . or until he fades away.'

'That's awful!' Jillan said in shock.

'Not that Miserath looks overly concerned,' Thomas added darkly. 'But it suited your purposes to see your brother undone, did it not, Miserath? You were probably party to it, weren't you? Tell us, what is the right punishment for deicide?'

The Peculiar's face remained unchanged. 'You do not know of what you speak.'

'But Wayfar is not entirely undone,' Aspin interrupted. 'In the mountains he is the greatest of the gods to many of our warriors. He is far from broken and blesses the faithful with powers over the storm.'

The Peculiar nodded. 'Beyond the Empire the old gods still hold some sway. Within the Empire, however, they are no more than haunting ghosts, movement glimpsed out of the corner of the eye, imagined voices and bad memories that will not go away. They are the restless dead. Wayfar is a cold, wailing wind who cuts right through you, but he is easily defeated by a thick coat, a raised collar and gloves.'

'Wouldn't mind some of those right now,' Ash complained through blue lips, his hands under opposite armpits. 'I won't be able to hold a weapon steady at this rate.'

'I'm hoping you won't need to,' Jillan replied.

'Nothing good can come of this,' Thomas warned. 'We are being led by the worst traitor ever known into a snowy and barren hell of the Saviours.'

'I thought you wanted to help free my parents,' Jillan challenged him. 'I do not have any other choice. If you've changed your mind then—'

'Peace, Jillan! I have sworn to help you, and help you I will. I still think it would be wise to remain cautious, however, for I cannot believe everyone here also wishes to help.'

The Peculiar yawned. '*You* have not always helped Jillan, though, have you, blacksmith? There is a word for someone like you: a hypocrite.'

'Oh dear,' Ash sighed.

Thomas's face began to turn red.

'Stop it, all of you!' Jillan yelled. 'If we're fighting among ourselves when there are just six of us, what hope can there be that the people will ever come together to fight the Empire? Perhaps the Saviours, Saints, Ministers and Heroes are a good thing if they stop us all fighting. Left on your own, you'd end up killing each other before you ever got to Hyvan's Cross. What use would that be, eh? My parents would never be rescued. *No one* would ever be rescued. Everyone would just end up dead.'

'I'm afraid that contrariness and self-division are an essential part of mortalkind, Jillan,' the Peculiar replied. 'I am the god of division, remember, and used to be worshipped for it.'

'Used to be!' Jillan stressed. 'Not everyone is like that. It doesn't have to end with everyone dead.'

'We will see, Jillan, we will see.' The Peculiar shrugged. 'Now is the time our group should be divided, though, for the city is coming into sight and soon there will be eyes upon us.'

At the top of the valley a large crag loomed out of the towering snow clouds. The way the soft stone of the crag had been moulded made Hyvan's Cross look like the horned and monstrous skull of an immense ice dragon. A high wall like a spiked collar had been built around the base of the crag. The dragon's cold breath came howling down the valley and blasted them harder than ever.

Ash's teeth rattled. 'Ye gods, who would want to live here?'

'Actually, it'll be far better once we're out of this valley,' Thomas told him. 'Several sides of the crag are out of the wind. And once we're through the gate, there's fairly good protection from the elements.'

'You're sure you can get us through?' Aspin asked.

The blacksmith nodded. 'I was here a year or so ago, to sell weapons. There are several markets a week in the city and plenty of traders come and go. There's always demand for good weapons in a place this big. With so many Heroes here, not all of them will have sun-metal, you see. There's a fair chance some of the guards will remember me for the quality of my weapons. And there is no reason why they would not believe you and Ash are my apprentices. People tend to keep their hoods up round here anyway, so your fairer hair shouldn't show up too much, Aspin.'

'Then Freda and I will leave you here,' Jillan said. 'Er . . . how do we do this, Freda?'

'Follow me, friend Jillan,' she replied, helping him down from the wagon and leading him over to the slope of the valley. 'Stay close behind me or I will not be able to keep the rock from crushing you.'

The rock woman began to sink into the side of the valley and Jillan stepped in after her. In a few blinks of the eye, they were gone.

'Miserath's gone too,' Ash commented. 'Vanished into thin air.'

'Good riddance,' Thomas breathed.

Ash shuddered and nodded his agreement.

In the village of Godsend Captain Hamir coughed into his handkerchief. He took the cloth away and examined it. Specks of blood. He prayed to the Saint and the blessed Saviours that he was just coming down with a seasonal chill. Fully half of his five hundred men had been taken by the contagion already, and more were reported each day. They'd tried everything to halt the spread of the illness, most recently filling the hospice with the sick, sealing it up and burning it to the ground. It had been a dark and grisly deed, far worse than anything he'd had to do fighting in the eastern region. It had always been his duty to protect the People, but now he was slaughtering them. He'd heard the screams of the dying in his mind every night since his order had been carried out and been unable to find sleep. Who was to say his dreams would have been any better than this living hell anyway?

Even worse, the torching of the hospice had done nothing to stop the plague. The physicker still reported as many new cases each day. Whether it was because the smoke from the hospice had carried the plague with it or whether it was because the town really was cursed – as many now whispered – nothing seemed able to keep death back. They said it was proof that the blessed Saviours had withdrawn their protection against the Chaos, as a punishment for allowing Jillan, his parents and Samnir to flourish among them, as a punishment for not having listened better to the warnings of their Minister, whose wisdom was now justly taken from them.

The one peculiarity to it all was that none of the children of Godsend – those who had not been Drawn, blasphemers liked to point out – had been affected. Parents had tried keeping their children next to them at all times, as a charm against the Chaos, but that had not saved them. Captain Hamir had heard of people bathing in children's urine and bleeding them for their protective humours, but that had not saved them either. Whenever a child was seen in the street, adults would come flocking and beg for a blessing and forgiveness. But the continued deaths said it was too late for forgiveness.

Since sealing the town gates, Captain Hamir had doubled the guards on them, for there'd been more than one attempt by the apparently healthy to escape. He'd had no choice but to order these deserting cowards cut down, to discourage any others from trying. Yet he knew it was only a matter of time before others did try. The longer the plague went on, the harder it would be to keep them under control. Certainly, some would give up, lie down and wait to die, but increasing desperation would eventually see the rest organise themselves. His main fear was that he would not have enough Heroes left to hold the gates, and then the wider Empire would be under threat. Therefore, he'd decided – with the agreement of the last surviving town councillor – to execute every last inhabitant of Godsend, children included, once he had only two hundred Heroes remaining on their feet. By his reckoning, the end would be just two days from now.

'Strange to know when you will die,' he observed to himself in his small hand mirror, as he combed his thinning hair. Clumps of it came out in the comb's teeth and he swallowed hard. 'Too old to be vain about it. You only need to stay upright and presentable for another two days and then your duty will be done. *Sacrifice and duty safeguard the People against the Chaos.* You have been lucky to serve so long. Yes, lucky.'

He didn't feel lucky even so. The Saint would know of his sinful thoughts, but the Captain could do nothing to stop them. He knew the Chaos had found its way into his mind. He knew he was infected. It was right that he died. He was resolved. The Chaos sought to plant niggling doubts in his mind; told him that he'd always been a faithful servant to the Empire and therefore deserved better; self-righteously claimed the Saint should be there with his People to save them or offer them comfort in their hour of need.

'No, Samnir was my fault. I always knew he was a wrong'un. I should have done something about it long ago. It was a disgrace that the holy one had to deal with it himself. A disgrace, Hamir, you hear? After that, why should the holy one feel any compunction to save us? We failed and betrayed him. We have probably broken his sacred heart. He probably cries at night for our lost souls . . . not that that monster ever shed a tear for those in New Sanctuary! Be quiet, you fool, or cut your tongue out. Traitorous tongue! Silence!'

Tears came to his eyes and he dashed them away with a hand. He caught a glimpse of his fingernails in the mirror and looked down. The bases of the nails were a deep purple, almost black. He knew they would soon crack and bleed. Not long after, he would be just one more dead body waiting to be thrown into the wagon heading for the pyres and mass graves next to the middens beyond the south gate, the same gate through which that damned boy had escaped and doomed them all. The Captain hadn't even known the boy. Fancy dying because of someone you'd never known. It was wrong really, just wrong. In many ways, though, much about his life had always felt wrong. Beneath the duty to the Empire and the sacrifice there had always been something that hadn't felt quite right. It had to be the Chaos, he told himself over and over. It would be good to be finally free of it. Free at last.

'Captain!' came an excited call from one of his men outside the door.

Crossing the small room in one long stride, Captain Hamir pulled the door open. 'What is it?'

'Someone at the gate.'

'Well, send them on their way.'

'But Captain, it's the Minister returned to us!' Eyes shining with hope.

Could it be, at this eleventh hour, they were now to be saved? Praise be! The Captain regretted his earlier sinful thoughts. He pushed his way out of his billet and went after the guard. He hurried to the top of the wall, careful of the patches of ice on the steps, and looked out over the north gates.

There stood the Minister, looking none the worse for wear, although perhaps a little thinner. A dozen paces behind him were a mule and a strange little fellow with a shaved head wearing a loincloth. Captain Hamir couldn't imagine how the fellow could stand the cold. Perhaps the savage was too simple to know any different.

'Captain Hamir, good day! What welcome is this? Will you leave me standing in the cold when my feet are sore from travel and I still need to offer up a prayer of thanks at the temple for having completed the holy mission allotted me by the Saint, and having safely returned to my flock by the good grace of the blessed Saviours?'

'Forgive me, Minister! The town has been sealed, as the plague is still among us and knows no mercy. If you enter in, then you may never leave.'

'Be of good faith, Captain.' The Minister nodded and smiled. 'Only if I enter in can I administer the blessing of the Saviours. Only if I enter in can the People be saved.'

'Minister, we rejoice that you have returned to us,' the Captain hiccuped, wiping bloody tears from his cheeks. His men could barely contain their celebration. 'What of yonder manikin?'

The Minister gave a brief glance over his shoulder. 'Be not afraid. This goblin is proof I have walked among the pagans. The power of the blessed Saviours protected me and the pagans fell at my feet, begging for Salvation. I took their holy man as my manservant so that he could lead them in their new service to the Empire. So, give praise, good People of Godsend, for I have converted the pagans and defeated the Chaos and its temptations, just as the holy one commanded.'

'O Minister, it is a miracle!' the Captain sang for joy. His men cheered, saluting the Minister with their shining weapons. 'We are saved, we are saved. I will be down this instant to open the gates myself, so that you may then pass among us. Praise be!'

Captain Hamir sprang down the stairs. How could he have ever doubted the blessed Saviours? He felt humble, he felt born anew. He couldn't help smiling. Single-handed, he threw up the heavy bar on the gates, where it would normally have taken two men. He pulled on one of the gates and the counterweight began to drop. One of his men pulled on the other and Godsend opened itself to Minister Praxis.

There was a blur and Captain Hamir found himself moving back through the air as if his feet had grown wings and lifted him up. Praise be, this must be how it was to be an angel! He hit the wall hard, smacking his head, and slumped to the ground. He looked down in confusion at the wooden shaft and feathers that sprouted from his chest. How had they got there?

The Minister came and crouched next to him. 'Apologies, good

Captain,' he whispered, 'but rest assured you sacrifice your life in duty to the blessed Saviours. It is all part of the holy one's plan to lure the pagans out and into a trap, so that they may be destroyed once and for all. Through me, he knows all that happens. At the same time the People of Godsend will suffer for their sins and for causing me to be expelled in the first place. Now I am returned and bring divine retribution in my wake. Accept my blessing, good Captain, for I am soon to be a Saint. Is the holy one already waiting within the town to welcome me?'

'N-no. There is only death here,' the Captain groaned as he watched the savages come pouring out from among the trees, their arrows picking off his men along the walls with disturbing and wind-favoured accuracy.

'No matter,' the Minister replied. 'I am sure he will come with the power of the blessed Saviours when he adjudges the time is right. Good day, Captain.'

Captain Hamir put his head back against the gate. Fancy dying like this. Still, it was as good as any other way, and probably better than some. It was better to die in battle than suffer a lingering death through illness, wasn't it? He no longer worried for the People of Godsend or the Empire, for they weren't his problem any more. He closed his eyes. Free at last.

'Freda, could you hear anything of what Wayfar was saying?' Jillan asked in the dark, more so that he would have a voice to hold on to, rather than because he had any real interest in the contents of the answer.

The rock woman slowed in her progress through the rock. 'It wasn't very nice to listen to, so I tried to shut my ears to it. There were a lot of bad words. Anger . . . and sadness. Some of it didn't make sense, as if his mind was broken like his body. Broken words. Then he begged for people to listen to him and answer him – anybody, anyone. So then I felt bad about not listening.'

Jillan knew something of how the god felt, or thought he did, crouched here in the dark, not knowing up from down. He couldn't see his hands. He was disembodied and lost. Actually, perhaps he could feel his hands, but hadn't one of the woodmen in Godsend lost a leg when it got trapped under a tree and sworn for the rest of his life that he could still feel it?

'So you did listen, then?' Jillan pressed.

'Yes, friend Jillan. It was like he wanted me to do something for him, but he didn't say what. Help him, I suppose. But I don't know how. Friend Jillan, we are under the city now. How should we find your parents? I sense many, many people.'

'I guess that they are keeping them in the punishment chambers, which are usually the lowest place in every town or city. Can you tell where they are?'

'Over here,' she chewed.

Where the hell are we? asked a faint voice. *You haven't got yourself killed and buried already, have you?*

Taint! Jillan shouted in mental relief.

Honestly, boy, you need to pay more attention. I've been shouting at you for ages.

Sorry. I couldn't hear you. Where did you go?

I suppose I shouldn't be surprised, what with Miserath's presence reducing me to a whisper and then Wayfar making such a din. He can be such a baby sometimes. Thank goodness he can't get down here into the rock with us. But this is the Saint's city, so you may lose me again soon. You didn't make any agreement with him, did you?

With who? The Saint?

No, you idiot. With Miserath.

I . . . had to. There was no other choice.

What? There's always a choice. Surely you've been through enough to know that by now. Having freedom to choose is the whole point. Jillan, what did you agree to?

Er . . . as part of the agreement, I can't tell anyone.

What! Oh, he's cunning. Look, telling me is just like talking to yourself. I'm in your head after all.

I can't. It's to help my parents.

There was a sigh. *No agreement with the Great Deceiver can turn out well. I leave you alone for five minutes and off you go dooming the entire world, your parents included.*

Don't say that! Jillan trembled.

What else do you want me to say, Jillan? That it'll all be all right? That you'll rescue your parents, you'll save Godsend and you'll all live happily ever after? I wish I could, I wish I could.

There has to be a way!

Does there really? the taint replied quietly.

Jedadiah had never liked small spaces. His body always felt squeezed and he couldn't breathe. It was even worse here because he was chained as well. They'd put manacles on him after he'd begun to panic as they put him in the cell and he'd lashed out and broken the heads of two of the guards. In the end it had taken six of them to wrestle him to the ground and get him in here. He'd cried and pleaded with them, but they'd ignored him. Even when they'd gone, he'd continued to beg until his voice had given out. He'd strained against the manacles for hours, all but cutting his wrists open, until his strength had also failed him.

He wanted to give up. He wanted to die. But there was some reason why that wasn't allowed. What was it? He'd been chosen somehow, and had promised never to give up. Yes, she'd chosen him. He saw her face before him and his breathing eased for a few blessed moments. His beloved Maria. And their blessed son, Jillan, whose eyes sparkled with such mischief but also such life, whose brow only creased in laughter with the joy he shared with everyone, whose smile was all the brighter for the unhappiness he showed when he saw misery around him, who never faltered when his will to help others caused him pain; Jillan, who made Jedadiah feel so humble, privileged and undeserving. Surely it was only what every parent felt for their child, but surely no child made their parent feel it more than Jillan. He was just a normal boy really, but was everything to Jedadiah, absolutely everything. He saw Jillan before him now and felt strength return to his heart and mind.

'You shouldn't be here.'

'I came to rescue you, Father.'

Jedadiah blinked. 'Jillan? How . . . ? You should be somewhere safe!'

Quite right. You should listen to your father.

'Nowhere's safe that I can tell, Father.' He pulled out his blade, lighting up the cell and causing Freda to step back into the shadows.

'That's sun-metal, Jillan!'

'Samnir's sword.' He smiled, effortlessly cutting away the manacles from his father's ankles. 'Freda, I can't reach the wrists. Can you do it?'

The rock woman slowly came forward and reluctantly took the sword, holding it at arm's length from her. She kept her eyes turned away, but managed to free Jedadiah without cutting him. The big man fell to the floor and groaned. Jillan looked down in shock, never having seen his father on his knees like this. He had always been the tallest and strongest man in the world, hadn't he? Jillan had always felt safe with him around. He couldn't bear to see him like this. His confidence suddenly fled and now he was scared.

Freda passed the blade back to Jillan and helped Jedadiah up, supporting most of his weight. 'Friend Jillan, should I take your father out of the city through the rock now?'

'I-I don't know. If my father can't stand, then maybe. It'll take a long time though, so they might discover he's gone before I can find mother. She isn't down here with you, is she, Father?'

Jedadiah shook his head. 'I'll be all right once the blood is back in my limbs. Just give me a moment. They took Maria somewhere else. It feels like she's not too far away. I can lead us there if we're lucky.'

Jillan shifted his weight from foot to foot impatiently.

You really haven't thought this through very well, have you?

Be quiet! It'll be all right.

'Okay,' Jedadiah said, in obvious pain. 'Let's go, since I assume you're not going to listen to me telling you just to leave us here and get away while you can.'

'I'm sorry, Father, I can't do that.'

'Stubborn. Just like your mother,' Jedadiah said with affection. 'Come on.'

Freda helped them out through the wall of the cell and they moved slowly along a low dank tunnel. They passed other cells, most of them empty but a few with unmoving occupants. Jillan was grateful for the dark so that he did not have to see too much.

They came to the foot of some worn stairs, at the top of which daylight showed. Jillan motioned the others to stay where they were and tiptoed up. A minute later he came back down.

'Two guards,' he whispered. 'Freda, can you go through the rock and hit them on the head?'

The rock woman looked unhappy at that. 'Do I have to, friend Jillan? I might hurt them so bad that they can't be mended again. Can't I just take each of you past the guards through the rock? I can find a quiet place where we can come out of the rock without anyone knowing.'

Less exciting, but eminently more sensible, eh?

'That's a better idea. You *are* clever! Can you take both of us at once?'

She shook her head. 'Your father is too big, friend Jillan. One at a time.'

Long minutes later the three of them were crouched in a natural blind alley that went up over thirty feet between rock faces. Hyvan's Cross was a maze of sandstone buttes and pillars, a place of narrow defiles, corkscrew paths and scalloped steps up and down. Nothing was quite flat or straight. The city had been created by the wind carving the rock, hollowing it out and engraving it with its will. It had been the home Wayfar gifted to his followers, a home where they might wonder at his divine artistry and lift their worshipful voices in harmony with the transcendent music of his breath. Yet his followers had not been able to match his divinity and had constructed stone buildings in the more open areas, hollowed out extra homes from the rock face, hung rope ladders from higher rooms and created aerial walkways with rope-and-plank bridges – all of which had made the notes of the air discordant and caused the wind to batter the crag, its voice becoming one of fury. The discordance between Wayfar and his followers had only grown, until the inevitable cataclysm of the Saviours' coming. The followers had fallen and were now mere shadows dancing and flitting chaotically through the city. The sound of Hyvan's Cross was an eternal lament to the fall of its god. The city had been gouged, tunnelled, mined and fortified as it had been bent to the will of its new ruler and the Empire.

Freda wept as she heard all this on the wind. It called to her, begging her to go to the temple higher up in the city. Yet she could not leave her friends.

'I sense Maria is that way. We should just try and walk like normal inhabitants,' Jedadiah whispered.

'Freda, it's probably best if you follow us through the rock,' Jillan suggested.

Freda nodded and sank from view.

Jedadiah and Jillan came out of their hiding place and made their way round wide columns, across small plazas and past cleverly terraced gardens. They passed a good number of women out browsing the goods of traders, squads of Heroes marching in files and children playing chase, but only received cursory glances in this place of so many.

'How are we ever to find our way out of here?' Jedadiah worried out loud.

Jillan knew his father had never liked crowds or the confined spaces of towns. 'Don't worry. Once we have Mother, all we need to do is follow the slope down. Thomas and my friends will be waiting near the gates into the city. I will pretend to be one of Thomas's apprentices and leave on his wagon. Freda can take you and mother through the wall one by one.'

'Thomas Ironshoe?'

'Yes!' Jillan grinned.

Jedadiah returned his son's smile and ruffled his hair like he'd always done before. Jillan had always seemed to mind it back in Godsend, but not now.

Freda came out of the rock, the small woman in her arms, and placed her before Jillan and his father. She watched curiously as the reunited family hugged each other for a long time, as if they would never let go. Jillan's father kissed the small woman and picked both her and his son up in one go. Jillan was laughing, Maria was crying. Why was the small woman crying? Yet Jillan and his father didn't seem to mind. Kisses, a caressed cheek, forehead rested against forehead.

Then Maria was pulling away. 'I prayed you would not come. Oh, why did you have to come here, my beloved son?'

Jillan looked crestfallen. 'But I had to rescue you, Mother.'

'It's all right, Maria. We're together again,' Jillan's father said, reaching for her, but she slapped his hand away.

'You should know better than that, Jedadiah!'

Jillan's father looked hurt. 'But we can go somewhere, leave the Empire,' he begged.

Pain in Maria's eyes as she squeezed them shut and said tightly, 'We have been Drawn, Jedadiah. We can never be free of the Empire. But the Saint will protect us. We can be a family again if we remain here.'

'No!' Jillan's father drew back aghast. 'This place is a prison. They will Draw our dear Jillan to the Saviours too, you know that. You cannot want that for him, Maria, not now we know how important he is. You cannot! What are you saying? Why won't you look at me?'

'Mother? What's wrong? Just come with us down to the gates, where Thomas and my friends are waiting. Then we can all go home. Back to our house in Godsend. Just like before. There is a plague there, but I think I know how to help everyone.'

Her eyes came open and she gazed proudly at her son, her smile brave and trembling, her eyes shining with tears of heartbreak. She could not deny him, could not help nodding. 'Then let us go, sweetheart, and be a family once more, if only for a little while. But you must promise me you will be brave, no matter what happens.'

'Of course, Mother.'

'Promise me, Jillan!'

'I promise.'

'Good. Jedadiah, help me as we go,' she said, squeezing her husband's massive hand hard and laying her other hand on Jillan's shoulder.

They made their way down through the city as quickly as they could without risking undue attention. Freda moved through walls and stayed in the shadows as she ghosted along behind them. Several times it seemed like they were doubling back on themselves but they always made sure to spiral downwards. Their footsteps echoed in the narrow passages as if there were an army coming after them from just around the last bend, and Jillan found himself glancing back time and again. *Nearly there, nearly there*, he panted in time to his footfall and heartbeat.

At long last they came to a wide tunnel through a squat bluff, beyond which they could see an apron of open ground down to the wall encircling the crag. Was that Thomas's wagon he could see down there inside the wall? Yes, the blacksmith was showing off his wares to a few Heroes.

They moved without hesitation into the tunnel, their strides lengthening. Like clouds passing over the sun, dark shapes began to move across the far end of the tunnel. Jillan craned his head left and right, trying to make them out. *No. Don't let it be anything bad.* Hard boots filled the tunnel, and then a voice all around them, dripping with menace, stopped them in their tracks.

'Is this how you repay my hospitality and indulgence then, little pagans? You think you can creep away without even a thank you? I know we haven't always seen . . . eye to eye, Jillan, but there is such a thing as basic manners. Not exactly courteous to be stealing my guests away, now is it? Did you think I wouldn't know? Had you forgotten that *the Saint always knows*? What say you, Captain Skathis?'

'Downright rude, holy one.'

Their way forward was blocked by dozens of men bristling with weapons. Jillan couldn't bear to turn back and face the leering Saint. They mustn't lose their momentum or all was lost. He began to summon the storm – it rose slowly within him at first, but the wind beyond the tunnel swirled with eagerness, like a prowling beast. Freda suddenly burst out of the ground in front of the men before them and began to lay about her. A Hero's jaw was dislocated, while another's chest was caved in with a mighty fist. The men fell back, but were well trained and quickly brought their weapons that had the reach to bear. A net twirled overhead. Freda stamped down, cracking the ground open and toppling more men.

Jillan raised his hands, sparks dancing around his fingertips. The stones at Freda's neck shone and she roared with renewed strength.

'Hold the line,' barked Skathis from behind them. 'Close in on them.'

A shocking blast. The sound of a sun-metal horn detonating all around them, unbalancing Jillan and his companions as well as a good number of the Heroes. Jillan's magic was snuffed out and Freda's eardrums burst. Cracks shot up her arms and legs and she wailed in agony, though none could hear it for the clarion call that rang and rang in the tunnel, echoing over and over and, if anything, building rather than fading away.

Jillan was on the floor. Dizzily, he looked around him. Maria was on hands and knees retching. Jedadiah staggered as if drunk, his eyes unfocused. Freda lay on her back, broken as if she was nothing more than the rubble of the tunnel floor. Heroes who had been just beyond the end of the tunnel picked their way forward, shafts of sun-metal levelled at the rock woman.

'Leave her!' came the Saint's mental command. 'I must have the boy. Nail him to the ground, quickly!'

'You promised you would not harm him,' Maria coughed.

'Ha! And what did you promise, wench? You have betrayed both the Empire and yourself.'

Jillan groggily called to the taint to help them, but it had been obliterated by the sudden power of the Saint. Only scraps and remnants remained. Jillan grabbed at them frantically as he turned his eyes towards the monster he now realised had haunted his dreams his entire life. It drooled hungrily at him, its hulking back brushing the top of the tunnel. The weeping sockets where its eyes had once been stared back at him knowingly.

'Do not fight me, Jillan,' it crooned. 'Give yourself to me and I will spare your parents. I offer you the blessing of the Saviours. I offer you Salvation.'

It intended to devour him. He knew it now. He scrabbled for the broken shards of his magic and drew from his core, from his own essence.

Saint Azual sensed Jillan stirring himself towards resistance and raised a sun-bright demon-horn to his lips once more, its bell the yawning mouth of a gargoyle. It was the weapon that had shattered Wayfar, and now it would decimate this defiant boy and his contemptible parents.

Freda felt things inside her snap and rupture.

You will die here, mourned the wind, *unless you come to me now.*

But my friends! she cried.

You have done what you can for them, given them everything you have. You could not have done more. To stay now would be an empty gesture and perhaps cowardly. It is harder to continue, I know. You want to die here with your friends, do you not?

I want to save them!

You cannot. So now what will you do? What of your promise to Norfred? What of your debt to the rock god? What of your promise to Anupal? Will you continue with these empty promises and gestures, Freda? Will you agree to an empty existence and meaningless death?

Always there was the guilt and the debt, always a demand for payment. Where did it come from? Would she never be free of it? Should she run from it, stand against it or submit to it? Did it matter what she did?

Blood bubbled up in her throat and her breathing became erratic. She was dying, she knew.

It does matter, Freda, the wind soughed. *Why else would Jillan struggle so? Of course it matters. I know it is more painful to continue, but if you decide to take on that pain, then your existence will be more than an empty gesture or promise, and your eventual death will be more than meaningless.*

Forgive me! she pleaded with the world and began to sink into the earth, where she would become one with the bedrock and allow it to remake her so that she might then begin the long and painful crawl up to the temple.

Jillan did not hesitate, lashing out with everything he'd been able to gather just as the horn began to sound once more. Lightning arced through the tunnel, clawing at Heroes and leaping for the despised Saint. The horn's energy intercepted it and the air between them boiled. A Hero tottered into the space and his armour sloughed off with his skin. Hot air burned the inside of his lungs and blood came sizzling out of every part of him. His eyes popped and the jelly inside them caught fire. He then all but vaporised, only a smear of carbon left on the floor showing he'd ever been a living, breathing creature.

Eldritch fire poured along floor and ceiling from where Jillan stood, setting light to a handful of Heroes and driving the others back. The flame licked around the Saint, but the energy coming off him kept it back. Jillan's wild magic howled and spiralled, whipping the roiling energy in the middle of the tunnel into a maelstrom, lines of power flying out in all directions, striking rock, burning holes through torsos and turning the place into an oven. The sound of the horn was drowned out and then an explosion tore out of both ends of the tunnel, flattening everyone and everything inside.

Concussion waves. Silence. Jillan realised he'd lost his hearing. He'd landed on top of his father, who'd instinctively been sheltering Maria with his frame. Jillan looked down at his glowing, smouldering armour and realised it had saved them from much of the damage. Others had not been so lucky, judging by the charred and smoking remains covering the floor. Saint Azual was holding up the arm which had held the terrible horn. The sun-metal instrument had melted in the crucible of their confrontation and engulfed the Saint's hand. The metal appeared to be eating into his wrist, and now his forearm. He might have been screaming, or shouting orders, but Jillan couldn't hear a thing, not even the taint. A burned Captain Skathis ignored his own pain, stumbled over to his master and sliced through the holy lower limb, the soldier's sun-metal blade instantly sealing the wound.

Saint Azual actually smiled. He gesticulated with his stump towards Jillan.

Jillan tried to move, but he was completely spent, the life energy within him flickering and stuttering alarmingly. The roof of the tunnel crashed down on him, and then he realised he was being lifted. His father – just like the time he had found him in Godsend. His mother was under his father's other arm. Jillan wanted to sob in relief, but lacked the strength even for that.

His head jolted up and down as if he were a rag doll. Had he blacked out for a second? They were outside the tunnel. Heroes were running up the slope towards them from all directions. The sky was a sheet of steel above them, the grey wall of Hyvan's Cross the entire horizon. They were still trapped.

Jillan was weaker than a newborn babe, but he realised something of his hearing had returned, for he could hear the unsteady crunch of his father's steps and the shouts of the soldiers charging towards them.

Jedadiah put down his wife and son, stepped forward and squared his shoulders.

'Samnir's sword,' Jillan whispered, the wind whisking the words to his father's ears.

Jedadiah spun back, grabbed the hilt at Jillan's waist and had the sword up just in time to meet the first oncoming blade. The sun-metal of Samnir's sword sheered straight through the other weapon as if it weren't there and took off the Hero's head in the same stroke.

Jedadiah booted the headless corpse back into the legs of the man coming on behind. He moved right and drove his sword point forward through a shield and into another man's chest. A Hero with sword held high came in from the left at the same time – Jedadiah knew he could not avoid him, so shifted his weight to move straight at him and then dropped his left shoulder to catch him in the stomach. With a mighty heave of his left arm, the hunter hurled the soldier over his head and back. The Hero hit the stony ground behind Jedadiah as Samnir's sword came free of the other man. Jedadiah fell back and plunged the blade over his right shoulder and straight into the Hero's gut.

'Beware!' Maria shouted as five more Heroes arrived while Jedadiah was still on the ground. She spat arcane words and inscribed patterns in the air. Three of the soldiers stopped in confusion as the air sparkled and refracted before their eyes, but the other two had come from the sides and not been caught by her cantrip.

One stabbed at Maria as she rolled. The blade sliced into her side but not deeply enough to finish her. She cried out and Jedadiah glanced in panic towards her. The soldier coming in was experienced enough to pick that precise moment to attack.

The point of Jedadiah's blade dropped slightly as he made to lunge to save Maria. The soldier thrust in with his own sun-metal sword over the top of his enemy's blade. Jillan's eyes went wide with horror. He tried to stop time; willed the blade to stop moving towards his father; prayed to Wayfar to blow it from its path; and watched as it moved agonisingly closer. Every instant was a lifetime lost. Should he close his eyes?

The Hero suddenly stood straighter, as if coming to attention. His hand came up to his front, as if looking to brush something invisible away before an inspection. Then he pitched forward, an arrow sunk deep in the middle of his back. There was a whistling noise and another shaft took down the Hero attacking Maria.

Aspin waved up to them and shouted 'Come on!' before quickly reaching to his quiver again. Heroes surrounded the mountain warrior, Ash and Thomas. Like Aspin, Ash worked with a bow, while Thomas hurled throwing knives with practised dexterity. There were archers all along the wall trying to take down Jillan's companions, but the wind bedevilled them and made a mockery of their aim. One sudden gust even turned an arrow back on its owner and skewered him through the eye. Yet a few of the arrows were tipped with sun-metal, and these cut through the air with fearsome power and accuracy, causing the wind to scream in agony and collapse in places. It was only Ash's perfect timing that allowed him to avoid such missiles at the last moment. Aspin and

Thomas, by contrast, were forced to retreat behind the cover of the wagon, so their ability to keep back the press of the enemy was severely hampered.

More and more Heroes were arriving with every moment, all driven by the voice of their Saint, now booming across the city. 'Kill them all, save for the boy!' A band led by Captain Skathis emerged from the tunnel behind Jillan and his parents.

'Look at them all. We'll never make it!' Maria cried as Jedadiah dispatched the three Heroes she'd bewitched.

'Oh, but I beg to differ,' crowed a golden youth descending from on high.

'What is this? An angel?' Jedadiah gasped.

'Far from it,' Jillan scowled. 'But he must help us.'

'I shall ignore such surliness, Jillan. These would be your parents, yes? I am glad to meet you at last. Jillan has told me so much about you. Well, Jillan, aren't you going to introduce us?'

'There's no time!'

'There's always time for manners, young Jillan. Oh, very well. If you would be so good as to run, I will ensure no harm comes to you. You, there, the father! I suspect you'll need to carry Jillan. That's it. Jillan can take the sword again. Off we go then.'

They raced down the slope. The Peculiar glided ahead of them, his arms and hands long flat blades that allowed him to take to the air one moment and scythe down Heroes the next. When a Hero raised a weapon in defence or to strike, the Peculiar would become a mist, sink his hands inside the combatant and then solidify again so that he could tear his victim inside out. The wind seemed reluctant to blow in his favour at first, holding him up on several occasions, but then it changed tack and moved him from foe to foe with increasing speed.

A squad of six Heroes came in attack formation for the Peculiar. 'Lay down your weapons and kneel to me!' the golden one thrummed and they stopped, mesmerised.

'I command here!' boomed Saint Azual's mental voice, reclaiming his men, creating a lull in the wind and tumbling the Peculiar to the ground so that he landed in an undignified heap.

The Peculiar took a moment to straighten his helmet, stand and rearrange the folds of his robe. 'This really won't do,' he announced as the six men bore down on him once more. 'Jillan and family, carry on without me. I will be with you momentarily.'

A blade sliced down at him and he made himself impossibly thin so that it missed. One blade came flat and low while another came flat and high. He became a winged serpent and snaked forward through the gap between them. He lashed right and left, sinking fangs and venom into the forearm of one and the thigh of another. All but instantly, capillaries around the bites showed green as lethal poison spread along limbs and into hearts. Twisting like the serpent, the men fell dead.

The Peculiar landed beyond the three remaining men, a beautiful youth once more. He spat. 'Eugh! Salty! You men should really watch your diets.'

But then Saint Azual entered the fray, leaping out of the tunnel and straight for the Peculiar in a single bound. The Saint was joined by the fast-arriving Captain Skathis, and the Peculiar was suddenly threatened by enemies from above and below. The Peculiar somersaulted backwards, just avoiding the Saint's taloned swipe. Captain Skathis rushed in and the Peculiar became a mist. As ghostly hands reached for the veteran's chest, the Captain's sword flicked up through the Peculiar's head and thrust the helmet of sun-metal off his brow, sending the headpiece rolling away down the crag.

'Argggggggh!' the Peculiar cried, his tongue elongating, vomiting out and running all the way to the ground. He clutched at his temples, his hands pushing through his skull as if it were mush. His knees buckled and then slipped; his thighs thumped end-on into the ground and then split open. His elbows drooped plastically and his jaw yawned down past his waist. His eyes ran like liquid down his cheeks. 'So many voices!' he belched. 'I am everyone!'

The Saint's hand smashed down on top of the Peculiar's head, pushing it into its bulging ribcage. Raking nails tore ribs apart and revealed the head nestled next to its own heart, teeth chattering as if about to eat the vital organ. The Saint bunched his hand into a fist and punched the head with everything he had, sending the mess flying, cartwheeling and flailing down the slope.

'You are no one! Nothing! *I* am the god here!' declared the Saint and then leapt for Jedadiah.

Jedadiah flung Jillan through the air and into the waiting arms of

Thomas just as the descending Saint's shadow engulfed him. Jedadiah planted his feet, raised his fists aloft, tensed and made himself as hard as possible. The wind connived to adjust the Saint's course as he came smashing down . . . and he found himself impaled by the living weapon Jedadiah had become. One of Jedadiah's arms audibly snapped and he crumpled into the ground, but he straightened the fingers of his other hand inside the holy one's body, to grab at his intestines and haul them out. Yet the guts slithered away and would not be held.

Doubled over, the Saint lurched back. Thomas had pushed Jillan behind him and now jumped in with his mighty hammer, intent on finishing the Saint, but Captain Skathis came in with his shield and a rank of Heroes to save his master.

'Thomas! No! Get Jillan out while you can!' called the crippled Jedadiah. 'The gates are still open. Now is the moment!'

The Peculiar alighted between them, seemingly unharmed by his gruesome experience, helmet firmly fixed back in place. 'Yes, now is the moment.'

Aspin and Ash continued to fire arrows, keeping the gates open for precious seconds longer and the archers along the walls a good way back. 'If we're going to go, we have to go now,' Ash panted raggedly, leaning all the way back to the ground to avoid yet another deadly shaft tipped with sun-metal. 'I can't keep this up.'

'Ironshoe, for the friendship you once bore me, take my wife and son safely beyond the walls. I implore you!'

Thomas nodded grimly. 'I will, my friend.'

'No! Father!' Jillan shouted hoarsely from where he leaned precariously against the wagon. 'Miserath, you promised you would help me rescue them. You promised!'

The Peculiar smiled gently. 'I agreed to see them safely to the gates of Hyvan's Cross, and that I have done. I am sorry, but I can do no more, for there is an aegis on your mother, a greater claim.'

'I will not permit it!' boomed Saint Azual, rising to his full height and scattering the men around him, the stench of his carrion breath all but overwhelming. 'You are the plague-bringer, boy! I will not allow you the freedom to spread your taint any further. You have murdered thousands of my People. Thousands! Your magic leaks from you continuously and infects the land like a cancer. Even your own mother has vowed to remain here and keep you with her so that your monstrous evil will be contained.'

'No!' Jillan shouted, thumping his fist against the wagon. 'Liar! It's not true! *You* are the monster.' Yet as he looked pleadingly from face to face, the sobbing of his mother, the sadness of the Peculiar and the way Ash sidled away to avoid direct contact with him told him it was just as the Saint said. 'Please! Noo! Mother, tell them it's not true!'

Maria looked to her beloved husband, her eyes begging him to understand, and then to Jillan, pleading for forgiveness. She threw back her head and screamed her agony to the sky. She was heard to the horizon and beyond, for the world all but stilled at the sound of her primal suffering. The horses in the wagon traces whinnied in abject terror. 'Jedadiah, my love! You *must* save him! You *must*! For all our sakes! For the Geas! For all life!'

'No!' thundered the Saint. 'I own your lives, as I own the People! Jillan, give yourself to me or I will end your parents here and now, end them with a mere thought.'

Jillan could not see for the tears in his eyes and the horror in his mind. All those people dead because of him. His own mother willing to betray him because of the monster he had become. And many more would die if he did not stop. 'Make it stop!'

His father was rising to his feet, cradling his broken arm against his chest. Jedadiah looked lovingly at his wife. 'I now know why you picked me all that time ago. It was for this one moment.'

'It was because of the man you are, beloved. A man who will stand with strength and passion where others will not. You have always humbled me.'

'And I have never loved you more than I do now. You have given me nothing but happiness and meaning, and a wonderful son. I could not have had more even had I lived a hundred lifetimes. Goodbye, my love.'

'Goodbye, my sweetest Jedadiah.'

'My son, you will obey me one last time and leave now. Your mother and I will hold the gates. Be brave, Jillan, for there is no pain next to our love for you. Ironshoe, take him out of here.'

Thomas nodded and threw a longsword from the wagon to his old friend and a pair of long knives to Maria. 'May the Geas protect you both!' He then scooped up Jillan and threw him over his shoulder. Jillan tried to fight, but was powerless against the blacksmith's brawn.

'Mother! Father! Please!'

Saint Azual hissed and took an angry and forbidding step forward. Ash and Aspin immediately trained their bows on him. Dozens of encircling Heroes raised their spears in response, awaiting their holy master's command.

'You have defied me for the last time, puny pagans! You think the Geas holds any sway in this world? Then let us see if it will protect you as I burst the hearts in your chests!' Azual sent out a magical command and Jedadiah, Maria and Thomas each paled and rocked on their feet.

'Oh, but that was poorly done, Saintling!' the Peculiar reprimanded as he placed one hand on Thomas's shoulder to steady him and gestured towards the other two. Maria slipped to her knees, but Jedadiah just about kept his feet. He gritted his teeth, gripped his sword tighter and raised it back to the guard position.

'You dare interfere?' raged the Saint. 'Your kind is long since broken! You have no rights or powers here!'

'On the contrary. My claim to the boy is greater than yours, and you are naught but a craven lackey of the elseworlders. As my will is their will in this, you cannot gainsay me when it comes to the boy. The parents are sacrifice enough to your petulance and delusion.'

Thomas finished cutting the horses from their traces and vaulted with Jillan onto the back of one, while Ash and Aspin mounted the other.

'Kill them all!' Saint Azual blasted out, his voice battering his own men as much as his enemies.

Jedadiah stood firm, swinging the longsword ferociously with his one good arm, hewing down one man and forcing another to stumble. He leapt back and the Heroes got in each other's way as they crowded in. Those towards the back of the press cast their spears, but the wind dragged the weapons down and buried them in the shoulders of those in the front rank. As the front row fell, they tripped and impeded those coming on behind. Jedadiah scythed forward with his blade again, cutting one prone man up under the armpit and then dragging the weapon on a continuing arc across a throat and through a man's upper thigh. Men cursed, screamed and shouted.

'Stand back, you fools!' Captain Skathis yelled. 'Forward together, on my mark. Archers ready!'

'They are escaping!' the Saint bellowed, smashing through his own men. One man's head was staved in by the heedless Saint, while another's neck was broken. The Saint raised his hand to bludgeon Jillan's kneeling mother into the ground.

'Geas, receive me!' Maria cried and threw her arms wide, releasing golden scintillations of her own life energy into the air. She'd given everything she had from the core of her being and sacrificed herself in one final act to buy Jillan and his companions a few more precious seconds in which to escape.

'Mother!' Jillan sobbed hysterically from the back of Thomas's fleeing horse, and hid his face.

The magic of Maria's death charm drifted through the Saint and stopped him dead in his tracks. She dragged him inexorably back towards his own mortality and death! His flesh withered where the golden motes touched it. Beyond the Saint, men began to fall as their bodies instantly petrified.

Using the last of his own power, Saint Azual released a red mist to smother the dancing gold and extinguish the battling mind and life force of Jedadiah. 'I will see you in Godsend, Jillan,' the holy one's voice echoed off the heavens. 'You have seen your parents undone, and next it will be your darling Hella, Samnir and everyone you have ever known. That's if the plague you bring doesn't rot them before I get there. You will destroy them all!

'And hear me, Miserath! We have unfinished business, you and I. I will look forward to tasting the blood of one who was once a god and making an end to you once and for all!'

Captain Skathis haltingly pulled himself up out of the mud and viscera, and crawled until he was before his Saint. 'H-Holy one, should we pursue them?'

'Fear not, good Captain, for they cannot escape the destiny of my will. I have drawn the pagans out so that they may await my judgement in Godsend. The enemies of the Empire have inevitably undone themselves and will serve as the means and witness to my rightful ascension. I will claim the power of the Geas, and then this entire world, for the blessed Saviours. So raise the army, good Captain, for now we march. Send to Heroes' Brook and Saviours' Paradise, so that their Heroes can join us and all the People can rejoice that the moment of their final deliverance from the Chaos is at long last here.'

CHAPTER 13:

To save us from what has already happened

'The old Saint's not looking too good, is he?' Ash commented in a flat voice as their horses plodded along the sunken road.

'Probably glad he's blind, so he doesn't have to look at himself in a mirror,' Aspin snorted.

'Seemed to see well enough,' Ash recalled.

'I think he sees through the eyes of others,' Thomas said gruffly.

'Bet that's a bit weird for him. Must get his left and right mixed up. Shaving'll be a problem, especially with just one hand,' Ash mused. 'Do you think he has to have people watch him crap so that he doesn't have to fumble around too much?'

Aspin stifled a giggle. 'Do the holy beings of the Empire crap like everyone else then?'

'Well, I assume so, since Azual was once just like you and me. If Miserath was here, we could ask him whether gods crap too. Where did he go, anyway?'

'Went looking for Freda,' Thomas replied, watching the road ahead so that the horses didn't trip on any exposed roots in the poor light. The last thing they needed was a lame mount. 'Said he'd join us in Godsend.'

'That's where we're going then?' Aspin asked.

'I reckon.' The blacksmith nodded. 'Need to warn this Hella and Samnir that the Saint's coming for them. Then we'll get out of there as quick as we can.'

'Never been to Godsend,' Ash said, rubbing his chin. 'What about you, blacksmith? Didn't I hear it said that Godsend produces a fine ale or two?'

How could they? After all that had happened! So many dead, and all because of him.

They are relieved to be alive, Jillan, that's all. They're giddy with it. Would you have them ride in funereal silence forever more? They've already been going a whole day and night. They're bored and tired. But they're sad too, and know that if they don't lift their spirits soon, they'll be incapable of facing what lies ahead. Despair would otherwise overtake them and they would deliberately put themselves in harm's way. Then you'd have even more to add to the body count.

No, that wasn't it. When he'd finally come out of his stupor to find himself tied behind Thomas on this horse, he'd woken up in a different world. It looked, sounded, smelt and felt like the old one, but there was something subtly different about it. It was colder, for one, and outlines were sharper, as if everything was somehow flat or lacking in depth. Colours weren't quite as bright either, or when they were they hurt his eyes. And the people he thought he knew weren't the same. They were exaggerated versions of those he'd known. Ash tried to be funnier; Aspin was too positive; and Thomas was more abrupt. These weren't his friends! They were shape-shifters or some such, trying to lure him away from his own world and those he cared about.

'I have to say I was impressed with your bow work, Aspin. And your fighting style. It was almost like a dance of sorts,' Ash told the mountain warrior.

Aspin smiled. 'It is how all my people fight. Balance and fluid movement, just as in the nature we see around us, in the nature created by the Geas. Any individual, be they young or old, can learn it if they dedicate themselves to a study and worship of the gods. The eldest among us are usually the most supple and deadly. It is a great compliment if someone elder than you even deigns to notice you. The older a person, the more important they are. Every man seeks an older woman, and every woman an older man.'

Ash frowned. 'Really? Our old people tend to be broken down and sit around complaining and farting all day. But maybe that is to be expected when their gods are also broken.'

There. It was as the doppelgänger of Ash had said. There was something broken in this version of the world. Something important was done or dead. Some innocence had been lost. The innocence within them had died and they'd become dark and twisted simulacra of themselves.

Just as your beloved parents died, Jillan. Just as something within you died. It is part of growing up, Jillan.

He closed his ears to the taint, the whispering and manipulative force that had caused all this to happen in the first place. He realised now that it had probably been there in his mind his entire life, influencing his actions and shaping events, even when he hadn't been fully aware of it: whenever he'd thought to ask troubling questions in Minister Praxis's class; whenever he'd thought angry things about Haal and the others; whenever he'd had fearful dreams; whenever he'd railed against the way things were. The taint had done all this, killed all these people and brought him here. Why? Why!

The taint sighed. *If the Empire is to fall, then many must die. But do not fear death. Be brave, Jillan, as your parents told you.*

Do not dare to mention them! I will not have you using them for your lies, like you use everyone else. For I know your tricks, who you are and what you want. You are Death! You seek to bring an end to everyone and everything. You want the Empire and pagans alike to fall. Well, I will not allow it, you hear! I want the killing to end! It must end.

In his mind's eye he saw his parents again, surrounded on all sides by enemies. For him they had committed terrible crimes and blasphemy. For him they had damned themselves. For him his mother had ended her life and his father had placed his flesh in the path of the Empire's swords.

Why me? I did not want them to die for me! I did not want the curse of this magic. I will never use it to kill again, Jillan vowed.

Magic is a matter of will, Jillan. Before they are Drawn to the Saviours, anyone can draw magic from within themselves and from the Geas, if they but have the will to do so. That will must want to change things, and then must be brave enough to take action against the established powers within their community. Very few dare to take action at such a young age, for they have behaviours, thoughts, belief and doctrine instilled in them from the moment they enter the world by others looking to own them. They are reprimanded and punished by supposedly well-meaning parents, who were similarly treated when they were young; they are schooled and castigated by fearful and fearsome Ministers; and then they are drained and kept short of necessities unless they dedicate themselves to the lifetime of labour and self-sacrifice demanded of them by the Saint and the Saviours. Magic is not some curse inflicted on you, Jillan, it is what you want of yourself and the Geas, and what you are prepared to do based on what you believe.

No! You are the cunning and corrupting Chaos. My magic has brought only death to untold numbers of people. It is as I have always been taught: you simply wish to unmake the Empire so that you may claim the People as your own. You are just as guilty as the Empire in seeking to own the People, yet where the Empire offers food, lives and communities, you bring only death. I will not kill for you any more!

Jillan, the mind is always quicker to remember the bad over the good. Your magic has not *brought only death. It cured Thomas of the plague, remember. It saved Aspin from the Saint. He would be dead were it not for you. Ash would certainly have died or lived forever alone if it weren't for you. Just as your magic is a part of you, so am I. We are one, Jillan. I am not some mystical taint; I am not the voice of your insanity; I am simply your more knowing self. You may call me the voice of your magic if you wish, but you and I are one. So of course I have always been here in your mind. Where else could I be?*

Intuitively, he knew the taint wasn't telling him everything; it was leaving out things it didn't want him to know. It was still seeking to manipulate him, still lying to him. How could it be a part of him when there had been times it had told him things he couldn't ordinarily have known? Yes, Jillan's magic had healed Thomas, but that had been an accident more than anything else. And who was to say Ash and Aspin wouldn't have been better off without Jillan, given that they were still far from free of the Saint and were more than likely going to end up dead anyway? In that respect, they'd be better off not staying with him. He resolved to try and get them to leave Godsend before the Saint arrived. Yet the taint would not leave him be, and was slowly driving him crazy with its perverting words and perceptions. It had got so that he couldn't trust his own mind, thoughts and instincts any more. He would therefore lie to the taint from hereon in and ask Miserath, when he next saw him, how he could block it out permanently.

'And who is the oldest among your people, then?' Ash asked.

'Oh, that would be our holy man, Torpeth. He's as old as our people, as old as the mountains, some say, but he's crazy.'

'Who isn't these days?' Thomas reflected. 'Don't need to be old to be crazy, although it seems more forgivable if you're old. I mean, look at you two youngsters. The millions of people of the Empire would say you had to be crazy to stand against them. Just what made you think it would ever be a good idea, eh?'

'Well, when you put it like that, perhaps you're right.' Ash shrugged cheerily.

'Matter of perspective, I suppose,' Aspin conceded guiltily.

'But if you're talking about Torpeth the Great,' Thomas added, 'then he really is crazy. Worse than crazy, in fact. Dangerous. Pray we never meet him.'

'Welcome to Godsend,' Torpeth called down amiably to Aspin, Ash, Thomas and Jillan. 'What kept you, Aspin Longstep, eh?'

'Shut up, fool,' Minister Praxis sneered and tried to cuff his servant round the back of the head. Torpeth ducked into a bow, however, and avoided the blow.

'Silence, both of you!' Chief Braggar shouldered them aside so that he could come to the wall and see those below. 'Ha! Longstep! You join us once all the fighting is done, I see.'

'Braggar. Where is Chief Blackwing? I bring ill tidings of more fighting to come. The Saint of this region marches towards us with an army of his Heroes.'

There were uneasy murmurs from the warriors lining the wall on either side of the north gates. A few spat contemptuously.

'You will address him as Chief Braggar, son Aspin,' snow-haired Slavin said sternly as he somehow contrived to create and step into a gap between the Minister and Braggar.

Braggar puffed up his chest and adjusted the necklace of mountain gems that signified his status. 'Ha! I say these are *not* ill tidings! The warriors of Wayfar have already defeated the so-called Heroes of the Empire in glorious battle. We rejoice at the prospect of bringing more to their knees in the name of the gods.'

'Even if these Heroes aren't a bit sick like the other ones!' Torpeth shouted as the warriors cheered their chief's words.

Aspin signalled his companions to dismount. Thomas got down and then helped Jillan. Aspin bowed low and shouted, 'Hail, Chief Braggar! We beg entry and shelter so that we may share more of our glad tidings with you and raise a toast to your wise leadership of our people and to the glorious victory you have already brought us.'

'I am minded to let them in, and I am sure I will hear no protest from you,' Braggar murmured to Slavin. 'Besides, it would be good sense to learn more of our enemy from them. But what say you, lowlander?'

Minister Praxis made a strangled noise and his eyes bulged as he stared down at Jillan.

'I think that's a yes,' Torpeth offered.

'Then make it so!' Braggar commanded, his voice ringing off the gates and the wall.

There was a moment or two of awkward silence. People shuffled their feet.

Slavin sighed and gestured to two of the warriors closest to them. 'Be so good as to get down there and open the gates. Then we can all get out of the cold.'

Braggar frowned. 'Where are our other warriors?'

'Some are out hunting, Chief Braggar, while the rest are at the inn,' Slavin managed to say without making his opinion on the matter evident.

'I thought the drink was all gone once we'd poured libations to the gods to celebrate our victory over the weakling lowlanders.'

'Apparently, they found another cellar.'

'What! And no one told me?' Braggar snorted like a bull. 'That . . . that is . . .'

'Utterly disrespectful?' Torpeth ventured.

'Yes, damn it! Disrespectful! Don't they know who's the chief round here? I am the favoured of the gods. I'll see heads broken for this!'

'Heads broken in the name of the gods,' Torpeth nodded.

'Yes!'

'The gods are sure to be very grateful.'

Braggar's brows came down and he lowered his head as if he had horns and was about to charge. 'You'd better not be mocking me, old man. Lowlander, get your servant under control or I'll have him thrown from the top of the gates.'

The Minister at last dragged his eyes away from the newcomers at the gates and blinked. He'd missed much of what had just happened, but saw enough to know Torpeth had been taunting the young chief again. The Minister's long arm shot out and he caught the holy man by the ear, giving it a savage twist.

The small man hopped up and down. 'Hey! That tickles! If you envy my ear and have become so attached to it, then you may have it, for I have another. But do not stand like a wide-eyed child before this spectacle, good chieftain, lest all the ale be gone before you get there. I hear your warriors belching and sniggering that you are not able to drink as much as they.'

Snow-haired Slavin silently rolled his eyes and looked to the sky.

'Silence, meddlesome slave!' the Minister screeched and turned Torpeth's ear ever more cruelly. 'On your knees!'

'Gah!' Braggar waved in disgust and shouldered his way from the wall. 'Slavin, bring your son and the others to the inn. I will make that building my meeting place from now on.'

Jillan saw Minister Praxis staring down at him with the sort of outrage and disgust that had always been evident when Jillan had failed to answer a question correctly in class or had done something he thought blasphemous. The same outrage and disgust with which the Minister had always warned them about the dark and sneaking thoughts of the Chaos and made Jillan feel so guilty. For the taint suggested dark and sneaking thoughts to him, did it not, and was therefore surely the voice of the Chaos? He felt dirty and sinful. He hung his head in shame. He was so overcome by self-loathing that he trembled wretchedly.

'What's wrong with him?' Aspin was asking, but Jillan hardly heard him.

'Exhaustion and grief. I don't think he's slept or eaten since . . . You know. He needs rest,' Thomas said.

A willowy white-haired warrior came out from the gates to meet them. His skin was tanned a deep chestnut from a lifetime spent among the high peaks. His face was criss-crossed like old leather, but his blue eyes were young and he moved with the grace of a man half his age.

There was a poise about him that said he was either holy or a deadly warrior, perhaps both.

Aspin bowed so deeply that his head almost touched the ground, and Thomas and Ash also felt it wise to incline their heads. Jillan already stood with his chin on his chest.

'Stand, my son. I am happy to see you here before me.'

Aspin stood proud before the elder. 'Honoured Father, these are good men, and I ask that you pay them notice. Here is Thomas Ironshoe, whose heart fills his chest and whose strength shakes the mountains. Here is Ash of the woods, who is a kindred spirit of the wolves, yet laughs with the wind. And here is Jillan Hunterson, brother to my heart.'

Slavin's blue eyes took in Thomas and Ash and gave them a gentle nod of acknowledgement each. Then his eyes passed to Jillan and looked upon him for long moments. 'Your brother is sorely afflicted. The road must have been hard on him. He can be excused an audience with the young chief for now.'

'I will take him somewhere he can lie down,' Ash volunteered.

Slavin inclined his head. 'Good. Aspin and Thomas need to present themselves at the inn directly.'

'The inn?' Ash asked with a raised eyebrow and a strange smack of the lips.

Slavin turned slowly back to him. 'It seems that the young chief finds himself most comfortable upon a throne of ale barrels.'

Numbly Jillan followed Ash into the wintry streets of Godsend. Water and blood lay frozen in the road's muddy cart tracks. The gutters to either side of the street were backed up with excrement and garbage. A body lay in one, eyes wide and mouth open, but it looked anything but human. It was so bloated and discoloured that it was more like one of the strange fish found in the deep forest pools. Despite the cold, the reek of the town was foul. Ash kept his nose buried in his sleeve.

They passed the veranda of a long house. An old man sat in a rocking chair at the far end, seeming to watch them. It was Old Samuel. Jillan had clustered with the other children of Godsend every evening to listen to his tales of the wide and wonderful world beyond the community's walls. The old man would puff on his pipe and tell them that if they were quick enough, and looked hard enough, they would see fighting dragons in the clouds of smoke. He said the dragons drifted up to join the clouds and became bigger there until they were ready to fly east and fight the barbarians, or to fly wherever there were enemies of the Empire. He said that the raindrops that fell were the tears the dragons shed when one of their number died protecting the People. The children had become sad or scared at this, but he'd laughed and reassured them that as long as there were clouds in the sky, there were always dragons watching over them and the Empire would always be safe.

There were no children clustered around Old Samuel now, and he wasn't smoking his pipe. He had no one to listen to his stories. Jillan had been beyond the community's walls and seen the wide and wonderful world. He now knew Old Samuel's stories had just been make-believe to entertain children. There was nothing in the sky crying or watching over them. Children did not always remain safe just because there were clouds in the sky. If anyone said otherwise, then it was a lie of sorts, and a dangerous lie.

For Old Samuel was dead. He sat in his rocking chair, a permanent look of pain on his face. His skin was mottled with purple and there were black trickles of dried blood down his cheeks and chin.

'There's no one around,' Ash whispered, as if he were scared he might disturb the dead. 'You don't think Aspin's lot have killed everyone, do you?'

Jillan shrugged disconsolately and trudged past him.

'No,' Ash said with relief. 'There's a child over there. See him?'

Jillan caught a glimpse of something a way off, but it was too small and quick to make out.

'And another one there! And there! They keep disappearing, like they're watching us but don't want to be caught at it. Shy, are they, these Godsenders?'

Jillan saw a couple clearly this time. Children quite a bit younger than him. He didn't recognise them. Where had they come from? It didn't matter, though. They were probably intent on avoiding the murderous mountain men and anyone who might have the plague, which by now had to be just about everyone in Godsend. It was probably for the best that they did, since that way there was a slim chance that one or two of them might survive long enough to get out of Godsend and find somewhere in the forest where there was enough food and shelter to see them grow into a free adult one day. They were right to avoid people, for too often people brought death. And there were no dragons in the sky watching over them.

'There are people in the houses, I expect, but they're all dying,' Jillan said. 'It'll be worse where we're going, because the southern part of town had most of the old and poor. They always get sick first, and are hardly ever strong enough to recover.'

'Er . . . okay. Say, you look like you're managing well enough now, Jillan. I was thinking . . .'

'Sure, Ash. I'll see you later. Go join the others in the inn. If you can't convince them to flee before the Saint gets here, then maybe you can entertain them with a song.'

The woodsman shifted his weight from foot to foot, hesitating. Jillan kept trudging on.

'I'll bring you some bread and a drink from the inn,' the woodsman called hopefully.

Jillan nodded without turning back and listened to Ash walk and then run back the other way. He couldn't blame him. He'd have wanted to do the same thing himself. To sit in a warm inn with a foaming ale and merry company. As a child, it was something he'd always dreamed his life would be. As an adult, he now realised it was something people did precisely to forget their lives. Brief moments of happiness and long moments of forgetting – all adding up to a sort of contentment and a way of getting by. It wasn't so bad. It was just a shame that such simple lives and pleasures didn't have a way of holding back plagues, armies, the fall of gods and oblivion. Such a shame. But he couldn't blame them. The streets and the world outside the inn were dark, scary, horrible places. Who in their right mind ever really wanted to leave a comfortable seat next to the warm hearth? No one, for oblivion lay just beyond the door. The vast hungry darkness of the void crouched, waiting for the innocent and unwary.

Which begs the question, dopey, of just what you're doing. Careful! There are more of those kids about, and they're closing in on you, herding you, I think. You don't think they've turned to cannibalism for want of food, do you? I bet they have sharp and pointy little teeth.

'One of my friends is out here,' Jillan explained. 'I have to find him. Otherwise, what sort of friend would I be?'

Er . . . an alive one? You'd be an alive friend. I'm sure your friend wouldn't want you as a friend if you were a dead one. Besides, he can probably find his way on his own.

'Actually, I'd already be dead if it weren't for him. Taint, payment is due.'

There was a silent gasp. *Where did you hear that phrase?* the taint asked shakily, but fled before Jillan decided whether to answer or not.

Jillan moved into the wide Gathering Place in the centre of Godsend and walked over to the Meeting House. He'd heard the patter of small feet behind and to either side of him, but they'd broken off abruptly as he'd left the narrow street. There was no cover in the large square for his stalkers to use, and they clearly lacked the courage to attack him out in the open.

'Hello, my friend,' Jillan said as he looked down at the chained and drooling Samnir. The once always clean-shaven soldier had an unkempt grey beard, which made him look far older than Jillan remembered. Yet Samnir did not look as gaunt or filthy as Jillan had feared he would. Had someone been feeding and cleaning him? There was a good blanket beside him too, which must have been why he wasn't yet dead of exposure.

'I've come to return your sword, Samnir, for I have had good use of it and do not need it any more. Let me see. What did you say when you first gave it to me? Ah. It is freely given and therefore yours to command.'

Jillan used the sword to cut his friend's chains and then laid it in his lap. He took a deep breath and called magic to him. As the storm began to eddy and swirl around him, power rose in answer from his core. 'Not to kill!' Jillan breathed to himself and gently trickled power into his friend.

After a few long moments, Samnir's body was completely suffused and sparks of excess energy danced in the air around his skin, but the soldier's eyes remained empty. What was wrong? Any more power would kill the old soldier. Jillan began to shake and sweat with the strain of the conjuring. If he didn't find an answer quickly, he might end up killing them both.

The taint sighed. *Can't have you killing yourself over something so silly, can I? The problem's with his mind, not his body.*

Mind? Mind! The Saint had disconnected Samnir's mind from his body. Rushing, but with little other choice, Jillan ran power through old synapses, saving, reforming and reshaping where he could. Breaking off, he fell back with a gasp. He prayed he had done enough.

He watched Samnir's dead grey eyes. Was that a flutter or a reflection of falling snow? Then a slow blink. A spark of life and intelligence.

'Saviours be prai— The gods be praised,' Jillan breathed.

'Jillan!' Samnir rasped. 'Look at all the trouble you've caused! I've a good mind to put you over my knee.'

'Samnir!' Jillan cried in delight and hugged the old soldier.

'Oof! Careful. You're either stronger than you look or I'm weaker than I should be. I'm absolutely frozen. And I've got piles to boot.'

Jillan felt hot tears on his cheeks, but they were good tears, tears that washed some of the pain and horror from his eyes, tears that blurred his vision kindly so that the world looked a little less grimy. 'And Hella?' he dared ask Samnir softly.

Samnir nodded. 'Who else do you think it was kept me alive? Ugh! What's that smell? It's me! Come on, Jillan lad, let's get you home and the two of us cleaned up. We should try to look presentable, or Hella will be turning us away from her doorstep before I can properly thank her or she can properly recognise you. I think you'll have to help me up. I'm stiff as f . . . er . . . a plank. Easy! Ow!'

They hobbled out of the Gathering Place towards Jillan's old home.

As they went, Jillan noticed nearly every door in the southern part of town had a big white cross painted on it as a mark of the plague. The doors and windows were shut up tight, some from the outside. There was no one to be seen except for an emaciated mongrel that was eating something red, and that growled as they passed.

'At least the odd chimney is showing smoke,' Samnir coughed. 'Otherwise, I'd think we walked through a graveyard.'

'The pagans from the mountains have left them alone, at least.'

'The pagans are no doubt fearful of the plague too. It's probably prevented most of the rape, pillage and looting that would otherwise have gone on.'

'I don't think Aspin's people are like that.'

Samnir gave him a wan smile and shrugged. Jillan noticed the old soldier was leaning quite heavily on him now that his cheeks had lost their brief flush of colour and he was beginning to shiver.

'Nearly there. Here we are,' Jillan said as they ducked the low overhangs of roofs and zigzagged between the old cottages, water butts and lean-tos near the southern wall. 'Oh.'

The door to Jillan's home hung forlornly from one hinge and bore the scars of where the Heroes who'd come to arrest his parents had kicked it in. Snow had drifted inside, and it seemed far smaller than Jillan remembered. For a second or two he was convinced that they'd come to the wrong place, that they must have got confused in the maze of streets. The top of his head had never brushed the door lintel like that, and he'd never had to turn his shoulder slightly to avoid knocking it on the jamb. And that was surely a toy version of his father's great wooden armchair. No, this wasn't his home. It was too dark and pokey. Far too cold, somehow colder than outside. It was . . . broken. He felt a lump in his throat, felt sick.

'Don't worry, lad. We'll have it set to rights in no time, you'll see. Look, there's wood piled there. I'll get the place warmed up. You go get us a bucket of water from outside. Jillan! Come on, lad. Do as I tell you. Put me down here. Go on now.'

Jillan blinked, standing stupidly with a full bucket of water in front of Samnir. He didn't remember having gone outside to get it, but he'd apparently done so. Hadn't he had to break through a layer of ice? There were grazes on the knuckles of one hand, which stung.

'Fill the kettle there and we'll get it on the fire. Give me a beaker of the cold stuff first though. I'm dying of thirst.' Samnir was slumped in the chair nearest the hearth: it seemed that just getting a few weak flames going had taken everything out of him.

Jillan did as Samnir told him and then went to the cupboards, most of which stood open. It seemed that some of his neighbours had been in and picked over his mother's winter stores before she was even properly . . . His sightless hands closed on a couple of pieces of hard bread that the thieves had missed, or didn't have the teeth to tackle. The bread had a pale mould covering it but would have to do. He dunked the pieces in water to soften then, skewered them on a toasting fork and then balanced them next to the kettle.

He breathed, watching the bread turn a darker green and then black. It smoked and popped. He didn't see it any more. He rested his forehead against the warm bricks of the chimney and closed his eyes for a moment, a blessed moment. You know what you have to do, he told himself.

His eyes came open and he pulled the bread out of the fire before it was completely lost. Soft snores came from Samnir's chair. Jillan was not about to disturb him, instead placing the bread on the corner of the table so that it would be within reach of the soldier when he awoke.

Then Jillan went outside and pulled the door gently closed behind him. He went to the nearest house with a white cross on its door and smoke coming from its chimney. He knocked several times and waited.

The Peculiar sat in the middle of the crossroads, one minute a picture of beatific contemplation, the next a brooding gargoyle. He'd been away from the world for too long, he knew that now. Time was as much a place as features of the landscape and its ridiculously short-lived people. It was incredible to think that the people of this world ever achieved anything, to be honest. How did they even manage to survive? Why did they bother? Probably because they didn't know any different, and because the elseworlders kept them blissfully ignorant of where everything was heading. If the people were to know, of course, they'd want to undo themselves rather than suffer the alternative. And that would be that: no more people, no more world and no more Geas. The elseworlders would suffer a moment of annoyance, but then be free to move on to the next realm and Geas, immediately forgetting the loss. For the loss would mean nothing to them; unless every realm they visited started to undo itself in the same way, meaning the elseworlders never recouped the energy they'd spent in spreading through the realms of the Geas, such that they became overstretched and thinned to the point of non-existence. But the odds of that happening were so remote as to be . . . well, non-existent, which just proved his point anyway.

He'd withdrawn from the world because he had expected the elseworlders to have it all over and done with quite quickly. Yet the stubborn and wilful nature of this people and Geas meant everything had become tediously drawn out. The world had remained in limbo, balancing between succumbing to the elseworlders on the one hand and tipping into suicidal oblivion on the other. Much to his surprise, neither had yet occurred. The world would teeter one way and look like it was about to fall, but then something unexpected would catch them all out and the world would rock back the other way. How long could it remain so unstable and still survive?

Was it chance that the world still survived? The elseworlders didn't believe in chance, of course, only complexity. The Peculiar differed from them in that, naturally, for was he not the Lord of Mayhem? For him there were no absolutes, although he conceded there were many near certainties, such as the way the formidably manipulative elseworlders had made particular eventualities inescapable. And the apparent certainty that nothing on this world could contend with the cosmic force that was the elseworlders, nor redirect their intent. Yet, just as the gods could not be omnipotent, so there could be no absolutes. Just as there were gods, there was sun-metal. Just as there was control, order and civilisation, there was himself, the Peculiar.

It was curious – no, *telling* – that he had been drawn back into the affairs of the world. He was still bound to this world and essential to it, it would seem. Either this signalled nothing was about to end or all the competing powers were finally colliding and about to settle things once and for all. All he knew was that he would either be bound here forever and lack the power to break free unless he secured sufficient amounts of sun-metal or, alternatively, he might manage to claim the Geas for himself, which wasn't entirely outside the realms of possibility, especially if he could keep the fragile Freda and unreliable Jillan alive long enough to do so.

He sighed. And so he crouched here at the crossroads. He pondered the dust patterns on the road. The raindrops that had formed the patterns were transitory, and yet they also left signs of their passing, signs that could interrupt the flow of that which came after. He was about to drag a nail through the dust when the ground trembled. At last.

Freda pulled herself up out of the ground and blinked as she looked around.

'Ah, there you are, my little mole.' The Peculiar smiled in welcome.

'I began to worry when you weren't there to help our friends at the gates.'

Freda's face remained as blank as stone, but he knew she'd be feeling a pang of guilt at his words. 'Is friend Jillan all right?' she asked. 'All the heavy men have marched out of the city. Where are they going? Chasing friend Jillan?'

'Precisely so. We should go to help him, yes?'

'I promised to take him to Haven.'

'Did you now? That's nice of you, dear one. Pretty stones around your neck, by the way. Very becoming. They bring out the colour of your eyes. Your boyfriend gave them to you, did he?'

Freda looked at her feet, kicking the road. He watched her for a moment and sighed.

'What's wrong? If I'm to take you and Jillan to – how many more temples is it? – then we're going to be together for quite a while. We shouldn't be keeping secrets from each other. Otherwise, it will be difficult to be friends, won't it? I presume you *were* going to mention to me that you found the temple of Wayfar, weren't you? That's where you were, wasn't it, while the rest of us were risking our lives helping Jillan? So come, dear one, tell me what's wrong. I promise I won't be mad.'

She looked up at him from under her brows, judging him, something he really didn't appreciate but had no choice but to tolerate on this occasion. 'You will want to kill all the heavy men, won't you? You like killing, Anupal.'

He raised an eyebrow, noting she no longer termed him friend. 'Dear one, you understand something of my nature, do you not? I have always been consistent and true to myself. I have been honest with you throughout. I have saved you from capture twice, and I saved Jillan at Hyvan's Cross, with a little help. Yes, my temper gets the better of me sometimes, and I get carried away, but none of us is perfect. I usually end up killing bad people or those that particularly irk me. I do not kill my friends. And I have already told you, I only try and do good things to make good friends. I am the same person as when we first became friends. I have not changed . . . but I sense you have, have you not, Freda? Perhaps you should be angry with yourself, therefore, rather than with me. Now shall we g—'

'But when someone disagrees with the things you do and you get irked, it does not make them bad. It does not mean you can just kill them,' she said slowly as she thought things through. 'I want you to promise not to kill so many people any more.'

'You what?' he exclaimed, barely keeping his pique and physical appearance under control. 'May I remind you I am the god of such things. You're asking me to change my fundamental principles, not to mention nature, just because of your squeamishness. It's going to be hard enough to help Jillan without you imposing childish restrictions like that. There are at least five thousand Heroes marching on Godsend, not to mention that lunatic Saint. For your information, I barely got away intact last time we met, not that you bothered to ask, thank you very much. Too selfishly interested in your own ends all of a sudden, eh? Got a bit big for our boots, have we? Shame on you, Freda! I thought you were better than this.'

'Promise me.'

'Woman, you're as stubborn as a rock!' The Peculiar glared at her, but it was clear she was not about to budge. Cursing under his breath, he finally came back: 'Look, I cannot offer you a binding agreement on this matter, but I can promise to try my best not to kill people unnecessarily. In return, when I do have to kill people, you'll just have to trust my judgement that it *was* necessary. As a god, I know and can foresee things you cannot. All right? Now, are we friends again?'

She beamed gratefully at him. 'Yes, friend Anupal. Thank you!'

'Good. Now can we please get going before we miss out on all the fun?'

'Race you to the next horizon!' she shouted and dived back into the earth.

'Hey! I wasn't ready. Look, I'm in charge here. Come back!' He smiled as he began to scheme his revenge on her.

Jillan's hands shook as if he had the palsy, and he saw double for a few moments. He could hardly stay upright on the stool by the bedside. So tired. But it was another life saved, and mercifully the nagging, insistent voice of the taint had now faded to less than a whisper.

'Saviours be praised! It's a miracle! Not even the Saint has done this for us,' sobbed the old man's granddaughter as she witnessed the dark blooms of the plague disappearing from her grandfather's skin. The man's eyes were now clear instead of rheumy and he smiled up at her.

'Nor will he,' Jillan said exhaustedly.

The man reverently touched Jillan's arm. 'How can I ever thank you? I feel so strange. My head is clear, clearer than it's ever been. I see everything differently now. It's as if I'd lived my whole life in a dream but never really known it. I will never hear a word said against you again, Jillan Hunterson. I know your parents too. They are good people, no matter what others say.'

Jillan smiled sadly. 'The Saint killed them.'

The man and his granddaughter gasped. 'Do not say so!' Shocked silence. Then: 'But our Saint has been known to kill innocents before. All know what went on in New Sanctuary. I am deeply sorry for your loss, lad.'

'Hush, Grandfather. People will hear you. And the Saint always knows.'

'I don't give a wet fart who hears! You weren't there, girl. You didn't see innocent throats cut as they pleaded for mercy, and the innards of your friends and family drawn out of them while they still breathed. So still your tongue! Saint Azual did those things or my name's not Den Arnesson.'

The eyes of the chastised girl were full of fear, but she bit her lip and kept obediently quiet.

Den turned back to Jillan. 'But you don't look too well yourself, lad. You have shadows round your eyes and your pallor is worse than Helga's day-old porridge. Takes its toll on you this healing, I can tell. Be sure you care for yourself first, else where will we all end up, eh?'

'I'll be all right,' Jillan said, putting on a brave face. 'Besides, there are still a lot of people waiting outside, some of whom are sure to die if they don't get attention soon.'

Den pulled a face. 'Well, I cannot argue with their having healing when I've had it ahead of them, I suppose. But you have a waxy look about you, so please be cautious with what you give or I'll never forgive myself for what I've already had from you. No, don't rise, master Jillan. Helga here will help me up so that we can be out and not be the cause of any overdue petitioner's death. I'll send Helga back with whatever victuals we can provide. That's my girl! Up we go.'

Jillan tried to watch them depart, but they were blurs by the time they got to the door. He had no idea what time of day it was or even where he was in the town. At first he'd gone from house to house, but as word had spread of the healing, more and more had come to him. He'd started in some abandoned house or other and a line of people had quickly formed outside. There was no end to them, no end. But he would keep going until he had nothing left to give. How could he not, when he was the cause of the plague and the death of so many? Still, he'd moved beyond the point of pain now and hardly felt anything any more.

'Come in,' he said blindly. 'Please, on the bed.'

There were heavy steps. 'J-Jillan, it's me.'

He knew that voice almost as well as his own. It had taunted and bullied him for years, although it seemed a little deeper now than he remembered. He looked up and met Haal's eyes. 'You.'

Haal raised his hands.

He's going to hit me. He's come for his revenge at last.

'I-I know what you must think of me. Please, just let me say this and then I'll go,' the hefty youth rushed. 'I'm sorry for the things I used to say to you, Jillan, and for that time when I . . . with Silus and Karl, you know.' He took a breath to slow and steady his voice. 'What happened was my fault, I know, and everything that happened to you after that. Pa was very angry with me – never seen him so angry – and told me I should apologise to your folks, but I didn't get the chance before they were taken away. So I'm apologising to you now. Not just because it was the last thing my father told me to do before he got the plague, and not because of anything Hella said neither, but because I know I did wrong and I really am sorry.' He looked down at his hands and fidgeted. 'Don't know what made me do it. I've never been as smart as you, have I, and that means when I get angry I do stupid things, see? Wish I wasn't so dumb. Pa said I'd never be smart enough to be an elder like him. I sure miss him. Wish I'd made him proud.'

Tears in his eyes, Haal fell silent. Jillan didn't know what to say. He'd never heard Haal say so much in one go before, and certainly never heard him say sorry for anything. The Haal he'd known before had always spoken with sneers, glowers and fists, but this boy was completely different. Jillan realised that in all probability, like Haal, he too must have changed. There'd been a time when he would have enjoyed nothing more than mocking his burly classmate, but now he couldn't understand why he would want to. They shared the silence for a while, and then Jillan finally said, ''Sall right, Haal. I was sorry about what happened to Karl. Didn't mean for it to happen.' He paused. 'Is your pa . . . ?'

Haal nodded. 'They took him out of the southern gate, with the other dead elders. Not many people went to the service. At the time we had no Minister to make 'em pay their respects, see, and everyone was right afeared of the plague.'

'Sorry I didn't get back sooner. I liked your pa. I could have tried to help. I dunno. My folks died too.'

Haal met his eyes and a sort of understanding passed between them. 'What're we gonna do, Jillan? Some townsfolk have been sneaking away now that there are no Heroes to stop 'em. Pagans don't seem to care. But it's not safe out there, is it?'

Jillan shrugged. 'It's no safer in here than out there, I reckon. I'll stay though, to save who I can from the plague.'

'I'll stay too then,' Haal replied. 'If you'll have me?'

Jillan frowned, not sure what to make of that. 'Sure, if you want. They told you the Saint's marching here with an army, right?'

Haal nodded. 'One of the pagans had been showing me how they fight. I en't afraid.'

Jillan nodded and waited. 'What?'

'It's my ma.'

'Bring her here then, Haal Corinson, and tell the next person waiting to come in.'

Haal actually ducked his head and tugged at a lock of his hair as he backed out of the room.

Too tired to make sense of it all, Jillan just sat and waited for a minute. This time it was Samnir, freshly shaved and wearing leather armour.

'Look at the state of you, lad! When did you last eat and sleep, eh?'

'I-I . . .' He struggled for an answer.

'Thought so,' Samnir replied as he put fresh bread, cheese and a bottle of water on the table. He folded his arms. 'You're not seeing anyone else till you've had that and I've seen you sleep for an hour. Don't speak. Eat! That's an order.'

Jillan didn't have the strength to argue.

After a brief sleep he was allowed to start healing again, all the while under Samnir's watchful, steely gaze. The soldier wouldn't let him see more than one patient every fifteen minutes, which, Jillan had to admit, seemed to be just about enough to spare him keeling over with fatigue. After a few hours Jillan managed to persuade Samnir to leave his post.

'I want you to find the blacksmith Thomas and a young mountain warrior called Aspin. They're friends of mine. They'll be helping Chief Braggar and Aspin's father, Slavin, to organise the defence. You'll probably find them near the inn. It occurs to me that the mountain men will not know much about scouting in forests in order to watch for the Saint's army. And they will not know much about how the armies of the Empire go about laying a siege and fighting a battle.'

Samnir nodded. 'And they won't know how to fight against an army equipped with sun-metal. The pagans captured a few sun-metal weapons when they took Godsend, but I doubt they know one end of such a weapon from another, let alone how to use one to best effect in a battle. Very well, I will seek them out, but you will need to swear to me you will pace yourself sensibly here.'

'I so swear as the Saviours and the gods are my witness,' Jillian replied with a smile.

Shaking his head, Samnir left Jillan to his healing. Jillan fell into a sort of rhythm with it and found that he became used to the way of using magic, recovering more quickly each time. He was soon able to see a patient every ten minutes.

Ash came to see him. He smelt strongly of alcohol and the whites of his eyes were bloodshot.

'You have to help me! I have caught the contagion, Jillan. My hands shake, my stomach and head are in terrible pain and I coughed up blood earlier.'

Jillan examined the woodsman's skin, nails, teeth and hair. 'You've got a hangover. You have no signs of the contagion.'

'But it's surely only a matter of time before I get it if I stay in this Saviours-cursed town much longer.'

'I think it's only those who have been Drawn to the Saviours who get the plague. Those who have been Drawn seem to lack the energy to fight it. That's why the children and the mountain men haven't caught it. But don't worry, Ash. If you do get it, then I'll heal you.'

'What's the point if the Saint's just going to come and kill us all?'

'Ash, calm down. What are you saying? That you want to leave Godsend before the Saint gets here?'

'I . . .' The woodsman nodded, his face flushed. 'It's only good sense, isn't it? There's nothing to be gained by staying. Jillan, come with me.'

'I must stay, Ash, to heal these people. Godsend is my home. There are people I care about here. And Aspin will want to stay for his own people, I'm sure. I can't leave him here to face the Saint alone when it was me who caused most of this trouble in the first place. I have a feeling that the mountain people wouldn't even be here if it weren't for the events I helped put in motion. I can't just leave them, Ash, you must see that. Besides, I'm tired. Tired of running from the Saint, tired of hiding, tired of always somehow owing him something, tired of feeling guilty, tired of begging for mercy. The only way for it to end is if I stay here. Can you understand that? But you can go, Ash. There's nothing for you here, I know that. And none will think any less of you for returning to your home in the woods, I promise.'

But everyone already thinks so little of him, it's not actually possible for them to think any less of him, is it?

Ash hung his head for a second as if shamed, before producing one of his nonchalant grins. 'Well, I'm glad you understand. I wouldn't want to disappear without having explained or said goodbye. We had some good times on the road together, eh? Saviours' Paradise, Linder's Drop, Hyvan's Cross . . . Quite a tour. Yes. Right, well, all the best, young Jillan. Hope to see you again soon. And go with the gods!'

They shook hands and the woodsman went to the door. He turned to give one last wave, a slightly apologetic grin, and then he was gone.

Coward. Or sensible? He can be sure of surviving the storm that's coming at least, although he might regret it.

A while later Samnir returned. 'It's getting late, lad. It's already dark, if you hadn't noticed. Next one is the last visitor of the day. I've given those still outside a numbered piece of paper each so that they have the same order in which to see you tomorrow. Don't worry. You'll be starting early and all of them are well enough to make it through the night. So here's the last one. I'll wait for the two of you outside.'

He knew who it was even before he saw her. He'd always been able to sense her presence, he now realised. The girl he'd so much wanted to visit him, and so much feared would actually do so. He'd almost been glad to have all these sick people to heal so that he then had some sort of excuse for not seeking her out. She terrified him; she thrilled him. What would she say about him having killed Karl and going on the run from the Saint? Would she hate him? He'd committed terrible blasphemies. Would she even want to look at him? But she was here! Had she come to condemn him?

Feeling sick, he slowly raised his eyes to meet hers. She smiled and it was as if nothing bad had ever happened. No one had died or been hurt. There'd never been a plague. The Saint was not hunting him. The gods had never fallen, and were only kind to the people. There were no ideas like the Empire and the Chaos. There were only the Geas, its healing magic and Hella.

'It's good to see you again.' She blushed. 'I was worried I never would.'

'Same here,' he mumbled, face hot. He stood and they moved together. They held each other for a long time, although Jillan lost all sense of what might be a brief moment and might be eternity.

'Father has said I should invite you for dinner. Say you'll join us.'

She was impossible to refuse. He grinned like a village idiot. 'Of course I will. There's no place I'd rather be.'

She took his hand and led him from the broken-down house. In the dark of the evening Samnir gave them a wave as if in blessing. 'I will see you here early tomorrow, Jillan. Enjoy your supper and remember something of what it is to be happy. Good night. And don't spend the whole evening gazing into each other's eyes. You need sleep, lad!'

'G'night, Samnir!' He yelped as Hella yanked on his arm and began to run. He stumbled and she laughed gaily.

Hella's home was in the north-west part of Godsend, where most of the traders had their establishments and stables. They followed the main route out of the southern part of town and were just entering the central Gathering Place not far from the school when a sneering voice came out of the night ahead of them.

'Well, well, well! It's the two children of the Chaos, returned to the scene of their original sin. Secretly pleased with your handiwork, are you, succubi? Think that you could scamper through the darkness without the holy agents of the Empire seeing you up to your schemes and conspiracies?'

Jillan and Hella clutched each other in terror, eyes so wide they hurt as they stared into the gloom. Hella squealed as a pale narrow visage revealed itself. 'The Minister!'

'To think that I was put out of Godsend because of you vermin. Yet my righteousness has prevailed and the People of Godsend have been punished for their lack of faith. The plague is divine retribution visited upon them, and you seek to undo it, do you not, evil boy?'

Jillan couldn't answer, dark memories crowding in on his thoughts He felt sick with hard-learned guilt. The old fears turned his bowels to ice, seized his heart and all but collapsed his lungs. A clammy thing slithered across his soul.

'He knows everything. I would dispose of you myself, but I have been told to keep you for him. He is coming. Nothing can save you! Damnation is yours!'

The Minister was coming closer. *Why won't my feet work!*

It's fear, Jillan, fear, whispered the taint. *Snap out of it! Back, back! For Hella's sake if not your own!*

Jillan pulled Hella back with him. She was as rigid as he was.

The Minister's long arm reached for them.

Flee!

'There's nowhere you can run. Nowhere you can hide. Come to me.'

Run!

The Minister lunged for them, and the spell that held them immobile suddenly broke. Jillan pulled Hella to the side and the Minister's long fingers missed their mark; and then they were dashing through the night with wailing threats and large slapping feet pursuing them. They ducked left and right, again and again. At one junction their hands came apart and they frantically grabbed for each other. Then they were away again, terrified they were about to run straight into another nightmare.

*

Jillan watched the door twitchily, always scared who the next person to come through would be. He'd thought about asking Samnir to stand guard for him, but he knew the soldier was needed to train the mountain men.

Besides, you can look after yourself well enough if you use your magic.

'I won't use it for anything but healing. Whenever I use it for anything like combat, people end up dead.'

Bad luck and details, that's all.

But people's lives weren't details, not to him anyway. They probably were to the Empire, though.

Halfway through the morning Aspin and Thomas stopped by to see him. They brought tea with them and Jillan gratefully warmed his hands around a cup. He'd hardly slept a wink during the night because of nerves and the desire to avoid his own dreams.

'What happened to you two?' Jillan asked as he noticed they both bore fresh grazes and bruises. Aspin looked like he was going to have quite a black eye.

The mountain warrior rubbed the back of his neck in slight embarrassment. 'Your friend Samnir has been training us. Likes to pick on those he thinks drank too much the night before. A way of teaching them a lesson of sorts, I suppose.'

Thomas grunted. 'Thought I knew my way around weapons, but nothing like him. Just about the only one who can stand his ground against him is Slavin. Still, I'll give Samnir his due: he's managed to focus the minds of some of the younger mountainers, eh, Aspin? They're suddenly beginning to realise what they're going to be up against. Won't be the picnic that taking Godsend was.'

Aspin nodded ruefully. 'Some of the scouts came back yesterday, Jillan. They reckon the Empire's army won't be here tonight, but probably by tomorrow evening. Doesn't give us long. You might want to ease up on the healing so that you're strong enough to fight.'

'I won't be using my magic in the fight. I'll use a bow and normal weapons like everyone else.'

His friends stilled as they absorbed that, then exchanged a glance. Neither challenged his decision, however, for which he was grateful.

'Hopefully, we won't need your magic anyway,' Thomas said, but his doubt was obvious.

'Chief Braggar is confident the gods will ensure our victory,' Aspin said.

I wonder how confident the gods are feeling about it, though.

As dusk began to fall, a curious little man came in with a female plague-sufferer. She lay on the pallet near Jillan, while the man crouched in the corner of the room. When the matronly woman had been healed, she left, while the little man stayed where he was and watched carefully as Jillan attended to the next patient, and the next.

Jillan looked straight at the man. He was naked except for a loincloth and had a clean-shaven shiny head. His body was all tendons and sinew, but he seemed strong and flexible for all that. His face was small and lean, but his eyes were large and seemed to show pictures of the world, many from the distant past.

'Can I help you?' Jillan asked politely, for want of anything else to say.

The man remained in his crouch and sucked on his gums. 'There's none to help me, I doubt. Not even the gods can change the past,' he said and wrinkled his nose up and down. 'Do you like pine nuts?'

'Er . . . actually, I do.'

'You do?' the man said. 'If I'd known, I'd have brought you some. Ah well, there it is. You can't save them all, you know, all these people.'

'Maybe not. It doesn't mean I shouldn't try, though.'

The man picked at one of his toenails and tasted whatever had been underneath it. 'Depends what's lost in the trying.'

For some reason he didn't entirely understand, Jillan found himself getting angry. Did this fellow remind him of Bion somewhat? 'Nothing is lost in healing people. Besides, what would you know about it?'

The man looked melancholy for a moment. 'That armour you wear was once mine. When I sickened of warfare, I gave it away or lost it in a game of dice, or some such. I think some other chieftain in these parts wore it for a while, but I lost track of it after that.'

Jillan's mind reeled. It wasn't possible. The ruins he'd taken the armour from had been ancient. So how old would this man have to be?

'I am Torpeth. Perhaps you have heard of me.'

Jillan shook his head. He hadn't heard that name, or had he? Had Aspin mentioned a Torpeth as they'd been reaching Godsend?

'Huh! No matter. I'm not as vain as I once was. The important thing to understand is that I was once very much like you, although probably more handsome, and that you are likely to end up just like me.'

Like this gnome? Crouched in the corner of a tumbledown house in a plague-riven town? Spinning riddles to work-weary strangers? How could that possibly be his own future?

You'd be surprised.

Torpeth pulled at the air beneath his chin.

'What are you doing?'

'Pulling on my beard.'

'You don't have a beard.'

'Maybe not. It doesn't mean I shouldn't try, though.'

Jillan hesitated. Damn the fellow! 'Depends what's lost in the trying.'

'And what do I lose?'

'I don't know. Your belief you have a beard?' Jillan hazarded, deciding Torpeth was completely crazy. Hadn't Aspin said just about as much?

'Hmm. There is that, I suppose. I'll have to go and ponder that. Just remember you can't save all, will you, eh?'

'Whatever you wish!' Jillan rolled his eyes and threw his hands in the air.

When he looked back, Torpeth was gone.

His remaining senses as sharp as they'd ever been, Saint Azual could smell the pagans in Godsend. He could taste their life energy on the air. He heard their drunken battle hymns. Through the eyes of the People, he saw them strutting about entirely oblivious to the fact they were being watched. There were pitifully few of them, meaning their total population could not be that large and would likely fall below a critical minimum when these were dead. Then the Geas would have no more people in the south beyond the sway of the blessed Saviours. At last his ascension was at hand.

The pagan scouts had been simple to capture, for they'd lacked any real ability to move silently through a forest. Of the six, four had resisted him to the end, and he'd drained them of every last drop of their life energy and nascent power. Yet he'd managed to break the minds of the other two when he'd Drawn them. These were completely compliant to his will and had been sent back to Godsend to report that the Empire's army would not arrive until two nights hence.

Faithful Praxis, do you hear me? Saint Azual called out mentally.

Yes, holy one. Command me!

It will be tonight. They will not be expecting us.

O master, I rejoice. At last the Chaos will be undone.

Make the preparations for our arrival, Praxis . . . or should I say Saint Praxis?

As is your will, holy one. Yet I have been unable to secure the boy. I have been watching him. He usually has friends around him.

Fear not. I shall see to that myself. Do not fail me now, Praxis, for deliverance is at hand. The blessed Saviours have intended this from the beginning and now their will is made manifest through us. They are the gods, our history, our future and our fate.

Praise be! Holy one, I but ask that I may witness the demise of the boy and the girl-child Hella.

You will see the boy suffer so much, and for such a long time, that he will ultimately thank me for his own demise. The girl I give to you.

O master, thank you! Never has such an unworthy servant known such love and kindness. I will ever follow your divine example.

Then you will not fail me, faithful Praxis.

In the evening Hella and Jacob came to sup with Jillan and Samnir at the cottage Jillan had once shared with his parents. Samnir had swept the place clean, set a good-sized fire in the hearth, plumped the cushions and scented the rooms with fresh pine needles, so it all felt cosy and homely.

'And see! I managed to rescue half a jug of red from those thirsty pagans,' the soldier said with a broad smile. 'Enough for a cup each, two if we water it down like old Linus the innkeep always used to do.'

The meal was a simple stew, but wholesome and filling. As Jacob reached for a piece of bread, the cuff on his shirt sleeve pulled back slightly and Jillan noticed discoloured skin around the trader's wrist. Out of habit, Jillan drew magic and sought to place a hand on Jacob, but the trader drew back quickly.

The moment did not escape the other two.

Hella could not help being upset. 'Father, why didn't you say anything? Let Jillan heal you!'

Jacob tried to shush his daughter. 'I didn't want to worry you unnecessarily. It's nothing, daughter. Samnir, how's the training going?'

Jillan recalled that when he'd met Jacob in Saviours' Paradise, the trader had urged him to hand himself over to the Saint. 'You would prefer to have the plague than let my unclean magic touch you, wouldn't you?' he said softly.

'Do you also hope my training of the mountain men is going badly, Jacob?' Samnir asked darkly.

'Father, no!'

Jacob met his daughter's eyes, anguish creasing his face. 'Hella, you're too young to understand. We are citizens of the Empire. Everything we have is because of the Saviours and their Saints. They help us keep the Chaos at bay. But we have allowed the dark magic of the Chaos, plague and pagans into Godsend. We must resist . . .'

But Hella turned her face away and stared at the wall.

'Hella, please!' Jacob begged. 'You cannot be so wilful. Show some gratitude. I have clothed and fed you your entire life. The *Empire* has clothed and fed you. These pagans will ruin everything!'

'What's there to ruin?' she demanded as she whipped her head back, fury in her eyes. 'We work and work and we have nothing to show for it. The elders, Heroes and Minister took any profit we made and any stocks we built up. You never stood up to them. You let them take everything. Did the Saint ever come to help us against the plague? No! Because he doesn't care about us. And now you turn down Jillan's help because of some stupid loyalty to that selfsame Saint. If mother were alive, she'd be ashamed of you. She'd call you a coward!'

Samnir slammed his fist down on the table and the cutlery and plates jumped. A beaker fell over and wine spilled into the wood. Hella yelped and Jacob leaned back as far as he could.

'You will both listen to me and then there will be an end to this, understand?' Samnir commanded, his grey eyes glinting like blades in the candlelight. Hella and Jacob nodded fearfully. 'Hella, you have no right to talk to your father so. You will show him respect for all he has done for you. I doubt it has been easy raising a daughter on his own. He has always been worried for you and done everything he can to protect you. He has smiled at cruel masters, nodded and allowed ruffians to steal from him, and bent a knee to those for whom he secretly has nothing but contempt. But what else could he do when it's not just his own life and future at stake? He has swallowed his pride and been less than a man all for the love of *you*, child. Where would you have ended up without him watching over you, eh? You know well that orphans are carted off to serve as retainers in the Great Temple. Have you ever heard of a retainer returning from the Great Temple? No. So let me tell you that their lives are horribly short. I have seen their ruined bodies, buried them even! So hear me when I say he is a stronger man than you can understand. I am not sure I could have been as strong. My selfishness would have come in the way and, were you my daughter, you would have consequently been dead long ago.

'As for you, Jacob, you talk of everything the Empire has given you without thinking of what it has taken from you. You have no freedom to think or believe anything except that which the Empire prescribes. You have no freedom to express your thoughts or be yourself. They have taken your very life and soul, man. You are a shadow of who you should have been. Even your own daughter struggles to know you. You have let the Empire take her father from her! You have let the Empire make an orphan of her, despite all your efforts. Is that what you want for Hella? And would you then allow them to take her and break her as they did you? Do you want to give your daughter into the hands of those cruel masters, people for whom you have a secret contempt? Well, do you?'

'No!' the trader moaned. 'Do not let them take her from me! She is all I have!'

'Yet you will lose her, and you will lose each other, if you do not let Jillan heal you.'

'Please, Father!' Hella whispered through her tears.

Shaking violently, Jacob looked into his daughter's eyes and held out his arms to Jillan.

Hella and Jacob had gone and Jillan and Samnir were just making up their beds when there was a quiet knock at the door.

'Who's there?' Samnir asked as he went near.

'Samnir, it is your mistress at last. You will open the door to me.'

Samnir stared at the door, his mouth hanging open, and his hand rose to obey. Sensing that all was not right, Jillan called, 'Samnir, wait! Who is it?'

The soldier pulled the bolt back and let in the late-night visitor. The newcomer was slender, dressed in a long black cape and wearing a grotesque wooden mask. The character of the face was beautiful and knowing on the left side, but ugly and leering on the other. Even so, it was one continuous visage and quite unnerving. At one moment the ugliness would seem honest and the beauty deceiving; the next the ugliness threatened pain and the beauty promised mercy. It was apparently a depiction of Miserath, but why would the pagan god come wearing a mask of himself? The mask was removed and a totally new face was revealed.

'Holy one, it has been so long,' Samnir whimpered and performed a deep bow.

'Rise, most cherished Samnir. You have aged but still cut a fine figure, eh?' The stranger's attention moved straight to Jillan. 'And this is the boy about whom there's been such a fuss. Good evening, my young fellow. I am Saint Izat and I have come to take you away from all this noise and hullabaloo. This region is positively putrid, no? I have no idea how anyone ever manages to keep their shoes clean. A chair if you please, darling Samnir. Sweet man.'

The Saint perched herself on the edge of the seat provided and looked Jillan up and down. 'A bit rough around the edges, but I'm sure you'll come up a treat after a scented bath or two.'

Jillan glared at the Saint, not liking her thin eyebrows and disconcertingly full lips. There was barely a line on the face of the Saviours' representative. This creature was clearly skilled at keeping expression from its face, to prevent others from reading its thoughts. What ambitions and desires did this Saint have that were so terrible they had to be hidden? What ambitions and desires did any Saint have, come to that? Nothing too savoury, that was for sure.

'Come to offer me Salvation, have you?' Jillan asked neutrally. 'Or to Draw me to the Saviours? Come to threaten me with damnation if I resist?'

Saint Izat smiled gently. 'I would be cynical too, if I had been treated as you have, Jillan. Saint Azual can be quite a zealot and a brute, I know. He misdirects his passion, you see. Things are different in the western region, my region, however. It is a garden of love and understanding. There is no killing and oppression there. Come with me! Bring your friends and you can live the life you've always wanted, you'll see! Leave this squalor behind.'

'But your region is still part of the Empire, is it not? The mechanisms of control in your region might be different to this region's – you may use loving arms rather than force of arms – but they are mechanisms all the same. In your region I would not be free to lead my own life the way I want. You would want to Draw all my magic from me, wouldn't you, just like Saint Azual? You may not like this squalor, but it is *my* squalor, where none may own, control or Draw me. Samnir, please show the holy one out.'

Saint Izat smiled again and tapped her thigh in amusement. 'Samnir is mine to command, my precocious and provocative young man. But I like you, so must now insist that you come—'

A heavy hand landed on the Saint's shoulder.

'Samnir! What is the meaning of this? How dare you lay one of your grubby hands on my holy person without my gracious permission!' the Saint squawked in outrage.

The fingers tightened.

'Samnir! Does your lust so fire you—'

A blade of sun-metal was pressed against the Saint's pretty throat, silencing her. 'Jillan has invited you to leave, holy one. I suggest you do so, before I fully recall the things you did when I was young to bind me to you. *Love* you called it? Why then do I only feel dirty and used? Hesitate one more second and it will be your last, *holy* one.'

Saint Izat came straight to her feet and Samnir walked her to the door and pushed her out. The soldier quickly slammed the door closed and double-bolted it. He put his back against it and slid down to the floor, his face pasty-white.

Through the wood at his ear came a gentle voice. 'You will be mine again, sweet Samnir, and you will beg for my love before I am through with you.'

Samnir stumbled back to the chair and stared and stared at the door.

Jillan poured the last of the wine into a beaker and pressed it into his friend's hand. 'Drink this. I thought you were going to kill her.'

'I wish I had,' Samnir said through rattling teeth. 'But it took everything I had just to get the blade up to her neck and hold it steady.'

In the dark Praxis finished loading the wagon with every bottle of wine and liquor he had in his personal cellar and drove it through Godsend to the northern gates. He called the pagan guards down to him and handed a bottle of the strongest liquor to each of them.

'From Chief Braggar, so that you may toast tomorrow evening's victory and help keep out the cold tonight. The Chief said he would take it as a personal insult if you did not finish your bottles within the hour, and also a blasphemy against the gods.'

The men laughed. They assured him they were of good faith.

'And an extra bottle for he who best proves his faith by finishing first!'

They cheered the Minister as he drove the remaining hundred or so bottles over to the inn, not far from the gates.

Jillan thought he wouldn't be able to get any sleep that night but entered his dreams as soon as he closed his eyes. He was in the middle of a ruined landscape once more, the blackened ground cracked, with lava flowing through caves below. He walked across the smoking crust of the earth, the roots of any trees long since burned away and their bulks toppled atop one another to make a charred pyre of the forest that had once stood here. The sky was a pall of soot and ash and the sulphurous air hurt his lungs. As he came over a slight rise, he found he walked upon the crumbling and powdery bones of the dead.

Again a large green hill rose high above him, a sea of humanity washing up its slopes only to be driven back by a waiting line of cruel-eyed heavily armed Heroes. The green of the lower slopes had long since been replaced by the red and brown of lost lives. Still people fought vainly against each other to be the first to reach the killing spears of sun-metal.

On the crown of the hill was a throne of skulls where the mutilated and mad Saint sightlessly surveyed his domain. He laughed as if watching a mummers' play. A woman in rags crossed the path of a stocky man, who twisted her head sharply round to break her neck. In her final instant of life her eyes fell on Jillan, and the Saint saw him.

The grizzly shape of Azual stood and pointed down at the boy. 'There is the one who has driven you to your deaths. See there! He stands behind you with the threat of his magic and you flee towards the verdant sanctuary of my hill. See how he has ruined the landscape all around so that you may have no haven elsewhere. See how he seeks to have you overwhelm this hill, your one place of safety. Turn on him! Do not allow him to force death upon you. Have your revenge! And the one who brings me his head will have a place at my side here in this restful garden.'

The wild-eyed mob turned as one to stare hungrily at Jillan. They began to race towards him. In the tumult the slow were trodden underfoot and smeared across the ground. Unfortunates were pushed into fissures, to fall screaming into the steaming lava. Children and babes-in-arms were dropped in the chaos, speared upon fire-hardened branches and broken on rocks.

'No! Stay back!' Jillan pleaded and spun away. He slipped and floundered on the treacherous remains of what had once lived here. 'Please!' He ran for his life, nowhere to go. He vaulted a tree trunk and leapt a yawning gulf with only just enough momentum to stop himself toppling into the fiery depths. An old man little more than an animated skeleton hurled himself across the gap after Jillan, fell short, caught the crumbling lip of the edge and frantically tried to haul himself up. 'Forgive me!' Jillan sobbed, and continued to run as the man fell into the molten rock below.

They came pouring around the small chasm. Fear and adrenalin gave him a new burst of speed and he outdistanced them by a handful of yards, but he soon began to flag while the mad horde did not slacken for a moment. Hands grabbed and tore at his clothing. They dragged him to the ground and clawed at his head, fighting to get a hold so that they could rip it from his shoulders. He bit hard on fingers, down to the bone, but the insane owners were oblivious. They gouged at his eyes, stuck sharp fingernails into his ears to burst his eardrums, ripped open his nostrils and yanked out handfuls of his hair.

His head came up, and he all but vomited his entire self out through his mouth. He screamed and screamed.

Samnir had him by the shoulders and was shaking him hard. A stinging slap to the cheek. 'I'm here, Jillan.'

'He's here!' Jillan cried in a cold sweat.

There were scratches at the front door and it shook as hands tried to pull it open. Kicking feet and barging shoulders rattled it in its frame. They called and howled bestially for his head. It was no dream. The People had come for him.

'The Saint's here!'

'How?' Samnir demanded frantically, pulling his sword free and facing the door. 'It shouldn't be for another day at least. We're not ready. We'll be slaughtered!'

Dawn was threatening when the last of the stinking pagans in the inn slumped into drunken unconsciousness. He snored as loudly as the others, a fly lazily circling his open mouth.

Minister Praxis shrugged off the arm the sot next to him had affectionately put round his shoulders and pushed the warrior's face away. Praxis climbed over the table, wove his way between the slumbering bodies and empty bottles and gained the door.

'At last! These animals will soon be skewered and set to roast over the greedy flames of their own corruption. Pigs!' he sneered in disgust.

He stepped out into the false dawn and all but ran for the gates. In his excitement he did not notice the shadow slip out of the inn after him.

The Minister could not contain himself. 'Master, I come to do your bidding! Glory be this moment, for the rising sun heralds the start of a new age of civilisation, a world where only the worthy will exist, a land where godly Saviours, their holy Saints and the People intermingle and become one. The day of eternal communion is upon us. Praise be!'

'Who goesh there?' slurred a boss-eyed warrior at the top of the steps next to the gates. 'Oh, it'sh you, lowla-la-lander.'

The Minister ignored him and went to lift one end of the bar across the gates. 'Master, your holy city awaits you!'

Good, Saint Praxis. We are ready. Quickly, for I am famished and would break my fast with pagan blood and bones! Quickly!

'Here! What are you about there, lowla-la-lander? Wanna hand?' hiccuped the warrior as he swayed down the first few steps and then, losing control, took the rest at breakneck speed. He bounced like a clownish acrobat at the bottom and shouted, 'Ta-da!' There were groans of protest from those on the ramparts above.

'Going for a walk then, lowla-la-lander? Don't think you sh-should really, not without an eshcort or something. Let me rouse shome of the others.'

Quickly!

The Minister bared his teeth, incapable of smiling at the vile semi-naked devil. He stepped in close to the Chaos creature, extracted a needle-like blade from within the sleeve of his ministerial longcoat and stabbed the weapon into the side of the pagan's neck. The Minister tried to saw the blade round to the front to prevent any scream, but the lack of a serrated edge meant he just waggled the blade in the wound. Blood sprayed into the Minister's eyes and mouth, and then over the hand holding the knife, making his hand slip.

Torpeth scampered towards the Minister, thinking to stop his betrayal before it could go any further, but at that moment Praxis turned his face away from his squirting gurgling victim and saw the holy man coming.

'You're too late!' cackled the Minister through his red teeth, as he abandoned the warrior and heaved up the other end of the crossbar. 'Now, master! Deliver us from evil!' There was a crash against the outside of the gates and they began to shudder open.

'Awake! Awake!' Torpeth screamed to the ramparts and the sky. 'Treachery! Awake to our nightmares made flesh! Awake, my people, or never wake again! Payment is due! Here is the moment of our true testing! The others are here with blade and flame! Oh where are the gods? Awake!'

Hands wringing and eyes rolling wildly, Torpeth ran for the inn as the flames of the sun began to devour the earth, and as Azual returned at last to Godsend.

Samnir pushed Jillan and his bow through the small window in the room where Jillan's parents had once slept, and then tried to squeeze out after him. The soldier got one arm and his head through, so knew he should be able to make it. He pushed off the ground with his feet, only to find himself caught in midair in the narrow aperture. He was hanging half in and half out, without sufficient purchase to drag himself through. He kicked with his legs as if swimming, tried to wriggle with his torso and pulled at the bricks outside with his one free hand.

Jillan took hold of Samnir's arm to haul him out.

Samnir slapped him away. 'Behind you!'

Out of the grey light came a ghoulish figure, its eyes fully black voids. 'Come to me, boy,' it snarled at Jillan in a many-layered voice as if there was more than one entity within it.

'Use the sword!' Samnir grimaced as he twisted his arm inside the house to push the blade of sun-metal past his body and head, singeing his hair as he did so.

Other ghouls came out of the grey, their movements jerky, as if they were pulled by invisible strings and another's will. The first ghoul lurched towards Jillan, who ducked, but the possessed Godsender fell on top of him, teeth gnashing at his cheek. Jillan craned his neck back and pushed against the man's chest with one hand, for his other was pinned beneath him.

'Hold on, lad!' Samnir shouted as he heaved himself forward a few more inches. There was a crash behind him in the house as the front door finally gave way.

Jillan realised Samnir wasn't going to get to him in time and flung out his arm to grope for the sword, his fingers curling around the hilt. The Godsender's teeth bit into his cheek and he screamed. He stabbed with the sword, its point going through the monster's temple and coming out the other side. The man's eyes cleared, returning to their normal brown; he blinked once and then fell dead on top of Jillan.

Jillan rolled the deadweight off him, pulled the sword free and immediately swung it through the neck of a slobbering maid who raked at him with her fingernails. The blade sheered effortlessly through flesh and bone and her head tumbled to the ground. It came to rest and stared up at him accusingly.

'I don't want to kill you!' Jillan cried in distress at a familiar man in the garb of a carpenter who lumbered towards him. 'Stay back!'

The carpenter cocked his head and spoke in the voice of the Saint. 'Then stop fighting me, boy. You have caused all this. How many must die before you submit to the authority of your elders and betters? They only have the best interests of you and the People at heart. You cannot fight an entire Empire, Jillan. Stop this before it is too late. Even now the pagans are being slaughtered because of what you started. Even now innocents are caught up and lost in the ensuing chaos. You have instigated a genocide, boy. They will all die!'

Jillan lowered the sword. 'If I stop fighting, you must stop the killing.'

'No!' Samnir shouted and kicked back against something hard, at last propelling himself far enough for his centre of gravity to drag him out and towards the ground.

He landed inelegantly, but rose quickly and punched the carpenter so hard in the face that the man spun all the way round. 'Give me that!' Samnir demanded, swapping the sun-metal blade in Jillan's hand for a normal long knife. He grabbed Jillan by the scruff of the neck and all but lifted him off his feet as he hauled him down the alley at the side of the house. There were howls behind them as the People of the Saint gave chase.

'They're not themselves,' Jillan cried in despair as Samnir hacked down an old couple ahead of them.

'I'll say!' Samnir replied grimly. 'But they never were the friendliest bunch, eh?'

They dashed out of the alley into a slightly bigger one and Jillan guided them through several twists and turns until they reached the main street. They slid to a stop, dozens of Godsenders spread out and standing motionless before them, waiting in the half-light. To their rear Jillan and Samnir heard the panting pack of hunters closing in on them. The eyes and heads of the Godsenders turned towards the soldier and boy and immediately saw Samnir's bright sword. In eerie concert, they came forward, silently at first and then with hungry snuffles and yelps of excitement.

'Shit! We're going to have to do this the hard way. Stay close to me, boy. We'll fight back to back if necessary. Jillan! Come on!'

The naked woman stroking Aspin's brow smiled dreamily at him and smacked him so hard across the face that she all but dislocated his jaw. That's not how the dream's supposed to go, he thought as he was brought violently awake. The woman grew stubble, her nose became wide and her brows heavy. She stank. 'Thomas?' he asked blearily, wondering if the blacksmith's blow might just have fractured his skull.

'The enemy are inside the gates!' Thomas shouted. 'Get your bow. Now!'

Thomas turned away, kicking others awake and bellowing for them to rise. Most struggled up, including Chief Braggar and Slavin, but a handful were so lost to drink that they didn't even stir.

The blacksmith got to the door of the inn, only to find it barred from the outside. There was the smell of smoke. Flaming torches were thrown in through the windows and the shutters slammed closed. A table that had seen liquor spilled on it during the earlier celebrations caught alight and fire roared up to the ceiling, billowing more smoke through the room.

'Awake, you dogs!' Thomas roared, backed up from the door and then smashed into it with his shoulder and powerful frame.

The door cracked and sagged. Thomas backed up again and hurled himself forward. The door burst open and Thomas went sprawling onto the ground. There were Heroes ready and waiting with swords of sun-metal raised. One immediately swung with his weapon at Thomas's head, but an arrow flashed out of the inn door and took the Hero through the throat. Mountain men jumped over Thomas, giving him life-saving moments to get to his feet and bring up his massive hammer.

Dozens of Heroes pushed at the pagans with their shields, trying to use weight of numbers to keep their enemy trapped inside the burning inn. Thomas flexed his mighty arms and chest and put deadly momentum into his hammer, its head crumpling shields, shattering ribs and bowling men over. More Heroes stepped into the gaps left in the wall of shields. Thomas swept the hammer again, smashing through two helmets and dashing a third man against the ground. Another swing, but this time a blade of sun-metal was thrust forward and the hammer was decapitated. Thomas now used its long handle as a staff, but the Heroes were at least six ranks deep around the inn, so he couldn't create more than swinging room for himself.

'For the gods!' came a full-bloodied battle cry, and Chief Braggar charged into the Heroes with head down, shoving the Hero in front of him back onto the sword of the man in the rank behind. Braggar held a blade of sun-metal that his warriors had seized when they took Godsend, and he used it now to carve a wide semicircle out of the front rank. Slavin stepped into the gap behind his Chief, a long thin spear in each hand with which he darted forward with unerring accuracy, spiking an eye here, a throat there, an open mouth and any unarmoured armpit exposed by a raised arm. No Hero had a chance to strike a blow at Braggar while Slavin protected him. Dying men loosed pathetic cries, begging for their blessed Saviours or their mothers to help them.

Aspin and several more warriors forced their way out of the inn, shooting arrows and casting short javelins. It mattered not that their hands shook slightly, for the Heroes were packed so tightly that it was hard not to hit one of them.

'One step forward!' cracked out a commanding voice at the back of the Heroes, and the ranks advanced as one, treading on fallen comrades as necessary and stamping down hard to establish a secure footing.

Thomas's staff had been chopped in two. He twirled the ends in his hands as short fighting sticks, smashing knuckles, blocking swinging attacks at the arm, cracking elbows, breaking noses and punching up under chins. He clubbed and drummed his way forward, knowing every step he took was another life from the inn saved. He was now right among the Heroes and knew that any moment could be his last. He increased his speed, his arms feeling like red-hot metal and his lungs working like bellows. He worked the iron in his muscles as if he were back in his forge. Roaring flames, stifling heat and blinding smoke were all around him. He fought the eternal dragon, the dragon of life and death, and laughed deeply, for this was the struggle he'd always been meant for, the struggle that gave him meaning, that made all his suffering and loss a wondrous joy.

Somehow, Braggar was still at his side, the bull-shouldered youth not about to be outdone by a mere lowlander. The Chief's bare torso was severely cut and burned all over, blood sheeting down his front and back, but each injury only seemed to add to his rage and strength. His eyes rolled with madness as he ran berserker, all thought for his own safety gone, any sense of self gone as he gave himself over to the elemental force and will of the gods. He'd won himself a second sun-metal sword and plunged forward with them as a dread and maddened aurochs would, twin points held low and threatening.

'Spears ready! One step forward! Thrust!' came the voice again, its commanding tone slightly shaking now.

Then Torpeth was running across the heads and shoulders of the Heroes, his ululating cry spooking the ranks and creating disorder as much as the small but devastating daggers in his palms. He leapt and landed with both feet on top of one man's helmet, going straight into a crouch and swinging his daggers down below his feet so that they punched through the man's ears to spike his brain. The near-naked holy man sprang up and landed his feet on either side of another Hero's head. The daggers sliced through the man's throat from both directions. He hopped onto another man, landing on one foot and kicking in the face of the man behind. Spears stabbed towards him, but he never stayed in one place long enough for them to arrive. He landed hard on another to break his neck and then jumped and skipped his way up and down the ranks, his every step and touch bringing death, every moment a final cry from a different member of the Empire's army.

'One step forwa— Argh!'

The mountain men now poured from the inn, coughing and spluttering, but most with weapons and all ready to fight. The force of over a hundred Heroes sent ahead to kill those within the inn had been entirely undone.

Thomas looked towards the north gates. The main body of Heroes was finishing off the mountain men on the walls and those who had been sleeping in the nearby barracks. Wave after wave of heavily armoured Heroes still marched through the open gates, and now the terrible figure of Saint Azual appeared. The region's ruler towered over all of them – apparently more formidable even than when Aspin and Thomas had faced him in Hyvan's Cross – the rising sun creating a glaring halo around his head so that it was hard for the several hundred surviving defenders to look upon him.

Jillan released his arrow and took the baker in the leg, the same baker who had always sold bread to his mother but now seemed intent on killing him. The baker hardly broke step and kept coming.

'Shoot to kill!' Samnir castigated him. 'We can't afford to waste shafts.' The soldier sliced and lopped off limbs that reached for him.

They were in a running battle along the south road, more and more of the Saint-possessed inhabitants coming out of side streets to swell the mob. They brayed for Jillan, for blood and the glory of the Empire.

The majority of the frenzied Godsenders came on behind Jillan and Samnir, but there was still a scattering of them ahead. Two came angling in at Jillan: he shot an arrow into the forehead of one and Samnir used his momentum to body-check and slam the other into the ground.

'Pick your feet up, lad,' Samnir panted, and cursed as an oversized lumberjack came across their path.

Jillan dared a glance back over his shoulder. 'They're gaining on us!' he cried in a panicky voice and fumbled an arrow from his quiver, only to drop it.

The lumberjack dived for Jillan, momentarily catching Samnir off guard. Big hands grabbed the front of Jillan's tunic and pulled him to the ground. Samnir stamped on the lumberjack's back, keeping him flat, sank his sun-metal blade into the nape of the man's neck and withdrew it. The soldier cut through the man's wrists and pulled Jillan up, one of the lumberjack's separated hands still gripping tightly to Jillan's front.

The pursuing townsfolk were now all but upon them.

'Head down and get to the Gathering Place, where we'll have more room to manoeuvre. Don't stop, whatever happens!' Samnir ordered fiercely, pushing Jillan on ahead of him.

'Jiiillan,' came a collective moan from behind them. Jillan dared not look back now. He was forced to discard bow and quiver so that he could run more freely. Besides, the weapon would do him no good in the close fighting that was surely about to descend on them.

His lungs burned and his legs shook with effort. 'We'll never make it!'

You will if you release me, you fool! the taint railed at him. *You've been given magic for a reason. Give up this self-doubt or the Saint has already won.*

'I can't! I can't!'

Release me! it howled, fighting his control.

Jillan dodged left and right, jumped and tore through grasping hands and then burst into the Gathering Place . . . where still more Godsenders waited for him. They turned as one towards him.

'Jillan, there's no escape. No more people need die.' The voice of the Saint came from a dozen throats.

Jillan, I can save you, save Samnir, save all these people!

'Here!' came a shout. Haal and several dozen others were running towards him, Den Arnesson among them. Jillan realised they were all people he'd healed of the plague, but he hadn't done so just for them to throw their lives away buying him a few more seconds of freedom! Many of those with Haal were old and clutched an assortment of domestic tools for weapons – how long could they last against a crowd ten times their number that had a single organising intellect?

Your magic gave them the freedom to choose, Jillan. Do not now take that away from them. You freed them from the trap of their own minds. They have meaning and purpose now. Better a meaningful death than a long and meaningless existence.

They were closer now and he saw determination in the set of Den's jaw, conviction in the eye of his classmate Haal and even joy in the bearing of a spry grandmother who held her breadknife in a firm grip. He was moved and humbled by them. He could not let them down. He ran to them as the masses of Godsend's population closed in.

Samnir was suddenly back at his side. 'To the north! Where the pagans should be, if any still survive.'

Jillan and his companions surged through the Gathering Place, skirting round the Meeting House. Every dozen yards one of those at the edge of Jillan's group was pulled down or overwhelmed, but the group as a whole managed to keep making progress. If anything, those the Saint controlled seemed to get out of their path so that they could keep moving.

'They're herding us! Corralling us,' Jillan shouted in alarm as his group entered the north road and saw the relatively few defenders that still stood against the numberless army of Heroes beyond. The people of the mountains and Jillan's small band were trapped.

The taint rose suddenly within Jillan as he beheld the giant the hated Saint had become. *You must let me strike at him before—*

'I! See! You!' Saint Azual mentally boomed and slavered. 'Good of you to join us, Jillan. You're just in time to see all your friends die. And see here! I even had your pretty Hella and her father join us. We wouldn't want them missing out now, would we?'

'No!' Jillan shouted involuntarily as he saw the girl he loved held fast by a group of lewdly taunting Heroes. The Saint laughed, knowing his final victory was only moments away.

Chief Braggar roared his defiance, brandishing two smoking swords of sun-metal and almost drowning out the Saint's own thundering tones. The mountain men rallied to the young but gods-favoured warrior.

'Wait!' Jillan cried despairingly.

But the brave mountain chief had no chance of hearing, and the battle rage still upon him meant he was lost to reason. Dead Heroes lay all about Braggar and he was painted with their gore. He was a terrifying apparition and an avatar of pagan vengeance. The Heroes in the first rank facing him could not help but recoil, battle-hardened though they were and despite the fact they were directed by their holy Saint.

'For the gods!' Chief Braggar screamed, the battle cry taken up by all his men. They rushed forward with fearless wild-eyed eagerness.

The mountain men formed the head of a spear, their Chief at the tip, Slavin and Thomas directly behind him, Torpeth, Aspin and another just behind, and then two hundred after them. The spear smashed into the wall of shields formed by the Heroes and punched straight through it.

Where Braggar stamped, the ground shook and Heroes lost their footing and heads. Where he looked, his shining eyes blinded and confused, and his enemy did not see their deaths coming. Where he breathed, the soldiers of the Empire choked and collapsed, clawing at their throats. Where he moved, the air burned and men were consumed by flames of blood. Where his spittle landed, those standing against him found their guts turned to water and their bodies paralysed by icy fear. The gods rode on his shoulders and their elemental powers were his to command.

When a rank of a dozen Heroes came for Braggar at once, Thomas would leap to protect the young warlord's left flank, while Slavin's willowy twisting spears would skewer those on the right. Where a Hero avoided or successfully defended against Thomas and Slavin, Torpeth would spring forward faster than the eye could follow, with an all but extra-sensory awareness of where flying weapons were and would be, and bring instant death with the slightest of touches.

One moment the Heroes were pushed back, the next they would push forward again, like waves battering against a beach. They poured around the sides of the spearhead formed by Braggar and his close companions, only to break against Aspin and the others. The dancing mountain men continuously spun and ducked, their churning motion impossible for their disciplined enemy to organise against. The pagans plunged through the Heroes, and Chief Braggar at last came face to face with the holy representative of the Saviours.

Saint Azual watched them come, revelling in the moment. What did it matter if five Heroes died for every pagan? Each pagan death was one less avatar of a free and chaotic Geas. Life by life, step by step, drop by drop, second by second, the time and self-defining power of the Geas was coming to an end. Soon there would be none but the boy left standing, and the boy would be all that stood between Azual and the Geas. The Geas, as powerfully connected to the boy as it had become, would have no other major avatar or hiding place except the boy. It would have to give itself entirely to the boy or risk losing both of them forever. Yes, the Geas would have to give itself to Jillan, and then Azual would claim the boy and Geas for himself. His moment of ascension and godhead was at hand. There would be no other gods either – none of those whining and mewling aborted gods of earth, air, fire and water! – for he would be the one god of all life, the supreme and defining will that would then turn to challenge the cosmos. The stars would be the dust beneath his feet and other worlds would be his playthings. He would hold the cosmos in his one hand . . . the one hand with which he casually reached out now and crushed the head of the pagan chief, mind, vital fluids and life squeezing out between his fingers. He raised his hand and let the heady juice drip into his mouth. How sweet and intoxicating was the essence of existence, the essence of this desperate avatar of the gods. And now he understood and foresaw these people in their entirety.

With what remained of the chieftain's body, Azual swept the ground before him, contemptuously smashing away the bothersome blacksmith and the sly snow-hair. The naked pagan priest predictably jumped over Azual's swipe and bounded up to deliver a fatal touch to the Saint's diaphragm. Azual's all-seeing mind – a mind which now knew past, present and future, a mind that was the defining alpha and omega of the existence written upon the pages of this reality – had known this final moment of presumption and defiance would come. It was almost anticlimactic, quite disappointing and somewhat tiresome now that it was here. Yawning mentally, he let his divine will be known.

'Cage!' Captain Skathis commanded, and sun-metal blades were raised in a tight mesh around the Saint's body.

There was no way through for Torpeth, and he had to contort madly in midair just to avoid dicing himself. The cage of deadly sun-metal pushed towards him and he back-flipped and tumbled away.

The mountain men cried out to their fallen gods as they witnessed the death of their chief and saw their greatest warriors cast down. Dismayed and despairing, they fell back, a number of them unable to disengage cleanly from the force of Heroes and quickly finding themselves unstrung. Torpeth and Aspin fought for valuable moments to allow as many as they could to escape, but had no choice but to flee themselves.

The Saint's laughter echoed all around them. 'See, Jillan, how many deaths you have caused with your overweening pride and refusal to kneel to another! See how you risk your beloved!'

'Spare them and I will give myself to you!' Jillan cried.

No! You cannot! It will be the end of all things. Free me!

The Saint smiled in satisfaction. 'And so it was always decided. Come to me and we will end this needless suffering and destruction.'

Jillan took a wooden step forward. Samnir's heavy hand clamped down on his shoulder. 'You cannot think of doing this, lad! Not after everything we have already sacrificed! Not after your parents' own sacrifice!' Jillan shrugged himself free of the old soldier and took another step.

The ground suddenly rumbled and pillars of stone rose ahead and behind the pagans, forming walls between them and their enemies. Freda climbed out of the earth, bright gems shining magically at her neck. The mountain men fell back from her, raising their weapons, but Jillan came and gestured for them not to be alarmed. A golden youth descended through the clouds of thick smoke billowing from the inn and alighted on the wall facing the Saint.

'Can it be? After all this time?' Torpeth gnashed, apparently beside himself. 'The whispering shadow? The Great Deceiver! Still the gods test me and demand final payment!'

The Peculiar looked down upon the Saint. 'It is here I must intervene. Have you not already been warned that my claim to the boy is the greater? Do you defy your betters, little Saint? I cannot allow it.'

The Peculiar glanced back over his shoulder and spoke so that only the defenders would hear and be compelled: 'Hide your eyes now, for otherwise your minds will be unhinged.'

With those words the Lord of Mayhem transformed himself into the shimmering image of whatever the Saint's army most desired. The Peculiar heard all their thoughts and fantasies, those of the Saint foremost among them, and made himself into them. He was the ideal of female beauty and carnal lust: her sex was vulnerable and promising; her lips were sumptuous, yielding and hungry; her eyes teased, undressed and pleaded; her breasts heaved with passion, the buds of her nipples erect and yearning; her slim waist gave way to pronounced hips and a sculpted behind that thrust out urgently. A heady musk filled the air that flared nostrils, dilated pupils, bared canines and made tongues hang. Then, conquering the remaining senses of those fixated on her, the Peculiar spoke in a shifting timbre that touched, seduced, commanded and compelled: 'Take your swords and put them to your throats. See how your Saint also finds a blade. Follow his lead and we will come together! That's it. All of you.'

'Friend Anupal, do you not remember your promise?' Freda asked in anguish, almost breaking the spell.

The Peculiar blinked. 'And you promised to trust my judgement whenever I decided there were those who had to die. Now don't interrupt me again, dear one.'

'No!' Jillan shouted. 'You cannot kill them all. You cannot avert one genocide by committing another!'

The Peculiar smiled coquettishly. 'Oh, but I can. Now, brave Heroes and Saint, push your swords—'

'Cursed god!' Torpeth spat, leaping impossibly high and landing directly behind the Peculiar on the wall. 'It was *you* who destroyed my own empire with your wiles and words. It was *you* who destroyed my army and people. It was *you* who broke the gods and gave this world to the others.' He wrenched the helmet of sun-metal from the vision's brow and kicked her from the wall. 'You cannot be allowed to do it again! The Geas will never be restored through your acts – it will only be diminished further. Out, devil! Away from all living things and this world!'

The Peculiar landed below, body and form at once dislocating, and looked up aghast. 'You! Torpeth the tyrant! Still alive. Petty Geas, what have you done!' The Peculiar's mask of beauty fell and there was a moment of insanity given physical form, a scratching itchiness inside the skull and a burrowing through flesh that felt like the carving Jillan had seen Ash try to sell in Saviours' Paradise.

The Saint leapt forward. Not hesitating for an instant, he broke a glass phial of blood against the Peculiar's dissolving teeth and jabbed a tapping tube into the god's liquefying flesh. A single sun-bright diamond of blood was distilled at the end of the tube, which Azual greedily lapped up with his long tongue, as the rest of the Peculiar trickled away into the earth.

The Saint threw back his head and screamed to the heavens as he grew back the hand he'd lost in Hyvan's Cross, his eyes were restored and he increased exponentially in stature. 'I am made anew! The power of creation is mine!' He raised the shining helmet of sun-metal, stretched it wide and lowered it over his brow. 'Witness as I am crowned a god!' His voice shook buildings to their foundations, toppling many, burst eardrums, rattled brains and was mentally heard the length and breadth of the Empire. Several Saviours were shaken out of the waking dream and knew a loss of self-control for the first time in their near-immortal existence.

'That could have gone better,' Samnir groaned from where he'd fallen. He coughed up blood.

'Kill them all!' the Saint demanded and used his will to force all the Heroes back to their feet.

'You said you would spare them!' Jillan cried out, his ears ringing so badly he thought he would pass out.

'That was before I became divine, you wheedling child! The girl will be the first to die.'

The taint was howling and howling, making it impossible to think. The ringing, the smoke, the blood, the death, the sacrifice: it was all too much! It was an unending assault, like a battering storm, a sort of spell that had been conjured over millennia to destroy the People and the Geas. It was a spell or consciousness that had seen countless generations sacrificed to its making. It was the magic of the Saviours. He saw it now. It was so colossal it all but eclipsed this world, just as Azual's prodigious size now cast a shadow across the whole of Godsend.

The Saviours had influenced and then controlled all of history and the lives of the People just to bring about this moment when the spell of their will would finally devour the Geas. And it was not just on this world. They would claim and devour the entire cosmos. Just to bring about this moment, their first moment of true creation, the moment when they truly claimed the power of all and became gods of the mind, of matter, of space and time.

All this he understood in an instant, and yet he could only care because of Hella. He had resolved not to use his magic to destroy anything again, but his resolve was as nothing when put next to losing her forever. He would not let them kill her, could not idly stand looking on when she was the only meaning left to him.

At last, having unknowingly resisted it from the first day he was born, he allowed his voice to become one with the taint's. He realised now that everything the Empire had ever said and taught had been designed to make the People deny and reject their own power, so that they could never become a threat to the Saviours. They'd cajoled, bullied and punished him into seeing his potential as something tainted, sinful and other. His magic was a tempting voice he should always suppress, it was a selfishness of which he should be ashamed. He should loathe, mutilate and sacrifice himself before ever thinking to use his magic. He should keep it in abeyance until the Saint had a chance to Draw it from him completely and claim it for the Saviours. How many millions had allowed the parasitic Empire to bleed them of their magic, freedom and selves? The scale of the crime was unthinkable. It would ultimately see the People and the Geas extinct, and the Saviours equipped with even greater power to visit cataclysm and apocalypse on other realms.

The taint was not the insidious voice of some corrupting entity. The taint was part of him. It was the stubborn and aggressive part of himself that believed passionately in things, that loved others passionately and would do whatever it had to in order to safeguard that which he loved. It was the part of him that challenged a bullying teacher, stood against a classmate intent on harming him and defied a genocidal Saint.

It was not even a question of releasing the taint. It was not an issue of giving himself over to it. It was simply allowing it to exist. It was sharing life with it. It was merging with it and becoming one with the storm, the storm of magic and consciousness. He now rose up with it, fully matching the overarching Azual. Jillan's eyes blazed as bright as the Saint's own and lightning arced between his fingertips.

'You will not touch her!' Jillan commanded the Heroes who had raised their swords to cut Hella down. The soldiers stopped and looked around in confusion, apparently at a loss as to how they had even come to be in Godsend.

'You dare!' the glorious Saint thundered, the displeasure of his look combusting the air around them. Then he released a killing red mist towards Jillan.

Jillan replied with a tempest, sweeping the mist away, and poured liquid fire at the leering deity. The magic washed over Azual, but fizzled away as he shrugged and renewed himself.

A mental blast from the Saint made Jillan cry out, for he did not know how to defend himself against such an invasion. Azual rampaged through Jillan's mind and memories: 'Come out, come out, wherever you are!'

Jillan sat having breakfast with his parents in their little house in the southern part of town. He whined that he didn't want to go to school, that he was feeling ill and that his mother should stay at home with him. 'He's not ill,' his father Jed decided on behalf of the family. 'Who are you afraid of, son?' The door rattled and the Saint's voice came from the other side: 'We both know who you're afraid of, don't we, Jillan?' Jed moved towards the door. 'Who's there?' Jillan leapt up from the breakfast table, begging his father not to let the Saint in, and fled to his parents' bedchamber.

He clambered out of the small window as he heard his parents being torn apart behind him. He raced through the morning towards the Gathering Place, where he knew his beloved Hella and his other classmates would be waiting. Long sharp fingers pinched him by the ear and

Minister Praxis dragged him into the school. All day the Minister punished them, until it was dark and Jillan was forced back out. The darkness was waiting to ambush him, he knew.

He ran and ran, bullies and killers on his heels, all the way to Saviours' Paradise. Aspin was in a punishment chamber calling for help, but Jillan dared not go down there because he knew the Saint would trap him. He fled with Thomas's wagon and the sick blacksmith, the sound of Aspin's cruel torture in his ears the whole time.

They made it into the woods and onto the hidden paths. He didn't want to go any further, but Thomas was forcing him on to Linder's Drop. 'No, Thomas, please! You don't understand. Linder's Drop is a dream. You must wake up!' The blacksmith shook his head. 'Ridiculous! If I'm not awake, but think I am, how on earth can I wake up?'

'How do I wake up?' Jillan cried to the forest. 'Geas, help me! Wolf, help me!'

And in reply the burning orange eyes of the wolf came out of the dark. 'Honestly, must you be so dense? You wake up by going to sleep,' the predator said in the voice of the taint. 'Lie down and I will watch over you. Quickly, before they find your trail again.'

Jillan closed his eyes and found himself in the ruined landscape of the Saint's mind. The green hill was there with its throne of skulls, but the throne was empty. All the People, the Heroes and the Saint were somewhere behind him, scouring the land in search of him. If he could get to the throne, he might be able to seize power here. He ran with all speed, his existence depending on it.

'NO!' boomed the ground and sky as Azual realised his own peril. To save himself, the Saint severed their mental link and they were facing each other in the eye of the storm above Godsend once more.

We are too evenly matched. I cannot overcome him.

Azual flew at Jillan, slashing with his talons, but Jillan's armour flashed and threw the Saint back. Jillan came in with fists, but Azual was more muscular and faster. He caught Jillan's chin with an elbow and then got him in a headlock. The death grip tightened.

Jillan called down lightning, and it struck Azual's helmet, the sun-metal absorbing the energy. Jillan poured flames upwards but these too disappeared into the helmet. His vision began to blur and develop spots. He attempted a mental blast of his own and that also went into the shining headgear.

The Saint hurled them both down into Godsend, Jillan landing cruelly on his spine. The violence of the impact and the eddies of the titanic forces the two of them threw at each other caused a concussion wave that flattened every being in Godsend and made them black out, all except Freda, who channelled the power of an earthquake towards Jillan so that he could hit Azual with it. Yet the boy reached up clumsily with his hand and only managed to find the Empire god's terrible crown again.

Jillan could hardly see any more. He was only dimly aware of his nemesis flipping him over; of Azual keeping one hand at Jillan's neck to carry on throttling him; of the Saint using his talons to slash at the fastenings of Jillan's armour to expose his chest; and the divine representative of the blessed Saviours extending the talons of his free hand.

'And now I will have your sacred heart, boy, to drink your life blood and at last have the power of the Geas as my own.'

Jillan drew the last of the power and life energy from his core, and whispered, 'Then it is my sacrifice and gift to you, holy one!' He raised two trembling fingers as if in benediction and trickled the last of his magic into the helmet of sun-metal.

The Saint laughed maniacally. As he began to extend his talons into Jillan's chest, a single drop of sunlight fell onto his hand. It burned through his flesh and bone. He frowned in annoyance and tried to renew himself, but the drop ran towards his wrist. With a mighty clash of his teeth, Azual severed the hand from him, discarded it and grew himself another. Another drop fell and began to burn.

Azual's head hurt. Molten sun-metal trickled down his face, searing through one of his new eyes, burning deep into his cheek, dissolving his teeth and coming out through the bottom of his chin. It dripped onto his chest and burned straight down towards his beating heart.

He frantically used all his power to renew and recreate his body, but the sun-metal ran faster and faster down his head and body.

'Pleaggge!' he belched. 'Save me!'

'I cannot,' Jillan mumbled, 'for you have already taken everything I have, holy one. Where are your Saviours now?'

Azual scrubbed at the blinding metal, only succeeding in spreading it further. He threw himself onto the ground and rolled to smother the deadly stuff or rub it off, but his movements became weaker and weaker, until he was all but still. For a few brief moments he seemed but a youth of Jillan's own age. Eyes streaming, the boy looked at Jillan and gave him a sad broken smile.

'We seem the same, you and I . . . Will you not help me, before it turns dark and the bad people come for me again? I've been trapped here in my room for so long. No. You should leave before they come.'

'I'm sorry . . . Damon? I can wait with you for a while. I don't think they'll be coming any more,' Jillan said with the last of his breath, and closed his eyes.

'Really? They're not coming?' the boy asked ever so faintly, as he became lost in shimmering heat and steam.

Moments later there was nothing left of the holy representative of the Saviours.

Freda came over to peer at the puddle of what was left and shook her head. 'It was as friend Anupal said. None can be omnipotent and the world still exist.'

CHAPTER 14:

Or end what has begun

The masked Saint and her children picked their way through the still bodies and debris that were almost all that remained of Godsend. Izat knew she would not have long to get to the boy and Draw him, if he still lived.

An unkempt but tall woodsman was suddenly standing in front of her. The Saint's children hissed and scattered.

'You should not be here, Unclean one,' Izat challenged him, the authority of her voice muffled by the mask of the Peculiar that she wore.

'Nor should you, holy one. Tell you what: I won't tell if you don't,' Ash replied with a wink. 'There'll be hell to pay if they find out you're in another Saint's region uninvited, won't there?'

'You know nothing of which you speak. Stand aside. The mad Saint is no more and I command here on behalf of the Empire.'

'Oh, I don't think the Empire's in any shape to be commanding anyone right now, do you?' the woodsman replied, looking around the body-strewn ruins and his smile becoming a wolfish grin. 'Why don't you just run along, Izat? That is who's behind that quite unbecoming mask, isn't it? Then there won't be any need for unpleasantness. There's been quite enough for one day, don't you think?'

Izat spluttered in outrage. 'How *dare* you address me in such a manner! I cannot let such impertinence pass without reprimand and censure. I insist you stand aside this instant. I would rather not sully my hands and rumple my robes with one so Unclean, but will not hesitate to do so if you do not immediately adopt a more reverent tone. The boy is a citizen of the Empire and thus I claim him. It is my divine right!'

'Enough of your primping, preening and posturing, Saint. What of the boy's rights?'

'He has none. He has not yet been Drawn. I will be his mother and father and make all decisions for him. Children, remove this upstart, being careful not to splatter me if you please. Quickly now!'

A dozen children stole out from behind semi-ruined walls and overturned barrels and sought to encircle Ash. There was a feral look to them, but the woodsman showed no concern. He shook his head. 'To think you would corrupt and use these children for your own dirty work. How can you, in all conscience, put these innocent children in the way of harm? Don't wish to risk chipping one of your nails, is that it? Just how is it that you are called holy? I say you are *not* holy, Izat. I say that it is time you and your kind were ended. My friend here agrees with me and has a voracious appetite. I'm surprised you haven't already started running.'

Izat took a cautious step back, turning her head this way and that in an attempt to identify a threat. She peered through drifting smoke and looked into pools of shadow. Satisfied there was nothing amiss, the mask turned back to Ash and the Saint stepped confidently forward, head lifted imperiously.

'You still don't see him, do you, Izat? I'm not surprised really, for he is the darkness and cannot be seen. He stalks you from within darkness too, little Saint. He is the *Chaos*! Are you afraid of the dark, children? You should be. Surely you see something in the deep, deep shadow beneath that wall over there? Are those just orange cinders drifting on the wind or are they the burning eyes of a black wolf watching and waiting for you? Look more closely. There! Didn't you see him blink?'

One of the children suddenly screamed and ran. It served as the cue for the others, and within moments they were all fleeing in panic, jumping over walls and zigzagging for all they were worth.

'The Chaos!' Saint Izat choked. 'It cannot be here! Wait for me!' Hurriedly she rid herself of her encumbering robes and mask and took off after the children.

Ash chuckled. He shouted after them, 'Make sure you sleep with the lights on, or the dark wolf will get you!' He watched them for a while, smiling each time one of them veered wildly away from a particularly large or dark shadow. He was satisfied they would not stop running until they'd completely left the region. Then Ash picked his way over to Freda, who was crouched protectively next to Jillan's prostrate figure.

Jillan's eyes fluttered open as the woodsman approached. 'I'm glad you didn't go too far,' the boy whispered. 'She tried to get me before, you know.'

Ash shrugged. 'It's all a matter of timing, Jillan. Some of us have it, and some of us don't.'

So pleased was D'Selle at what had happened to D'Shaa's mad Saint and the town of Godsend, so smug was he that D'Shaa must surely now suffer fatal punishment and her region be given over to him, so entirely vindicated did he feel, he just could not bring himself to mind too much that his own Saint, Izat, had failed to capture the boy. The millennia of humiliation with one so immature as D'Shaa as his peer, and the further affront of his attack on her being frustrated by Elder Thraal's inexplicable decision to release the Peculiar, were at an end, with victory and the inevitable reward D'Selle's alone. His careful planning, effort and genius had shaped this world and made his will manifest. Surely now none had better claim to ownership of this world than he: D'Shaa had disgraced and condemned herself; D'Zel of the north, in having ambitiously Declared for D'Shaa, would be lucky to survive certain censure; and D'Jarn was an irrelevance for not being able to tame the east. Even Elder Thraal's judgement would now be in doubt, for had he not saved the disgraced D'Shaa? The Council of Elders must surely be wondering if Elder Thraal had outlasted his use and time as Watcher. They must surely be looking at D'Selle and wondering if he would be a more suitable candidate. Watcher D'Selle! Elder D'Selle! His name would be spoken in the far reaches of the cosmos and all would know that a new power was rising, a power that could lead his kind to salvation where none had yet managed to do so.

D'Selle passed along the infinite corridors of the labyrinthine Great Temple, undoing untold numbers of retainers with his mere presence, but hardly noticing it. They aged so quickly when one of his kind was near that they were of no moment or consequence. They were fallen leaves, grains of sand, drifting dust.

He ascended to the First Sanctum, the only place his kind ever came together in numbers. It was here that the exercise of the Council's judgement and will was witnessed. He climbed with mounting excitement, eager to see D'Shaa undone. Never before had he seen one of his kind ended. He twitched at the wonder, terror and thrill of the prospect. When was the last time he'd known something *new*? And this wasn't just the discovery of some new flower or insect. It was something that would tell him more about his existence and own kind.

He hurried into the perfectly spherical chamber, rings of seats rising from the bottom of the sphere to the top. The majority of his kind occupied the seats of the largest ring, which was halfway up, and the rings just below it. His own rank, of course, sat higher up, where there were fewer seats. Elder Thraal sat in one of the highest circles, all alone. Clearly, the other elders had resolved to remain in their near-permanent repose. D'Selle put aside his disappointment: he would not be replacing Elder Thraal today then. No matter – he was sure to have more and greater opportunities in the near future, once he'd claimed the spoils of his most recent victory.

He began to ascend the stairs to the circle of his own rank, wondering when D'Shaa, as the Subject of Judgement and Will, would be led in to stand at the bottom of the sphere.

'No, D'Selle!' spoke Elder Thraal's mind into the silence of the First Sanctum. 'You will rise no further.'

There were mental gasps from the gallery of rings. D'Selle's eyes dilated to their extremities. D'Shaa sat in the higher circle! She should be here below instead of him! How could this be? No! He was not the Subject of Judgement and Will. No! Treachery!

D'Selle sought to leave the sphere, but the Will of the whole held him in place. He could not stir even a fraction. His thoughts were deliberately slowed so that he could not escape into the waking dream.

'Mine is the voice of Judgement,' Elder Thraal mentally intoned for all to hear. 'D'Selle, organising intellect of the west, ordered his Saint into the southern region without the prior invitation or permission of D'Shaa, organising intellect of that same region. That alone is deserving of censure. Worse, D'Selle's Saint was tasked with removing a primary agent of the Geas from the dynamic of control I had already instituted. The primary agent was the boy Jillan, who was controlled in a dynamic between D'Shaa's Saint and the Peculiar. If D'Selle's Saint had managed to remove the boy, the dynamic of control would have become an uncontrollable gyre of destruction. All know of what the Peculiar is capable. The foreknowing Council is in no doubt that the Geas and this world would have been lost to us forever. Therefore, it is the Judgement of all that D'Selle put our Will and our kind at fatal risk. The Will of all is that D'Selle's existence be ended. With the permission of the Council, D'Selle's sustaining energies will be divided among the rest of our kind. Raise him to the centre!'

D'Selle was dimly aware of his feet leaving the bottom of the perfect sphere and the power of his kind's Will drawing him to the exact centre. He slowly spun in space, their black eyes hungry voids. They began to Draw his energies from him. Here, at the end, he understood his own existence and the nature of his kind.

Elder Thraal settled himself back into his chamber. All had passed as he'd intended. He'd elevated the inexperienced D'Shaa precisely to draw out and destroy the overly ambitious D'Selle, but also to see the highly dangerous D'Zel hampered by a self-preserving Declaration. Even more, it was Elder Thraal who'd encouraged D'Shaa all that time ago to make the erratic Azual her Saint. It had served to make her region unstable and to draw out the pagans and Geas. Now the Geas was inescapably connected to the boy, who would inexorably lead them all to Haven. At long last the Geas would be claimed by the Empire, and the Declension would have the power to continue spreading through the cosmos. This world would serve as a jumping-off point. And it was *his* will that made it a reality. The Declension would have no choice but to raise him to a rank of cosmic dominion.

There were none of any lower rank left to challenge him: D'Shaa was now probably the most pre-eminent of the organising intellects, but she would be too busy appointing a new Saint and trying to wrest back proper control of her region to get up to any mischief. Just to be on the safe side, however, he would instruct her to make the zealot Minister of Godsend her new Saint. And it was time to recall General Thormodius and his army from the east. They would see to it that the south was subdued and culled, and that Godsend was wiped from history once and for all. The lack of a sizeable army would also force Saint Dionan to adopt a new approach towards the barbarians and pagans in the east. After all, the pretence of peace could often prove more subtly subversive than the contention of war. *Now, who to make the new organising intellect of the west? Hmm.* And some task for the Disciples might serve several purposes at once, not least of which was removing them from the Great Temple and their positions guarding the Great Saviour himself.

She put her lips to his and kissed him, gently at first and then with a passion that was painful. He didn't mind – far from it. It was only when he couldn't breathe any more that he pulled her away from him. He gasped and panted and then looked at her with an embarrassed smile. He took her hand.

'You're shaking.' Hella laughed. 'One minute you're taller than the sky and pouring down magic on a holy Saint, and the next you're scared of a kiss.'

'I am not! Anyway, so what if I am?'

'Haven't you kissed many girls before?'

'Of course I have! Loads. How many have you kissed, then?'

'I don't kiss girls!' she giggled.

'That's not what I meant.'

'I know, silly. I was just teasing.'

'Oh,' he said, feeling foolish. He scratched his head and looked down at his feet. Then he looked back up at her, smiled and laughed out loud.

She threw her arms around his neck and kissed him again. This time he made sure to breathe through his nose so she would never stop.

With a sword of sun-metal bent round his head the Peculiar crouched, watching Jillan and the girl kissing beneath the tree. He would let them have this moment – not because he was sentimental, but because it was important the boy have something or someone to keep him motivated and willing to sacrifice himself during the times and trials ahead. If the boy did not develop some sort of attachment here and now, the Peculiar would not be able to manipulate him so easily in the future. So let him have this.

The Peculiar knew a moment was both a place in time and a force. Brief and apparently inconsequential though it might seem, applied just so it became the infinitesimal fraction that tipped something of incalculable magnitude out of kilter. A kiss could destroy worlds, perhaps the entire cosmos. *Just look at how my theatrical but precisely timed stand upon the wall lured Torpeth into ripping the sun-metal helmet from my head, in turn for the vainglorious Azual to place it upon his own brow, an act that ultimately proved his undoing. See how my giving but a single drop of my power to the Saint finally forced Jillan to embrace his power and become the weapon of my will. Ah, how simple and easily controlled is this world. Neither the Geas nor Empire can hope to stand against me, the Lord of Mayhem. Indeed, the Geas and Empire are as easily manipulated as the boy himself. My place in the cosmos will soon be fully restored.*

And all I have to do is wait. I will not insist that the boy fulfil his end of the binding bargain that we made upon entering Hyvan's Cross until he has restored himself. First let him break bread, raise a toast, share stories and swear lifelong friendship with his pagan comrades-in-arms – Aspin Longstep, snow-haired Slavin and the troublesome Torpeth – before they must return to the mountains to bury Braggar and choose a new chief. Let him toil, laugh and smile next to stoical Samnir, stubborn Thomas, dear Freda, Ash the Unclean, Jacob the trader, solid Haal and sweet Hella, as they begin to rebuild Godsend in the time ahead. Let him engage in this labour of love and begin to think of starting a home with his beloved, as the season of spring sees the forces of life renewed. Let him not fear the newly fled Praxis and Captain Skathis for some while to come. Let the people and Heroes of this region, now freed of the control of their Saint, begin to know themselves. Let them look upon the world in wonder as if seeing it for the first time. Let the Godsenders take this boy into their hearts and build a town that will stand against the Empire and cause the elseworlders no end of trouble. Let these mortals remember what happiness is, so that they will have something other than the boy to sustain them and will not resist me unnecessarily when I come to take him from them. Let them offer him up in sacrifice to the God of Chaos and let them worship me again, as the people did once before.

Here ends the first of three
Chronicles of a Cosmic Warlord.

Jillan's struggle continues in the second chronicle:
GATEWAY OF THE SAVIOURS.

A note from the author

I grew up reading Raymond E. Feist, Michael Moorcock, Stephen Donaldson and Harry Harrison. I studied Christopher Marlowe and Edgar Allen Poe at university (along with a few other writers, obviously). Mix it all together and you end up with a style of fantasy that is darker than the average and sometimes called 'gothic fantasy' or 'metaphysical fantasy'. At its heart, it attempts to take on some serious considerations about this thing called life, but often ends with an amused shrug, an ironic quip or a simple toast raised and shared by friends. It seems that it is the journey that counts more than the destination. To put it more poetically perhaps:

Tread lightly, love deeply and love joyfully,
for we are stalked by time and shadows.

On this journey, I could not have come so far without the help of many, many people, including all those who purchased copies of my first three books: *Necromancer's Gambit*, *Necromancer's Betrayal* and *Necromancer's Fall.* Without the sales statistics you provided, I suspect I would have remained a struggling author for another twenty-five years. I have to make special mention here of my good friend Oliver Flude (www.oliverflude.com), who provided the necessary book covers in exchange for a few pints of (pretty thin) ale, and did the original sketches for *Empire of the Saviours* to boot.

Which brings me to my wondrous editor Marcus Gipps, who did so much to help *Empire of the Saviours* secure a deal with Gollancz. Thank you for letting me spell 'forever' as one word. Thank you for letting me spell it 'woodsman' instead of 'woodman'. And for the faith!

Lastly, I would like to thank those fantasy authors who still keep me intrigued and inspired: George R. R. Martin (of course), Peter V. Brett, Robin Hobb, J. V. Jones, Paul Kearney and anyone who has ever written a Gotrek & Felix novel.

Enough wittering from me. Time to get *Gateway of the Saviours* finished. For the latest: www.ajdalton.eu.

Turn the page for a preview of
the sequel to *Empire of the Saviours*

Gateway of the Saviours

Dust. As strong as the seals on his father's chambers were, the dust of the realm still found its way inside to cover everything. It was in the air, invisible but there, like so many things. It coated the inside of his throat and made his eyes run constantly. It was a permanent taste in the back of his mouth and he could feel it causing damage down in his lungs. When he moved, it caused irritation between his robes and his body, and sores at his joints. There was no escaping the dust, for it was pretty much all that was left of his realm. Certainly, there was still enough rock below ground to shelter his kind, the Declension, but the surface was a lifeless wasteland continuously scoured by the solar winds of their erratic and failing sun. Some said that there was less and less rock each year; as the dust storms blew, they exposed that which lay beneath and tore hungrily at it.

Some said that it was time for the Declension to leave their home-realm once and for all, before they were ground down to nothing along with the Geas of the realm. Another faction, led by his father, insisted that to abandon the Geas – that which had given the Declension life in time before remembering – would be to commit suicide as a people anyway. His father's faction was in no doubt that the Geas could be saved with the blood tribute supplied from all the lesser realms ruled by the Declension. This faction even claimed that, despite the failing sun, life could be restored to the surface once the volume of tribute became sufficient to both sustain the Geas and feed the ground properly. It was imperative, therefore, that the Declension continue to spread through the cosmos in search of new realms to conquer and from which to draw resource. To do otherwise, most believed, would be to see an end to their kind one way or another.

Ba'zel swept the dust from the smooth surfaces of his father's chambers for the sixth time that day and then used his limited magic to push the dust out through the seals. Why he bothered he was not entirely sure, for there would only be more dust to remove as soon as he had finished the current sweep. His father said the chambers would become uninhabitable if they were not constantly cleaned, but Ba'zel suspected his father actually just wanted to keep his *unstable* son occupied and out of trouble. After all, many other lines of the Declension used retainers for such menial labour. Besides that, the repetitive nature of the work also reminded Ba'zel of the sort of drill Mentor Ho'zen put him through each day in order to discipline his *unstable* mind and fitful magicks.

Those who were *unstable*, of course, were a threat to the future unity and common goal of the Declension. Such individuals were therefore confined and closely watched. All young were naturally *unstable* and most of the time kept within the chambers of their line, in part to protect them from less influential – and thus more desperate and predatory – elders of other lines. But an *unstable* youth would only be tolerated for so long, even within their own line. If they did not quickly show signs of developing some discipline, then all their blood and life energy would be fed back into the Geas, in the hope that they would be reborn with a greater willingness to mould themselves to the wider and long-term needs of the Declension. It was the only way their kind could survive, Ba'zel's father had explained . . . and had also begun to mention with increasing frequency of late.

Ba'zel knew he was running out of time. If his lessons with Mentor Ho'zen didn't soon start showing more success, then there wouldn't be any more lessons. There wouldn't be any more anything.

And his skin wasn't thickening and hardening the way it should, either. He was as pale and soft as one freshly reborn. Whenever he was permitted to come close to the realm's surface, even relatively diffuse light from above would sear him and cause him agony. Ba'zel's father had used the power and position of their line and faction to secure Ba'zel *extra* time in the realm's sun-metal chamber, to which some lines were not permitted access for generations at a time. Yet the privilege had only succeeded in partially blinding Ba'zel and covering his body in large, weeping blisters. The last time he'd been forced into the sun-metal chamber, he'd felt the blood boiling in his veins as if he were being cooked alive. He'd screamed for days after.

Time was running out. If he could not form the stone-like skin that was normal in his kind as they matured, then he'd be of no value to the Declension, either in the home-realm or any other realm. Now, whenever his father returned to their chambers, his eyes would only regard Ba'zel briefly before turning away. The very sight Ba'zel presented spoke of wrongness and being *unstable*. His father's disappointment and disgust were increasingly palpable. His father would mutter about how Ba'zel's motherhad also been *unstable* – the only thing Ba'zel had ever heard mentioned about his mother – and would then question Mentor Ho'zen intently about how the lessons had gone that day. Then no more would be said until Bazel's father went from their chambers the next morning.

Yes, time was running out. The cleaning now forgotten, Ba'zel agitatedly paced backwards and forwards. It wasn't his fault his skin wouldn't harden. For all Mentor Ho'zen spoke of how mental discipline could overcome any pain, it wasn't Ba'zel's fault that both the sun's cursed light and sun-metal threatened to kill him, was it? He told himself he did all he could to master Mentor Ho'zen's impatient lessons. Yet what could he do? Would his father be proud of him if he meekly submitted to his blood and life energy being fed to the Geas? Or be even more ashamed? Or would he be just relieved, perhaps?

Feeling eyes on him, Ba'zel turned to look at the small and pathetic creature crouched in the cage in the corner of the room. It was from some lesser realm or other and served as a supply of blood and life energy for him and his father. When younger, Ba'zel had fancied that the chitterings and doleful eyes of the creature had denoted intelligence – a thought that had made Ba'zel more than a little queasy when drinking its blood at first – but his father had been adamant that the creature was nothing more than the lowest type of animal, and that Ba'zel should never think to do anything as stupid as naming it. It was *not* a pet. It was unworthy of affection of any sort.

'What should I do, creature?' Ba'zel asked.

The creature did not reply, of course; just continued staring vacantly at him.

Ba'zel reached out and lifted the latch, letting the door of the cage slowly swing open. The creature now always displayed the lassitude of one drained too many times over the years: the frenzy of its early days had long since disappeared. It could not pose any real danger. Its muscles were wasted and it seemed old and spent. All it had eaten for the length of its captivity was the thin and negligible waste he and his father produced – and that diet only seemed to have contributed further to the creature's gradual decline. The creature trembled and crammed itself into the far corner of its home.

'Yes, it is frightening, is it not? Are you worried you will get into trouble by leaving? Do you think I have opened the door so you can be drained for the second time today, perhaps for the last time in your life?'

Ba'zel sighed. 'Do you even understand I have offered you freedom? Perhaps you are right to fear freedom, creature. Beyond these chambers you would not last more than the blink of an eye. Perhaps it is safer to stay in your prison, then. Yet to remain can only mean a slow death for you. I do not know, but perhaps you have come to desire it, to be finally left alone.'

The creature whimpered plaintively.

'I know. Perhaps then there is no true freedom and therefore no escape. Only the choice of a slow or quick death. I understand why you would want to remain – so that you might cling on for as long as possible. Me, I think I would prefer it to be quick.'

Ba'zel hesitated. 'You see, the Mentor is late coming today. It is the first time that has happened. He has not sent me a thought saying he is ill or has been appropriated by a more influential line. I do not think he will come at all, creature. And I find I cannot even endure waiting for him, or waiting for my father to return. If I can get past the seals, I will leave, and allow the sun, some elder or the Geas to consume me. Goodbye, creature. I hope . . .' *What should one say at such a time, to such a primitive animal?* '. . . I hope you achieve the manner of death you most desire.'

So saying, Ba'zel shook the dust from his grey out-of-chamber robes and put them on. He also retrieved his ceremonial mask from where it lay near the tomes of his line, since it might offer him some protection from the light. Moreover, given that the mask was usually worn by those wishing to conceal both the shame of their hunger and their identity when on their way to the feeding pools, it might encourage others to give him something of a wide berth. Small though he might be, his kind were at their most unpredictable and dangerous when desperate with hunger.

Ba'zel tried to calm his mind, trotting through the trope with which

Mentor Ho'zen started every lesson. Now, what was the mental phrasing with which his father sealed and unsealed their chambers? Ba'zel knew its signature, but had never attempted to frame anything so complex himself. For an inexperienced or *unstable* practitioner of magic, there was considerable risk in attempting such a weave. If he could not keep the threads separate throughout, they might form a loop in which his mind was caught for the rest of eternity. He would become disconnected from his body but be trapped within it, fully aware but powerless to command it. Or he might spin the threads into an *unstable* pattern that would unravel just as he was passing out of the chamber. The damage done to him by the dust of this realm would be as nothing compared to a stone wall becoming solid right as he was in the middle of it. Or, then again, his father might have set deadly traps and triggers to snare anyone who attempted the seals except himself.

Best not to think about it, Ba'zel told himself. *Calm. Say the trope again. That's it. Calm.*

'You must act with confidence!' Mentor Ho'zen had always instructed him sternly. 'A weave begun with doubt and uncertainty will never be stable enough to succeed. Don't look at me like that, young Ba'zel! You know confidence is not some character trait – it is merely a behaviour to be learned and used with discipline. Discipline, leading to confidence, leading to a stable weave. Otherwise, the first weave you attempt in earnest will likely fail and that will be the end of you. Without discipline, there is only death. Are you confident, young Ba'zel?'

'Yes, Mentor Ho'zen!' Ba'zel always replied as confidently as he was able, but always with a slight hitch and tremor in his voice to betray him.

'You are the scion of a powerful line and must be proud of that. Our kind looks to you for leadership. It wishes you to be strong so that our people can be strong, so that we will succeed in every realm we touch, so that we will be *saved* as a people. You must become a Saviour. Anything else would be a betrayal of your kind. Now tell me again. Are you confident, young Ba'zel?'

He understood the words and ideas behind them, but as hard as he tried, he never quite seemed able to embody them. He wondered if there was a weave to help him with embodiment, but that was just circular daydreaming. Without the confidence to cast the weave, he would never be capable of the magic to capture the confidence he needed.

Calm. A clear assertion of will. There is nothing to lose. If it goes wrong, that will be that and you'll never know any different. It will be a relief of sorts.

His breathing stopped and his heart stilled. He was as still as the stone. He asserted his will so that his essence became contiguous with the barrier. Again he asserted himself, to create separation on the other side. His robes and mask snagged within the rock and he felt panic begin to well within. His heart was about to flutter back into life! *Calm, calm!* His every instinct screamed that he should try and force the material through, but he knew that would be to give in to the panic. *Calm, calm! Just stop! Become part of the stone again. Now ease into the separation once more. That's it, that's it. Calm.*

With a cry he fell into the corridor beyond his father's chambers, dust pluming up from the floor and temporarily blinding him. He coughed, his heart beating so hard that it felt as if it would punch its way out of him through his back. He felt broken inside, but he'd made it.

He'd made it! Perversely, he wondered if his father would be proud that Ba'zel had found the discipline to achieve such a weave. But no, any such pride would be as nothing compared to the outrage his father would feel upon learning that Ba'zel had, without permission, wilfully left their chambers. His father would be disgusted by such an act of disobedience, for it was yet further evidence of his son being so *unstable*. This act alone would warrant Ba'zel's immediate sacrifice to the Geas.

Was it too late to go back? He was trembling now, the weave having drained him. He was probably too weak to return to the chambers, as further attested by his sudden thirst and hunger. In any event, he could not bear the thought of becoming a caged and cowering creature once more, always waiting to be drained to the point of death. Besides, Mentor Ho'zen would not be coming again: there were no more lessons to be had back in the chambers, no more chances to show his discipline. And even if Ba'zel did return, his father would no doubt sense he'd tampered with the seals and exact immediate and final retribution.

He no longer had a home. Where to go? He couldn't think clearly though, so desperate was he for sustenance. Instinct told him he must seek out the feeding pools. He could almost smell and taste the blood from here, despite its distance. He salivated and had to wipe his chin.

He rearranged his robes, settled his mask back into place and strode quickly through the warren of corridors his people inhabited beneath their realm's surface. As he reached the main tunnels, he lifted his chin so that he would not display anything but confidence to an observer. So intent was he on reaching the pools, so fixated was he on feeding to renew himself, so concentrated was he on his purpose, he hardly had to feign any sort of confidence of will.

Suddenly, coming towards him out of the gloom was a large, prowling elder. The elder's nasal aperture widened, either in hunger or in order to identify this approaching stranger. Unable to control his response, Ba'zel found a growl issuing from his throat. Displaying such indiscipline in front of another was shameful, but it succeeded in startling the elder; and they passed each other holding close to opposing walls of the corridor. Fantasies of attacking the elder crowded Ba'zel's mind. It took some effort to dispel them: if he started giving in to such impulses, he wouldn't survive very long at all.

He'd only been to the feeding pools once before. When he'd been very young, his father had brought him before the members of his faction to be ritually anointed in the blood that fed the Geas of their realm and people. It had been a deliberate and public display, for his father was ever the politician, even within his own faction. But Ba'zel had ruined everything by slipping and falling into the deepest and thickest of the pools. He'd been at the point of drowning when his father, after considerable deliberation, had finally submitted himself to the indignity of diving in to save his son. The ancient robes of their line had of course been ruined, and rumours about Ba'zel being ill-omened had been whispered ever since. His father had never been able to forgive him. How could he?

The corridors of the warren all looked much the same, but Ba'zel had no trouble sensing the direction of the feeding pools. Both the blood and Geas called to him, promising him life from death. It was all he could do not to break into a run, but to do so would be to show such a loss of control that it could not be tolerated in the presence of others.

He would be attacked en masse by every elder in the area, and torn apart so that not one scrap of him remained.

The closer he came to the pools, the more elders he sensed around him, some standing like statues, some secreted in the walls and others lurking in the shadows. Their thoughts hummed just beyond the range of his hearing and limited magic.

They would know him for one that was young. He sensed eyes turn towards him. Minds probed him. His nerves jangled – would they sense that too? He could not bear the scrutiny. They would find cracks in him and force them wide, exposing the soft and vulnerable flesh and being below.

He ground his jaws together in fear, praying the mask would hide the telltale reflex. The edges of his jaws crumbled and became dust in his mouth. Dust. Suddenly, he dragged his feet to make long trenches in the dust; and kicked the stuff up into the air. He turned his thoughts to dust and crouched lower. They were already coming for him, long limbs slashing through the air.

He kicked more and more up, tumbling to stay within the fog and away from the extended, scything forearms and legs. He kept his thoughts drifting and billowing and escaped into a small tunnel off the side of the main space. The larger elders would be unable to pursue him here unless they decided to use valuable energy coming through the stone. He stumbled farther away, knowing that every stride he took would make him less and less worth the effort of a chase.

His body shaking with exhaustion, he went to hands and knees and crawled on. If he were to meet an oncoming elder now, it would all be over. Yet he sensed the tunnel led away from the feeding pools and up towards the surface, so it was likely to be little frequented. The deep drifts of dust certainly suggested it was rarely used.

Gasping, he allowed himself a moment's rest, sitting back against the parched and crumbling wall. It sucked at him, as if trying to leech the last of his life energy. He struggled to breathe, his body wheezing worse than it ever had before. He pulled the mask away, thinking that would help, but it only allowed more choking grit and heat to get at him. *So thirsty! Calm, calm. Just wait for those below to settle, then try for the pools again. Perhaps at night, when it will be quieter.*

But foreign thoughts of surprise, shock, betrayal and then outrage came seeking him out. His father had now discovered his absence from their chambers.

Ba'zel! thundered the thoughts. *Where are you? Yes, you hear me. What have you done? You will return here at once! I will not repeat myself.*

Ba'zel whimpered and cringed lower against the wall, putting his arms around his head, as if that might somehow keep his father's anger at bay.

How dare you? You are no son of mine!

Pain stabbed at Ba'zel's temples and he came close to passing out. *Calm*, he prayed. *Calm!*

There were long moments of terrible and threatening silence. If Ba'zel had had the will and energy to answer his father, he would not have known what to say. What could ever be said that would excuse the shame he was bringing on his father's line?

When his father's mind spoke again, it was with more control. He sounded conciliatory now, almost patient as he said, *Ba'zel, there is no need for this. It is not too late. Come, let us talk, you and I, before you are discovered by others. Like you, I am afraid. Afraid that the other lines will discover you are alone outside our chambers. Afraid that they will mean you harm, particularly the enemies of our faction. They will seek to use you against me. I am afraid that they will declare you* unstable *and a risk to our kind that can no longer be sustained. After all, what sort of young would be outside the chambers of their line without escort? Come to me quickly then, before you are discovered, and we will talk.*

He almost believed his father, so desperately wanted to believe him. Imagined talking together as if they were both elders. But Ba'zel was no elder. He was an *unstable* son who was unworthy of any exchange of words each night his father returned to their chambers. No, he was less than that – for had his father not just said Ba'zel was no son of his? He was . . . the creature in the corner. Less than a pet. He was unworthy of affection of any sort. He could believe his father was afraid for himself, afraid for his position and faction, perhaps even afraid for his people. Beyond that, however, Ba'zel knew his father lied. If he were able to return to his father's chambers, there would be no conversation. Just as there would be no more lessons, there would be no more talk, and no more mercy.

Will you defy me then by not answering? his father whispered in disbelief, anger beginning to tinge his words once more. *Truly you are beyond help. Any discipline you may once have displayed has either completely foundered or has always been the sort of mimicry mere animals adopt. How dare you risk my line like this? I knew I should have let you drown all that time ago. As it is, I must now suffer the shame of putting out a clarion call to all our kind about your escape. I must beg them to kill you on sight. Were I not to do so, and it were discovered I knowingly put our entire kind at risk with one so* unstable, *then my life would also be forfeit.* A moment's hesitation. *So be it.*

And the call went out, first as a keening whirl of thought, and then, as it was taken up by others, as the howl of a hunt. Ba'zel pushed himself away from the wall and frantically scrambled up the small tunnel. They would not hesitate to come for him through the stone, now that he'd been declared a threat to all his kind. How long did he have left? Seconds?

There was no hope of ever getting close to the feeding pools, but he furiously focused his mind on the place so as to mislead those searching for him. The tunnel began to narrow as he forged up and he feared he would become stuck, but the walls were becoming softer, reluctantly allowing him to keep moving forward. The soft edge would make separation for those coming through the stone more difficult. He deliberately kicked dust up into the tunnel behind him – not that it required much effort in the desiccated surroundings of this realm.

Panting and coughing hard, he kept his head down and pushed on. The top of his head and his hands began to burn and he knew he must be close. He could not see anything but a blinding whiteness. He pulled the hood of his robe over his head and wrapped his hands in its voluminous sleeves. It helped a little, but he could feel his skin start to bubble and crack. He gagged as he smelt the sweet iron of charring flesh and burning blood.

With a final surge, he pushed through an avalanche of sliding sand and suffocating dust and out onto the barren surface of the realm. He knew better than to open his eyes immediately, having come close to being blinded permanently by the realm's cruel and ancient sun on a number of occasions. Winds tore at his robes, seeking to pull back the material and sacrifice him to the angry and ailing eye of the heavens.

Ba'zel wrapped himself as tightly as he could and tottered away from where he had emerged.

He was fortunate that he seemed to have come out into the tail end of a storm, for its energies would make him hard to follow for a while. On the other hand, it kept him deaf to pursuit and disorientated when it came to direction. And he needed to find his way off the surface as soon as possible, for he would not be able to survive here for more than a handful of minutes. His entire skin felt aflame and the agony was only increasing. How long before he passed out or lost all feeling and sense of self?

His lungs felt like they were shrivelling up, all the moisture drawn out of them. He staggered in the direction of the storm, casting his mind out as far as he could. Eddies and currents burned across his internal vision. He stumbled on the shifting, sinking surface, barely keeping his feet. A hacking cough racked his body and there was blood at the back of his throat. Shadows loomed through his mind now, filling him with darkness. Was he entering the void already?

He risked opening his eyes a crack and fancied he could see dark shapes among the swirling dust devils. He sloughed closer, all but at the end of his strength.

Sifters, hear me! he begged. *I have nothing to offer you but the last of my life.*

The narrow besailed giants stood with long limbs rooted deep in the surface. Every so often a leg would ponderously rise and anchor itself elsewhere, as a sifter repositioned itself with the changing wind. Ridged and textured flares of skin stretched between their thin bodies and upper limbs. The skin gently glowed as it absorbed particles of energy from the storm and filtered any remaining sustenance from the fine dust of the air. The sifters always travelled in the wake of the storms, feeding as best they could.

Some said that the sifters had once been close cousins of the Declension, but had chosen to adapt themselves to the realm's surface rather than hide below. Others said the strange and unsightly creatures could never have been related to the Declension and must have been a lesser race, cast off by the unknowable Chi'a in the time before remembering, when the Chi'a had apparently passed through this realm – as they had so many other realms – on their Great Voyage. Still others claimed that the sifters were a simple indigenous life form of this realm, of extremely limited intelligence and entirely reactive, just like the plantforms of other realms. What all agreed on, however, was that the sifters were completely harmless and possessing of so little life energy of their own that it was not worth the effort of bleeding or consuming them.

To Ba'zel, who had nowhere left to go and no other hope, the sifters were worth his every last effort. He slumped to his knees, which quickly began to become buried. He would be pulled down or covered over soon, for he did not have it within him to rise again. This would be his dusty grave. As the last of the energy and moisture was whisked from him, the dry husk of his body would begin to collapse. It would be blown to the winds in the next storm and the last of his essence would be sifted from the air by the silent giants. He would be nothing but a few motes of dust lost in the endless storm.

The last of my life is yours to do with as you will. Command or use it as you wish. Or spurn it if it is of no worth to you. I am sorry. I have and am nothing else. Should you be able to, tell Mentor Ho'zen and my father that I tried my best and that I am sorry for their shame. I did not wish to be so unstable. *I wish it could have been otherwise.* He smiled grimly. *For see where being* unstable *has brought me. See what it has won me. See what it will make of me. See how I am nothing but dust.*

The final eddies, currents and patterns of energy faded from before his mind's eye. He could feel nothing but a sort of weightlessness. Frenziedly, he tried to find his body and its pain, but there was nothing there. He couldn't even hear the storm. Or taste the sapping heat or the blood from the ruptures and lesions inside him. Or smell anything of substance. Here it was, then. A last few moments of floating. Or a disembodied floating forever.

We will command, use and spurn you then! came the whisper.

'What?' he croaked. 'Who are you?'

We have taken you up in the fold of our wings. You will be protected for a while, perhaps replenished. We will take you to the Gate.

'The Gate? Why? What would you have of me?'

You agree to being commanded, used and spurned by us?

'Yes.'

Then leave this place.

He felt fear. 'Can I not stay here with you?'

There was a pause. *No.*

'But . . .' But what? He had no right to ask anything of them. No right to ask anything of anyone. No right to ask anything of any realm, or of the cosmos. No right to existence. 'You would not have me become dust?'

One day. One day you will become dust and return to us. All the cosmos comes to us as dust eventually. In this way, we know of realms in the furthest reaches of the cosmos. It is inevitable that you will return to us.

'But you have spared me from that now, in your mercy. Why?'

So that you may leave this place and find the other realms of the Declension.

'You want that?'

Yes and no. It grieves us. Look at what has become of we sifters – as you call us – and our realm, because of the Declension. You will see what is being done to other realms by them. This end may be inevitable, we do not know. It is enough for us that the Declension reject you – because of that we shall spare you, for now, and allow you moments in other realms.

'What purpose will I have to give me discipline and meaning there? I must have discipline and meaning or the existence will be terrible beyond enduring. I would rather be dust.'

You must find discipline and meaning in enduring, then, as we do. You must search for new purpose even if you cannot discover it before becoming dust. It is all we know and can tell you. But we are here now. We command you to leave and to remember your promise to us.

Ba'zel was gently lowered back to the ground before he could even ask exactly what it was he had promised. He shielded his eyes as he watched the sifter lever itself away. Although its movements were slow and measured, it was soon lost in the white and grey storm once more. Ba'zel's skin began to pain him again and he knew he had to get moving. He'd been brought to a slope where the ground was firmer than elsewhere. There had to be rock just below. He ascended the slope and looked into the gaping mouth of a wide tunnel. He wasted no time hurrying down, out of the light.

He did not know this entrance but sensed great energies at play not far away. He navigated his way through long well maintained corridors, peering anxiously in all directions at intersections, expecting to see the flicker of rapid movement at any moment; but all remained deserted. It was through these corridors that the lesser races were marched from the Gate of the Waking Dream to the place of bloodletting at the feeding pools. For their own protection, these races were kept under close guard at all times, and lurking elders were regularly swept from the corridors. That meant that even if his people had now established where he was, they would have to come some distance before he was in sight. For the first time since leaving his father's chambers, he genuinely began to believe there might be some chance of escape.

With a measure of renewed energy, he ran for the Gate's chamber. Although he possibly had a good lead, the elders could move with frightening speed, and some possessed arcane magicks far beyond his understanding. Mentor Ho'zen had made mention several times of great magicks that could potentially alter space and time. What if Ba'zel's pursuers were to slow time down so much in this corridor that he never reached the chamber? He prayed such a spell would require more preparation and energy than was immediately available to those coming after him. Yes, he sensed them now! They'd entered the corridors and were swarming after him in massive numbers.

Panicking now, he flew round the next corner and saw the doors to the chamber ahead. As he raced forward, an enormous guard stepped out of the shadows of an alcove to the side of the doors and levelled a trident of rarest sun-metal at him. The glare of the weapon hurt Ba'zel's eyes as much as the sun itself, and he slid to a halt with a cry of shock and pain. The guard was an elder of prodigious size. The scars criss-crossing his hard skull marked him as one of the most experienced of the warrior lines. There would be no defeating or eluding him.

'So small?' the elder observed with a mixture of disgust and amusement. He sniffed. 'Young, too. I would not usually deign to notice one such as you, let alone do you the honour of raising my weapon. I can only wonder at the oddity of your being able to cause so much trouble and disorder. There is no power of significance within you, so what lack is there in our kind that has allowed you to come so far? Has your instability somehow already affected us? Surely it is not some sort of infection that has weakened us?'

Ba'zel's mouth had never felt so dry. 'I-I . . .'

'See how you waver,' the warrior sneered. 'There is no confidence of will about you, no discipline of being. You are not even worthy to sully the points of this trident. You should be dispatched like the lowest animal, and never fed back into the Geas. Your existence cannot be permitted an instant longer!'

The elder took a deliberate step forward, the movement breaking the spell of paralysis in which Ba'zel had been caught. Words tumbled from his lips so quickly that they had barely formed in his mind before he spoke them out loud. 'The Eldest sent me! *She* bids you stand aside and allow me entrance to the chamber. Further, you are to render me whatever assistance I might require, even falling on your own weapon should I command it. But I will not command that, for you are unworthy of such mercy. Instead, you will guard these doors against those coming on behind me, do you understand?' He finished with a gasp, hardly believing what he had said. None would dare mention the Eldest, let alone invoke *her* authority, lest they wanted to attract that unforgiving and eternal being's attention.

The guard growled but had no choice but to fall back. Even if he suspected Ba'zel of lying, failure to obey instantly the very idea of the Eldest's authority was enough to warrant death. It would be for the Eldest – not a mere guard – to punish any using *her* name in vain. And the punishment would be more terrible than could be imagined. There were various stories of members of the Declension immediately committing suicide upon fearing they had used the Eldest's name inappropriately – death was preferable to the alternative, and if their bodies were then fed to the Geas they would be reborn with wiser wills and tongues.

The guard's eyes were impossibly wide as Ba'zel came forward. 'Surely you are insane. Your mind is gone rabid. Your line must have mixed with another race, for you are not of the Declension,' the elder hissed. Yet he opened the doors and let Ba'zel pass.

There was a *boom* as the doors closed behind Ba'zel and he was sealed inside the chamber. His eyes went straight to the shimmering portal atop the dais in the middle of the wide circular space. The light coming from the Gate of the Waking Dream was the first Ba'zel had seen of the other linked realms of the Geas. Watchers both in the home-realm and the other realms held the Gate always open by keeping the same shared images of place in their minds. It seemed that just as thoughts could be shared between realms, so the realms could be materially connected. Mentor Ho'zen had spoken about the different realms actually being different levels of existence and consciousness – the Declension naturally being the highest, with their superior magic and elevated consciousness – but Ba'zel had only been able to follow the explanation in a general sense. He'd understood that it was only right a tribute of life energy was drawn from the Geas of every other realm in order to feed the Geas of the Declension's home-realm. The faction of Ba'zel's father claimed that, since all the Geas across the realms were linked, the potential fall of the Geas of the home-realm represented the potential collapse of all the other realms as well, the end of all life!

The lesser races were fortunate, then, the Mentor had carefully elucidated, that the Declension had discovered the means to travel between the realms and to sustain the Geas of their own realm. The Declension were indeed the Saviours of every realm. They were the intellectual and spiritual leaders of the known cosmos. They were light and hope in what would otherwise be just an empty and eternal void.

And of all the races in the realms of the Geas, it was only the Declension who could steer the realms towards the truly divine and eternal, who could lead others on the Great Voyage. For was it not the Watchers of the Declension who had first searched the cosmos with their minds for trace of the ancient Chi'a who had gone before them? Was it not these selfsame Watchers who had finally sensed and shared in ancient memories of the Chi'a elsewhere in the cosmos? Had they not thereby discovered other realms of the cosmos through which the Chi'a had passed on their own Great Voyage before travelling beyond? Had those Watchers not then influenced the dreams of, and whispered new ideas into, the minds of the races of those other realms, until the same thoughts and images were synchronised and shared between the realms and material travel between them was possible? Indeed, was it not the Watchers of the Declension who, with each new realm occupied, were able to probe further into the cosmos and deeper into the shared consciousness, in order to discover yet more realms and levels of existence? Yes, it was the Watchers of the Declension who would ultimately lead them all to divinity and eternity.

The Gate of the Waking Dream was therefore a holy place of sorts to Ba'zel's kind. He went to his knees, so awed was he by its beauty and meaning. Although it was radiant, it did not hurt his eyes like most other light did. He saw images from different realms drifting and twisting before him. Perhaps they were more than images, for they looked entirely real, if extremely distant. He didn't understand much of what he saw, and that only served to overwhelm him more. He had never seen such vibrant colours. The Gate made his own realm seem muted and drab by comparison. *He* felt muted and drab, utterly inadequate before it. How could he presume to approach such wonder? He would only begrime it, cover it with dust.

A figure slowly came around the Gate and placed itself between Ba'zel and the portal.

'F-Father! You h-have found me!' He would have grovelled and writhed on the floor in an abject display, but his father's glittering black eyes held him in place.

His father's voice was like stone cracking. 'Did you think I would not know the mind of the least of my line? How is it you have not ended this already, you wretch? Are you so *unstable* that you are utterly insensible to the horror of what you are? Quickly, end this before others come and I am further shamed! Or must I lower myself further still by doing it for you?'

Something told Ba'zel not to reveal that the sifters had told him to leave the realm. 'Father, the Declension say I am no part of them. Can I not just go elsewhere, disavowing any claims to line, name, race or realm? I will be a different race of my own, a lesser race if you will. I will work in the deepest mine in some other realm. Can the Declension not simply forget I exist? Can they not just leave me be?'

'Fool!' his father replied with an impatient stamp. 'You will always be a part of the Geas of this realm. The Geas is old and occasionally sick. The creation of those who are *unstable* like you is but a symptom of its illness. Left unchecked, those symptoms can become devastating in their own right. You must be destroyed! Even were you to attempt the Gate to travel elsewhere, you would not have the strength and discipline of mind and magic to survive it. And were you to survive, the Declension would have no choice but to send one of the . . .' and here his voice unconsciously dropped to a whisper as he pronounced the word '. . . Virtues after you. Better you kill yourself here and now. Do so at once! I insist!'

'Father, spare me! Please!'

'You have the temerity to ask yet more of me? You are despicable and shameless in every way. I see I must end you myself!'

His father bared his stone fangs and raised clawed hands. Ba'zel responded with a snarl and a yell and leapt forward. His father had not expected this of his son, just as no elder would expect it of a younger one. It could only be a futile gesture, after all, and none of the Declension would ever indulge themselves in such a waste of time and energy. So why would Ba'zel attack? What could it mean? Was there something the elder still did not know about his *unstable* son?

Ba'zel's father swayed back in momentary confusion, then he blinked. Of course. The futile attack was precisely the sort of nonsensical behaviour one might expect of the *unstable*. With a roar he lunged forward again, with deadly eviscerating intent.

But the moment's hesitation proved enough. It decided whether Ba'zel would live or die. Landing just short of his oncoming father, Ba'zel dropped through the stone floor. As his father flew over the top of him, Ba'zel swooped back up into the chamber behind and past his father. Ba'zel leapt for the Gate.

'Son! I beg you!' his father shouted in appeal.

Never had he heard his father's voice break so. Never had he heard him use such words. Ba'zel hesitated and looked back round at his parent.

'Kill yourself! Please!'

And Ba'zel stepped into the Gate and the maelstrom of the cosmos.

Mentor Ho'zen fidgeted as he sat in the chambers and presence of Elder Starus, the head of the Faction of Departure. The scrutiny of one so large was of course terrifying, but the blood lamps that burned around the chamber also made it difficult for the Mentor to control himself. The lamps were an outrageous display of wealth and power, of course, for every other member of the Declension – save perhaps the Eldest herself – made do with lamps of tallow rendered from the bodies of those fed to the Geas, or lamps of the black oil from decomposing bodies. But Elder Starus was no fool – he also knew that the cloying heady scent of burning blood and the frisson of life energy released into the air kept most of those with whom he dealt completely distracted and at a disadvantage. Despite his best efforts, Mentor Ho'zen's nasal aperture flared hungrily and he shamed himself.

Elder Starus smiled knowingly. 'I heard Elder Faal's pathetic call about his *unstable* son having fled his chambers. All went as we intended, I take it?'

Mentor Ho'zen smiled weakly and whined, 'Yes, Great One. Ba'zel escaped entirely on his own. There is nothing to suggest any other parties were involved. Elder Faal may ask why I was not with his son for lessons that day but I will simply inform him I was ill. He will not suspect me. He has always believed Ba'zel actually was *unstable*. I made sure of that.'

The elder nodded. 'And Ba'zel is dead?'

The Mentor hesitated. 'No, but he went through the Gate. Surely one of the Virtues will be sent after him.'

'Hmm. He is worse than dead then. Faal is shamed and the influence of his faction must become diminished. If we are fortunate, he will become distracted with grief, although I suspect he is not so weak. I wonder if there is a way, however, that we can start a rumour that he is properly grief-stricken yet hiding it. If so, we might see him entirely dropped by his faction. Wouldn't that be something! Perhaps if we point out he seems to have been keeping to his chambers much more of late . . . I will give it some thought. In the meantime, Mentor, I am well pleased.'

So saying, the elder waved forward a retainer who had been waiting with two goblets from a tray. The elder took one goblet and then gestured for the other to be taken to the Mentor.

The Mentor gave the unworthy retainer but a passing glance and eagerly took the proffered blood, for his nasal aperture had already caught an exotic and intoxicating scent from the goblet. Yet he caught himself and sensibly waited for the other to drink first. Elder Starus was apparently in no mood to rush, and so the Mentor was forced to wait in agony as the other first shifted his bulk so that he was more comfortable and then chose to speak expansively. 'I saw you notice my new retainer, Mentor. It has of course had its ears put out and its tongue removed. It represents a lesser race from the fifth realm, you know. I have been promised that it will last longer than the races of the other realms, which is just as well, for the blood of its race isn't much to savour.

Retainers just don't seem to last as long as they used to. It's quite an inconvenience.'

Mentor Ho'zen made a polite desperate noise.

'Now, this blood,' the elder continued, 'is from the *sixth* realm. It is quite a rarity, for the race that donated it seems particularly short-lived when coming into our proximity. Apparently, there is a great problem with supply, even for the Saviours in that realm. But I am assured it is worth all the effort of collection.' The elder sipped at his goblet experimentally and pulled a face. 'Not as fresh as it could be.' He put the goblet aside. 'But tell me what you think of it, Mentor. I'd be interested in the opinion of one as learned as yourself.'

Mentor Ho'zen wasted no time in finally trying the blood. It was so imbued with life energy that he found it utterly addictive. He guzzled it and could not lower the goblet until he'd completely drained it. Immediately, he was giddy. He burped and grinned apologetically. 'Potent, Great One, quite potent. Indeed, that is my most potent opinion.' He giggled. 'My most *learned* opinion, I should shay . . . say!' Light-headed and suddenly brave, he blurted, 'And it ish alsho my learned opinion, Great One, that we should now shpeak of the poshition of influence within your faction that I wash promished.'

'Indeed?' the elder responded mildly. 'You would presume to make demands of me within my own chambers then?'

'Cshertainly not, Great One!' the Mentor slurred. 'But I cshertainly think it'sh time we dishcussed the poshition.'

'That is demand enough.' Elder Starus sighed. 'Very well, you may approach and receive the mark of my line.'

Mentor Ho'zen rose to swaying feet, stumbled forward and then knelt. Elder Starus extended his huge hand, placed it on the Mentor's head and then squeezed until the learned skull broke open.

'Ahhh. Now this is far fresher. Forgive me, Mentor, but I have always found the blood of our own kind more to my taste. Even in death, you serve your new faction well, for now it is certain that there is nothing linking Ba'zel's escape to us. I will see to it that you are properly fed to the Geas and prayers are said so that you will be reborn into the position of influence that was promised you.'